T0382002

THE
SOUTH
WIND

ALEXANDRIA WARWICK

**SIMON &
SCHUSTER**

London · New York · Amsterdam/Antwerp · Sydney/Melbourne · Toronto · New Delhi

First published in Australia in 2025 by Simon & Schuster (Australia) Pty Limited
Level 4, 32 York St, Sydney NSW 2000

First published in Great Britain by Simon & Schuster UK Ltd, 2025

1 3 5 7 9 10 8 6 4 2

Simon & Schuster UK Ltd, 1st Floor
222 Gray's Inn Road, London WC1X 8HB

Simon & Schuster Australia, Sydney
Simon & Schuster India, New Delhi

www.simonandschuster.co.uk
www.simonandschuster.com.au
www.simonandschuster.co.in

The authorised representative in the EEA is Simon & Schuster Netherlands BV,
Herculesplein 96, 3584 AA Utrecht, Netherlands. info@simonandschuster.nl

Simon & Schuster strongly believes in freedom of expression and stands against
censorship in all its forms. For more information, visit BooksBelong.com

A CIP catalogue record for this book is available from the British Library

Hardback ISBN: 978-1-3985-3368-4
Trade Paperback ISBN: 978-1-3985-3386-8
eBook ISBN: 978-1-3985-3260-1
Audio ISBN: 978-1-3985-3261-8

Map by Robert Lazzaretti

Printed and Bound in the UK using 100% Renewable Electricity
at CPI Group (UK) Ltd

To Mr. Simmons, who gave me music

PROLOGUE

THE CHILD WAS BORN INTO SILENCE.

Initially, the midwife believed her to be stillborn. No cry cracked the gold-tinged dusk, no almighty declaration of arrival. Dense lashes fanned her round cheeks, which appeared to have been sapped of all color and warmth. Yet there was a subtle stirring, the weak flutter of a pulse. Alive, but only just.

The child required immediate healing. But her mother, sickly and frail following that long, laborious birth, lifted a trembling hand and gestured for the midwife to approach. The child was passed into her mother's arms. *So slight, my daughter.* It would be the queen's last thought, for she took one final breath and was still.

When the king learned of his wife's passing, he screamed, and tore the window drapes from their rods, and pleaded with the highest deities, and wept. The child was rushed to the palace physician who, despite his best efforts, failed to stabilize the flagging newborn. The blue tinge to her skin, the sporadic hitch of her chest—she would not survive the night.

The king was powerless. He did not understand why misfortune had befallen him, of all people. Was it fate? Retribution? Why should his child enter this world, only to be snatched from him on the heels of her mother?

And so, he went to Mount Syr, the holy site that stood watch over Ammara's blistering sands. Upon summiting the bare, rocky peak, he fell to his knees before the dais, atop which rested an empty throne. It was there the king called upon the Lord of the Mountain, the mightiest of those primordial gods.

When a cloaked man materialized before him, the king prostrated himself. The Lord of the Mountain was as vast as he was broad, his face shielded by the cowl of his cloak. In the hours that followed, the king bargained for his daughter's life. Wealth, power, even the realm itself—the king offered all that he was worth. But the Lord of the Mountain was merciful. He agreed to save the child's life—for a price. In a rush of desperation, the king accepted the deal without question. And thus, the trap was set.

Later, after the bargain had been struck, the king entered his children's bedroom. His sons slept soundly, unaware of their mother's passing. He kissed their brows, then approached the crib where his newborn daughter lay. She was awake. Color had returned to brighten her brown cheeks. Her small mouth pursed as she gazed up at him with wide, dark eyes.

Believing himself to be alone, the king began to weep. He failed to notice a shade of a figure hovering over the crib alongside him. Nor did he witness the phantom's shadowy hand press onto his daughter's brow.

Sleep, crooned the voice.

Sleep, my beauty.

PART 1

THE BUD

1

FORTY-SEVEN DAYS.

My stomach cramps at the sight, yet I carefully mark an *x* through the number, one of dozens recorded in the pages of my journal. Tomorrow, day forty-six will follow, then forty-five, forty-four. I wonder if I might not end it now, in the small study attached to my bedchamber. Topple the candle wavering atop my desk. Surrender to the smoke. Defeat the curse before it defeats me.

A bell clangs. Its echo leaps from the shining rooftops of the city's prosperous upper ring to the stately, wind-eroded pillars of the Queen's Road. I smooth the wrinkles from my dress with a trembling hand, for the time has come sooner than I wished.

Pushing to my feet, I move to the window. An enemy approaches Ishmah's border. From my vantage point overlooking the Red City, I observe the line of soldiers snaking across the raw, sunburned earth. Sunlight glints against a thousand hammered shields.

The gates will open at Prince Balior's arrival. There will be a feast held in his honor. The streets will swell with citizens, oleander blooms plucked from the public gardens and tossed onto the cracked, dusty roads. For this enemy is welcome.

My palm lifts, pressing flat against the windowpane. For twenty-four years of my life, my left hand has lacked the opal rune that would identify me as a married woman. But my twenty-fifth nameday approaches. If I am to do my part in securing my people's survival, then I will wed this prince, whom I know nothing of.

We must all make sacrifices.

Returning to my desk, I spot the journal lying open, rows of numbers etched in blackest ink. A rush of despair consumes me, wholly and completely. Forty-seven days seems like an age, but chill mornings will bleed into stifling afternoons. Time, unable to alter or slow.

I hurry toward my wardrobe, hauling open the doors to reveal a collection of brown, gray, and black dresses. Utterly lackluster, painfully drab. I brush them aside to reveal a smaller collection of jewel-colored gowns. I am Princess Sarai Al-Khatib of Ammara, yet I am not even allowed a bit of color or sparkle. Father's word is law.

Reluctantly, I tug two colorless dresses from the wardrobe, accidentally knocking my violin case from where it had been shoved in the back corner. It topples onto the rug with a muffled thump.

I wince, kneeling to pull the leather case onto my lap. Fahim would scold me for my carelessness. But Fahim is not here.

My throat tightens, and after returning my instrument to its place in the back of the wardrobe, I hold up both dresses in the mirror. Linen of dull brown, which blends into the mahogany of my skin, or ivory, which promises purity? My mouth curls bitterly. Brown, most definitely.

Gathering my heavy locks of ebony hair, I weave a ribbon through the plait that begins at the crown of my head. With a steady hand, I apply kohl to the corners of my dark eyes. A threadbare cloak drapes my shoulders, sandals strapped across my oiled feet.

After a slow, calming exhalation, I head for the door, murmuring, "Duty to one's kingdom is duty to one's heart." I must, of course, fulfill my duty in greeting Prince Balior. But not now. Not yet.

I cannot escape the palace quickly enough.

The immense edifice engulfs a hill amidst the stately homes of the upper ring. Despite Ishmah's moniker—the Red City—its palace walls are alabaster pale: glossy marble, weathered limestone. They curve into hollowed ceilings and deep, romantic archways, everything exquisitely tiled in mosaics.

One pillared corridor flows into another, with spacious, open-aired chambers concealed in cleverly designed niches, their ceilings exposed to the elements. An occasional courtyard shaded by tall fronds materializes as a burst of yellow brightness amidst the sheltered passageways and still pools.

As I turn a corner, movement in my periphery snags my attention, and I slow, angling toward a dark shape near the vast double doors leading to the Library of Ishmah.

The man is broad of chest, an unnatural stillness swathing his form. He wears loose ivory trousers and an emerald, knee-length robe. A white scarf wraps his hair, shielding the lower portion of his face from the boiling sun. Though I cannot see the man's eyes, I experience the intensity of his gaze, as if the sharpest of arrows pierces my breast.

It cannot be. Years have eroded much of my past, yet some memories retain their clarity. I swear I recognize him. "Excuse me—"

But the man retreats down a side corridor. By the time I reach the end of the hall, he has vanished.

It takes a moment for my heart's rhythm to settle. I must have been mistaken. The man was likely a traveler who lost his way. When he does not reappear, I hurry past the library toward the stables. Generally, I would bribe the watchmen at the palace gates to let me pass, but not today. Due to the prince's arrival, the palace is doubly guarded. None may enter or depart without the king's permission, including me.

But a secret passage hidden in the stable walls grants me access to a cool, dark tunnel, which deposits me beyond the palace grounds in the upper ring. The Queen's Road cuts south through Ishmah, with the perpendicular King's Road stretching east to west. Tidy, single-story homes hewn from red clay line the streets, and glorious windows of stained glass reflect colored light onto the paved road. Drought has touched everyone in Ishmah, including the wealthy. Where hedges once ornamented green lawns, only sand and shriveled branches remain.

Dressed in my nondescript cloak, I blend in with the passersby easily. The roads narrow. The jeweled windows vanish. The stones underfoot fracture to gravel, packed soil, dust. In the lower ring, wagons multiply, and stalls spring up to clutter the streets. Merchants hawk their wares as unruly children scrabble underfoot, chasing a herd of goats through the crowd.

Eventually, the road squeezes to a thread, halting anything aside from foot traffic. An arched entryway marks the entrance into the souk.

It is, on the best of days, disorderly, and on the worst, absolute madness. Beyond the crumbling wall, alleyways fold around sharp corners, the area so littered with carts, tents, and stalls that it is impossible to pass through without knocking against *something*. The offerings are varied and numerous. Colors assault my vision and scents dizzy me with their potency. Fruits and nuts and grains, pottery and tapestries and useless trinkets.

"The Red City's finest rugs! Buy now!"

"—can't agree to a lower price, I'm afraid I'll have to go elsewhere—"

"What did I tell you about eating things off the ground?"

Coins are passed into outstretched hands. A young mother attempts to shepherd her five children through the rush. Always, there is more. Shallow bowls of hammered copper, inside which pile small hills of spices acquired along the Spice Road: the fired red of sumac, the ochre of cumin, turmeric, ginger. As I ease around a bend, I accidentally jostle a young man carting a crate of live chickens. He snarls at me; I snarl back. Then, suppressing a smile, I hurry onward.

A door dressed in peeling yellow paint lies slightly ajar at the end of the lane. I slip inside, into cool darkness tinged with the warm, earthy scent of sandalwood.

Children seated on colorful woven rugs occupy the small room I have found myself in. At the front sits a wizened woman draped in a frayed shawl. Her name is Haneen. She perches on a three-legged stool, her milky eyes staring sightlessly. As though having sensed my arrival, her mouth curves. But of course that is impossible. How is a blind bard to know that the princess of Ammara attends her weekly storytelling hour?

"Now," she begins, her voice like a creak of aged wood. "Where did I leave off?"

The air stills as the room holds its breath.

Last week, our fierce and loyal Aziza enlisted in Ammara's army by disguising herself as a man and declaring her grandfather's identity. War was coming. And if Aziza was to save her grandfather from being conscripted into the army, then she must become his replacement.

Training was ruthless. These soldiers were strong, agile, prevailing. Aziza was the weakest by far. None knew she was a woman. She was forced to bathe far from camp in the dead of night and hike back before dawn. But Aziza didn't give up. One month passed, then another. Her muscles hardened. Her will became unbreakable iron.

I listen to the tale of Aziza with the desperation of one who fears it might all be stripped away. This transportive narrative, a glimpse of what *could* be. As the story slowly unravels and the hour slips its knot, I find myself in awe of this bold, selfless woman, who managed to overcome unsurmountable odds.

One night, Haneen continues, her tone darkening, *Aziza was not so careful. She failed to realize that Omar, one of the men from her unit, had heard her leaving the tent to wash. He wondered where she was going and decided to follow her.*

The children gasp. Even I catch my breath. I did not wish Aziza to be discovered. She was brave—braver than I hoped to be.

After arriving at the small oasis where she bathed, Aziza shed her clothes and began to submerge herself when the scuff of a boot stopped her cold.

"Yousef?" the man whispered.

There is a pause. I expect Haneen to go on, but she merely sits there, more satisfied than the fattest of cats drunk on cream.

"What happens next?" a young boy cries. "What happens to Aziza?"

She grins. "You will have to return tomorrow to find out."

The slap of my sandals travels the length of the palace corridor with the percussive rhythm of hide drums. I have nearly reached the throne room when someone drawls, "I hear celebrations are in order, Princess Sarai."

I slow, angling to the right. A buxom woman draped in yellow silk reclines against one of the smooth pillars—and she is not alone. Three noblewomen flank her. My pleasant mood promptly sours. Dalia Yassin.

Somehow, I manage to plaster a close-lipped smile across my mouth. "And what, exactly, are we celebrating?" *That dress makes you look like an old goat.*

Dalia bats her eyelashes. "Why, your forthcoming betrothal to Prince Balior, of course." *You don't deserve him, hag.*

My smile wanes. That information has not been publicly announced. Then again, countless cooks, attendants, handmaidens, and stableboys are employed by members of the court to snoop and pry, including Dalia's family, one of the oldest and wealthiest in Ammara.

"Although, I'm not sure if *celebration* is the right word," the woman goes on, easing off the pillar, arm outswept in an absurd display of dramatics. Her followers gaze on, captivatied. "King Halim must be truly desperate for a match if he is selling you off to the enemy."

My eyes narrow in warning. "That's not—"

"But who can blame the man?" she cuts in smoothly. "It's not like you're getting any younger. A princess in her mid-twenties with zero prospects? Well," she *tsks*. "That is a shame."

A furious blush flames red across my cheeks. What is worse? This poison she spews, or the fact that I cannot deny its verity? In my younger years, I was too busy studying music to make a strategic match.

"I myself had my pick of eligible noblemen." She glances at her nails. Rich, glossy pink. "My husband is lucky to call himself mine."

Lucky. That's not exactly the word I'd use. "Didn't I hear your husband married you to help pay his father's gambling debts?"

Our audience titters behind their hands. Dalia grows so red I am convinced she will succumb to fever.

"I'll have you know that I was tutored alongside one of Prince Balior's cousins as a child," she seethes. "So I would take care with your words."

I offer a wide, toothy grin. "You should have kept in touch."

The noblewomen's gasps trail me as I stride purposefully toward the throne room. Two expansive doors painted the pale blue of the midmorning sky open with a groan. It is vast, this chamber—the great belly of the palace. Guards ornament the walls. Archers, unseen but for the points of their nocked arrows, command the second level. Gleaming marble tiles toss light from the high windows onto the mosaiced ceiling.

A long, woven rug connects the entrance to the dais in the back of the room. King Halim occupies the most impressive seat: a deeply cushioned chair that drips with jewels. To his right sits an equally impressive yet slightly smaller throne. It has been vacant since my mother's passing nearly twenty-five years before. To his left, three additional thrones: mine, Amir's, Fahim's.

Upon reaching the dais, I kneel. "Father."

"You're late."

The drop in my stomach is a feeling I know well. Lifting my head, I glance around. The chamber is empty. "Our guests have yet to arrive."

He stiffens. "Excuse me?" His voice is low, dangerously so.

"So long as I am seated before they are," I say, "why should it matter that I am a few moments behind schedule?"

"It matters because *I* know that you are tardy. I have spoken to you about this before."

I regard Father coolly. King Halim was once an impressive man. The breadth and solidity of his shoulders, arms, and back. The curve of his proud belly. He stood taller than most men, black beard shining and full.

But the man who surveys me now is but a shade of my father. His musculature has wasted with disease. He looks frail beneath the folds of his ivory robe. The skin around his jowls hangs loose with age.

"And what of Amir?" I press. "You and I both know he struggles with timeliness."

The king is not amused. "Amir is not tardy *today*. He is on his honeymoon, as you well know. Do you expect your brother to be in two places at once?" He does not allow me the opportunity to respond before he adds, "Tardiness is unacceptable for someone of your station. See to it that it doesn't happen again."

I bite into the soft flesh of my inner cheek. Too easily, my tongue sharpens, its barbs threatening to spew forth. I remind myself of what's at stake: my kingdom, my life. "Duly noted," I clip out.

Father grunts in acknowledgment as I rise, taking my place on the smallest throne. Only when I am settled do the doors open once more.

"Announcing Prince Balior of Um Salim to His Majesty, King Halim Al-Khatib of Ammara."

A man, tall and well-built, strides through the doors. Twelve men dressed in loose, ebon robes flank him, scimitars hanging from their belt loops—his personal guard, I assume.

The prince is young, not yet thirty. Handsome, though even the most pleasing countenance may obscure a rot beneath. Black hair curls over his ears, and color reddens his sharp cheekbones from the sweltering heat. A fairer complexion than I am used to, though if he were to spend considerable time outdoors, his skin would likely turn as brown as mine.

For many years, the realms of Ammara and Um Salim were at war. And who could blame the larger realm for attempting to invade? Ammara is rich with wealth, particularly its capital, Ishmah, though the people of Um Salim do not know just how much this prosperity has waned. Twenty-five years of drought, for which I am to blame. And there is the threat of the encroaching darkwalkers to consider, too.

Prince Balior is a preeminent scholar who has studied the region's oldest myths. Father hopes his research will prove useful in finding a way to break my curse, end the drought, and halt the darkwalkers' infiltration of our land. If Prince Balior's negotiations with King Halim are favorable, our separate realms will soon marry into one.

Of course, the prince cannot know that his bride-to-be is cursed, or that the kingdom he hopes to one day rule is doomed. I will need to take care with how I approach discourse concerning his research findings. It weighs on me, this secret. Only Father is privy to it.

"Your Majesty." Our guest kneels, blue headscarf brushing the snowy tile. "I am honored."

Father considers the man's prostrated form. After a moment, he states, "Rise, Prince Balior. Our Lord of the Mountain shines upon you. I trust your journey was fair?"

He sweeps to his feet with a fluidity I do not often witness. "It was. My men and I are humbled by the welcome."

"And where are your soldiers now?"

"Beyond Ishmah's walls. They await your permission to enter."

King Halim presses the tips of his fingers together. "Unfortunately, Prince Balior, I cannot permit your army to pass into the capital. Not until the wedding ceremony is complete. This is for the protection of my people. I'm sure you understand. Your personal guard will of course be accommodated inside the palace."

The prince frowns. His eyes flicker with some indecipherable emotion. This, he did not expect. While I agree with Father's decision, it's not exactly a hospitable introduction. But Prince Balior bows, saying, "I understand. Though, it has been a long journey—I cannot expect my men to return to Um Salim after having just arrived here."

"Naturally," the king replies smoothly. "They may camp beyond the wall as we await the ceremony." Father gestures to me, though does not glance my way. "My daughter, Princess Sarai Al-Khatib."

The prince regards me curiously. I dip my chin toward our guest, my smile thin and cutting.

King Halim continues, "I'm hopeful that we'll reach an arrangement benefitting both Ammara and Um Salim in the coming weeks."

My hand in marriage. My freedom exchanged for Ammara's survival. In less than thirty days, the tattoo marking the left hand of every married person in Ammara will be inked on my skin.

"Thank you, Your Majesty. Ammara has much to offer—"

Though Prince Balior continues to speak, my attention cuts to a sudden motion within the stillness of the chamber. A figure slips through one of the side doors behind the guards. Broad, sure-footed: the man with the white headscarf I saw loitering outside the library.

A rush of defiance sends me to my feet. "Halt! What business do you have with the king?"

The archers located on the second level angle their arrows toward the intruder. A hundred scimitars slide free of their scabbards. Prince Balior's personal guard hastily forms a shield around their sovereign.

Father's eyes flash in my direction. "Sarai. This man is a guest."

"A guest who slips through the back door," I snarl, "no better than a fox in the brush?" How did he get past the guards? Unless he has killed them? Unrest has bled into the realm's widening cracks. As drought creeps toward its third decade, people's desperation intensifies. "Step forward."

For someone so broad, he moves with startling lightness. Something about the motion sends an odd shiver across my scalp.

"Sarai!" King Halim's rage is total. "If you do not take your seat this instant—"

I am both dreaming and awake, for though the man's face is partially veiled, I am certain I have seen it before. "Remove your scarf, sir."

He lifts a hand, catching the fabric between two fingers. The cloth unwinds: nose, mouth, jaw. That face, bared and horribly familiar. My stomach drops as the South Wind speaks in a voice reminiscent of a deep, ceaseless current.

"Hello, Sarai."

2

A SLOW, PRICKLING CHILL ICES MY BLOOD. IT LEADENS MY LIMBS, encases my heart and lungs in impenetrable crystal. I am both Sarai of past and Sarai of present. I am eighteen years old and twenty-four. I am inspired, cherished, adored, then deceived, broken, alone. My throat squeezes so tightly I fear I will faint.

But I do not faint. No, that will simply not do. Vulnerability is the enemy.

Notus—known to all as the South Wind—regards me with eyes like clear, deep pools. I have not seen his face in five years, yet he has aged not a day. I have touched that face, kissed that face, loved that face, despised that face. How appalling that I still consider it beautiful. Skin of deepest brown and black, impenetrable eyes. A broad, stocky torso swathed in emerald and cream. The South Wind, who sees much, speaks little.

"Sarai!"

Father's voice is distant, a wavering sun beyond the thickened haze. I force my legs to move—down the steps, across the tiled floor, expression fixed into one of intense loathing. The leather binding on the hilt of Notus' scimitar appears fresh, newly wrapped. It is the only change I perceive.

"Guards!" I shout, halting an arm span away from the South Wind. "Take this immortal to the dungeons to await my arrival."

The flare of Notus' dark eyes reminds me of volcanic rock, forged fresh by blistering heat. A breathless pang grips me. I promptly squash the emotion.

"You have no such authority, Sarai," Father snaps, voice laced with displeasure. "Notus is here at my behest. As such, you will treat him with respect."

"You must be mistaken, Father. If you recall, he deserted Ammara years ago. According to our laws, desertion is punishable by death."

The chamber falls silent.

When the king speaks, it is with a chilling lack of warmth. "You dare to question my decision?"

"No, Father." I respond without removing my attention from the South Wind. He will witness neither fault nor crack. "But we have laws for a reason. I suggest we make an example of him."

The South Wind is, after all, immortal. As a god, he cannot be killed except by a god-touched weapon. The only sword in this room that could kill him is his own. Why, I could slide that scimitar of his through his chest if I chose. But a swift death? That is a grace he does not deserve.

"Return to your seat, Sarai."

Father's command cuts severely enough that I flinch. I must obey, yet some deep-seated part of me fears the South Wind will vanish should I turn away.

"There's no need to treat me like a child," I say. "I am only trying to help."

"If you act like a child, then I will treat you like one. Notus' presence does not concern you. Return to your seat. *Now!*"

Many of the guards shift uncomfortably. Even Prince Balior gazes on with sympathy.

Somehow, despite my weighted legs, I return to the dais with a smooth, unfaltering stride and settle onto the immense throne. For the entirety of my life, I have despised this chair. Today of all days I am acutely aware of how it swallows me.

I turn toward the king. "Father—"

"Not another word." Then, lowly: "You dishonor me."

His strike lands precisely where it is intended. Heat climbs my chest and paints my face in shameful red. I did not mean to dishonor Father. I only wished to protect him from this banished god.

Notus continues to scrutinize me with an impassive expression. The strength required to maintain such a mask is too great—strength I do not possess. I drop my eyes. After this embarrassment, I doubt Prince Balior will be keen to bind his life to mine. Have I ruined the only chance of saving my life, the lives of my people, before it has even begun?

When the barest of breezes stirs the hem of my dress, my attention flits back to Notus. This, too, I remember: his emotions and the wind, forever intertwined. I glance at his hands, from whence those winds come. Broad palms and callused brown skin. Even now, my body remembers their weight.

King Halim dismisses the South Wind with the promise to discuss matters later. I do not watch Notus depart. The doors heave open, hammer shut.

It is an age before the king speaks again.

"Prince Balior, I want to apologize for that deplorable scene." He regards the much younger man with meaningful remorse. "My daughter—"

"There is no need for an apology," Prince Balior replies, hands lifted in a gesture of goodwill. His personal guard has since retreated, having returned to their stations. "Ruling a kingdom is quite messy, as I'm coming to learn. I do not fault your daughter in wanting to protect your best interests."

A wave of unexpected gratitude warms me. It is a kindness I do not deserve.

"If we are to wed by the month's end, I daresay I would be foolish not to put this incident behind us." A small, secret smile plays about the prince's mouth. "I look forward to spending time together, Princess Sarai."

I nod, though my attention slips its knot, sliding over the throne room doors where Notus departed moments earlier. I force my eyes back to Prince Balior's. "I look forward to that as well."

King Halim lifts a hand, and an attendant steps forward. "Ilan will show you to your chambers. I imagine you are weary from the long journey. Tomorrow, we feast in celebration of your impending nuptials."

The prince bows low. "I appreciate your hospitality, Your Majesty. I look forward to dining with you and Princess Sarai. Good night." Then he takes his leave.

As soon as we are alone, I round on Father. "Why?"

He slumps back into his chair with a sigh. Time has faded the scarlet cushions to the color of rust. "Why *what*, Sarai? I need specifics. *Why* is not enough."

King Halim is no fool. He will make me spell it out. Very well. "Why have you allowed Notus to return unpunished?"

"Because I have need of him. Our realm has need of him. As of this morning, he has accepted a position in the Royal Guard."

"Guard?" I struggle to catch my breath. "Why have you placed Notus in a position of power?" Why welcome him back into our home with open arms? My hands tremble. I fist them in the folds of my dress.

"Must I explain something so obvious?" he snaps. "Fahim was never so slow to understand and did not waste his breath asking questions."

It always takes me by surprise how swiftly the grief rises. Despite five years having passed, it still feels as if my brother's death occurred yesterday. Bright, beloved Fahim, the eldest of Father's sons.

"I did not realize my concern was a waste of breath," I reply stiffly. "I will be sure to temper it the next time I believe our realm to be under threat."

He pinches the bridge of his nose, as though my hurt is an inconvenience. "You know what I meant."

I don't, actually. But I keep that bitter thought close. "I do not see what is obvious about allowing a deserter into the Royal Guard."

"Deserter or not," Father explains, "Notus is the strongest person in this realm. You know as well as I do that the drought has weakened Ishmah. Years of failed harvests, and we cannot even afford to feed our people, much less an army. Darkwalkers gain strength by the day. Many have fallen prey to their hunts."

I know. Of course I know. Ishmah, strategically hewn from the valley's clay walls, once utilized the annual floodwaters to supply its extensive irrigation system, including numerous wells, reservoirs, and canals. But rain has not fallen in Ammara for over two decades. The capital's high walls, carved with runes to repel the darkwalkers, provide adequate protection from the beasts. Yet each passing year, they seem to multiply. Some claim darkwalkers have already infiltrated the city, but I have seen no such evidence.

As for the South Wind, Father is right. Notus is the only person to have ever entered the labyrinth and return alive. His power will help quell the darkwalkers—even if that means admitting him as a member of the Royal Guard.

"Times are changing, Sarai." The king surveys me with eyes touched by fatigue. "Sometimes we must take drastic measures if we are to endure the worst of what's to come."

He appears defeated. Perhaps I should not have behaved so recklessly in Prince Balior's presence. After all, Father risked everything to save my life as a sickly infant. I owe it to him to be dutiful. "I understand, but how can you trust that Notus will not desert us a second time?"

"I trust him, Sarai. That's all that matters."

"He turned his back on our kingdom!" *On me.*

His expression hardens. No matter my concern, no matter my hurt, my feelings will always be deemed as insignificant in the eyes of a king. "I have not forgotten," he replies, "but I have forgiven. Perhaps it's time you do the same."

3

ROSHAR HAMMAD. ROYAL TAILOR.

The plaque displays a tidy script carved into the wood's pale grain. My mouth quirks at the ornate penmanship, its dramatic flourishes. The original plaque had been modest, uniform, unremarkable. In other words, far too dull for the likes of Roshar. Muffled conversation drifts through the door.

"I said a two-finger hem, not three," a man barks. "Don't give me that look. Redo it. I don't care how long it takes."

There is a pause.

"Are you insinuating I do not know the difference of an inch? My dear, I have clothed the royal family for a decade. I have designed *the* fashions of the season for the highest governmental officials, the wealthiest of merchants, and the most influential families. You dare suggest I do not know something as fundamental to tailoring as *inches*?" Whoever he speaks to utters a quiet response. "That's what I thought."

Lifting a fist, I knock.

The door cracks open, then pulls wide. Large, hazel-green eyes swim with irritation behind a pair of wire-rimmed spectacles. A blink, and the man frowns. "Sarai?"

"Is this a bad time?" I whisper.

Beyond his shoulder, three women and two men crowd around an article of clothing spread across a large table. They stare at me in unease, likely wondering why the princess has come knocking.

"For you? Never." Roshar snaps his fingers. "Everyone out."

A flurry of cotton, a rush of lemon-scented air, and we are alone.

Quiet presses upon my ears. With space enough to breathe, I enter the room and collapse onto a cushioned armchair near one of the many windows. Beyond, the sky is brutally clear. I cannot remember when clouds were last stitched into its blue fabric.

Tilting back my head, I close my eyes. Deep breath—in, and out. And again.

"Rough day?" asks Roshar.

If only he knew. I pinch the bridge of my nose, willing the tension between my eyes to dissipate. "I've said it before and I'll say it again. I would trade places with you in a heartbeat."

Roshar *tsks* as though I'm admitting to some horrible offense. "You can't mean that. I may be the royal tailor, but at the end of the day, I am still a tailor."

Yet he is unburdened, and free.

I glance around the room. It is draped in riotous color: ruby and citrine and amber and jade. Heaps of fabric weigh down the long tables shoved against the walls. Various works-in-progress hang from the ceiling, including a long, ivory robe embellished in silver thread.

Roshar is equally embellished: scarlet trousers, tawny robe, white headscarf. I am forever in awe at how far my friend has come. Ten years ago, he was but a lowly apprentice. Now, he is tailor to the royal family.

"What's on your mind, dear?"

Nervous energy bristles under my skin. It flows down my left arm, through my fingertips, into a subtle *tap-tap* against the chair arm in a rhythm I have not thought of in years. Even now, the melody that accompanies this rhythm shimmers against my eardrums in a ghostly echo of the past. I flinch and curl my fingers into a fist.

"Once again," I say, "I fear I fall short in my father's eyes."

"Is that all?" he asks with too much knowing, taking a seat in a neighboring chair.

No. It is not even the half of it.

"I never say the right things. I continually dishonor him. My actions are humiliating, disgraceful, unwanted." I clench my jaw in an effort to ward off the rising shame. "Sometimes I wonder if my father wouldn't prefer that Fahim were here in my stead." And me buried beneath the earth.

Roshar's expression falls into a rare somberness. "You don't mean that."

"I do," I whisper. I very well do.

Reaching out, he takes my hand between his thin, bandaged fingers. Blood spots the cloth where one too many needles have pricked him. Customarily, no man may touch an unmarried woman. But why should I not accept comfort when it is offered? I am to die in just over a month, and the affection of a friend is much needed. Besides, Roshar prefers men in his bed, not women.

Springing upright, Roshar moves to the opposite side of the room and returns with a plate bearing a small pomegranate tart. Wordlessly, he sets the plate in my hand, passes over a fork. "You look like you need it."

My smile wavers in gratitude. "Thank you." I was born into privilege, Ammara's riches my inheritance, yet I have but one friend. I do not trust the women at court. They slip their fingers between the bars as though I am a bird in a cage, offering me morsels, crumbs. Apparently, I am only good enough for favors.

"All right." Roshar plops onto a stool upholstered in olive green fabric, a cup of refreshing mint tea in hand. "Tell me what happened."

Gently, I tap the tines of my fork against the plate. "I met the man I am to eventually marry this morning."

"I see." He takes a sip. "Let me guess. He was dreadfully dull."

I shrug. "I haven't formed an opinion of him yet." Though I appreciated Prince Balior's effort to shield me from Father's ire. These initial weeks, the prince and I will court, until the engagement is formalized. Then: marriage. "And . . . there's more."

"Oh?" Roshar perks up, takes another sip.

I abandon all propriety and shove the entire pastry into my mouth. Through bulging cheeks, I manage, "Notus has returned."

Roshar spews his tea everywhere. "What!"

I mop the tea from my face with a square of cloth, mouth quirked. "Must I repeat myself?"

He snaps into motion: across the room, to the door, the window, back to the stool. "By the gods, Sarai. You can't just drop this information into my lap without warning." Gradually, his astonishment hones itself into a bright, eager curiosity. "When did this happen? Why? Have you seen him? I need details."

I respond around the sweet acidity of pomegranate jam. Our meeting occurred just this morning. No, I was not aware he had returned. Yes, Father knows of his presence. Oh, and he appointed Notus as a member of the Royal Guard.

"The Royal Guard? Oh, goodness. I need to sit." He collapses onto the stool, fanning himself with one of his sketches. "Does Amir know?" A sharp gasp sounds as his hand flies to his mouth. "Can you imagine the bloodshed?"

My stomach quivers with unease, and I set the plate aside. Perhaps I should not have eaten so much so quickly. "No," I reply. "He's still on his honeymoon." Lucky him, that he should be granted the opportunity of seeing the world while I am expected to remain here, forever tied to the prince. "I'm sure it will be fine. He has more important things to worry about than petty revenge."

Roshar's gaze communicates his disagreement, but thankfully, he doesn't press the issue. "How are you though, truly?" His eyes soften behind his glasses. "It's been years since he left, but . . ."

But time is treacherous. Seasons may have waxed and waned, yet I stood before the South Wind mere hours ago and felt as if I were once again a girl of eighteen.

"Honestly?" I swallow painfully. "Confused." It took years to rebuild my life. During that time, I'd grieved not only Notus, but Fahim as well. I decided then that vulnerability would never again hold power over me. My heart would belong only to myself.

Roshar squeezes my fingers in solidarity. "That is valid. Expected, even." He frowns, perhaps noticing how my hand trembles. "What's your plan?"

"Plan?"

"I assume you are already plotting how best to murder the South Wind?"

My mouth relaxes into the smallest curve. "How did you know?"

"How will we do it? Tell me." He leans forward with all the eagerness of a young pup. "You know I'm always here to help bury a body."

I do know. And I appreciate him for that. But I do not wish for Notus' death. Merely his suffering.

"I'll need time to think about it," I say.

Seeing that my mood has improved slightly, Roshar wanders to a far window, where he halts. "Oh, my." The glitter of his rings catches the light as he rests a hand over his chest. "Sarai. It's him! He looks even more handsome than I remember." He glances over his shoulder, notes my sour-faced expression, and winces. "Honestly, dear, you have eyes. Tell me he isn't one of the most delectable men you've ever seen!"

Despite my knotted gut, something tugs me gently, then with insistence, toward the window overlooking the central courtyard, where a rounded, crumbling structure the color of bone squats. For twenty-five years, the labyrinth has shadowed the palace's very heart. It was built immediately following the bargain King Halim struck with the Lord of the Mountain. In exchange for my life, the all-powerful god required a stronghold secure enough to contain a beast for all eternity. That should have been the end of it.

When the annual floods failed to appear the following year, however, Father suspected something was amiss. He returned to Mount Syr, demanding an explanation. It was then the Lord of the Mountain revealed the true price of his benevolence.

In exchange for my life, Ammara would suffer a slow decay. No longer would the summer rains enrich the soil, swell the dams, quench the farms. Though I would live, it would be a cursed existence. For on my twenty-fifth nameday, the Lord of the Mountain will return to claim my life.

Shifting my attention to the far side of the labyrinth, I watch Notus circle the courtyard. Every so often, his hand drifts to the hilt of his scimitar. That quiet gaze, always seeking, never still.

Once a decade, seven men are sacrificed to the beast imprisoned within the labyrinth. A blasphemous creature, its appetite must always be satiated. No matter the efforts, none could slay it. Notus, however, arrived in Ishmah six years ago promising to slay the beast. He was unsuccessful. To this day, he is the only one to have escaped the labyrinth. In a way, it makes sense that he should be the one to guard it.

"Look at his shoulders, those *thighs*." Roshar bumps his hip to mine. "I wouldn't mind having those wrapped around my—"

"Roshar!"

His high, cackling laughter chases my outburst. I shake my head, then shove him for good measure. He only laughs harder.

Abruptly, he straightens, nose pressed against the glass. "And who is this?" An eagerness whets his tone. "Your future prince?"

My eyes cut left. I spot Prince Balior emerging from the guest wing of the palace. The moment he enters Notus' line of sight, the South Wind slows.

They regard each other across the expanse of baked stone. Prince Balior glances at the labyrinth, frowns, then approaches Notus. I lean closer, face plastered to the searing glass. God and prince, ex-lover and future husband. They converse for an uncomfortably long time.

Roshar angles toward me, mouth pursed. "One woman caught between two men. There are worse things in life."

I am not so certain. The god who broke my heart, or the man I must bind myself to for the remainder of my days, whether I want to or not?

When Prince Balior advances toward the labyrinth's arched entryway, Notus sidesteps, blocking his way forward. Though I cannot read the South Wind's expression behind the headscarf shielding his face, I imagine his response to be low, calm, thrumming with command. None may approach. That is law.

Eventually, Prince Balior gives up and returns to the guest wing. I step back from the window. The air has grown heavier, if possible. These walls sag inward, smothering my skin.

"I need air," I mutter, heading for the door.

"Wait!" Roshar scurries after me. "Take this."

He offers me a second pomegranate tart. I peer at him in exasperation.

"You're going to need it," he says.

Amir is scheduled to return to Ishmah with his new bride in a matter of weeks.

His timing could not possibly be worse. Between the South Wind's return, Prince Balior's arrival, and my own impending death, I do not have the mental capacity to pile yet another worry onto my plate. And I dread how our reunion might unfold. We did not part on the best terms. I begged him not to go, but Amir would not be swayed. Our argument grew heated. I ridiculed his lack of leadership. He mocked my inability to cope without him. Then he left. Without a proper goodbye, without . . . anything. Three months later, the memory remains bitter.

The palace staff are already deep in preparations for my brother's return. It is to be expected. One day, he will bear the weight of a crown on his head, a kingdom on his shoulders. The responsibility was never his to carry, but such is life, changing as unexpectedly as the sands. I do not envy him this fate.

A wall of scorching heat blasts me as I emerge into the courtyard. A few attendants scurry between the various wings, carting baskets of laundry or cleaning supplies. Sunlight boils the stone slabs underfoot. The labyrinth gleams with an alabaster shine.

I circle the structure twice, but Notus is strangely absent. Is it possible the king called for him in the time it took me to travel from Roshar's workroom? The labyrinth is rarely left unguarded. Still, a sentinel may fall prey to the beast. It is not unheard of. Prior to Notus' presence, King Halim struggled to retain guards. Too easily, they were lured inside.

As for the door to the labyrinth, it is constructed from neither clay nor sand nor metal nor stone. A symbol bearing a likeness to the moon or sun has been carved into its face, with a triangle slicing through its center. When my hand hovers over its surface, a whiff of frigid air billows against my palm.

Hello, Sarai.

I startle and whip around. "Notus?"

No one is there.

Disquiet slinks through me, and I hurriedly return to my chambers. There, I sit at my desk and remove my journal, which I open to the most recent page of numbers. An unending line of x's, which will soon cease to exist. Tomorrow, day forty-six. My heart palpitates at the thought.

I glance toward the window. Sundown. I'm late for my lesson.

The south wing's main passage overlooks a light-filled atrium, a large garden sprouting from the first floor below. It holds a collection of climbing wisteria, fragrant laurel trees, and still pools bordered by pebbles. As I turn a corner, I hear it. The muffled reverberation of the violin's lower register, followed by the slurred notes of an ascending scale.

My breath catches, and I slow upon reaching the music room, peering through the partially open door.

A wizened man swathed in pale yellow robes sits near the window overlooking the palace orchards. Ibramin: the greatest virtuoso of his generation. Brightened by a beam of waning sunlight, instrument cradled between shoulder and chin, he shifts from first position to third, the bow drawing forth a sound of deep anguish, notes warbling with a slow vibrato. I press a palm to my chest, teeth gritted as my eyes sting with feeling.

I have performed every manner of concerto, sonata, romance, caprice, partita, and show piece. I have mastered every étude, memorized every scale in every key. This, I do not recognize.

But I cannot deny its beauty, and its ache. When the music reaches its resolution, I am released from its painful spell. I wipe my eyes, loose a long, shuddering breath. Once my emotions are under control, I enter.

Ibramin smiles in greeting. "Good afternoon, Sarai." He rolls his wheeled chair toward me. "I anticipate you've been working diligently this week?"

Every week without fail my teacher asks this. And every week without fail I reply, "I have."

It matters not that I haven't touched my instrument in years. I can barely look at it without thinking of Fahim, for he, too, loved the violin, was an even greater prodigy than I. We often took lessons together before his duties as heir forced him to abandon the endeavor. Granted, my career as a concert violinist is unusual, considering my station, but Father encouraged me to pursue music. I believe it helped him feel closer to our mother, who had once been an accomplished violinist herself.

Crossing the room, I settle into a chair opposite Ibramin. A faded green rug ornaments the floor, while shelves stuffed with sheet music span one wall. My life can be measured in memories of this place and all that I've achieved.

I am four years old, the smallest of violins placed in my chubby hands.

I am eight years old, drilling scales and études for four hours daily.

I am twelve years old, debuting with the Ishmah Symphony Orchestra.

I am fifteen years old, and my reputation precedes me. I perform in the most prestigious concert halls throughout Ammara, at every major city along the Spice Road. I witness places I have never been, things I have never seen.

I am eighteen years old, and in love. I practice with a frenzy I have never before experienced, joy unfurling with every singing note.

I am nineteen years old, and overcome with sorrow. When I tuck the violin beneath my chin, the music does not come. I place the instrument in its case, shove it into the back of my wardrobe. I abandon it, and myself.

"Sarai?"

I startle. Ibramin regards me in concern. "Apologies, sir," I say. "My mind was elsewhere. Did you say something?"

"I asked if you would play something for me. *Winter's Lullaby?*" He searches my face, seeking what, I am not sure. "You always loved that one."

I shift uncomfortably in my chair. He is right. I do. *Did.* "I don't know if I feel up to playing," I respond, as I do each time he asks. "It has been a tiresome day."

"Will you at least try?"

The pleading in his voice does not go unnoticed. *Try.* It does not seem so perilous a word. Harmless, really, without any expectation attached.

Generally, Ibramin and I spend lessons reviewing music theory and counterpoint. Most days, we sit in silence. I pretend to study, and he pretends I have not completely abandoned music. But sometimes . . . sometimes, he asks me to perform. Always, I decline. But today? Something new.

I nod in compliance, watching as Ibramin wheels to my side before offering me his instrument. A deep red varnish coats the flamed maple back. My violin's coloring is much lighter in comparison, a uniform gold with darker whorls near the tail piece.

As I accept the familiar weight of the violin, my throat narrows, and I remember all that I wish to forget.

There is Fahim's face, the pearly flash of his laughing mouth as I watched him perform. Then, years later, the fatigue dulling his once-bright eyes. There is the unease of silence during meals where merriment had once thrived. There is his bedroom door, my palm resting against the cool wood, confusion and fear intertwined after he'd failed to come down to breakfast. And there is what lies beyond that door, which still haunts me to this day.

"Will you play?" Ibramin asks.

Gently, I return the violin to its case. "I will not."

4

The following morning, there's a knock on my door.

"From His Majesty," the messenger states, the king's waxen seal still warm when I pluck the parchment from the man's grip.

Prince Balior will join us for dinner tonight. I expect your arrival promptly at seven. Do not be late.

Biting the inside of my cheek, I crumple the parchment in my fist. "Please notify the king that I will be in attendance," I inform the messenger, then shut the door.

Quiet seethes into my chambers, slithering through the cracks in the floor. An echo of an old panic eats at me.

Moving toward the window, I peer out over the Red City. A blistering flare of color daubs the horizon. The sandstorm is miles off, yet it cloaks all in a red haze: ideal conditions for a darkwalker attack.

I cast my eyes down to the palace grounds below. A figure, blurred behind the encroaching dim, shifts across the courtyard with an effortlessness belonging only to the divine. *Of course* the South Wind is practicing his swordsmanship, and *of course* he would do so bare from the waist up. At this hour, the air still holds a chill, but sweat glazes his muscled torso, threads of black hair plastered against his neck. Admittedly, I have never met anymore more gifted with a sword. It is to him as the violin once was to me. I watch the shift of muscle as he cuts down an invisible opponent, and my face stings with heat. I may loathe the immortal, but I'm not dead—yet.

I force myself to turn away, no matter how compelling the sight. Ishmah calls to me. I cannot stay.

After tossing on my cloak, I quickly descend the stairs, taking a few lesser-known corridors to reach the smaller western gate. As an adolescent, I would often escape into the city when Father's expectations began to feel particularly taxing. Hours I would spend, exploring the public gardens, the crooked footpaths of the souk. When Father discovered my disobedience, he sealed the gates, forbidding me to enter the city without an escort. In retaliation, I bribed his watchmen.

"Your Highness." A middle-aged man named Mohan dips his chin in acknowledgment. The younger guard beside him, Emin, beams at me.

One by one, I drop five gold coins into each of their palms. "I will be returning in approximately two hours." *Clink, clink.* "If Father asks after me"—*clink*—"you know what to say."

Mohan flashes his teeth as the gold disappears inside his fist. Emin appears positively giddy over his heavier pockets. "You were last spotted reading in one of the gardens and asked not to be disturbed."

I have trained them well.

It does not take long to reach the Old Quarter. Head ducked, hood shadowing my face, I dive into the vibrancy of the souk, skirting the area where farmers congregate, their wagons and carts cluttered together like toys in a chest. Aromas of onion, garlic, and pepper wend through the mill of patrons, layering themselves upon the mouthwatering scent of grilled meat.

And yet, the produce is diminished, touched by disease. The grains are shriveled, the fruit scarce and picked over. Farmers are forced to travel many miles to the nearest oasis for water, which depletes year after year. It is not enough to sustain the city. But we do what we can.

A stall near the end of the lane draws my eye, and I halt, shock rooting me in place. A woman sits behind a display of black iris, calmly biting into a bruised peach. Velvet petals painted the black of a deep well. The forbidden bloom.

King Halim ordered the removal of black iris from Ishmah decades ago. It was a lengthy affair, and thorough. Every dusky bud ripped from the flower beds, the gardens, the smallest pots sunning themselves in kitchen windows. All imports were permanently banned. If black iris is discovered in a citizen's possession, the penalty is death.

For that is how I am to die, according to our Lord of the Mountain. A prick from the thorn of Ammara's most beloved flower.

Which begs the question: How did *this* woman manage to slip past the gates with the deadly blooms? I glance around. No one seems to detect the flowers, or care. She is breaking the law, yet I do not wish for her to die. It is so hard to make a living in this drought-stricken land. As long as I do not touch the flower itself, I am safe.

I browse another cart farther on. This merchant sells fine necklaces of hammered copper and silver, among other things. I frown, touching the surface of a small, ruby-inlaid mirror with a fingertip. I'm certain I saw something move within the looking glass. As I peer closer, my hand stills.

I need not spot the South Wind to sense his presence. It arrives as a cloud of heat against my nape, the scent of salt and hot stone. I grit my teeth against the unexpected ache. My body remembers that scent viscerally.

"If your plan is to stalk me without notice," I drawl, "you are doing a poor job of it."

"Does your father know you're here?" he asks in a low, welling pitch, more vibration than sound.

"You are well acquainted with King Halim." Despite my quickening pulse, I continue to peruse the merchant's offerings. "I imagine you can answer that question yourself."

Notus enters my periphery then. This large, broad, sturdy man who, despite our similar height, overwhelms the surrounding space. It enrages me, that he should still have this effect on me. I shove the feeling down as deep as it can go, grinding the sentiment beneath my heel until it is dust.

"The guards put your life at risk in allowing you to enter the city without an escort," he says in disapproval. "That is no laughing matter."

I tuck my tongue against my cheek. Clearly, gold is not enough to guarantee their silence. "I am Princess Sarai Al-Khatib," I state, plucking the mirror from the table and lifting it to the sun. "I may do whatever I like."

"Your position grants you certain privileges. Of that, there is no doubt. But you must consider the dangers, Sarai—"

My head whips toward him. "Do not speak to me so informally, sir."

I do not believe the South Wind is breathing. Then again, neither am I.

Deliberately, I place the mirror back onto the table with the utmost care. I will my spine into hardened brick, my mind into stone. Yet my heart is wounded. I feel its cry beneath my ribs, for to look at this immortal is to remember all that I have lost. I once believed I was enough for the South Wind. Certainly, he was enough for me. All I wish now is to ask him why. *Why* was I not enough? Was I too hotheaded, too ambitious, too proud?

Eventually, Notus dips his chin in compliance. "Forgive me, Princess Sarai."

My throat thickens with an unexpected rush of sorrow. For there was once a time when I was Princess Sarai to all but him.

"You've been following me," I manage to choke out. "Why?"

A woman hauling a massive barrel of grain cuts between us in an attempt to squeeze through the hectic market. The South Wind steps to the side until she has passed. "Your father asked me to keep an eye on you."

"And that's the only reason you're here?"

Notus does not reply, and my heart sinks. It is all the answer I need.

Pushing past him, I delve deeper into the chaos of the souk. The storyteller's hour nears. On the heels of misery, always, is anger. Who is he to speak of danger? He cannot understand how high the palace walls rise.

Frustratingly, Notus follows, carving a path with ease through the throng. We pass a cluster of women dyeing fabric in large wooden tubs.

"Are you capable of developing your own opinion," I challenge, "or must you always do the king's bidding?"

"Your safety is the king's priority."

I scoff, sidestepping a malnourished dog as I turn down a calmer path between two buildings. "How ironic."

"What, exactly, is ironic about this situation?"

"If Father wished to keep me safe, he would have stationed you as far away from me as possible."

Despite the obvious insult, Notus' tone remains even-keeled. "You are not making his life any easier by placing yourself in harm's way. Do you think a cloak will stop someone from recognizing you? Hurting you?"

Harm's way? What utter horse shit. "The Old Quarter is one of the safest areas of the capital," I retort. "Even if I were recognized, no one would dare lay a hand on me. It is in everyone's best interest to uphold security." Ishmah is, after all, the heart of Ammara's trade. Due to our depleted resources, the majority of its citizens depend on goods acquired from far-reaching villages, and increased crime would only lead to a decline in business. They would not risk losing their livelihood to hurt me.

"You are not as safe as you are made to believe." He slots into place behind me, his wide frame a blockade against the rising tide of pass-ersby. This, too, I remember: how his body would shift in a reflection of mine. "There have been reports," he continues. "Two women were reported missing by their families just this week. Last month, a young man was found mutilated in an alley, evidence of a darkwalker attack."

My blood sparks with dark energy, a dull pulsation of climbing rage.

"Even today—"

I spin around. Only quick reflexes prevent Notus from slamming into me.

"Stop it," I hiss. "You're trying to frighten me. It will not work. This is *my* home, *my* realm. You are a visitor at best, an outsider at worst."

Notus gazes at me steadily, brown eyes watchful above his face scarf. Emotion flickers there and is gone. Sorrow, if I am not mistaken.

"Let me be absolutely clear," I say, stepping aside so a harried mother carrying two swaddled infants can pass. "There are no darkwalkers inside Ishmah's walls. They have never been breached. Your fearmongering has no place here."

My pace quickens as I push onward. No longer do I neatly skirt those in my path. No, I knock those smaller and weaker aside, elbowing my way past women carting large skeins of cotton and wool. Meanwhile, Notus dogs my heels, an unwelcome shadow at my back.

"Will you inform the king of my outing?" I call over my shoulder, turning into another alley. Notus matches my stride with frustrating ease.

"That depends." He sounds scarcely out of breath. "Will you continue to explore the market despite your father's orders?"

"I will do as I please."

"Then I have no choice but to notify him of your whereabouts."

At this point, I would be thrilled to lose him, whether he informs Father or not. The faded yellow door at the end of the lane is a welcome sight, and I 'm rushing toward it when Notus catches my arm. "Where are you going?" he demands.

Despite the power of his grip, his fingers tighten only enough to halt my forward motion. "Let me pass," I snap. "I'm late for the story."

"Story?"

I wrench free of his hold. Do I wish him to know I sit at a grandmother's knee to hear her tales? No. But I have failed to shake him loose. "I visit the storyteller often. I started attending when—" I shake my head, unwilling to mention Fahim's passing. "It's harmless. Just a handful of children listening to an old woman speak. If you wish to be of service to my father, then make yourself useful and stand watch."

Notus eyes the battered door with deep mistrust. One end of his scarf has pulled lose, but he tucks it back in place, strands of black hair poking free of the cloth. "I would prefer to accompany you inside. What if one of them is a threat?"

I scoff. "They're children, Notus. I'll be fine."

He merely glares at me. "I'm serious."

"As am I. These people don't know who I am. I want to keep it that way. Stay here." Spinning on my heel, I slip inside, grateful for the darkness that cools my rising frustration. Quietly, I settle in the back of the room. Haneen has already begun to weave her threads. Hopefully I have not missed much.

Aziza snatched up her tunic, hurriedly shrugging it on to cover her nakedness.

Omar stared at her in bewilderment. "You're a woman."

Aziza lifted her chin in defiance. Yes, she was a woman masquerading as a man in their nation's army. The punishment was death. "And? Will you turn me in?"

"You know that I must."

Her lip curled in disgust. "You would have lost your life in the last battle if not for me." The first few weeks of training, Aziza had wondered if she would survive. But she had learned. She had pushed herself when others had languished. She had refused to accept defeat.

Omar scanned their surroundings, as if only now realizing their isolated location. Aziza glanced at where she'd leaned her sword against a nearby boulder. Omar eyed it as well.

A few children gasp in panic. A slow grin spreads across my mouth as I lean forward, watching the woman's milky eyes flicker deviously.

"Don't do it," Omar warned as his hand went to his own sword.

For whatever reason, Omar's mistrust after months spent side by side in combat made Aziza's heart sink. "Kill me then," she whispered.

Omar frowned, yet he did not shift any nearer. Perhaps he was recalling how Aziza had saved his life. "Why would a woman choose a soldier's life?"

"I took my grandfather's identity to protect him. He would not have survived the war."

Omar was quiet for a time, gazing out over the river. Eventually, he said, "And when your secret comes to light? I will be connected with that deceit. I, too, will face certain death."

"Then we must keep it between ourselves."

When Haneen stops for the day, the children begin filing out, chatting amongst themselves excitedly with the promise of next week's tale. I spot Notus near the door, blending into the shadows. My mouth thins as I stride over to him. "I told you to wait outside."

The South Wind takes stock of the room. It is sparsely furnished, wanting. The old bard perches on her stool, head canted in our direction. Despite my attempts to corral him out the door, Notus will not budge.

"This is where you go when you leave the palace?" he questions.

I restrain myself from clobbering him on the head. He may as well shout that I am Princess of Ammara for all to hear. When I glance at the storyteller, I find her smiling.

"Outside," I growl. "Now."

Notus allows himself to be herded back onto the street, though I am not so naive as to believe I am physically capable of maneuvering him. As we begin our return trek to the palace, a brassy clang tears across the city. The warning bell. Three tolls signal an approaching sandstorm. Five tolls warn of darkwalkers.

Two, three . . . The ringing stops.

It is impressive how swiftly the streets empty. In moments, Notus and I are the only ones left standing in the alley. He looks to me. I look to him. "We should get back," he says.

Clearly. A few strategically selected shortcuts through the souk deposit us onto the King's Road. The wind rises. Its scalding gusts blast through the streets, groping at my dress and tearing at the hood of my cloak. Soon, the palace gates are in sight.

Of course, Notus continues to shadow me. I turn to glower at him. "Isn't the bell your cue to help secure the city?"

He meets my gaze squarely. "I will once you're safe inside the palace. King Halim doesn't want anything to befall you, after what happened to your brother." They are too quiet, these words. "My condolences—"

I stiffen. "That is why you returned? So you could apologize for something that has nothing to do with you?" I feel the barrier rise, brick by crumbling brick. "Fahim died five years ago."

You were not here, I think. The words choke me. I dare not utter them.

The South Wind stares at the ground as though his life depends on it. "I wasn't aware. It saddened me to learn of his passing," he says lowly. "I enjoyed your brother's company, for however short a time I knew him."

Another thing I have tried to forget: the image of Notus and Fahim sparring, bare torsos pouring sweat. My brother had been an excellent swordsman, but the South Wind was something else entirely. Sometimes, I suspected Notus let him win.

"It is cruel that a hunting accident took him so young. I'm truly sorry for your loss."

A hunting accident. That was the explanation King Halim gave to inform Ammara's population of Fahim's death. But nothing could be farther from the truth.

"Your brother," Notus continues, "was a good man."

He is mistaken. Fahim was not just a *good* man. He was the best.

"Why did you come back?" My voice quavers, and I fear it will fracture into a thousand pieces if I allow it. I vowed never to reveal such weakness, yet I am burdened by the echo of my past, its wretched refusal to die.

Something shifts behind Notus' eyes. It frightens me, tears open this unhealed wound within me, and once more, I am bleeding out unseen.

Hurriedly, I turn away, breath short, chest tight. Whatever emotion he has expressed, I do not care to acknowledge it.

"Sarai—"

"Never mind. It doesn't matter anyway." My heart stutters with the uncontrollable urge to flee. "Tell the king what you will. It will only reinforce what I already know: that you are little more than a mindless dog, lacking any thought or willpower of your own."

When I enter through the palace gates, the South Wind does not follow.

5

"Announcing Princess Sarai Al-Khatib."

The double doors to the dining room open simultaneously, revealing a long table laden with silverware, which sparks stars in the low candlelight. King Halim and Prince Balior have already arrived, the latter rising to his feet upon my entrance. The prince has donned a pale gray robe intricately threaded at the collar, and a matching headscarf. Father dictated that I wear red: the national color of Um Salim. Thus, I am draped in cloth of rich scarlet, heavy as clotted blood.

"Princess Sarai." The prince bows low, a lock of mahogany hair falling across his brow.

I dip my chin in greeting. "Prince Balior."

Father's disapproving glare cuts toward me. *Do not disappoint me*, it warns. Inwardly, I sigh. "Thank you for joining us this evening," I manage to say. "I hope the food will be to your liking."

"I'm certain it will be." Catching my eye, he smiles tentatively. "Though I admit I'm more eager for the company than the meal."

My smile sours before it has the chance to form. "Then I hope I will not disappoint." Despite my attempt at pleasantries, my irksome encounter with Notus this morning has refused to loosen its grip on me. Even now, my blood continues its prolonged simmer.

With a curt nod, I cross the dining room, disregarding the men stationed along the room's perimeter. The bell tower tolls the seventh hour as I settle into the cushioned chair. Right on time, as promised.

King Halim, who sits at the head of the table, appears sunken in the low light. His violet robe hangs like bands of old skin from his arms. The sight pains me. Though having not yet reached his seventieth year, the king has failed to fully recover from a recent illness. For months, he was bedridden, liquid flooding his lungs. Despite the royal physician's remedies, his strength has continued to erode. I notice the effort this attendance costs him, and I worry he may overtax himself.

But Father would only dismiss my concerns if I voiced them, especially in front of the prince. So I brush my unease aside and focus on the matter at hand as the attendants begin serving our meal. Prince Balior. Thirty-two years of age. The eldest of King Oman's sons. And, if negotiations are favorable, soon to be my betrothed.

There was a time when I fought against fate. But it is a sacrifice I must make. Ammara will benefit from Um Salim's vast army, its rich, fertile grounds. Once I am gone, it is my hope that I will have made a deep-enough connection with Prince Balior that he will do everything in his power to protect my realm and its people.

King Halim begins to cut into his spiced lamb. "I hear you are an accomplished horseman, Prince Balior."

Our guest appears wryly amused. Shy, even. "I would not go so far so as to call myself accomplished, though I have ridden since boyhood. Father and I would often venture into the mountains for days at a time. They are among my most cherished memories."

Well. At least the prince is humble.

"Perhaps you are unaware, Prince Balior, but Ishmah boasts some of the fastest horses on this side of the desert." Father slides a sliver of meat between his teeth. "I guarantee you will find no swifter mount."

And just like that, he has commanded the prince's attention. "Do you breed them?"

"We do." King Halim is too proud a man. "The herd is small, yet healthy."

Prince Balior dishes a spoonful of date-studded rice into his mouth. The motion draws my eye, and I watch the darting of his pink tongue. When his gaze catches mine, I immediately look elsewhere, fearing I have overstepped.

After a moment, he clears his throat. "I would be interested in seeing the herd. I've a stable at Um Salim. Perhaps, once negotiations are over, we could discuss crossbreeding our species."

"Crossbreeding?" King Halim sounds appalled. "Absolutely not. The bloodlines must remain pure."

One of the attendants refills the prince's wine before returning to his station along the wall. "Pardon my ignorance, Your Majesty." It is a solace, his voice, the sedate response of one who seeks to cool that which has begun to spark and burn. "I only thought we might both benefit from the transaction. The strength of my horses paired with the swiftness of yours. Could you imagine such a creature?"

It is compelling, his vision. What is the harm, truly? Then again, Father loathes change.

"Perhaps," the king concedes.

"What about you, Princess Sarai?" Prince Balior turns his curious gaze onto me. "What do you think of this enterprise?"

The unexpected shift in attention takes me aback. I haven't the time to spin my words, soften them into something more palatable. "Seeing as I know little of horse breeding, I'm probably not the best person to ask."

The prince appears even more intrigued. "But you are familiar with horses, no?"

I do not glance at King Halim, though I certainly feel his gaze on my face, likely warning me to mind my tongue. "I am, yes. My mother was fond of them, or so I was told." Even after all this time, the reminder stings. "She would know better than I."

Prince Balior suddenly stiffens, having realized his misstep.

"I apologize." He looks to King Halim, whose expression possesses a smooth blankness of which nothing can penetrate. "It was not my intention to stir up painful memories, Your Majesty. Forgive me for my blunder."

No one is more surprised than I when the king gifts it. The exception is likely circumstantial.

As a child, I often prodded Father for information about my mother. The color of her hair, the scent of her skin. What sounds she loved most in the world. But he refused to offer me the smallest crumb. According to Amir, her death destroyed him, for he loved her as the sun loves the earth. My heart breaks at the thought.

As I spear a glazed carrot, I catch sight of a shadowed figure out of the corner of my eye. My mind blanks. I'm not sure how I could have possibly overlooked the South Wind's presence. I know his shape like no other.

Dressed in indigo robes and an ochre headscarf, he stands motionless against the wall. The small copper pin adorning his chest signifies his position in the Royal Guard. When his dark eyes meet mine, my chest hollows out.

"... and an accomplished violinist."

Wrenching my gaze from Notus, I glance at Father in surprise. He regards me expectantly, eyebrows raised.

"Do you still play?" Prince Balior studies me over the rim of his wineglass.

It is an effort to hone my focus on the conversation, rather than the god swathed in indigo. *Accomplished violinist.* Father truly uttered those words. I have graced Ammara's most esteemed concert halls, toured with the realm's preeminent orchestras. Yet I have never heard Father express pride in my achievements.

With surprising serenity, I reply to Prince Balior, "Not in many years."

"That is a shame." He takes another sip. Red droplets sheen his mouth. "May I ask why you stopped?"

My chest pulls taut, like a network of strings. The prince cannot know the burden this question carries. No one ever explained to me that when a loved one passed, pieces of you died with them.

"I suppose I lost interest," I murmur.

Prince Balior continues to regard me inquisitively. His interest draws up my guard. I smile blandly in response.

"I confess that I knew of your musical triumphs long before our introduction," he continues. "My mother once acquired tickets to one of your concerts. You were scheduled to perform the Jerashi Violin Concerto with our National Symphony Orchestra."

At the time, I was performing five nights a week. Ibramin encouraged me to explore opportunities beyond Ammara's borders, including competitions. *She was born for this*, he'd told Father. *You cannot keep her small.*

Unfortunately, talk with Um Salim soured due to political differences. King Halim was too stubborn a man to set aside his opinions for the sake of my career. He could not have known how heartbroken I'd been to learn the opportunity had been dashed. I cried myself to sleep every night for a month.

"Tensions were high between our realms at the time," I explain. "Father believed it best that the tour be contained to Ammara."

Prince Balior coughs uncomfortably, then sips his wine. I down the remainder of my drink, my skin prickling under the South Wind's scrutiny. King Halim ogles me as though I have gone mad.

"You will have to forgive my daughter," Father eventually grits out. "She has . . . quite the imagination."

My lips curve bitterly. "I was simply explaining to Prince Balior the reason I was unable to perform."

"That's enough, Sarai. When your opinion is requested, I will call on you. Kindly return to your meal before you spoil the rest of the evening."

I hold the king's enraged gaze. He is pale—too pale. Sweat dots his brow and upper lip, and I am reminded of his deteriorating health. I swallow my shame, for I did not mean to cause him additional stress. My hands tremble as I slice into my lamb. The knife shreds the meat's soft pink center.

A wave of hot air brushes my nape, almost like a caress. My head swings toward Notus. He clasps the hilt of his scimitar in one white-knuckled hand. For once, he is not looking at me, but at Father. The chill of his expression makes my hair stand on end.

As one of the servers piles another scoop of rice onto my plate, I consider the best means of escape. I could feign illness: a sudden fever, perhaps, or wooziness. But I fear the consequences of an early departure. Though I hold no love for this prince, I understand the importance of our union.

Discussion veers toward current events. Prince Balior is aware of our drought, though he does not realize it is the work of dark forces rather than nature running its course. Apparently, Um Salim does not have darkwalkers to contend with, though the prince has heard of them. Both men discourse on how best to distribute resources and aid Ammara's struggling farms.

Eventually, conversation turns to our courting. King Halim dictates how our time will be spent. Breakfast in the mornings. A ball in three weeks' time. Trips to the public gardens and aviary, so that Ishmah's citizens will grow used to Prince Balior's presence.

Lifting my glass, I quickly sip my wine before I do something rash, like toss the liquid into Father's face. Unsurprisingly, he does not ask my opinion on the matter.

"And how many children do you desire, Princess Sarai?" the prince inquires.

My throat spasms around the liquid, and I choke, spewing wine across the table. Ruby droplets stain the white tablecloth.

A babe in my belly. A child yanking on the hem of my dress. The heaviest stone around my neck. How many children do I desire?

None.

I have always known this. Whatever maternal instincts the noblewomen at court claimed would surface, I never experienced them. Perhaps, if my mother were alive, or if I had not developed in the shadow of my early demise, I would think differently. But I know the grief of growing up without a mother, and I would not wish that pain on any child of mine.

"You must produce a male heir, of course." Father's iron tone, edged in denial. He is hopeful Prince Balior will find a way to break the curse. I am not so sure. "You will make that a priority once wed."

I swallow down my protest. Nothing can break me. "My will is Ammara's will."

A small sound draws my attention to the South Wind, who continues to stare at me without attempting to hide it. I'm almost certain it was a scoff. As if he knows anything about the trials I face.

"Prince Balior." I offer our guest my warmest smile. "Since you are so fond of horses, would you care to accompany me on a ride tomorrow? The weather should be ideal." Granted, the stretch of desert separating Ishmah from Kir Bashab—Ammara's largest oasis—will be brutal, but once beneath the cover of dense forest, the temperature will be downright pleasant.

Prince Balior grins in return. What pleasing features he has. Had I not been so distracted by the South Wind's unwanted presence, I may have noticed sooner. "I would be honored, Princess Sarai."

At this, my smile widens, a bit too brittle, a bit too bright. "No need for formalities." I look to the South Wind as I say, "Just 'Sarai' will do."

6

DAWN FLAMES THE DESERT SANDS, YET THE RED CITY STILL sleeps.

I arrive at the stables early to saddle the horses. Lamps flicker from their posts, producing small wells of amber light. The horses stir as I pass, dropping their heads over their stalls. Hoda, marked by a white star on her sandy forehead. Khaleed, whose coat is black as pitch. Shielded by stacked bales of hay, I am merely Sarai, a woman in the stables with the horses.

Zainab greets me with an expectant nudge against my shoulder. Of course, I have not arrived empty-handed. I present her the apple from my pocket. She consumes the fruit with an exuberant crunch.

"Hello, darling," I coo, unlocking her stall door. "It's been some time, no?"

Too long. Since Amir's departure, Father's expectations have climbed so high as to be nearly out of reach. I must attend every social event, every tedious political dinner. I must answer graciously. I must remember names, policies, ranks, titles. I must smile, always smile. Ask questions. Be happy, eager, *engaged*.

My throat cinches painfully, and I press my forehead against the mare's muscular neck, struggling to breathe. Sometimes I feel as if I am little more than an ornament, something polished to catch the light, drawing the eye for a brief interlude.

Last night's conversation returns in waves of increasing apprehension. I cannot shed the image of a babe in my belly. If Prince Balior possesses the answers we seek, that is what the future will hold for me. And if he does not? I will have wasted my final days catering to the whims of others.

It takes longer than usual to saddle Zainab. She prances in place, for she understands the weight of a saddle signifies a long, hard run. I cannot fault her for that. It is what she loves best. Generally, it is the hostlers' responsibility to saddle the mounts, but I prefer completing the task myself. I have so little control over my own life. It feels necessary, taking matters into my own hands.

I'm slotting the metal pin into Zainab's billet when an unexpected whisper of heat teases the ends of my hair. My skin tingles from the sensation.

Without turning around, I say, "Are you to be Father's errand boy in addition to his guard?"

Hay crunches beneath the South Wind's heavy tread. "I'm not here to deliver a message."

"Then why are you here?"

When he fails to respond, I turn to face him. Tendrils of ebony hair poke from beneath his equally black headscarf. His eyes, glittering like beetles on hot desert rock, sit beneath thick, strong eyebrows. Even after all this time, he is still the most handsome man—god—I have ever laid eyes on. The Lord of the Mountain must truly hate me, to test me this way.

"I am to accompany you on your ride," he says.

I bite back a particularly venomous response. Lovely. Absolutely lovely. "If you recall from last night's discussion, I will be properly escorted. Prince Balior will see to my well-being." Turning my back, I tighten the cinch before moving to saddle Essam, a handsome chestnut with coal stockings. I'm surprised Father is allowing the prince to ride him, considering his aggressive temperament. Not even I am allowed to mount King Halim's prized stallion.

"With all due respect," he goes on, "Prince Balior is a stranger. Until your union as husband and wife is made law—"

"You mean until he is in my bed?"

A muscle twitches in Notus' jaw. I am petty enough to claim it as a victory, though paired with the triumph is the confusion this interaction holds, because there was a time when the only person I wished to share my bed was the immortal standing before me.

With admirable effort, I refocus my attention on Essam. "There will be time enough for Prince Balior and I to get to know one another. I understand you're not from this realm, but these are our customs. Courtship, then engagement." Which can only be broken if one of the parties renounces it. "A longer engagement is the norm, however, there are advantages to a shorter one such as mine—"

"You are not engaged," he clips out.

And why should that bother him, I wonder? "Not *yet*," I say with a smile.

The gleam in the stallion's golden eyes is my only warning before he lunges, teeth clicking shut where my hand had been moments before.

"Brute," I growl. He sidles toward the stall wall, making it impossible for me to secure the saddle.

The South Wind presses forward. "How can you trust that the prince's intentions are noble?" An unmistakable edge roughens his tone. It is so rare a thing I'm temporarily distracted from my task and fail to see Essam lunge until his teeth are clamped around my elbow. I swat at him. He rears. The saddle slips from his back. Heavy hooves slash toward my face.

A warm band of air wraps itself around my waist and snaps me back into a hard body. Notus exhales, breath stirring the crown of my head, and I am falling into memory: our bare legs tangled in pale sheets, eve darkening the open window of my chambers. Notus' head tipped back, his mouth parted, his low, agonized groan shivering through me as I played between his legs with hands and tongue and lips until he spent himself in my mouth . . .

I swallow thickly. My nipples rise to points beneath my dress.

As though sensing my body's response, Notus curves one large hand around my hip bone. "Sarai." Low and impossibly deep.

Wrenching free of his grip, I stumble toward the opposite side of the stall. I have been careful to avoid sharing space with the deity who discarded my heart as if it were nothing more than a filthy rag. It hurts that I still remember. That my body still remembers.

I'm no corpse. I am incredibly aware of this immortal's virility, the span of his chest, the hard cut of his muscled arms. Now he is here, forcing himself into my life, and I haven't the slightest notion why. He left. Clearly, I was not enough for him to stay. So why does he pretend to care about me?

The South Wind studies me for a moment before saying, "You claimed you never wished to marry. Why now, after all this time?"

"That's none of your business."

Yet Notus does not retreat. Rather, he steps forward, pushing me further into the stall. The dry scent of the desert air clings to his robes.

"You conform to your father's wishes. This isn't what you wanted for yourself."

He is right. I hate that he is right. "Time passes. People change. I'm not the naive girl I once was." My teeth clench as I fight to contain all the emotion I've repressed over the years, the pieces I've buried longing to tear free. "Perhaps you did not know me as well as you thought you did."

Brushing past him, I grab the saddle from where it had fallen and toss it onto Essam's back.

"Perhaps," he concedes, angling toward me. "But I still find it hard to believe that you would be so foolish as to place your trust in a man you have known for a handful of days."

"Prince Balior is trustworthy."

"You are certain of that?"

Something in the South Wind's tone gives me pause. "If King Halim claims Prince Balior is trustworthy, then he is. I trust Father's judgment." I hesitate, then ask, "What business did he have at the labyrinth yesterday?"

Notus' eyes narrow in suspicion. "How do you know the prince visited the labyrinth?"

"The *how* matters not," I clip out. "Though I noticed you'd deserted your post when I arrived at the courtyard." I maneuver Essam against the wall, keeping him pinned while I attempt to secure the billet. The stallion, however, possesses a much wider girth than my mare. I struggle to slot the pin through the hole.

"Let me."

The South Wind's warm hand covers mine. His callused palm is rough against my skin. I should retreat, yet my traitorous body continues to respond to his proximity. Gods, what is *wrong* with me?

I promptly withdraw, angling away so Notus will not notice my quickening breath. He finishes saddling Essam with ease. The brute does not even bite, as if calmed beneath the immortal's firm yet gentle touch.

"Does Father know you abandoned your station?" I demand. "I suppose I should not be surprised, seeing as how disappearing is what you do best."

Notus stiffens, and pain darkens his eyes. I'm not prepared for how swiftly his expression eviscerates me. It is not enough to blindly hurl barbs and hope they scar. I seek to wound him as he wounded me. That is fair. Justice. But in witnessing his pain, the only thing I feel is an awful, curdling guilt. The truth is this: I loved him, would have given my life for him. Then he was gone without a word, without . . . anything.

"I realize that what I did all those years ago hurt you," he whispers hoarsely. "But you do not know the full story."

My lips quiver. I struggle to speak. "Then what is the full story?"

The blacks of his eyes are an impenetrable shell. "I would rather explain when you are more in control of your emotions. And preferably not in the stables where anyone can eavesdrop."

A small, biting smile crooks my mouth. "Sounds like excuses to me."

The South Wind regards me calmly. He neither cowers nor folds. Always, he plants his feet. He is the rock upon which the wind breaks. I envy him that ability. "I was called elsewhere on your father's orders. That is why I was not at my post the other day. If you want to tell your father, be my guest. But it's pointless to tell the king what he already knows."

"Tell me what?"

I turn. Flanked by four men, King Halim stands in the stable doorway, posture flattened, wilting in the insufferable heat.

Do I trust the South Wind's word, or might there be more to his claims than he is willing to reveal? Ignoring Notus' warning glare, I reply, "That there has been a misunderstanding, Father. Notus seems to think he is to accompany me on the ride."

"That is correct." The king appears unperturbed by my obvious distress. "He will be your chaperone."

Chaperone. Am I a child or a woman grown?

"I'm not certain I understand why I need a chaperone in addition to an escort, Father. Prince Balior is already accompanying me, and I've visited Kir Bashab frequently, as you know. I'm familiar with the trails."

"Do not act dense, Sarai. It is not becoming of you." A sweet reek perfumes Father's robe: the incense used to help rid his wasted body of illness. On the days he is well enough to leave his rooms, the physician encourages him to take walks for his health. The king often visits the stables for this very reason. "You know as well as I do that the dark-walkers grow stronger. I will take no chances."

"And you know as well as I do, Father, that darkwalkers do not typi-cally emerge in broad daylight," I counter, though recent occurrences would suggest otherwise.

"Must you always argue for the sake of argument?" he snaps. "Notus will accompany you. That is final." He begins to exit the stables.

I should be used to the sight of Father's retreating back, but it has the unsettling power of reducing me to a child, mindless with panic at his refusal to stay.

"All my life you have brushed me aside." Despite the rigidity of my posture, the stubborn thrust of my chin, I am ashamed to hear cracks in my voice. "Yet now you act as if I am suddenly dear to you?" Whether or not he acknowledges it, Father remembers my relationship with Notus clearly, for once it came to light, it proved just how little he truly knew his own daughter. Is this punishment, I wonder, for having gone behind his back in my younger years, for seizing my heart's desire?

Slowly, the king turns to face me. His expression hurts to look upon. "I don't know what's come over you of late, but remember that everything I do is to keep you safe. Time is running out, Sarai. What else do you expect me to do?"

I glance at Notus, who is frowning in mystification, likely at the king's vague exclamation. There is some truth to what Father said. I would not be here were it not for him. He risked everything to save my life when I was a newborn. Perhaps I am being ungrateful.

Prince Balior abruptly appears in the doorway, hair freshly combed, beard oiled and trimmed. The rising sun hangs as a red star above his shoulder.

"Prince Balior. Welcome." Drawing him near, King Halim bestows a kiss on the prince's cheek. "I trust you slept well?"

"Indeed." He bows to me. "Princess Sarai."

I smile wanly, suddenly regretting having made this commitment to spite Notus, for I am left drinking its poison. "Prince Balior."

The prince's gaze flicks to the South Wind before settling once more on the king. "May I ask what the pastries that I received for breakfast this morning are called? They were delicious."

"Ah." A rare grin creases Father's face. "They are our prized apricot tarts. I will ask the cook to send a fresh batch to your rooms upon your return."

With that, the king departs, and we mount our horses. Prince Balior appears comfortable enough atop the stallion, directing him with a firm hand while Notus saddles a roan gelding. The prince regards the South Wind for an uncomfortably long time. "Will your guard be accompanying us?"

I offer him a strained smile. "Unfortunately."

Five miles west of the capital, the landscape sheds its skin. Sand dissolves to hardened earth, parched red rock that wavers beneath the blistering air as the Ramil Mountains near. At the foothills, a ring of shocking greenery interrupts the otherwise monochromatic landscape, a thick density of tough, woody trees. Ishmah sits as a smudge in the distance, a rust-colored stain against the gilded backdrop of spreading dunes.

After sipping from my waterskin, I tuck the small container into the bundle of supplies tied to Zainab's saddle. Sweat dampens my underarms, though my light linen dress ensures I do not overheat.

"Do you require a reprieve?" I ask Prince Balior as we ride shoulder to shoulder. "There is shade up ahead."

"Unnecessary." He sits astride the stallion's broad back, reins slack in one hand, sweating quite profusely. Color slashes the paler skin of his cheeks. "The sooner we reach Kir Bashab, the sooner we can return to the palace—and a cooling glass of mint tea."

My mouth quirks. "That's fair." From what I recall of my studies, Um Salim is located at a much lower elevation. Its coastal position provides a cool sea breeze that Ammara lacks. "It's not much further," I reassure my riding companion. "The journey will be worth it, I assure you."

"I trust it will be." There is a pause. "What is that formation in the distance?"

I look to where he points. Splayed across the flattened mountain-top, an ancient stone structure reflects the white light of the sun. "That is Mount Syr, the holiest site in Ammara." Visited during the annual Festival of Rain, the monument contains a large dais and a vast stone chair that may have once been a throne.

"I see." Clearly, I have piqued Prince Balior's interest. "Might we stop for a short visit?"

I wince. Normally, I would agree, but I doubt our chaperone would permit an unplanned detour. "We don't have the time, unfortunately."

The prince frowns in disappointment. Again, he peers out at the holy site before facing forward with a sigh. "So many of our beliefs can be traced back to those ancient places. Even the labyrinth is a wonder.

Though your guard would not allow me to approach when I visited it the other day."

"I apologize for that. It is a measure of security, but I'm sure we can make an exception." I offer him a small smile. "I will speak to Father."

Sweat continues to drip down Prince Balior's face, which he wipes with the cloth of his sleeve. "There's no rush. If I am to one day rule Ammara by your side, all that is yours will become mine. There is time yet to explore it."

I stiffen in response to his word choice. All that is mine will *not* become his. It will be shared.

Abruptly, the prince drops his voice. "Who is he, by the way? Your chaperone?"

I fight the urge to glance over my shoulder, where Notus sits astride his gelding. "He is the South Wind."

Surprise flickers across my companion's expression. "He is immortal, then? Weren't he and his brothers banished from the City of Gods?"

Of course Prince Balior would have heard of the Anemoi, the Four Winds, divine brothers who possess enormous power, a wellspring always overflowing. And the prince is correct. Ammara is not Notus' home. It is simply the place he was banished to.

"I didn't realize he was loyal to King Halim," the prince continues, a slight frown creasing his brow.

I hold my tongue. If I am to present Ammara as the image of strength, I do not wish to weaken it with the truth: that loyalty likely has nothing to do with Notus' return.

Silence settles between us for a time. I'm rocked side to side as Zainab picks her way down the dusty path, small stones skittering beneath her hooves. Eventually, I find the courage to speak. "I apologize for the scene with my father earlier."

He offers me a quizzical smile. "What scene?"

My expression thaws somewhat, that old shame dissolving far more readily than usual. The man is too kind. "Father and I do not often see eye to eye. He believes I require additional protection beyond the capital."

"King Halim loves you. I cannot fault a father for looking after his daughter."

Yes, and I do not make his life easier with my poor behavior.

Navigating Essam up a small incline, Prince Balior says, "These darkwalkers. They grow stronger, do they not? It makes sense that he would fear for your safety."

The nearer my nameday draws, the tighter Father's hold on my life. I can hardly breathe most days. "I suppose."

"Maybe there's something I can do to help."

It is what I have hoped for, desperately. A willingness, an open door. The darkwalkers are a concern, yes, but I also suspect they are linked to my curse. Investigating them may uncover clues about my fate. But I must tread lightly, for I must be eager, but not *too* eager; distressed, yet not completely consumed by despair. "I would welcome any insight, Prince Balior. But I don't seek to place this responsibility onto you." I lower my eyes. Desperate times. I am not above using my feminine wiles to manipulate the situation. "Surely you would rather spend your time exploring what Ishmah has to offer? Our temples are beautiful, as are the public gardens."

Something plucks at my dress. I whip my head around, but Notus is staring off into the distance. I narrow my gaze. I'm certain it was his winds.

"I have no objection to visiting the gardens," says the prince. "But I packed most of my research, if you're interested in taking a look. I might be able to shed some light on how to combat these creatures. Or at the very least, learn where they come from and what they want."

"I am indebted by your generosity, Prince Balior. Thank you. Though I had hoped we might spend time together *without* a chaperone," I confess.

He glances sidelong at me, Essam tugging at the bit. "Who is to say we cannot?"

I straighten in my saddle. A rule breaker? Perhaps we are a better match than I thought. "What are you thinking?"

"I'm thinking we might find a way to lose your chaperone, if you're amenable."

As a matter of fact, I am. Fighting a smile, I carefully scan the terrain. Higher we ascend, small clouds of dust kicked up by the horses' heavy hooves. Sparse, stubby brush claws through cracks in the rock, and cliffs sketch the horizon: plunging valleys, narrow ravines. Notus will not be easily lost. He watches, and he listens, and he knows.

"See that gorge?" I jerk my chin toward the red stone piling in the distance. "It is only wide enough for one person to pass through at a time. Halfway through, the trail will split. Take the path on the right. It will lead you to Kir Bashab. I'll draw Notus away and backtrack to you." I know this land as I do nothing else. The sand is in my blood.

The prince's grin is positively wicked. "This should be fun."

Notus follows our descent toward the gorge. Its smooth, red walls reach upward impressively, shielding the sky above but for a thin blue ribbon. Notus glances between me and the prince, eyes slitted against the harsh glare. I cannot read his expression.

As instructed, Prince Balior goes first. I make a show of securing my supplies to buy myself some time. Notus angles his gelding toward me. "I don't trust him," he mutters.

This again. "You do not know him." I dab the sweat from my forehead with a square of cloth.

"Neither do you."

My fingers tighten around the scalding leather of the reins. I welcome the burn. "You speak of trust, but you don't even know the meaning of that word. Or did you forget that I once trusted you wholeheartedly?"

Some unnamable emotion flares to life in the dark wells of his eyes. "There are things I would explain to you," he says quietly, "if only I were certain you would listen."

All too easily, the past is present. "You had every opportunity to inform me that you were leaving Ishmah all those years ago, yet you did not. You never even told me *why*." If he had informed me, I could have prepared myself. If he had provided a reason, it might have spared some of my pain. "Was it about your father?" If I recall, Notus didn't have the best relationship with him. It was one of the reasons I opened to him so quickly.

"That's none of your business," he growls.

A retort sparks along my tongue, but I snuff it out, swallow it down. He is right. It is none of my business. But it wounds me, his reluctance to share.

Wheeling my mare around, I dig in my heels and plunge into the canyon.

Bent low over Zainab's neck, I fall into the staccato of thundering hooves, the trail cutting this way and that. The sound of Notus' pursuit erupts against the canyon walls.

He is an excellent rider, though his larger gelding cannot slip around the corners as swiftly as my streamlined mare. The trail divides. I angle left, squeezing through the shallow curves cut into the rock. Again, the trail splits. This time I go right, backtracking until the trail empties onto an expansive plateau. I sight Prince Balior in the distance, trotting toward the stretch of forest leading to the oasis, and I race to catch up. By the time Notus emerges from the canyon, we will be far from sight, deep in the thickening shade.

A low-hanging mist kisses my skin as I enter the wood, and I slow to a walk, tilting back my head to peer through the holes in the canopy, this dappling of sun and shade. Shortly after, we reach the oasis, its stunningly clear waters hemmed in by dense walls of stone.

Laughing, I swing down from my mount. "That was brilliant."

"Indeed." Prince Balior dismounts with a flourish, hair windblown, attractively disheveled. "I wasn't certain you had it in you."

My smile falters. It was a harmless comment. But the sting I experience is very real. "I was different as a child. Less afraid."

"Weren't we all?"

I rub Zainab's velvety nose before she wanders off to graze. Essam drinks deeply from the still pool.

The shock of the prince's hand on my lower back is enough to snap me to attention. I shift out of reach, suddenly wary. In Ammara, no man is permitted to touch an unmarried woman. And the prince is far closer than is appropriate. "Is there something I can help you with, Prince Balior?" At my back, the oasis laps gently ashore. But the lack of wind is strangely eerie.

He lifts his palms, fingers splayed wide in a gesture of innocence, though confusion clouds his expression. "I merely wish to spend time with you, Sarai."

"Then you can do so at a respectable distance."

"Respectable?" He laughs as though I have told the most delightful jest. "Surely that hardly matters, considering our imminent union?"

His words don't sit well with me. Of course, not everyone in Ammara abides by tradition—my past relationship with Notus is evidence enough—but I have given the prince no indication that I am eager to part with my people's customs in this instance. "You forget yourself. We are neither engaged, nor wed."

"Yet." At this, he smiles, a bit too sharply. "What difference is another month? Your father intends to announce the engagement quite soon, if I'm not mistaken. It is not unheard of to touch one another during courtship, so long as it is done behind closed doors."

"Another month makes all the difference," I state, unwilling to yield to his warped ideology.

Prince Balior stares at me. I am suddenly aware of how tall he is. A sword hangs from his belt loop. I assume he is skilled with the weapon. "I don't understand," he says, taking a step forward. "I assumed you abandoned your chaperone so that we could have some privacy."

"I did." I ease back a step, nearer to the oasis. The large boulders bordering the water prevent escape. My only option is to turn back the way we came. "But not for that reason. Don't you wish to converse without being a spectacle?"

He shakes his head as though amused by my willful obstinance. "Sarai." The curl of his fingers suggests the desire to clamp with possession. "Before long, our separate realms will become one. Why wait? No one ever has to know."

Years earlier, I cared little of the consequences when I fell into bed with the South Wind. It was Notus to whom I gave my virginity. If Prince Balior learns that I am impure, it is entirely possible he will withdraw the marriage offer.

"We have not known each other for very long," I say, struggling to soothe the alarm that has awakened, "so let me be clear. Until we are wed, we will not engage in any physical touch. We may spend time in each other's company. That is all. I should hope you would respect the wishes of your intended."

The prince scoffs. "*You* requested that we spend time alone together. *You* sent your chaperone away. You all but *begged* me to touch you."

"I did not *beg* for anything!" I snap.

"Your eyes told me otherwise."

As my heels brush the edge of the water, a harsh breeze fractures the glassy surface of the oasis. Prince Balior stands nearer to the horses, blocking my way. Likely he recognizes the advantage of such a position, for he makes no move to give ground.

"Step aside, Prince Balior."

His mouth twists into an ugly shape. "By all means." He sweeps out an arm mockingly. "I promise not to touch you without your permission."

I do not trust his word, this man I must marry. But Zainab is my only means of escape. She shifts in agitation as the wind strengthens to a howl, the air crackling, alive with sensation. Essam startles, bolting toward the trees as my attention snaps skyward. A sudden haze coats the sky overhead, its edges melting from brightened amber to a sickly yellow pall. Then a massive boom cracks the earth, and all at once, the sun goes dark.

7

AN IMMENSE FUNNEL OF WIND CARVES UP THE DARKENED SKY AND plummets toward the earth. It hits the ground with a shattering roar, an incensed mass of air and sand and debris. An uprooted tree crashes to my right. Zainab rears before fleeing into the forest.

Only I am spared the vicious gusts that snag cloth and snap trees. Eyes slitted against the spitting sand, I watch a blurred silhouette materialize behind the swirling cyclone. The South Wind: he who commands the hot summer winds.

The debris peels open, allowing Notus to stride forward through the funnel unharmed, though the wind snatches his headscarf and flings it elsewhere. For the briefest instant, his eyes meet mine. Here, now, I understand that I have glimpsed only the surface of this ageless god. Fool that I am, I had assumed to know his depths.

The terrifying blankness smoothing his expression is wholly new. It is a degree of rage I have yet to witness from the South Wind. Mortifyingly, I feel an unwelcome pulse of desire between my legs.

Prince Balior shouts as he's yanked skyward, tossed clear across the oasis. He slams onto the opposite bank and is still.

Too still. The motionlessness of broken bones. A budding horror creeps through me. *Get up.* By the gods, if Notus has killed the prince—

Miraculously, he stirs. I should go to him. He is, after all, an honored guest, my intended. But his earlier behavior has left a horrid taste in my mouth. It is not something I will soon forget.

And so I watch. Prince Balior stumbles upright, swaying. Blood trickles from his hairline. Then, carved silver blurs beneath wavering heat: Prince Balior has drawn his sword.

Notus tosses his hand. A gust of wind knocks the weapon aside. Prince Balior stumbles. Rage whets his features, curls his mouth.

"Will you hide behind your powers?" he spits, fury bleeding across his cheeks as he rounds the oasis toward his adversary. "Or will you fight me man to man?"

I glance between them, wondering if I should interfere or let them tear each other to pieces. I don't want Prince Balior to come to harm. But Notus is not easy to read. Some part of me is compelled by what may come.

The South Wind levels his fathomless gaze. "I am no man," he states coldly. "I am a god."

Prince Balior throws the first punch.

The South Wind ducks. He hits the prince low in the abdomen, forcing him back. That only enrages Prince Balior further. Again, he jabs, teeth bared. Catching the prince's wrist, Notus swings him in a circle, releasing him so he's launched through the air.

He hits the ground. The South Wind strides toward him, expression thunderous, his eyes the black of eclipsed suns. The force of his tread cracks the stone underfoot.

Closer he nears. He is shorter than the prince, certainly, yet broader, studier, uncowed. Prince Balior lifts a hand to ward off whatever strike may befall him.

But Notus only grasps the front of the man's robe and yanks him up, nose to nose. A small, twisted part of me revels in watching Notus having been brought to his lowest instincts. I do not consider him to be a predator, but in this moment, there is no doubt that Prince Balior is prey.

Unfortunately, I am too far away to eavesdrop. Whatever Notus says, it causes the prince's face to go ashen. Notus shakes him, and the prince grits his teeth, then nods.

Dropping the prince onto the ground, he returns to my side, shoulders bunched, tension knotted beneath his skin. "Are you hurt?" he demands.

I stare at him, too stupefied to process his concern.

"Sarai." The low growl brushes against me like a physical touch. He takes a step closer. "Are you hurt?"

I look to the prince, splayed out like a discarded rag across the cracked earth. "I'm fine." I am most certainly not fine. "Though perhaps you should ask the man you flung across the desert whether he is fine."

"I don't care about the prince. I care about *you*."

To that, I have no words. None.

Actually, that's not true. I have a handful, a select few. "You were out of line." In the distance, Prince Balior struggles to his feet. He brushes the dust from his robes. All his limbs seem to be in working order. I *should* feel relieved. Yet I don't.

"No," he says, and his next step eliminates the remaining distance between us. Our bodies all but collide, my chest brushing his as I inhale, the hot, coiling air of the desert calling back the memories of a bygone time. If I were to lean forward a hair, my nose might graze his jaw.

"Let me be absolutely clear, Sarai." He peers unblinkingly into my eyes, and I dare not look away for fear of missing the reshaping of his emotion into something new. "If I were not certain that killing the prince would mean all-out war against Ammara, I would have done so without question."

His rage renders me breathless. "Oh."

Notus frowns, and his gaze slips to my mouth, which parts of its own volition. "You cannot marry him," he says.

I struggle to swallow. "Excuse me?"

"A man who does not respect your boundaries, who threatens your safety, whose impudence may bring misfortune onto Ammara?" He tugs free a strand of hair caught behind my ear. It is so natural a gesture I fail to recognize what he has done until he has already dropped his hand. "He's not good for you, Sarai. I saw the fear plain on your face.

Tell me, is that the sort of man you wish to bind your life to? What of your people? Your realm?"

My shield is forged from unbreakable iron. It cannot be broken, not even by the fear that he is right, the fear that I am wrong.

"You overstep, Notus. As you can see, I am safe." I sweep an arm toward our surroundings. The land, the sky, the rising trees, and me. Alone, as I have always stood. "Now, I must collect our horses, and my guest. Father will have my head should I return without them."

The moment we enter the palace stable yard, Prince Balior dismounts, his face a motley of streaked sweat, sunburned skin, and grit creasing the lines bracketing his mouth. Dust dulls the vibrant cobalt of his robe.

Father will be furious.

In what ways will Prince Balior retaliate? Will he demand a meeting with the king? Will he pack his bags and return to Um Salim, our courtship dissolved before it was made known?

"I wish I could say the trip was enjoyable," the prince bites out, passing the reins to one of the hostlers, "but we both know that's a lie."

I'm sorry, I might say, though am I really? While I may not condone Notus' assault against Prince Balior, my husband-to-be did not respect my boundaries. Indeed, he viewed them as obstacles to overcome.

I quickly dismount. Zainab noses the ground for bits of dried grass sprouting through the cracks in the stone. Hours in the saddle have left my legs sore, my patience thin. Whether or not I agree with his behavior, Prince Balior has his use. "On behalf of King Halim," I say, "I wish to extend my sincerest apology."

"Apology?" Terse, disbelieving laughter belts across the stable yard. "Begging your pardon, Princess Sarai, but I do not care for an apology. What I want," he says, "is justice."

Justice. The word drips cruelty.

"I understand," I say, hoping to soothe his boiling ire. "The South Wind will be punished for this. You have my word."

Prince Balior cuts a glare in Notus' direction, though the ruddy tinge to his cheeks suggests embarrassment over his speedy defeat at the oasis. The South Wind has dismounted and proceeds to unsaddle his horse. He remains at the perimeter of the stable yard to offer us privacy. His hearing, however, is keener than most.

"If this were Um Salim, your *chaperone* would never have returned to Ishmah alive. I question King Halim's integrity, that he would allow an untrained animal into his service."

My chin lifts, spine steeled, legs braced in aggression against the prince. Personal insults I am well equipped to handle. Insults against the king? Unacceptable.

"My father is the greatest king Ammara has ever known," I snap. "Take care with the words you speak, Prince Balior."

He meets my glare with one of equal ferocity, though I'm almost certain a bit of fear lurks beneath his outrage. Standing paces away, his guards await their orders. For once, I am thankful for Notus' presence. He possesses the strength of a hundred men. Now that the prince has witnessed the South Wind's power, it is unlikely he would risk an assault.

In the end, Prince Balior looks away first. "Do you want me here?"

I'm so blindsided by the question that I do not immediately respond. "Of course I do." What else is there to say? The truth will not extend my life. It will not save my realm.

"I know when I'm not welcome." Again, he looks to Notus. "The South Wind was prepared to drive his blade into my heart. It makes me question whether he is a mere guard, as you claim, or something more. I do not like to share what is mine."

Mine. A pretty bird in a cage. I swallow the words bristling on my tongue.

"I promise you," I say. "There is nothing between us now."

"You said *now*. Does that suggest there once *was* something between you?"

I do not seek to lie. It is too complex a web. But I fear the truth will drive Prince Balior, and his research, back to Um Salim.

"Please." It is painful, this word, yet I voice it nonetheless. "It has been a difficult morning, and I don't wish this miscommunication to sour negotiations. The attendants will draw you a bath. You will feel better once you have washed and rested. Then we will talk."

Irritation is creased in the lines pleating his features. But he nods and quits the stable yard, his guards accompanying him back to the guest wing. After passing Zainab to a hostler, I veer toward the palace as well, eager for a hot bath and peace.

"Sarai," Notus calls.

I remind myself of who I am: Princess Sarai Al-Khatib of Ammara. My time is not an obligation.

As expected, his heavy footfalls trail me, sturdy, yet with that unexpected swiftness that mirrors the wind. To my left, the labyrinth gleams alabaster white, thin cracks clambering up its eroded walls. My attention momentarily falls onto the entrance, and I pause, eyeing the swirling symbol carved into the door.

Hello, Sarai. Won't you step into the dark?

Notus catches my wrist. "Don't touch," he warns.

I startle and come to. Somehow, I stand less than an arm's length from the veiled, ancient doorway, a dry chill pulsating against my outstretched fingers.

The first threads of apprehension ooze through me. I do not remember approaching. Nor do I remember reaching out my hand. The voice that invaded my mind has since dissolved.

Pulling free of Notus' grip, I continue toward the palace. Cool, jasmine-scented air plumes in invitation as I pass one of the gardens. Moments later, Notus cuts off my path. Color flushes the wind-roughened skin of his cheeks. He has yet to replace his headscarf after the incident at the oasis.

I find myself studying the planes of his face, the heavy shape of his jaw, the slope of his forehead. It is unfair for something so loathed to be wrought with such splendor.

"Will you ignore me for the rest of the day?" Notus demands.

I quirk a brow. He is absolutely livid. What does that say about me, that I find him all the more compelling for this display of emotion?

"For the rest of the day, and for all the days after, until you are gone from my life." With a neat sidestep, I turn a corner, taking a shortcut to my chambers.

Notus' footsteps follow. "Did he touch you? At the oasis?"

I halt in the middle of the corridor. My pulse beats a tattoo against my neck. "And if he did?" Slowly, I turn to look at him. "Would you care?"

The South Wind hesitates before stepping closer. The breadth of his shoulders eclipses the sunlight filtering through the high, circular windows. "Maybe I would care. Have you thought about that?"

Of course I have thought about it. And that is exactly the problem.

I'm about to respond when movement draws my focus farther down the hall. A small group of noblewomen loiter near one of the marble statues, heads bent in conversation. My stomach drops. I recognize Dalia immediately.

"Not here," I mutter. "Someplace private so we're not overheard."

Notus looks to where Dalia flutters her fingers in our direction. The way she drinks in the South Wind makes me want to claw out her eyes.

Thankfully, Notus trails me without question, lengthening his strides to keep pace. "Well?" he quips, as soon as we are out of earshot.

"Well what?" I snap.

"You didn't answer the question. Did he touch you?"

I shake my head in frustration. As if he needs another reason to attack the prince. Anyway, answering truthfully feels a little too much like defeat. "No, he didn't," I growl, more maliciously than I intend. "Now would you drop it?"

"I'm only trying to protect you. I cannot do so if you do not let me in."

"I let you in once," I choke, the words like shattered glass in my throat. "I will never make that mistake again."

I turn away, but the South Wind slips in front of me, grabs my arm. "Stop. Just . . . stop."

His hand is so large it completely swallows my upper arm. And yet, it is gentle. It has always been gentle, his touch.

My gaze lowers, drawn by the glimmer of gold circling his wrist. All goes still inside me. "What is that?" When he attempts to retreat, I pull up the long sleeve of his robe, revealing a delicate bracelet of hammered gold, shaped like an arrow.

A gulf opens inside my mind. Its roar swells, dousing all rational thought. For I, too, have a bracelet identical in shape, only fashioned of lead. Notus bought them from an artisan, years ago. He'd gifted mine to me on my nineteenth birthday. Two arrows. For I had pierced his heart as he had pierced mine.

"Why are you wearing this?" I whisper in a trembling voice. My eyes lift to his, fever bright. "Explain."

Suddenly watchful, he swallows, lifts a hand to his neck, expression pained. "I have always worn it."

That cannot be. "You're lying."

"It is not a lie."

I flinch away from him, unable to bear the implication that he has worn this symbol of our shared love these past years.

"Sarai—"

"Stop. I don't want to talk about this."

"I am trying," he grinds out, "to do what is right by you, by your father, by your realm. What more do you want from me?"

Too easily, the noose slips tight around my neck. The truth is, I haven't an answer for him. What do I want? Not this. Never this.

"Nothing," I hiss. "I want nothing from you." Spinning around, I stride down the corridor, my footfalls slapping loud against the tiles.

Notus' scoff reaches me. "And you call *me* a liar?"

I halt. Were Father in this position, he would continue onward. He is not someone who needs the last word. But I am not my father. It is a bitter thought as I whirl around, my gaze burning with the potency of a thousand desert suns.

Yet when I look at Notus, all that flame is swiftly doused, for I recognize the sorrow within those black eyes as a reflection of my own.

"I know you, Sarai," he murmurs. "I know when you're hurting, when you're frightened, when you've been brought so low as to feel nonexistent. I do not wish to cause you any more grief than I have, but the fact is, I will be here until Ishmah is declared safe from darkwalkers, and I do not know how long that will be. Can't we at least *attempt* to discuss what happened between us?"

My spite folds onto itself, small, smaller, a piece of coal that burns hotter and brighter over time. If I could, I would tear my heart free of my body and wander the earth without its insufferable weight. But if I were to discuss my wretched emotions with the South Wind, I fear that I would fall to pieces, unable to find the strength to put myself back together. Some days, it is all I have anchoring me, this ire.

"We cannot," I say.

He appears pained, yet departs without argument, for which I'm grateful. It is a small grace, this empty corridor. No guards to witness me sag against the wall, eyes closed, body trembling with a combination of rage, confusion, and self-loathing. Five years, and my shields are brought low with but a handful of hurled accusations.

"Lover's quarrel?"

I startle, snapping upright to face Prince Balior. Arms crossed, he leans against the wall, dressed in a clean gray robe, hair damp from his bath.

I regard him pointedly. "It's rude to eavesdrop."

The prince is properly abashed. "These halls are not exactly conducive to privacy. You sounded distressed."

"As you can see, I am well, though tired after our outing this morning." And in desperate need of a wash. "Are you feeling rested?"

"I am, thank you." He gives me a lingering once-over. "You and the South Wind do not see eye to eye."

I brush my palms down the front of my dress. "You were right before. The South Wind and I have a history. I knew him as a young girl. There was a time when I almost believed myself in love with him."

"I see." It is steady, his gaze. "And now?"

Stepping forward, I slot my smile, however hostile, into place. "Prince Balior, if you are as observant as I believe you to be, you must know that the only thing I feel for the South Wind now is revulsion. You have come to request my hand in marriage, and I truly hope that we will soon be betrothed. Might we discuss our impending nuptials over a pot of tea?"

His smile spreads. It is positively triumphant. "Sarai," he says. "I thought you would never ask."

"I need your help."

Roshar glances over at the blue velvet chaise on which I currently lounge. Apparently, the chaise cost him an entire month's wages. The price is absolutely absurd, but I must admit it's the most comfortable chair I've sat on in my life.

"Of course you do, my dear." He lowers the square of cloth he's using to polish his rings. "What is it you need from Roshar?"

I pick at a stray thread on one of the pillows. "You're adept at conversing with men."

"*Adept?* Sarai, honestly. *You* are adept at conversing with men. *My* skills are unsurpassed."

Well. I certainly cannot argue with that.

"I'm to meet with Prince Balior after dinner tonight. What are some topics of conversation I can broach with him? If we are to wed by the month's end, surely we should be able to speak of more than just politics."

"An established man like Prince Balior? Shouldn't be too difficult." Lips pursed, he lifts one hand, watching the bejeweled rings spear facets of color onto the wall. "Compliment his hair. Tell him he smells delicious. Fawn over how strong he is, how brilliant and intriguing and clever. Inflating a man's ego is all but guaranteed to get you into his good graces."

Except I do not desire to be in the prince's good graces. I desire for our union to be fair, honest, respectful, supportive. I am aware that I'm leading him astray. But I cannot afford to follow my conscience when death looms.

"What of your hobbies, pastimes?" Roshar asks.

Hobbies? I gave up music long ago. It seemed a pointless pursuit with death just around the corner. Oh yes, let me show Prince Balior my journal of numbers, this obsession with tracking my demise. That would surely be a mistake. "I have no hobbies."

"What about . . . horseback riding?" he adds with telltale mischief.

I narrow my eyes at him. "Spit it out, Roshar."

"I heard you and the prince had a little rendezvous this morning— with Notus as your chaperone."

"Who told you that?"

"Don't you worry about where I gather my information from. How was it?"

A gossamer breeze blows in through the open window. I sigh and rub my eyes. The unease I felt earlier hasn't diminished, but seeing as Roshar is a horrible gossip, I am reluctant to add fuel to the fire by informing him of Prince Balior's improper behavior. Better to skip that part. "Notus may have . . . attacked the prince."

Roshar gapes. His mouth hangs open for one heartbeat, two, then snaps shut. "Do you think he's jealous?"

"Of Prince Balior?"

"Think about it," he insists, leaning forward. "You're to marry this prince from another realm, but if I recall, at one point you were hoping Notus might ask for your hand in marriage."

A small sting hits nearest to my heart. He's not wrong. I'd never wanted to marry . . . until Notus. Then, I'd wished to bind my life to the South Wind in all ways. But Notus is immortal. It did not seem fair to promise him forever when I would live to only twenty-five years of age. To this day, he does not know my secret.

As for the jealousy . . . It may be petty, but I want to draw the green-eyed rise from the South Wind. Proof that I am not so forgettable as he made me believe. But all I have received in return are reminders of his duty to Father. "As he continually states, he's just doing his job at keeping me safe. And anyway, he's the one who left."

Roshar winces. He was there when I learned the South Wind had departed without so much as a farewell. He gathered my broken pieces and patched the cracks to the best of his abilities. If not for Roshar, I fear I might never have clawed my way free of the dark. It is something I will never be able to repay him for.

"You're right," he says with a dismissive wave of his hand. "Why are we talking about Notus when you've a delectable man wanting to marry you? Tell me more about this prince of yours."

Later that evening, I arrive at Prince Balior's chambers. Ten soldiers guard his door. It is more than Father posts at his own quarters, though I suppose when one finds oneself in an enemy nation, one cannot be too careful.

Before I'm able to knock, the door opens. Prince Balior is dressed in a knee-length robe, brown trousers, and bare feet.

"Princess Sarai." He dips his chin in greeting. Surprisingly, no flattery sweetens his tongue. I cannot blame him, after what he endured in the desert.

"Prince Balior." Brushing past him, I take a seat in the sitting room, and the prince selects a chair adjacent to mine. Two of King Halim's men join the sentries outside. Technically, as an unmarried woman, I am not allowed in his rooms unaccompanied, but my guards know better than to speak against me.

A small tea set graces a round table placed between the two chairs. The prince pours the scalding liquid into a hammered copper cup. "Sugar?" he asks.

"No, thank you."

He passes me the cup before stirring sugar into his own drink. The spoon clinks against the metal rim.

A deep sigh leaves the prince as he settles back, tea in hand, to regard me with eyes darkened by remorse. "I wish to apologize for my behavior earlier today. It was unacceptable, and I am ashamed to have made you feel uncomfortable. I promise it will not happen again."

I sip from my drink. The mint leaves have been steeped to a sharp bitterness. "I appreciate the apology." Do I believe he is regretful? Perhaps. "The heat can make any sane person mad."

"Some more than others." The tonal shift implies he speaks not of himself, but of the South Wind.

Slowly, I lower my cup onto the table. This dread has loomed in the thick of my mind for most of the day. It must be addressed.

"I am utterly humiliated by what happened at Kir Bashab," I say. "Should you wish, I will go to Father about the matter and discuss what actions can be taken. You were right. What kind of example are we setting by allowing this display of violence to stand?" There must be consequences, even for the South Wind.

Unexpectedly, the prince does not appear pleased by my words. Hours earlier, he was forceful, aggressive, adamant. Now he is relaxed, ponderous, at ease.

"After some thought, I realized I may have gotten carried away before," he replies. "I can't blame the South Wind for protecting a woman he believes to be in peril."

My eyebrows wing upward in surprise. "That is an abrupt change of opinion." Though I find myself experiencing a sliver of relief that he does not wish to punish his adversary.

"Yes, well . . . Notus sought me out earlier and apologized. We came to an understanding." He sips, slowly. The motion commands my full attention. "Moving forward, I do not anticipate there being any bad blood between us."

"Oh." I blink in stupefaction. This is . . . good. So why the unease?

"Well, I'm pleased to hear the issue has been resolved. But I want to reiterate that I stand by what I told you earlier. There is nothing between me and the South Wind. There hasn't been for a long time."

"I'm glad to hear that." This, paired with a brief smile. "When we marry, there will be no man in your life but me."

He stares at me long enough that I grow uncomfortable. It's not a threat, though it certainly sounds like one. Pushing to my feet, I wander to the window, peeling myself away from his focus for a moment. Carved red stone edged in violet: Ishmah at dusk.

"May I ask you something?" Turning, I take in the man I am to marry. He regards me with unusual intensity, a foot propped casually over one thigh. My skin tingles beneath his scrutiny.

"Anything," he says.

"What do you hope to gain from this alliance?" I gesture to the desert beyond the still-warm glass. "As a whole, Ammara is far smaller than Um Salim. And our wealth, while extensive, is dependent on continued trade along the Spice Road, which has declined in recent years due to drought. If the lack of rain continues, I fear my realm will face famine. As far as I can see, our marriage will be a disadvantage for you."

The prince frowns as he pours himself another cup of tea. A spoonful of sugar follows, a gentle *clink* as he stirs the sweetness into the steaming liquid. "I admit that when King Halim first broached the subject of an arranged marriage, I declined the offer." He lowers the spoon, takes a sip, gaze direct. "You're right. A union to Ammara *is* disadvantageous to Um Salim, especially considering our harvest is not always robust, and more mouths to feed would strain our agricultural fields. Life, however, is not always about the best economical choice."

With all the care of a young child handling glass, he sets down his cup. "I wish to tell you a story, if you are amenable?"

I am properly intrigued, for I dearly love stories. "Go on."

"When I was a boy, I accompanied my father to Ishmah. At the time, our people were suffering. A sandstorm had decimated the region; the year's harvest failed. Our only option was to call on King Halim for aid.

"Many days we spent in this palace, these very rooms. At times, discussions extended well into the evening. But at the end of our visit, King Halim agreed to loan a year's worth of gold to Um Salim, which was used to rebuild our cities and villages. I have never forgotten that kindness." He drops his head forward, staring down at his interlaced fingers, brow furrowed. "You ask what I hope to gain from this alliance?" His gaze lifts to mine. "A generous, more prosperous world."

It reassures me, his reasoning. For I, too, believe in such generosity. "That is admirable, Prince Balior. Thank you for sharing." There is a silence. "During our ride earlier, you mentioned we might discuss ... certain matters."

"Ah." He smiles. "How could I have forgotten?" The prince gestures toward his desk and its precarious stack of books. "After doing some preliminary research," he says, "I've found mentions of shadow beasts in a select number of texts. From what I gather, they absorb or, say, *extract* souls from living bodies. Is that correct?"

A shudder grips my frame. "Essentially, yes."

"And you don't know where they hail from?"

"No."

He rubs at his stubbled jaw. "Do you know why your Lord of the Mountain trapped the beast in the labyrinth?"

As it turns out, I do not. "Why do you ask?"

"According to my research, it's possible the beast comes from the same realm as the darkwalkers. Or, at the very least, from an adjacent realm. Some sources claim the beast was once not a beast at all, but an immortal, forced to submit to the power of the labyrinth. If we were to discover *why* the beast was trapped, it could shed light on the matter." Prince Balior *tap-tap-taps* a finger against the stack of books, then shakes his head ruefully. "I daresay I am boring you with my observations."

"Not at all," I assure him. At this point, I would welcome any ideas, no matter how far-fetched.

He smiles at me gratefully, as if he has found himself in front of less-than captivated audiences before. I certainly know the feeling. "Consider this: If it's true that the labyrinth's power forces its prisoners to become beasts, then it can be assumed the beast would return to its previous form when no longer bound by its prison. Right?"

Helplessly, my lips curve. The prince is more animated than I have ever seen him. "Right."

"And if it *is* from the same realm as the darkwalkers, then might it not also know how to eradicate the creatures, or return them to their birthplace?"

My mouth parts, hangs open a moment, then snaps shut. "That is an excellent question, Prince Balior." And it gives me much to consider. What if the beast is somehow connected to my curse? In discovering more about the labyrinth, it may be possible I can free myself from that which ails me.

While Prince Balior searches his collection for additional information, I peruse the material on his desk. A slender volume tucked beneath miscellaneous records gives me pause.

The book is old as Ammara is old. A tattered cloth cover coated in grime. Pages so brittle I fear they will dissolve beneath my touch.

It is the symbol marking the cover of the book, however, that captures my gaze: an enclosed circle, like the whorl of a shell, overlapping a small triangle. The tip of my finger finds the curved iron edge, though I do not recall reaching toward it. I trace the raised swirl, my focus sliding out. The warmed metal turns icy enough to burn.

Sarai.

I snatch back my hand, awareness bleeding through my system. Warmth. Sun on my face. I stand near a window, though I do not remember ever approaching it. The labyrinth sits bone-bright in the courtyard below.

When I cast a glance over my shoulder, I find Prince Balior poring over texts, face pinched in concentration. My attention returns to the book resting against my stomach, which twists in unease. This symbol . . . I have seen it before. And then it comes to me. The raised whorl gracing the cover of Prince Balior's book is the same one etched in the labyrinth's doorway.

8

SARAI. THE TIME IS NEAR. I CAN GIFT YOU WHAT YOU SEEK.

Bolting upright in bed, I glance around the room. The fire has cooled to coals. Red flickers beneath the gray ash.

My mind is clouded water. No matter how frantically I rifle through the murk, I cannot recall what it is that woke me. I lie back, close my eyes, yet sleep evades me. Too warm—I toss off the blankets. Too chilled—I drag the thick wool onto my shivering body. Caught in a black spin, my thoughts spiral down. When dawn cracks open the world's hardened shell, I am no nearer to sleep than I was hours ago.

Unfortunately, I haven't the privilege of lying in bed until my thoughts sort themselves out. Moving to the window, I peer at the courtyard below. There the labyrinth stoops, a darkened stain in sunup's pearly light.

Yesterday evening, I watched Prince Balior visit the labyrinth once again. From the safety of my bedroom window, I looked on as he stood there for an age, peering into the shadowed veil. Then he returned to the palace.

Twice now, he has visited the labyrinth since his arrival over a week ago. Despite my desire to discuss his research further, I hesitate, fearing my desperation will expose my true motive in wanting to learn more. Beyond that, the waiting is painful. Seven days have trickled by, and the prince has not offered further insight about the labyrinth, nor the beast within. Why should I not investigate myself, now that I know where to look? And there is only one place I can think of that would provide the information I need.

I quickly dress and descend the stairs to the first level. Hexagonal tiles adorn the walls in shades of turquoise, azure, aquamarine. At the end of the corridor: twin doors of oak.

The Library of Ishmah is my mother's legacy. It is here she remains, her memory enveloped in brittle parchment and dust. According to Father, she adored the written word and would read to my brothers nightly. Following her passing, the entire south wing was reconstructed into what is now the greatest repository of knowledge the realm has ever known.

The three-story structure is a spectacle of polished wood, woven tapestries, and tarnished brass. A massive fireplace anchors the main chamber. Sizable armchairs offer comfortable seating for visitors. Currently, a few researchers occupy the tables near the far wall, analyzing ancient records. Last growing season, we received clay tablets from a faraway realm, the capital city of which is dominated by an enormous tower.

To my left, a bespectacled man draped in scarlet robes sorts through a pile of scrolls behind a long counter. Above the counter, painted script reads: *As long as there is knowledge, there is light.*

I approach the head archivist. "The Lord of the Mountain shines upon you," I say in greeting.

He startles, eyes comically wide behind his glasses. "Your Highness! My word, this is a surprise. Do you require privacy?" He scans the room beyond my shoulder, likely noting the curious stares. "I can have the library vacated for your convenience."

"That won't be necessary, but I would appreciate your assistance"— my voice drops—"and your discretion."

Straightening, he sets the scrolls aside. "I see." His voice has lowered to match mine. "How can I assist you?"

Two men in yellow robes—archival apprentices—gather a pile of documents from the counter and retreat to the special collections housed in the back stacks. It is then I realize the library has fallen silent—no hiss of parchment, no delicate murmurings. I turn, glaring at those attempting to eavesdrop. Immediately, they return to their reading.

"I came across a symbol recently and would like more information on it," I murmur to the head archivist. "Do you have a piece of parchment?"

He offers me the requested material, along with a quill and pot of ink. As I draw the whirled circle, the man's brow creases with concern. "This is the symbol you saw? Are you sure?"

"Yes. What does it mean?"

"This is the symbol of our Lord of the Mountain."

I see. That would make sense, considering it was the Lord of the Mountain who necessitated the labyrinth's construction. "What else can you tell me about it?"

He traces the symbol ponderously. "Not much, unfortunately. The swirl is said to represent power over storms. The small triangle is believed to represent Mount Syr." He frowns. "I wish I could offer more."

More than I expected, less than I'd hoped. "That's all right. I still wish to research the labyrinth regardless. I assume you have documents on file?"

The head archivist straightens from his hunched position over the counter. "As I mentioned to Prince Balior yesterday, Your Highness, all texts associated with the labyrinth have been placed under restricted use."

"Restricted use?" Unease worms through me. "By who?"

"King Halim."

That does not sound like Father. He has always been a champion of knowledge and learning. "Surely my station would allow me to override this restriction."

He dabs his forehead with a square of cloth. "I wish that were so." The cloth disappears inside his clenched fist. "The decree was signed by the king. Only the one who authorized the document may be granted access."

I peer down the gloom-shrouded corridor where the archival apprentices vanished minutes ago. Father would not censor information unless it posed a threat to the realm. "Is that where the restricted documents are held?"

"Your Highness, I cannot say."

It is all the affirmation needed. Rounding the counter, I stride toward the back stacks.

"Your Highness—"

I brush past him. Far from the central atrium, the shelves narrow, the air cools, the light dims. "Where are the documents? In here?" I try one of the doors. As soon as my palm grazes the brass handle, the metal grows icy to the touch. I snatch back my hand with a pained hiss.

"Your Highness, *please.*" The man slips between me and the door while attempting to push his glasses back up his sweaty nose. "I ask that you refrain from entering rooms without the king's permission."

I'm still attempting to process what just occurred. "What sorcery is this?" I demand, pointing at the door.

The head archivist opens his mouth. A small sound of distress squeaks out. "Sorcery? I don't understand."

"The door handle. It's cold as ice."

"What?"

"Touch it," I press.

He hesitates, then grabs the brass handle firmly, confusion crimping his mouth. "Begging your pardon, Your Highness, but the door handle feels perfectly normal to me."

How is that possible? Again, I reach for it, but the moment metal grazes skin, the handle grows frigid. A heartbeat later, the discomfort forces me to withdraw.

"All the doors are locked," the man insists with evident apprehension. "They cannot be opened without King Halim's permission. I would request it for you, but considering his illness—"

"Excuse me?" My gaze narrows. "What have you heard?"

He is unable to hold my stare for long. "I have heard only that he is ill and keeps to his rooms."

Not even Father's advisors are aware of his declining health. It is why he has called Amir back from his honeymoon sooner than expected. "How did you learn of this?"

"The palace attendants talk." He swallows, pushes his glasses up his nose with a trembling hand. "I do not wish to lose my position, Your Highness."

My head drops forward. How easy it would be to demand entrance. But this man is a citizen of Ishmah, and I, as its princess, am its emissary. My station comes with certain obligations that I can neither escape from, nor alter, nor discard.

"Apologies," I whisper to the head archivist before departing the stacks, and the library, entirely. He need not worry that I will violate the king's decree. Not while the library is occupied. I simply need to return at a time when there are none to witness my transgression.

Later, when the sky unfolds in panels of black silk, I light my lamp.

Beyond my bedroom window, stars fleck the horizon like tossed salt, bright and plentiful. Slipping a thin sleeping robe over my nightgown, I belt it at the waist and ease my door open, lamp held high over my head. A wash of orange light warms the hall. Empty, as I anticipated.

The quickest path to the library is via the east corridor. Unfortunately, that requires bypassing Father's chambers, which I will not attempt. Thus, I find myself hurrying down the more obscure passages, tucking myself into shadowed nooks to avoid detection. The air is frigid, tinged with sweetly scented jasmine. I am a woman alone among the tall pillars of stone.

Two men guard the entrance into the library. Thankfully, they appear to be sleeping. Of course, at any other time this would be completely unacceptable, considering their job is to, well, *guard*, but I am not going to complain. Breath held, I tiptoe past them and ease open one of the doors. It emits a soft creak of sound, but the men do not wake. I slip inside with them none the wiser.

All is drenched in moonlight. The plush armchairs have been vacated. They sit as softened statues, basking in the pool of alabaster. A smoky odor lingers, the charred logs having cooled in the fireplace's wide stony mouth.

Rounding the front counter, I proceed down the stacks housing the special collections. I do not bother searching the shelves. If material on the labyrinth is restricted, it will be placed under lock and key.

As I did earlier today, I attempt to open the door slotted between two of the shelving units. The brass handle burns the moment it brushes my skin.

I drop my hand in frustration. I don't understand. Why can't I open the door? And why did the handle feel perfectly normal to the head archivist?

To my left lies a separate passage, tapered, barren of shelving, with doors spaced at regular intervals along the wall. All seven possess brass knobs. When I try to open the first two, I find both locked, metal icy to the touch.

Deeper I venture. My slippers scuff the ground, wooden floors transitioning to cracked stone, ceiling slanting low. I try doors three, four, five. Locked. As I attempt the sixth door, something clicks behind me. I whirl, lifting the lamp toward the darkness. "Hello?" When a pulse of frosty air unfurls from the corridor's depths, I swallow, retreating a step. "Notus?"

My voice echoes faintly. There is no response.

Calm yourself, I soothe. But my heartbeat has begun to lurch with a speed I cannot hope to tame. The corridor seems to squeeze in around me, stone walls crowding inward, and for a moment, I am certain the shadows change shape.

I tighten my grip on the lamp. Only one door remains. At this distance, I'm able to glimpse the curved handle of tarnished brass. Whatever Father knows about the labyrinth, he did not want me, or anyone else, to discover it. That is reason enough to press ahead.

But this door is not like the rest. The handle grows warm beneath my fingers, uncomfortably so. A gentle push, and the door opens fluidly. Its hinges make not a sound.

Beyond: darkness, or so I presume. I lift the lamp high. It catches the long shelves of a bookcase. Sparse and windowless, the space is occupied by a desk cluttered with open books and unfurled scrolls, atop which a lone candle burns.

I stare at the flame's weak flutter, a singular brightness guttering in a pool of hot candlewax. The candle has been burning for some time. And yet, no footprints disturb the floor, which is coated so thickly in dust I can only assume no one has entered this space in centuries. The question remains: who lit the candle?

The hair along my arms spikes upward. If I had any sense, I would leave and not return. Dark things lurk here, things that do not wish to be found. But instinct wars with the desire to uncover secrets of old. What, exactly, does Father hide?

As soon as I cross the threshold, the candle extinguishes itself. It is so dark my lantern barely pierces the blood-thick gloom.

I begin sifting through the documents, though I'm not certain what it is I'm searching for. Some tomes are written in unfamiliar languages. Others contain charts and maps. I untie a red ribbon binding a large scroll, skimming the elegant script. No mention of the labyrinth, nor of the darkwalkers, nor of the beast. I set it aside and choose another book at random. An old journal? Flipping to the first page, I begin to read.

When I ponder my existence, I am cruelly aware of my own atrocious nature. But as I wander the halls of my prison, I feel myself changing. My fingers have begun to stiffen. My shoulders have widened, my back has grown hunched, forcing my arms nearer to the ground. I write my story now so that I do not forget who I once was.

It was not my mother's fault, you see. It was her husband's, that selfish King Minos, who spurned the sea god's generosity by failing to sacrifice the snow-white bull he was gifted. When the sea god learned that no sacrifice had been made, he enlisted the help of our dear goddess of love. To punish King Minos, the goddess beguiled the queen—my mother—with a powerful enchantment, and when she cast her eyes upon the divine bull, she became enamored with the beast. And that was how I was conceived.

From the moment of my birth, I was spurned. The progeny of a woman and bull? Brute, monster, swine. It was clear I did not belong. But no one treated me so poorly as the self-proclaimed Lord of the Mountain. He asserted that I was a threat to all of god-kind. It was he who demanded that I be cast out from the City of Gods.

Yet the Lord of the Mountain had a secret of his own. Oh, he was adept at hiding it. But why should anyone question him? I knew of the horrors committed against him. Perhaps he felt shame in seeing my unnaturalness reflected back at himself?

The Lord of the Mountain is the reason I have found myself bound to this cage, through no fault of my own. He, who decided a beast was unfit to walk among his flawless, faultless gods, and through negotiation with a pathetic mortal king, demanded a prison be built to contain me in endless walls of stone. The truth is, I do not know if I will ever escape the labyrinth. I have learned not to hope. But if you somehow manage to unearth this scrawled plea, I ask that you come find me.

Find me, and I will grant you what you seek.

9

FIND ME, AND I WILL GRANT YOU WHAT YOU SEEK.

My fingertips quiver against the journal as I stare, slack-jawed, at the ink bleeding through the thin parchment. Once a decade, seven men are sacrificed to the beast. King Halim claims it is the only way to mollify the creature that paces the labyrinth. But what if the beast doesn't wish to devour these men? What if it seeks escape, to enact revenge on those who imprisoned it?

The deeper I ponder the matter, the more I am convinced of the injustice of it all. The beast is right. Why should it be punished for its existence? Why not the king, who failed to sacrifice the divine bull? Or the Lord of the Mountain?

I pause, quickly returning to a previous sentence. *Pathetic mortal king* . . .

My blood runs cold.

Not the king who failed to sacrifice the bull. The king with whom the Lord of the Mountain negotiated to construct the labyrinth, a bargain fulfilled to save the life of his ailing daughter: King Halim. And if the beast escapes, it could very well go after Father for having played a role in its imprisonment. I cannot let that happen.

I'm so focused on scouring the stack of books that I fail to realize the temperature has dropped until my teeth begin to chatter. When a low, faint hiss echoes from a distant chamber, I whirl, wielding my lamp like a weapon. "Hello?"

A wave of cold sweeps into the room.

Like a foul fog, it reeks of decay, raising the hair along my body. I remain frozen, entrenched in the stone floor. Something grazes my nape, and I whip back around, swinging the lamp wildly to strike whatever it is that touches me.

Nothing is there.

My heart beats so rapidly its rhythm bleeds into a dull hum. Time to leave. It is absolutely time to leave.

But I can't guarantee that I will be able to return—these records are too valuable. So I gather them into my arms as swiftly as my shaking hands will allow. Again, that skittering hiss, like nails over stone: nearer, just beyond the threshold.

I toss aside the heaviest tomes and cram as many of the smaller books as I can reach into my arms, never mind that they are centuries old. Then I grab the lamp and bolt for the door, peering out into the hallway. The entire corridor is obscured, steeped in a dim so thick it coats my hands. I squint, seeking any movement, when my lamp gutters.

Darkness blots my vision. I am entombed.

My fingers spasm around the lamp handle. I'm no warrior. I'm a violinist, with no skill in combat. I know how to run, how to shrink, how to hide, but little else. Whatever lurks beyond sight, it is large, that much I know, for the shifting air heaves against me in great waves, suggesting something massive stirs it into agitation. I dare not breathe as, heart careening, I retreat back into the room and slowly, slowly ease the door shut.

A glassy fear masks my thoughts. I am naught but a body crafted from dread and bone, driven by instinct, fingers fumbling for a lock, finding none. The door handle has nearly rusted through and is unlikely to hold against a forced entry.

I continue to retreat, using touch to guide myself around the desk. I now understand how foolish this mission has been. No one knows of my whereabouts. Down and down my thoughts spiral, amplifying the hysteria until I reach a place of such brutal clarity that I am momentarily separated from the fear: my lamp. It has been extinguished, but there must be a means of lighting the wick.

Carefully, I place my stolen books onto the desk and begin pulling open the drawers. The ground trembles with the unmistakable rhythm of a four-legged gait, and the scratch of nails over stone makes my jaw twinge. With shaking hands, I grasp hold of what feels like flint and steel. Two, three, four strikes, and the wick of my lamp catches. Light drives the shadows into hiding—and draws the creature's attention as well.

There is a scratch at the bottom of the door. A single nail dragged across the warped grain. The whiff of decay is stronger now, layered with a faint trace of woodsmoke. As I gather up the books, something heavy pushes against the ancient door. It bows from the pressure, groaning, and I shrink against the desk, teeth chattering as my gaze flits from corner to corner. There is nothing. No window, no means of escape, and now—

The door shatters. Something tumbles forward, a mess of elongated limbs, jutting bones, and oozing shadow patched across a body that appears to have been wrenched apart and stitched back together haphazardly. Its fangs are so numerous they bulge outward, dripping black fluid.

Darkwalker.

My mouth is dry as the desert sand. How did one manage to slip into the capital? The city gates, carved with protective runes, are shut prior to sundown.

The beast's head snaps toward me. I scream and stumble backward, narrowly missing the snap of its teeth. The books tumble from my arms. I snag one within reach, tuck it close to my chest—this one small hope that might lead to further information about the labyrinth—and dart to the opposite side of the room. Two steps later, the darkwalker cuts off my escape.

I pivot, ducking beneath its jaw to scuttle back toward the desk, the only shield in proximity. The creature is massive. Overwhelming. I've barely time to throw myself sideways as it strikes, toppling the desk as it rushes past. The beast rams snout-first into the wall, and I'm up, sprinting for the doorway.

I cut left, back toward the main atrium. I didn't realize how deeply I'd ventured from the special collections, for the narrow passage continues, on and on, an endless stretch of shadow. My lamp swings wildly in one hand, the other clutching the book. A furious roar rattles the air. Then my foot catches on a crack in the slab, and I stumble, hobbling awkwardly as pain licks through my ankle. Another crash draws my attention over my shoulder where the darkness seethes. It is coming.

I'm steps away from the back stacks when a great stench rolls forth. I abandon the lamp, force my legs faster, the pain in my ankle a distant memory. Turning right will lead me to the main atrium, the library exit. But the darkwalker is mere steps away. If I continue toward the main chamber, it will tear through my body long before I ever reach safety. I'll need to lose it in the stacks.

I veer left. The beast, too bulky to make these hairpin turns, rams into the wall. Grit showers down from the ceiling, and I dart along the shadowy aisle. The brightness of bound parchment flickers past as a *thump* sounds from behind, followed by a groan of wood. The shelving unit to my right wobbles.

I reach the end of the row. A corner—the worst place to be. When I peek around the shelf, I find that the beast has reoriented itself, sniffing the area as it seeks my scent. I wait until it turns its head, then dash down another aisle. If I move carefully and quietly, perhaps I can evade the darkwalker long enough to reach the front counter.

I place as much distance as I can between myself and the beast before ducking behind a row housing scrolls of Ishmah's recorded history. A darkwalker's sense of smell is keen. Its hearing and sight, less so. I can use that to my advantage.

With the stolen book still pressed to my heaving breast, I slide a bookend free from a shelf and ease around a bend, ears straining to catch the slightest sound. There—a handful of rows away. Its sniffling grows louder. Breath held, I launch the bookend as far as I can in the opposite direction of the front counter.

It scuttles toward the crash with a shriek. I duck behind another row before it realizes I'm on the move. If not for the small, cutout windows in the vaulted ceiling, I would be navigating the stacks blind.

When the beast fails to find me, it returns to its previous position, smashing into one of the shelves in the process. I watch it wobble from a distance. The idea emerges sleek and fully formed. I grasp its smooth shape in hand and consider my next move. If I can lure the darkwalker to the very end of the stacks, I can tip the shelves against one another, potentially trapping the beast beneath their weight long enough for me to flee the library.

Unfortunately, I'm on the wrong side of the room. To lure the beast, I must give it something to chase. Which means I will need to run faster than the toppling stacks, timing it just right.

The moment I ram the shelf hard enough to tilt it forward, the darkwalker catches sight of me. I dart down a row, leading the beast to its demise.

The shelf crashes into the one before it. Then that, too, tilts. It creates a domino effect, ancient texts and centuries-old documents tumbling to the ground in bits of parchment and dust. When I reach the penultimate row, I am near collapse. The final shelf topples forward as I dig deep for that last bit of speed. But I am not quick enough. My fingers catch the bookshelf. Momentum hauls me around, so fast my feet slip out from under me. I slam into the floor.

Seconds before the bookshelf crushes me, I scramble backward. The darkwalker strikes, quick as an asp. I scream and scuttle sideways, wiggling into the small space created by the collapsed unit propped against its neighbor.

"Sarai!"

A sob of relief builds in my chest. My fingernails scrabble at the stone as I drag myself forward through the scrolls and maps and tomes, while the darkwalker, steps behind, is destroying everything in its path searching for me, the parchment ripped as easily as dried leaves. I do not stop. Every fallen book is an obstacle to overcome. "Notus!" I cry back.

"Where are you?"

Teeth clenched, I push through the next wave of exhaustion. It is too far, his voice. My gasps are ragged, my throat inflamed. I haven't the breath to respond. The plan has failed. And I have blocked my only way out.

"I'm in the back stacks!" I scream. "Hurry!"

The darkwalker is too preoccupied demolishing the shelving to notice when I wiggle free on the opposite side of the aisle. At the next doorway, I duck inside, hobble behind the open door. Breath held, I wait.

It emerges from the stacks as something constructed in my nightmares. Pits for eyes, broken wisped tail. Saliva drips from its long, serrated fangs.

Wherever these darkwalkers hail from, I am certain it is a place of darkness, the chasm of some demonic hell. Prowling forward, it lifts its snout to the air. I watch it through the crack in the door. Once it kills its victim, it sucks out their soul through the mouth. *I am marble*, I think. *I am stone.*

Even my thoughts have stilled, as if they, too, fear to attract the beast's attention. Snout pressed against the crack, it exhales a noxious breath.

A blast of wind shatters a nearby shelf. Yellowing parchment spews in countless directions. The darkwalker whirls, a furious roar tearing from its throat.

My vision has adjusted well enough that I can make out a broad shadow taking shape across the room. Relief weakens my knees. If I didn't have the wall to support my back, I would absolutely liquify into a puddle. A cyclone sprints through the space as Notus unsheathes his sword and steps into a beam of moonlight. His eyes are blackest fire. His face is a thundercloud. This deity, who will topple cities, exterminate armies, send realms into ruination. He is the South Wind—he who commands the summer winds. Tonight, blood will be spilled.

He hacks low with his sword, and a thin blade of air slices across the room. The darkwalker dodges out of range, scaling one of the shelving units. When it reaches the top, it launches toward Notus, who blasts it sideways with another forceful gust. The darkwalker crashes into the wall. Dust clouds the air. The South Wind then catches the debris in another funnel of wind, using it to force the creature in between two narrow shelves. Even from this distance, I feel the wind's dry heat.

He swings his sword. Misses. The darkwalker swipes at Notus, who neatly sidesteps, stabbing it in the hindleg. I shrink back as a roar blasts from its mouth. His power isn't enough. The only means of killing a darkwalker are with salt, a strike to the heart, or decapitation. The darkwalker seems to know this and tries to keep its distance.

It retaliates with another vicious swipe, three long claws gouging his upper thigh. I bite my lip in worry. But that, I realize, is the South Wind's intention. To place himself in a position of vulnerability, to feed the darkwalker's bloodlust, to ensure it is so overcome by the desire to drag Notus' soul from his body that it forgets itself.

It tears at his arms, shoulders, and back. Blood soaks the fabric of his robe. The South Wind neither falters nor slows. He takes the beating as the beast draws itself into a frenzy. The reek of blood is overpowering.

He cannot die, I remind myself. But he can be severely wounded, maimed. When the darkwalker next strikes, Notus maneuvers it into a corner, using his winds to bind the beast's legs. It snarls, gnashing its fangs as he steps closer, scimitar raised. "Return to the shadows where you belong, beast." His sword descends. It gleams bright silver: a falling star.

Steel punctures the creature's skull, parting it as easily as water. Then Notus severs head from body. The darkwalker collapses in a heap of reeking flesh. Until, at last: silence.

My breath remains locked away inside my chest as the South Wind lifts a hand to his face. If I'm not mistaken, it quavers. "Sarai?" Slowly, he turns, scanning the collapsed shelves. Moonlight brightens the layers of dust, crystallizing it into new-fallen snow. He stalks toward the destruction, chest heaving. "Sarai!"

Taking a breath, I step out from behind the door. "I'm here."

Notus spins toward me. Fear has ravaged his features so severely that it has done the impossible. It has aged him.

I'm shaking so hard my knees buckle. Notus catches me with a muttered oath, drags me against his chest, and bands his arms around me so tightly I feel as if he is an extension of myself. Our hearts beat in sync: melody and countermelody. Gradually, the warmth of his body thaws my stiff, frozen limbs.

"Sarai." His frame trembles. And yet, sheltered in his arms, I have never experienced such security. "Are you hurt?"

I shake my head, face pressed against his sweaty chest. I can't speak.

The South Wind lowers his nose into my hair. He is sturdy. He neither bends nor breaks. My fingers clamp on fistfuls of his robe. I do not let go.

"How did you know I was here?" I ask.

"Some of the guards are loyal to me. One overheard you asking about access to the restricted documents yesterday. I assumed you would return. The sentries posted outside the library informed me once you'd entered. I heard your scream . . ." He falters, his tone vulnerable enough to communicate all that he feels, even if he cannot bring himself to speak those words aloud. It makes me bleed. I hate that it makes me bleed. "Tell me what happened."

So I do. I tell him of Prince Balior's research, the symbol that graces both his book and the labyrinth entrance. I inform him of the abandoned corridor and its locked doors. I speak of what I learned: the story of how the beast came to be.

For a time, Notus is quiet. "Where are those documents now?"

"I dropped them," I say. "This is the only book I was able to grab." Pulling away, I offer it to him. Plain gray cover, perhaps fifty pages thick.

The South Wind touches the slim volume with a frown. "If those books can help us unravel the mystery of the labyrinth, then I will return for them."

"No!" My hand clamps his forearm. "You can't go back there."

His features have been pressed by rigidity for as long as I've known him, yet now they soften with a rare, tempered amusement. "You do know that I am immortal, right?"

"And what of your wounds?" I gesture to the blood clotting the front of his robe. "You can bleed. You can feel pain. Why should you risk certain injury for something we are not sure will help?"

Our eyes lock. The unexpected drop in my stomach precedes the drop of my hand. And now I have said too much.

"Please," I whisper. "Not tonight. Wait until morning, if you must." In the brightness of day, it is unlikely a darkwalker will venture into the sun, though as time goes on, it seems less of a deterrent for reasons unknown. The only question remaining is how this creature slipped into the palace. Was it sent? Did it somehow find its way into the capital? How suspicious that I found it in the palace library, of all places. Could it have possibly come from one of those locked doors?

"How much does Prince Balior know about the labyrinth?" Notus abruptly asks.

"I'm not sure." I search his gaze for answers. I find none. "He hasn't told me much."

Again, a silence, stretching longer than it did previously. "What?" I ask. Something has captured his thoughts. I wish to know what has the power to do so.

The South Wind rubs at his jaw, as if massaging away the tension there. He seems reluctant to speak. "Have you considered whether the prince's motives are entirely unselfish?"

I narrow my eyes in suspicion. "What do you mean?"

"Prince Balior already has an established interest in the labyrinth. Now you learn that the beast promises to give whoever releases it what they seek. What if that is power? Why should Prince Balior bind himself to Ammara, a smaller, weaker realm, unless he hopes to gain something by it?"

His voice falls into the blackness of the ruined stacks surrounding us. I stare at his stern, unwavering expression, its shades of gray. My heart rejects the notion that I could be so easily fooled.

"I see what this is about." I cross my arms, shake my head in frustration. "Firstly, you are forgetting that Father arranged my marriage to Prince Balior, not the other way around. Secondly, Prince Balior *is* a scholar who researches myths within the realm, so of course he has some interest in the labyrinth. Lastly, why would the prince seek to harm Ammara by releasing the beast when he intends to bind himself to this realm through marriage? It makes absolutely no sense. The only reason you're bringing this up is because you hate to see another man claim my hand in marriage."

His eyes flicker dangerously. "That's not it at all."

I'm sure. "So, you have no issue with my upcoming nuptials?" I press, hand propped on my hip.

Notus sighs, glancing up at the ceiling overhead as though he might find a bit of patience there. Interestingly, he fails to answer the question. "What if Prince Balior doesn't intend to honor the marriage, only use it as a ruse to gain access to the labyrinth until he has succeeded in his plan?"

That, I did not expect. Here I was, placing my own pieces on the game board, when Prince Balior may have been shifting their positions while my back was turned. What if Notus is right?

What if he is wrong?

If I end the courtship, I sacrifice my best chance at obtaining information to break my curse. It's possible this has all been a misunderstanding. And if I act against it? In believing Notus' claim, I allow suspicion to cloud my gaze. I substitute research for nefarious motives. I brandish my future husband a traitor.

"I understand where you're coming from, Notus, but we have no evidence to support your suspicions. I can't make a decision on what *may* be."

"That's fair," he says, because of course he attempts to see both perspectives, despite the disagreement. I admire him for that. "But there is something I would like to show you."

At this point, I really have nothing to lose.

Moving silently, we depart the library, then the palace itself. As we stride down the Queen's Road, the South Wind says, "Is that bakery in the lower ring still there, the one that makes those honey cakes?"

"It is," I say, glancing at him sidelong. Quiet steeps the residential streets, but a few windows glow with candlelight.

He shortens his strides to match mine. "Do you ever . . .?"

"Sometimes." It feels too vulnerable, this admission. That I still visit the bakery I once considered *ours*.

Notus smiles, which in turn makes me smile. "You always did love their honey cakes."

Indeed, I did. Still do.

This is not a road I wish to revisit, yet I find myself saying, as we turn a corner past one of the smaller shrines, "Nadia asks after you on occasion." Between the two of us, the old woman had her favorite, and it certainly wasn't me. Not that I can blame her. Notus' quiet nature endears him to even the most cantankerous personality.

"We could always drop by," he suggests casually, casting me a suggestive glance. "No harm in it, right?"

My head snaps toward him in surprise, and despite the walls I have erected around my heart, I feel the slightest crack forming. Nadia begins her baking quite early—hours before dawn, if I am not mistaken. "What about the thing you wanted to show me?"

"It can wait."

Well, I'm certainly not going to reject the opportunity to eat a honey cake fresh out of the oven.

The bakery is located at the end of a crooked lane shrouded in deepest shadow. We knock. I'm not expecting Nadia to answer the door at this hour, but to my surprise, she does, a wave of warm, sugar-dusted air billowing out onto the street. Flour coats the old woman's apron and hair. One look at the two of us, and her entire face brightens. "Princess Sarai! And . . . is that Notus?" A girlish gasp escapes her. "My word, it is. Look at how you've grown!"

I bite back a shock of laughter. The woman has no idea Notus is immortal. He hasn't aged a day since he left.

"Let me guess," she says, eyes twinkling with mischief. "You're here for the honey cakes? Don't you think that I've forgotten."

Notus ducks his head sheepishly. "Guilty."

All right, even *I* find his reaction adorable. It must be something in the air.

"Lucky for you," she says, "they've just come out of the oven. Just a moment."

When Nadia disappears into the back, the South Wind murmurs, "There's a bakery in the City of Gods that is renowned for their cinnamon biscuits. Father would take my brothers and I when we were young." He stalls there, as though unwilling to cross an unseen threshold. "Next door was the armory, and after purchasing a few sweets, we would wander the shelves of weapons. One day, Father told us each to select one."

His hand drifts toward his blade. "Boreas selected a spear. Zephyrus a bow, and Eurus an ax. But I didn't care for a weapon. I had no desire to spill blood. If allowed, I would have chosen to spend my days researching obscure texts. But Father didn't like that. After all, I was one of the Anemoi. There was nothing more pitiful to him than a god unable to defend himself."

And this is how I had originally come to know the South Wind. Years before, Notus had arrived in Ammara intending to slay the beast within the labyrinth. In the weeks, and then months, of his time at court, we came to know each other just like this: through story.

"It is how I came by this sword." His fingers twitch around the hilt. "And I decided that I would become so brilliant a swordsman that none would be able to force my hand. It would be my shield. I would be free in all the ways that mattered."

I understand. Truly, I do. That is partially why I practiced the violin so diligently. I witnessed how easily Father had stripped Fahim of his dream, despite his advanced skill. I would become greater, so great that there would be no question that I belonged to music, and it belonged to me.

"For what it's worth," I whisper, "you are a fine swordsman. You should be proud of how far you've come."

Notus gazes at me for a long, breathless moment. "Thank you," he murmurs.

Moments later, Nadia returns bearing a tray of round cakes crisped at the edges. I select two. They're still warm.

When she disappears into the back again, Notus gazes down at his dessert with a small, sad smile before slipping it into his mouth. Maybe it is this night. Maybe it is how present the past feels in this moment, but I do not like seeing the South Wind so forlorn.

"Your father was wrong to pressure you into becoming something you're not," I tell him.

He shrugs. We stand near enough that the motion buffets warm air against my side. "We cannot change others. I have learned that lesson again and again."

"We should allow ourselves to choose what makes us happiest," I say, holding his gaze, "don't you think?" I slip the cake between my teeth.

His eyes flicker, then drop to my mouth. "Sarai—"

The pang in my heart hits unexpectedly. I step back. "It's late," I say, but the words do not come as easily as I'd hoped. "What is it you wished to show me?"

He nods stiffly, though I do not miss the hurt clouding his expression. "Of course, Princess Sarai."

After bidding Nadia goodbye, we head west. Here marks signs of industry, the whiff of smelted metal billowing from cooling forges, wood dust layered like a pile of snow atop the pitted road. As we ascend the rise of a hill, Notus grips my arm, forcing me to slow.

Initially, I do not understand what I'm looking at. Then the clouds part. The moon drenches the land below in silver. I see horses, the sheen of dented armor, the dusty earth packed by the tread of a thousand boots.

An army.

Turning toward Notus, I demand, "Does Father know of this?" After all, King Halim specifically informed Prince Balior that his army was forbidden inside the walls until our marriage was legitimized.

"Not that I'm aware of. I only discovered it this morning." The South Wind runs a rough hand through his inky hair. I remember all too well the sift of those silken threads. "Maybe Prince Balior's interest in the labyrinth *does* pertain to his research. But consider this: Why would he bring his army inside the city unless he intends to use it?"

I am caught between tomorrow and today, the threat that was promised, and the threat that is current. The South Wind is right. Marrying Prince Balior would grant him significant power over my land and people, regardless of his motives surrounding the labyrinth. His army is evidence enough. It is too great a risk.

"You were right," I admit, the words pitifully frail. Hooves thud against the distant earth as the prince's soldiers corral their horses into a vast pen. Gods, how could I have been so stupid? "I trusted Prince Balior too soon. And now I fear I have invited an even greater threat into Ammara."

"It's not your fault," Notus says. "But King Halim must know of this."

I agree. And we've no time to waste.

10

"I wish to speak to Father."

Ali, who has guarded King Halim's private chambers for the last decade, replies, "Unfortunately, Your Highness, he is not present at the moment." At his back stretches double oaken doors, cut no thinner than a hand width. Even as a child, I was not welcome to enter Father's rooms without an appointment. Always, I must knock as a stranger would.

"Then where is he?" I demand.

"He is in a meeting, Your Highness."

This early in the morning? It is not yet dawn.

At my side, the South Wind shifts his weight, features pressed into fine creases. He, too, distrusts this meeting at so inconvenient a time.

Together, we hurry toward the war chamber, marked by doors paneled in gold, and flanked by four guards. At our approach, a broad-shouldered man bearing a long, pointed spear steps neatly into my path. "King Halim has asked not to be disturbed."

"I must speak with the king," I snap.

"I cannot allow that, Your Highness."

The South Wind edges forward so that we stand shoulder to shoulder. The display of solidarity momentarily takes me aback.

"Princess Sarai has ordered you to stand down," he murmurs, voice no louder than what is required for intimate conversation. "May I remind you that she outranks you tenfold and has the power to order your execution for obstruction of justice, should she desire it? Now step aside."

The air begins to stir, roused to life by the South Wind's budding ire, and the guard flinches back. He glances to his comrades, who appear equally fearful. Inwardly, I smile. I never claimed pettiness was beneath me.

A low groan as the doors open wide enough to grant Notus and I entry. At the disturbance, the two men occupying the long table stretching the length of the war chamber glance up in surprise. King Halim—and Prince Balior.

It is so vast a space my footsteps echo against the pale stone walls, the gleaming slabs of marble gracing the floor. Father regards our unexpected appearance with reproach. Meanwhile, Prince Balior regards me curiously before his gaze flicks to Notus. The blacks of his eyes flatten with a distaste he does not attempt to hide.

"Father." With the ease of practice, I soften my expression, the tense pinch of my mouth. I smile warmly at Prince Balior, as if in silent apology of the intrusion. After all, he is our guest. "May I speak with you in private?"

King Halim digs the tips of his fingers into the cushioned arms of his chair. Its rust-colored upholstery paints his complexion with a yellow tinge. "Our meeting is still in session. You will have to wait."

"The matter is urgent."

"As is this meeting," he retorts, "which is now delayed due to your interruption."

An all-too-familiar heat begins to pinken my face. I stand tall by force of will alone. Indeed, the rules are clear. But I am trying my best to do what is right. "Please."

"I will not repeat myself."

I am your daughter, I wish to say. But I know what will occur, should the situation escalate. And after? When I have been shamed into silence, as if my emotions are a burden, and must be hidden as such? My mouth shuts, my words swallowed. I say nothing at all.

"Your Majesty." The South Wind steps forward, drawing Father's attention and, as a result, his anger. "I apologize for the interruption, but Princess Sarai would not interject unless the matter was as pressing as she claims."

In this moment, I am a body with two minds. The woman who seeks to push aside any existing fondness for Notus, and the girl who leans toward him as though he is star bright. Even when I have treated him contemptuously, the South Wind still attempts to shield me. I do not deserve this kindness, but I appreciate it nonetheless.

"Very well," King Halim growls with a wave of his hand. "You have the floor. Speak your concerns."

All eyes come to rest on me. My heart flutters in uncertainty. I ask myself if I am willing to step from this cliff's edge without knowing what awaits me at the bottom of the drop. For my people, for my realm, there is only room enough for *yes*.

"Father, I strongly prefer that we speak in private." The prince's attention continues to shift between me, Notus, and the king. "As I'm sure you would agree, I do not want to burden Prince Balior with news of Ammara's toils."

"If Prince Balior is to one day oversee Ammara, then he should be given a full image of the realm's current state."

My intention was to discuss my concerns with Father, calmly and concisely. I would lay out the information, no matter how implausible, though the implications are grave, and the details are few. Maybe I'm overthinking and forcing connections when none exist. But I fear what will happen to Ammara when my twenty-fifth nameday arrives and I am forever gone from the world. There is the army inside our walls. There is Prince Balior's interest in the labyrinth. There is the beast, who seeks escape. No matter my fading days, I must find a way to force the prince—and his army—out of Ammara.

"Father—"

"Damn it, Sarai. Spit it out."

Well then. He asked for it. "I cannot marry Prince Balior."

Silence.

It is drowning, this stillness. Prince Balior sits frozen in his chair. Notus stares at me with rare bewilderment. King Halim's mouth hangs open, jowls quivering. For half a heartbeat, I fear I have driven him to insanity.

Then Father lifts a hand to alert the guards. "Please escort our guest from the room."

Prince Balior shoves to his feet. "I mean no disrespect, Your Majesty, but don't you think I should hear what Princess Sarai has to say, considering I'm the topic of conversation?" A thin film of venom coats his words.

It takes a great effort, but eventually, the king stands as well, using the table for support. It hurts to watch him struggle for balance. But I know better than to show outward concern over his health.

"I apologize, Prince Balior. Please excuse Sarai's behavior." Despite his lack of stability, the king's voice rings with strength. "She has not been feeling well of late—"

"I am feeling perfectly fine, Father," I say through gritted teeth. Oh, if there were no witnesses in the room, I would have a story to tell. "If I could speak with you *privately*—"

"This heat would make anyone mad," he goes on in response to Prince Balior. "Why, just yesterday—"

The lump in my throat thickens, and I turn from the king. I'm not sure why I try so hard to be heard when it is clear he does not care to hear my voice.

"Sarai."

The touch of a gentle hand on my arm draws my attention to Notus. His eyes soften as they rest on me. They promise sanctuary. What fool am I, that I might reach out and collect what is promised? I never wished for Notus to see me in this pitiful, weakened state. If I am not strong, if I am not assertive, if I am not self-reliant and encased in armor, then I am vulnerable. And that simply cannot be.

"Was this your plan, Your Majesty?" the prince demands. "Lure me with the promise of an alliance. Then, when my guard is brought low, humiliate me?" His voice, which has climbed in volume, pelts the stone and marble of the room.

"Not at all, Prince Balior." I hear it then—the king's panic, which in turn ignites my own. As the prince paces, his gestures grow wild, an outlet for a fury that swells and overwhelms. In attempting to avoid conflict, have I in actuality set the spark?

"I have journeyed over twelve hundred miles through desert sands to get here. Now I'm expected to return home without a wife, without a union, as if this was no more than a holiday?" The prince barks an incensed laugh. "It is absolutely the worst treatment I have ever received in any kingdom or realm. You promised me your daughter's hand," he argues. "Now you're going back on your word?"

King Halim's face is so deep a red I half expect him to burst into flames. "I assure you, Prince Balior, that *no one* is going back on their word, least of all me. Like you, I am hearing of this for the first time. My daughter is simply confused ... heat-stricken."

Prince Balior smiles cuttingly. "I'm sure."

With a heavy sigh, the king lowers himself onto his chair, bent in defeat. I glance at Notus, failing to mask my fear. If Prince Balior retaliates, Notus will protect Father, protect Ishmah, protect the realm. This I know. "I swear to you, Prince Balior, I would *never* disrespect you in this manner. I ask only for your forgiveness."

The prince glances between me and the king in suspicion. "I have your word, Your Majesty, that you were not aware of what Sarai would say?"

"*Princess* Sarai," Notus growls to the prince in warning. "Do not address her so informally. You are not yet betrothed."

Prince Balior studies the South Wind with arms crossed, posture loose, mouth slanting into his cheek. "As it turns out," he says, "that *is* what King Halim and I were discussing—before you so rudely interrupted." He slips from between the table and chair to circle the room, bypassing the guards stationed along the walls. When he begins to approach, Notus steps between us, hand gripping the hilt of his sword. Distaste curls the prince's upper lip. "The king and I have reached an agreement. Princess Sarai and I are soon to be wed."

My head whips toward Father, who refuses to meet my eye. We had an agreement, he and I. Yes, I agreed to an arranged marriage. But first, I would meet this prince and determine his character. Father promised that we would discuss my betrothal following the courtship before a final decision was made. Now he has gone behind my back and made this decision for me, without my consent?

And now my alarm has burrowed deep. I cannot separate myself from it. Because if Prince Balior's motives are as nefarious as I suspect, my options have been reduced even further. I did, indeed, have a plan. And now Father has ripped a hole clean through it. No water will hold. It must be patched—quickly.

"Is there something I have done to offend you, Princess Sarai? Is that why you refuse to marry me?"

Prince Balior's question draws my attention. Peering around the South Wind's broad back, I regard Um Salim's adored prince warily. For a heartbeat, I wrestle with the absurd desire to press my palm flat against Notus' spine, absorb his heat and strength.

"No, Prince Balior." Lies.

"You're sure?" He cocks his head curiously. "Because if that were the case, I would hope we might discuss it like reasonable adults."

"It's not that," I say. He cannot know the why. If I mention the army, the darkwalker, the beast, who is to say the prince will not retaliate? No, to abandon this plan, the reason must be sound. Indeed, it might be the only clear-headed decision I have made since the prince's arrival.

"I cannot marry you," I explain, "because Notus and I are engaged."

11

THE SOUTH WIND MAY BE A PILLAR BESIDE ME FOR HOW MOTION-less he stands. Even the air hangs in suspension. His winds have died, wholly and completely.

"Excuse me?" King Halim's features are so twisted they appear to have gone to war with one another.

I consider my response. Too meek—I toss it aside. The next: too forceful, teeming with resentment. That one will not do either. I discard them all, each one lacking, until I unearth the very core of myself, this polished, hardened heart of metal. "I believe you heard me well enough, Father."

He chews on the inside of his cheek, gathering himself. "Whatever hoax this is, Sarai, I do not appreciate it. Have I not been giving you enough attention? Is that why you feel the need to jest?"

Once a king, always a king. No matter that I am his daughter, disrespect will not stand in King Halim's court. "It is no hoax, Father." It takes an effort to smooth the raw edges of my response. His assumption stings more than I care to admit. "Notus and I are engaged."

"Since when?" he barks.

"Yesterday evening."

My attention slides across the room to Prince Balior. He, too, is immobile, carved in equal measure by affront and disbelief. That is to be expected. The fury igniting his dark eyes, however, is potent enough to send me back a step. It is too wild a thing.

"Meaning no disrespect, Princess Sarai, but I was with you yesterday evening, roaming the palace grounds." The prince smooths the front of his robe, giving motion to his evident frustration. "At what point did Notus have time to ask for your hand?"

A perfectly valid question, for which I have no answer.

"Princess Sarai and I crossed paths in the corridors," the South Wind says. I glance at him in surprise. He is a flawless image of placid waters, as though this is all unfolding exactly as intended. "I wanted to make sure she arrived at her chambers safely, but I couldn't wait. I asked then."

Prince Balior appears moments away from stabbing Notus through the heart. After casting a glare in the immortal's direction, the prince turns to me, his expression deeply wounded. "You told me there was nothing between you and the South Wind," he says. "Was that, too, a lie?"

I am acutely aware of Notus' heated gaze razing the side of my face. I refuse to look at him. "Not exactly," I begin, wetting my lips, "but after some reflection, I wondered if I had been too quick to judge his past actions—"

Prince Balior scoffs and turns from me. "I can't listen to this anymore."

I look to King Halim, who glowers at me, hands clamped around the arms of his chair. "Explain."

Does he demand this of me as a father, or as a king?

"I'm not sure how else to explain it," I say with notable composure. "Yesterday, Notus asked for my hand in marriage. I accepted. Should the gods will it, we will be wed."

Father shakes his head. His gaze is so cutting I imagine he wishes to chisel this image into something else. "You tread too soft of sand, Sarai." That I have accepted Notus' engagement without Father's knowledge—without anyone's knowledge—is cause for potential scandal.

I startle as the strength of Notus' fingers encloses mine, and my eyes leap to his. He does not understand what is happening, yet he stands with me. A gratified warmth blooms against my sternum, which I tuck aside for consideration at a later time.

"Your Majesty," the South Wind says, with the bass resonance of canyon winds, "Sarai speaks the truth. I've asked for her hand in marriage. I understand it is sudden and that it may complicate matters—"

"You're damn right this complicates matters!" Spittle flies from Father's mouth. "I don't know what marital customs exist in whatever realm you hail from, Notus, but in Ammara, they are not to be treated carelessly."

"I do not treat your customs carelessly, Your Majesty." The solemnity with which Notus speaks rings in the way only truth can. "However, I understand my actions may suggest otherwise. I have only the utmost respect for you, Princess Sarai, and your realm. All I wish is to bring your daughter happiness."

My fingers twitch inside his palm, and Notus tightens his grip in what I convince myself is comfort. A past version of myself—young, naive—at one point wished to hear this sentiment. Now, I'm uncertain whether the South Wind speaks the truth or is simply going along with the ruse because he hopes to foil the prince's reprehensible plans. Would it matter, in the end? If I'm promised to another man, Prince Balior will leave Ammara. There would be no reason for him—or his army—to stay.

With calm resolve, I inform King Halim, "As you know, Father, Ammara's customs dictate it takes two parties to consent to an engagement, but only one to break it. If you cannot honor the fact that I'd already accepted Notus' proposal before this meeting, then at least honor the traditions of our realm." So long as Notus and I refuse to renounce our betrothal, the king hasn't the authority to prohibit it. This is our law. And it would be in poor taste for the king to disregard the laws of the realm in front of a visiting prince.

Father blinks once, twice, before a bit of laughter slips out and unrolls in hoarse waves of disbelief. Notus and I exchange a wordless glance. Across the room, Prince Balior observes the South Wind with crossed arms, his expression downright scathing.

"I see what this is about," the king manages once he regains control of his emotions. "It is a jest. A means to get my attention. Well, you have it. I admit, I have not been present enough, Sarai, but please understand there are more important matters at hand. Enough of this."

"That's not it, Father. Not at all." And it hurts unbearably that he would make light of a very real, very unmet need in my life.

He sits straight-backed in his chair, mood darkening. "I arranged this with your future in mind. Prince Balior is what you need. What we *all* need."

Does he think I don't understand? Of course I do. Without Prince Balior's research, darkwalkers will continue to infiltrate. But if I am to protect my realm from a potentially larger, more insidious threat, this is my only path forward.

Quietly, I say, "Please, Papa."

Something fractures the king's expression. Sorrow, perhaps, or grief. I have not called him this since I was a child. But it is what I have always yearned for: to reach for Father, knowing that he will reach back.

"King Halim." Prince Balior turns toward him. "You assured me that a union between our realms was guaranteed. Now I learn that your daughter is promised to another man?" His lip curls. "I have traveled far, and for what? To be publicly humiliated by a second-rate royal and this foreign scoundrel—"

"That's enough," Notus cuts in.

The air coils onto itself, a serpent in its nest. The South Wind's black eyes lock onto Prince Balior in warning. Sensing the mounting tension, the guards stationed along the walls reach for their swords.

Quietly, Notus says, "Remember whose home you occupy, Prince Balior. Do not think to disrespect the royal family."

A deep flush inflames the prince's cheeks. "This whole thing reeks of deception," he growls.

"There is no deception on my part, Prince Balior." The king lifts a quavering hand to rub at his eyes. "I don't know what madness has overtaken my daughter, but I assure you this union does not have my blessing."

"Blessing?" he hisses. "What good is your blessing when your hands are tied?"

"Now, let's not get ahead of ourselves," Father says hurriedly, seeking to console his prospective son-in-law. "An engagement can be broken as swiftly as it is made. Once Sarai has come to her senses, I'm certain she will renounce their engagement, and everything will go ahead as planned."

But the prince will not be pacified. "Princess Sarai was promised to *me*." He lunges for me, fingertips grazing my elbow before a wall of wind plows into him with enough force to send him careening against the wall. He hits it with an *oof* and drops to the marble floor.

A wretched howl tears through the war chamber, ripping curtains from their rods, snatching maps and documents from the table. At once, guards surround King Halim, who stares at Notus with a combination of awe and fear. Those spiraling gusts gather closer to the South Wind's body as he advances toward Prince Balior. He is an impossibility, a living, breathing body of wind. Unsheathing his sword, he tucks its curved edge beneath the man's chin.

"If I *ever* see you lay a hand on her," Notus growls, "you will learn the true depth of my wrath. Do we understand each other?"

Prince Balior's face has gone ashen. He swallows, then nods, flinching back when Notus removes the blade from his neck.

The South Wind's dark promise feeds through my bloodstream with surprising heat. I am ashamed that it has the power to render me weak in the knees. Notus is calm, always calm—until he's not. I can't allow myself to hope that he protects me for any other reason than duty.

Father glances at the prince in uncertainty. Our guest's behavior has likely given him pause, as it has given me. Angered or not, assault is unacceptable.

And yet, Father has too much pride to change his mind. He turns to regard me in disappointment. "You are the Princess of Ammara."

"I am also your daughter."

"Nonetheless, you and I had an understanding. Now you go back on your word?" Then, softer: "What would Fahim think of your selfishness?"

Only years of practice allow me to swallow the gasp before it escapes. His barbs, which never fail to pierce the softness of my heart. So long as Prince Balior is present, I cannot tell him that I fear he is being deceived.

"Think of me what you will, Father, but a decision has been made and my mind will not change. Notus and I will wed at the end of spring." Time enough to break this curse, to oust Prince Balior. If I fail, it won't matter who I marry, for I'll be dead.

"I forbid you to speak of this mockery," the king bites out. "You do not have my blessing. Nor do you have my respect." He tosses out a hand. "Dismissed."

As soon as the doors of the war chamber shut at our backs, Notus withdraws his hand from mine. The absence of his touch carries an unexpected chill.

"You better have a good explanation for this," he mutters.

As a matter of fact, I do not.

But I merely flash my teeth in a feral grin, burying my uncertainty and sorrow with all the rest. "Follow me." This is no place for private conversation.

As soon as I turn the corner, Notus must realize where our destination lies, for he strides ahead of me, descends a nearby staircase, taking the shortcut we utilized in those early days of our budding relationship. Eventually, we reach a small garden, its shadowed alcove framed by laurel trees and ornamented with night-blooming orchids. Moonlight cascades in hues of snow and silver through the circular windows cut into the ceiling high above.

I have not returned to this refuge in half a decade. In fact, I have avoided the entire western wing. It is here that the South Wind's rooms were once located, rooms I found myself in most nights, tangled in damp bedsheets, pressed against heated skin.

I remember our first encounter.

The morning hung wet and heavy as sopping wool. Father searched for me, demanding I attend dinner with some visiting dignitaries later that evening, but I had refused and sought solace among the plants, who would not attempt to recast silver into gold.

The scuff of a shoe drew my attention to the garden's entryway.

A man stood partially shielded by vines, his eyes cool and unfamiliar above the scarf shielding the lower portion of his face. I glared at him, not at all in the mood for company. He wore no weapons. I could not decide whether it was the mark of arrogance or foolishness. Hours later, the South Wind would be properly introduced, but I could not have known then what purpose he had in the palace.

"Who are you?" I'd demanded.

Shaking my head to clear the memory, I step forward into the garden, exchanging *then* for *now*. I cannot say for certain what emotion grasps hold. There is no separation between sorrow and longing, bitterness and grief. All are woven into the same tapestry.

Dropping onto a bench beneath a trellis, I sigh. "That went about as well as I expected it to." I massage my temples wearily.

Notus glares into the gloom dripping shadow onto the foliage. A muscle tics in his jaw, the most irritated metronome. He will not look at me. I hate that I am weak enough to desire otherwise.

"Well?" I say. "Speak your thoughts, if you have them."

His attention slides to me momentarily before flitting elsewhere. "Why does it sound like *I* am to blame for that ridiculous display? It wasn't as if I was an informed participant."

I stare at him, perplexed. "Of course you're not to blame."

"But you are angry."

"I'm not angry."

"Yes, you are." That dark, penetrative gaze manages to strip me of flesh, muscle, down to bone. "Perhaps you have simply lived with anger for so long you no longer recognize its face."

I haven't the words, only this murky pool cloaking my heart, in which I see nothing, not even my own reflection. The conviction with which he speaks only solidifies how uncertain I am. Why does fear so often manifest as ire? He cannot understand these grains of sand I attempt to collect in my outstretched hands. They slip through my fingers and are gone.

"I'm sorry," I murmur. He's right, of course. It's unfair to place blame onto the one person who is willing to stand by my side through this mess. The hurt I feel toward Father is irrelevant. He has insulted me plenty over the years, but that dig about Fahim was too raw, too fresh.

I open my mouth to respond when Notus drops his head into his hands. "Some forewarning would have been nice."

"I know." I bite the inside of my cheek. At the very least, the pain helps push thoughts of Father aside. "It likely doesn't matter, but I didn't know I was going to say those words until they'd already left my mouth. I didn't exactly have a choice."

"Of course you have a choice."

Even as my irritation boils toward the surface, I tamp it down. Notus could have outed me as a liar, could have renounced the engagement and put an end to this. But he didn't. For that, he has my gratitude.

"I just ... I couldn't see it any other way," I whisper. "Time is a luxury we can't afford. If Prince Balior intends to release the beast from the labyrinth, I won't make his quest for power any easier by marrying him. I'd hoped that by taking marriage off the table, he would be forced to leave the city and take his army with him. I didn't anticipate Father's stubbornness—or that the prince might consider staying to court a woman who has committed herself to another."

He lifts his head. "What of the position you've placed me in, or your father? What of the consequences I will soon face for appearing to having asked for your hand?"

A bit of guilt digs at me. Once again, he is reminding me of all the ways I have made some imprudent decision of desperation. "Father may be stern, but he is no fool. He would not make an enemy of you, no matter how displeased he is about our engagement."

"Will you continue to make excuses?"

For the second time in as many moments, I am left unbalanced, exposed, vulnerable. "I've already apologized. I take full responsibility for placing you in this situation. I can understand what a burden it must be for you," I choke, the words like shattered glass in my throat, "to tie yourself to me through marriage. But worry not. This is only a ruse until Prince Balior gives up and departs the capital."

"That isn't what I meant," he says.

I'm sure. "What is this really about, Notus?"

Moonlight dusts his fathomless eyes. Even after all this time, I struggle to identify his emotions. "You don't want to marry the prince. But nor do you want to marry me."

Eighteen-year-old Sarai would have argued differently.

He eases nearer, the ferns framing the garden path rustling against his ankles, stirred to life at his passing. "I am a tool," he goes on.

Better a tool than a victim. Better the needle than the thread. "If that's how you choose to perceive this, then that is your own prerogative. But I was under the impression you disliked the prince. Aren't you glad to be rid of him?"

Notus eases onto the bench beside me, our shoulders brushing. A whiff of warm, salted air hits my face, and I swallow, fighting the urge to bury my nose into his neck.

"A man like Prince Balior will not accept defeat," he says.

I am well aware. In rejecting the prince's hand, I damn myself and my realm. Prince Balior was to be our salvation. Now I fear he will become its ruination.

"Prince Balior will beseech Father to reconsider his stance on Ammara's customs. He will threaten war and demand our marriage be established. But I will not bend. And Father will not stand against our union."

"How can you be certain?"

As if it is not already obvious. "You are the South Wind," I tell him, and when he turns his face toward mine, I find our mouths separated by the smallest distance, warm shadow spiced by breath. "You are formidable. Immortal. Our greatest weapon in defeating the darkwalkers. But more so, you are an incredibly powerful deity, and Father would not wish to anger you for fear of retaliation."

"I would never bring harm to Ishmah," he says.

"I know." It is why I trust him now, despite swearing never to do so again. "But Father doesn't know you as I do. We can use that to our advantage."

"And what of Prince Balior's army? Who is to say he will not retaliate to this disgrace with force?"

It may take time—days or weeks—but eventually, Prince Balior will lower his blade, lift the white cloth of surrender. He will not wish to steep in this humiliation.

"Prince Balior is too proud to resort to threats," I explain. "He wants his victory to be earned, not coerced."

"Sarai—"

"I know," I rush to say. "And you're right: I've placed both you and Father in difficult positions. And I'm sorry, truly. I know how it feels to be trapped into something you don't want. But what's done is done. Now I must figure out how to protect Ammara to the best of my ability."

It is not surrender. I am not baring my belly to the god who shattered my heart. But as much as I wish otherwise, Notus' cooperation is necessary. I'm no longer the girl I was. My skin does not tear so easily.

"Will you help me?" I implore him.

The South Wind's gaze leaps to mine. Those shining pupils gleam with a focus so acute I am temporarily left wanting. All of this, every effort, to bind myself in appearance to the immortal I despise. For Ammara. For my people. Nothing and no one else.

In the end, it is Notus who looks away first. "What must I do?"

12

THE FOLLOWING AFTERNOON, NOTUS' BELONGINGS ARE MOVED into the chambers adjacent to my room. In the hours since declaring our betrothal to King Halim, I did what I rarely do, and I tossed breadcrumbs to the court. The story unfolded like so: Darkwalker sighted in the library yesterday evening. None were harmed, though extra security measures have been put in place to protect the royal family. The South Wind's presence is a necessary precaution.

I'd hoped that his proximity would grant us the opportunity to unravel the mystery of the labyrinth without interruption. Unfortunately, Notus seems to avoid my company at all costs. Some mornings as I lie in bed, I listen through the shared wall as he dresses for the day. By the time I gather the courage to approach his door, he has already departed, none the wiser to my increasingly vivid dreams, which feature his broad hands and swift fingers. Sometimes, I fall asleep with my hand between my legs, skin stinging with perspiration following a particularly sweet release.

A week after the darkwalker sighting, I inform my maidservants that I will be taking breakfast in my chambers rather than in the dining room. It is early—before dawn—but I want to catch Notus before he leaves. Too easily, he slips from my grasp. Today, I will not allow it.

Grabbing a robe from my wardrobe, I wrap it around my nightgown and belt it at the waist. Then I cross to the interconnecting door between our rooms. Ear pressed against the wood, I listen to the rustle of clothing as he dons his uniform. When I knock, the rustling stops.

Then, the South Wind's slow footfalls, their undeniable approach. I catch my breath, neutralize my features as the lock flips and Notus pulls open the door.

He wears a pair of trousers and a tunic so thin that the curl of chest hair bleeds through the fabric. The disheveled state of his hair suggests he has run his fingers through it repeatedly—or someone else has. As soon as the thought forms, I discard it. I've heard no indication of Notus hosting guests. And I refuse to consider the possibility.

"Good morning." I offer him a smile. "Would you care to join me for breakfast?"

He stares at me. "Breakfast."

"Yes, breakfast. According to some, the most important meal of the day." I gesture toward my sitting room, where two place settings await, in addition to assorted fruits, fresh bread, sliced vegetables with hummus, and steaming tea.

Notus looks to the spread, back to me, back to the spread, back to me.

"I don't bite," I reassure him.

"Much."

My mouth parts in surprise, and bit of laughter slips out. Well, he's not wrong. "Look." Boldly, I rest a palm on his chest, over the hard kick of his heart. "If we're going to convince Prince Balior that he's lost the battle, we need to be a little more . . . *convincing*."

His gaze drops to the hand on his chest. The drum beneath my palm quickens. "A love match." He lifts his head, eyes darkening in both wariness and understanding.

My face warms, and I snatch my hand away in sudden retreat. "It was once." It takes more strength than I care to admit, to voice that aloud. "Obviously, circumstances have changed, but I believe we can put on a decent front, don't you?"

He scrubs a hand along his jaw. "I suppose . . ."

"Great." I tug him across the threshold. "Then we'll need to practice. Obviously."

"Of course," he replies smoothly.

He takes a seat. I take a seat. We sit near enough that, were I to angle slightly to the right, our knees would touch.

"Tea?" I inquire. At his nod, I pour him a cup. Notus returns the favor. He even adds a spoonful of sugar, just how I like it. I watch him beneath lowered lashes as he takes a sip. After a period of silence, he sets the cup on the table.

"So," he says.

I straighten in my chair. "So."

"How do you suggest we go about this?"

That is a question I have examined thoroughly, in varying shades of light, at every manageable angle. And I still haven't the slightest clue.

"To be honest, I'm not sure." At the very least, this discussion requires a full stomach. I dip a carrot into hummus and pop it into my mouth with a satisfying crunch. "We'll need to spend time together." My eyes dart to his face, then away. "Not that I care to humiliate Prince Balior further, but if we can rub salt into the wound, it should be enough to drive him from the city."

The South Wind pauses with the rim of his cup at his mouth. He does not appear thrilled, but at least he doesn't argue. "Very well. How should we spend time together, aside from sharing breakfast?"

"To begin," I say, "it would be a little easier if you stopped avoiding me. How are we to put on a convincing front if you fail to attend meals with the king?" Despite his ailing health, Father remains keen. He will know something is amiss should Notus continue to stay away.

He looks away guiltily. Through the windows, Ishmah's shining rooftops glint beneath a yellow sun. Mount Syr shimmers in the far distance, reduced to a smudged hill of barren rock. "I've my duties to attend to."

Somehow, I knew Notus would say this. "Can't someone cover for you?"

A muscle pulses in his jaw, but he nods, saying, "I'll ask around. I . . . suppose it couldn't hurt to question if the guards have seen anything suspicious regarding Prince Balior or the labyrinth." When he next catches my gaze, a little zing of energy darts through me. I hurriedly shove a cucumber between my teeth. "It could help determine our next step."

I nod, chewing as fast as I can. Mouth half full, I manage, "It might offer additional insight about the b—" Except instead of *beast*, a fat glob of saliva slips from the corner of my mouth.

A rush of heat consumes my face. By the gods. Snatching my napkin, I wipe the saliva from my chin while Notus looks on, holding back laughter. I glare at him, and he clears his throat, saying, "What will happen when the prince has returned to Um Salim?"

Right. Because once Prince Balior is out of the picture, there will be no need for this charade. "We'll need to break the engagement."

The South Wind shifts in his chair. The toe of his boot nudges my ankle. I try my damndest not to examine that touch too closely. "I imagine you've already formulated a story for the court?" He sounds ... indifferent? Frustrated? Difficult to say.

"No." Crumpling the napkin in my fist, I reply, "But don't you worry. I'm sure I'll think of something."

"Sarai."

I startle, my surroundings coming into focus. I'm sitting across from Ibramin in the music room. At his back, the wide bay window frames the palace orchards, pink blossoms clinging to bare tree branches.

"Apologies." I offer him a wan smile. "I was momentarily distracted. What were you saying?"

He drums his fingers against the strings of his instrument. The bright, percussive sound suggests a rare impatience. Inwardly, I wince. My lesson began nearly an hour ago, yet instead of completing my counterpoint exercises—today's topic is melodic shaping—I've spent the majority of that time trying not to think of Notus, with various levels of success.

"The Ishmah Symphony is performing tonight," he says. "I have an extra ticket. Do you wish to accompany me?"

My initial shock gives way to something far more tender and bruised. I cannot remember when I last attended a concert, one where I was not performing myself. "Father expects my attendance for tonight's ball, unfortunately. Perhaps another time?" Before Ibramin can respond, the bell tower tolls the hour of three, signaling the end of our lesson. I'm up and heading for the door. "I'll see you next week, sir."

"I will not be here."

I pause with my fingers curled around the door handle. Slowly, I turn to face Ibramin. "Oh? Will you be visiting family?"

"No, Sarai." He sighs, glances down at his instrument. "I am leaving Ishmah."

The first tendrils of unease begin to slink through me. "But you're coming back, right?"

He lifts his eyes to mine. "I do not know."

My mouth opens, then snaps shut. I swallow, force my mouth open again. "When did you decide this?"

"Last month."

"And you did not think to tell me?"

"To be honest, I did not think you would care."

It stings, though I cannot blame him for the sentiment. Distance is my only shield. What might happen if I allowed it to fall? Betrayal, deception, disappointment, suffering. My grip tightens around the handle. I fight the urge to pry it free of the door. At the moment, it is all that holds me up. "It feels like you're giving up on me," I whisper.

"No, Sarai." The sound emerges warped. "I haven't given up on you. How could I? You are an exceptional violinist, one of the greatest the world has ever known. It has been an honor and a privilege to teach you." The lines mapping his face deepen, sadness pressed into his expression as a seal is pressed into wax. "I stayed these past years because I hoped you would find your way back to music. But every year I grow older. There are others I might teach and shape into accomplished musicians such as yourself."

I hear him plainly, but I fear how things will change. My legs itch to flee. I might haul open the door, dash down the hall until I reach my chamber, its shadowed interior. But I think of these past five years. Ibramin has met me for lessons every week despite me having failed to touch my violin. He deserves my patience, my understanding, my respect.

"Do you already have someone in mind?" I ask, releasing the handle and wandering back to my seat. I perch on the edge, hands fisted in my lap.

"There is a boy from Mirash whose teacher claims he has advanced beyond her capabilities. The boy's family requests that I take him under my instruction. He is four years old."

The age at which I myself began taking lessons.

It shouldn't matter. Ibramin is not bound to teach me forever, and it is not fair to demand that he stay. But it feels like a betrayal that he is choosing this boy, who has all the potential in the world, over me: a failure.

But I am nothing if not polite. I straighten in my seat, saying, "The boy would be beyond lucky to have you as a teacher."

The old man rubs the curved body of the violin: shoulders, waist, the swell of a woman's hips. "If you decided to pick up your instrument again," he says, "I would stay. I would do all that I could to help you return to your previous proficiency."

Even the thought threatens tears. "It's too painful," I whisper.

"I know." Wheeling his chair closer, he reaches out, rests his dry, papery hand atop my fist. Though he says nothing else, Ibramin understands. He loved my brother as a son.

Few knew of Fahim's gift. Ibramin built my brother's musical foundation as he had built mine, hours and days and weeks and months and years. At age fourteen, Fahim was invited to debut with the Ammaran Philharmonic. He told me it was the happiest day of his life.

A week later, Father bid that Fahim begin focusing seriously on his duties as heir. No more violin. The hours dedicated to practicing would now be spent learning about trade, policy, war. I remember the sound of Fahim's weeping through the shared wall of our bedrooms, that heartbreak of unrealized dreams.

And after? A measured slide into a darkness none knew. I do believe something died in my brother that day. No matter the ease of his smiles, no matter the frequency of his laughter, there would forever be an absence, a hole in his spirit.

"Father should not have made Fahim choose the crown over music," I whisper, suddenly overcome with anger on my brother's behalf. Could there not have been space for both love and duty, freedom and obligation?

Ibramin's eyes widen at the unexpected statement. But he says, "Music is grief, yet it is also healing and wonder and joy. Remember that. Remember the ways it has shaped you. Remember how it nurtures and heals."

I stare at the curve of his fingers on mine, their ends toughened by calluses. With a pained swallow, I push to my feet. "I appreciate your concern, sir, but I must be going. I wish you safe travels. Best of luck with your endeavors."

Melancholy veils his gaze as he responds, "May the Lord of the Mountain shine upon you, Sarai."

Back in my chambers, I set my violin case on the ground and flip the locks. The instrument is a masterpiece of curved red wood and ebony fixings—a gift from Father. My pinky catches the thin, tightly wound E string, gently plucks. Its high, tinny ring draws the fingers of my left hand into a subtle curl, as though they seek their home atop the fingerboard.

The piano's opening chords of Lisandro's Sonata for Violin return to me now. Drawing the violin onto my lap, my fingers begin to move. I shift into third position, then sixth, picking through a complex run of sixteenth notes. Eventually, I falter, unable to remember what comes next.

I kneel in place for a time, staring at my violin, before returning it to the case and closing the lid. What is the point of returning to music if my life will end?

Which reminds me. I approach my desk, where my journal lies open. Twenty-eight days remain. The sight sobers me, and I hurriedly shove the blasphemous evidence into the desk drawer.

With the ball to commence in a few hours' time, I begin to prepare. Father believes I will change my mind about Prince Balior, and so continues to uphold the image of celebration. I slide on my breezy, sky-colored gown as though it is armor. Silk slippers, threaded with the smallest opals. A pearled clip to secure my elaborate braid, and kohl to frame my eyes.

Reaching behind my vanity, I remove a small box, inside which rests a slender, arrow-shaped bracelet hammered from lead—the twin to the bracelet Notus wears. If we are betrothed, it is customary for the woman to wear a piece of jewelry gifted to her by her husband-to-be, as a symbol of their commitment to one another. It will also serve to reinforce my engagement to Notus in the eyes of Prince Balior.

Mouth pursed, I pluck the bracelet from the box and slide it onto my wrist as a knock sounds from the door. "Just a minute!"

I open the door to reveal a tall, slender man clothed in a robe so lavish, I am convinced the gods snipped the sunset sky into strips of pink, ginger, and violet and wove them into this exceptional garment. A full, well-groomed beard frames his jaw. It is dear to me, this face, yet I have not seen it in months.

"Amir." I'm forced to grab the doorframe before my knees give out from shock. "I thought you weren't arriving until next week!"

"Our mounts were fast." His teeth flash in a grin I have sorely missed. "I thought we might surprise Father."

"He will be pleased that you have returned early."

As we regard one another, I fight the urge to retreat and slam my door shut.

"Are you well?" He searches my gaze, suddenly uncertain.

"Of course." I am not aware of how tightly I'm gripping the door-frame until my nails dig into the soft wood. I force them to relax. "Why do you ask?"

"You do not appear enthused to see me, is all."

I lift a hand, rub at the twinge in my chest. He looks healthy, bright-eyed, kissed by salt and sun, heat and wind. He looks, I think, free.

"Of course I'm glad to see you," I whisper. Though paired with this truth is always a bitterness, that he may leave Ishmah and seek happiness beyond the palace grounds, while I am left behind, always behind, to wonder where another of my loved ones has gone, and why.

We embrace, my smaller frame tucked against him. Amir smells of mint and wood polish. His absence has stretched for three months, and much has changed in that time. "Tell me of your honeymoon," I urge. "Was it as amazing as you hoped it would be?"

"It was all that and more—so much more. We weren't ready to come home."

Pushing his way into my room, he takes stock of his surroundings. A warm breeze puffs against the window drapes and stirs the ends of his headscarf, which has unraveled from his face, the strip of fabric draping his shoulder. An opal rune tattoos his left hand. Tuleen, his wife, is inked with an identical marking.

"And how is Tuleen?" I am nothing if not polite. She is, after all, my sister-in-law. The future queen of Ammara. I try to see her as such, as opposed to the woman who stole my brother from me.

"She is well. Currently resting—it was a long journey. You will see her this evening." He turns to face me with an intensity I shy away from. "Are you sure you're all right, Sarai?"

Guilt claims space alongside my heart. What might I say? That I have but a handful of weeks to live? That I have bound myself to the immortal who broke my heart in order to save Ammara from a man who seeks to destroy it? That I am always grieving, always furious, always searching, always falling short? This would be so much easier if Father hadn't forbade me to mention the curse to anyone, including Amir, who remains uninformed of my early demise.

When I do not immediately respond, he moves toward the window, perhaps sensing my desire for space. "I ask because Father informed me of your betrothal," he explains.

I straighten in sudden alarm. "When?" Amir doesn't appear upset. I would have expected a barrage of spitting curses.

"Last month when he wrote me. Well, forthcoming betrothal, I should say. I am relieved to hear negotiations with Prince Balior have gone well. He is an excellent match for you."

My trepidation grows thorns. "That's all you heard?" I question. "Nothing else?"

He peers at me over his shoulder curiously. "What else should I have heard?"

I shake my head, waving the question away. If Amir doesn't know of my engagement to the South Wind, then I am not going to mention it. His opinion of Notus is far from favorable. In fact, he might despise him more than I do. Amir has never forgiven the South Wind for how he hurt me.

As my brother claims one of the armchairs near the window, I sit across from him.

Quietly, he asks, "How is Father?"

I am a terrible princess and an even worse daughter. What do I really know of my father, my own flesh and blood, but his iron capacity to rule? His health declines, yet I do not visit him.

"Stable since you departed, though he has been bedridden more often of late."

Amir grits his teeth. He and Tuleen returned early from their trip due to the king's flagging health. There are things Father must teach Amir before his passing. We have known this for some time, but I am not ready to face the knowledge that he will soon be gone. As will I.

"I ask because he mentioned the growing unrest throughout the realm in his letters," he says.

I hesitate. "There has been a significant increase in darkwalker sightings the past three months. He is right to be concerned." According to a few attendants I overheard in the halls, two men from the upper ring were reported missing. This is unusual. The wealthy are located farthest from the city gates, but apparently this man and his son had taken a trip to a nearby town. They failed to return.

"He claims this match between you and Prince Balior could bring an end to the darkwalkers."

I nod. "That is what he hopes for." And the cover story given to Amir. "But I believe we might be able to combat this issue ourselves, without the need for outside help."

"What are you implying? Prince Balior's strength would be a boon to us in eradicating these beasts. If any managed to enter the city, or the palace—"

"One already has."

He startles, eyes bulging, hands clamped around the arms of his chair. "What? When, and where?"

I wince, rub the sharp throb in my temples. "In the library a little over a week ago. I was completing some research after-hours when one appeared and chased me through the stacks."

Amir gapes. If I were not so uncomfortable with the topic of conversation, I daresay I would find his expression humorous. "You weren't hurt, were you?" He gives me a quick once-over. "How did you get away?" Every evident point, every curved bone in his face, fixes rigidly with disbelief. "I mean no offense, but you're not exactly the most, shall we say, athletic person."

"And you're not the most, shall we say, tactful person, brother dear." I offer him my sweetest smile. "I was lucky. It was dark, and they can't change direction quickly." And there was Notus, of course. I would be dead if not for him.

Amir demands, "Father knows about this?"

On the night of my attack, I had every intention of informing Father of the infiltration. But I was a woman with her back against the wall, her days dwindling. I feared Prince Balior's retaliation if he knew the reason for my sudden change of heart. So I said nothing. Not that it mattered. King Halim learned from the men guarding the library what had occurred. Regardless, Notus returned to the library later that night to search for additional darkwalkers, after disposing of the body. He found nothing, though the head archivist nearly lost his mind when he saw the extent of the destruction.

"He is well aware, Amir."

My brother nods. "Good. Though I will likely demand another search of the palace grounds. We can't have those beasts threatening your intended, now can we?"

Now, I think. Now is the time to mention my suspicions, qualms.

"To tell you the truth," I begin slowly, "I have concerns about the prince."

Amir tugs on his beard, eyes narrowing in question. "Prince Balior is a good man. Honorable, accomplished, well-respected. Whatever gossip you have heard amongst the court, I suggest you distance yourself from it. That sort of talk will rot your brain."

My brother means well, and I do love him. But Fahim was the only person with whom I felt safe enough to share my vulnerabilities. He knew how the palace stifled me, my longing for adventure. Yet I failed to recognize his struggles until it was too late.

But I do what I have always done. I draw my mouth into a curve. I crease my eyes with joy, mirth. Whatever strain I experience, I bury it. "You're right," I grant. "Gossip is not becoming of me."

13

A BEAD OF SWEAT SLITHERS DOWN MY SPINE, SLIPPING ALONG THE notched bones. This was a mistake. Who wears a long-sleeved dress in the middle of summer? I do, apparently. I fear I will melt before the stars materialize.

The ballroom doors lie open to the eastern gardens. Drooping branches and trimmed hedges offer shady reprieve beneath their foliage. Guests wander the garden paths, drinks in hand. I cannot count their number. Visiting dignitaries from neighboring realms, governors from far-flung cities along the Spice Road, aristocrats whose coin purses run deep.

Amir and I loiter near a pillar at the perimeter of the ballroom. Across the vast chamber, Father overlooks the festivities from his throne atop the dais. As afternoon cools to night, he begins to sag into the opulence of his seat.

The palace physician checks on him every so often. He offers the king a draught that is continually refused. I bite my lower lip in worry. Father should not be here in this condition. He is better off resting in his chambers.

Amir seems not to notice. He downs his drink—the second of the evening—with an air of utter woe. Meanwhile, I scan the area for a set of broad shoulders. I've yet to spot Notus. I do, however, spy Dalia accompanied by her small entourage. The smirk curling her luscious mouth twists my gut in apprehension.

"To think my days will be spent rubbing elbows with people I despise," Amir moans. "No wonder Fahim avoided these events."

I glance sidelong at my brother, Dalia momentarily forgotten. He is right and he is wrong. Fahim was always the most animated of King Halim's children. But after Father forced him to abandon the violin, he withdrew. His studies grew more demanding. He often skipped meals. In the year leading up to his death, I no longer expected his presence at dinner. I can imagine how unbalanced his life became, forever crushed beneath our father's impossible expectations.

Angling toward my brother, I ask, "Are you ready?" No further clarification necessary. From the crimp of Amir's mouth, he knows of what I speak.

"It doesn't matter whether I'm ready or not," he says. "I don't have a choice, do I?" As soon as the words escape his mouth, he frowns, his features tinged with a familiar bleakness. "I suppose Fahim hadn't a choice in becoming king either."

I recall such a look in Fahim's eyes—an overwhelm of responsibilities. That in turn sparks panic, for I do not wish Amir to befall the same fate.

"Amir." I grip his arm hard. He glances at me, startled. "If ever there is a time when you feel lost or like you aren't sure who to turn to, please come to me."

For a long while, we stare at one other, caught in the pain of memory. "I will," he promises.

As I turn to face the gathering, a slender woman escorted by an elderly man—her father, I assume—greets my brother with a kiss on his cheek. "Hello, darling," she says.

Amir smiles, gathering Tuleen into his arms. She tucks herself against his side joyfully. I try not to stare. Is it envy I feel? Awareness of my own loss, a happiness I had once lived before all burned away?

"Our Lord of the Mountain shines upon you, Sarai." Tuleen's voice reminds me of the desert winds: low and airy.

I brush a kiss to my sister-in-law's cheek. Her scent, perfumed with night jasmine, clings to my nostrils as I retreat. "And you, Tuleen."

She glances at my brother, but Amir's attention has been captured by a group of advisors at the far end of the room. They call him over, and he excuses himself, winding through the mingling, the drinking, the swaying.

Tuleen fiddles with one of the buttons on her elaborate green gown. It is a shade lighter than her mossy eyes. "Congratulations. I hear you are soon to be betrothed to Prince Balior." She gestures toward me, then drops her hand, as though self-conscious of the gesture.

"Thank you." I sip my drink, continuing to scan the room. Of course Tuleen would think that. As promised, Notus and I have given no indication of our engagement. King Halim clings to the hope that I will see my error before the court realizes circumstances have changed.

"We will have to celebrate," she says.

I make a noncommittal sound. If she wishes to celebrate my engagement to a man who is no longer my betrothed, that is her own prerogative, but I, unfortunately, will not be in attendance.

Tuleen opens her mouth, hesitates, then promptly closes it. Inwardly, I sigh in relief. There can be no greater waste of air than trivial small-talk.

Why Tuleen chooses to remain in my company when there are plenty of noblewomen eager to converse, I have no idea. Like me, she grew up at court, having been born into an old, aristocratic family. And that is precisely why I keep her at arm's length. These noblewomen are hungry for weakness. The slightest crumb will soon be devoured.

"You look lovely this evening," Tuleen suddenly says, with a desperation that sets my teeth on edge. "Where did you get your dress?"

I tap my fingertips against the glass, considering how much trouble I would be in if I removed myself from this conversation. My relationship with Amir has suffered enough strain the past few years to risk it.

"This was commissioned by Roshar Hammad. He is the best tailor in the realm." If only he were here! Roshar delights in these functions—scandal is what he loves best.

"His work is exquisite," she says, eyeing my gown. "I love the detailing near the bodice. Are those music notes?"

I glance down. The pads of Tuleen's brown fingers trace what is undoubtedly a collection of eighth notes. I've worn this dress on three separate occasions, yet this is the first time I have noticed this embellishment.

"Quite fitting for a musician," she says, and drops her hand.

I set my glass onto a nearby windowsill, feeling suddenly overwhelmed by fondness for my friend, that he would stitch musical notation into my gown, allowing me to carry music without my knowledge.

"And you look very …" I peer at my sister-in-law, grasping for possible compliments. "Healthy."

Her expression falls. Unsurprising, as it is a word used to describe livestock, not a pretty woman draped in silk. "Thank you," she responds. "That is kind of you." She then glances toward the ballroom doors. "Your intended is quite handsome."

My head snaps around. But—no. Prince Balior has entered the room, resplendent in white silk. His eyes hook into me with predatory intent. I regard him calmly until he moves off. That is fine. It is not his face I have fallen asleep thinking about these past few nights.

"He is," I agree curtly. And yet, my attention continues its wandering. Dalia has slithered closer as the evening has progressed, and now I begin to notice a few guests glancing at me in distaste. I look down, thinking perhaps I've spilled something on my dress. Not a speck.

"What is his personality like?"

Why are we discussing Prince Balior? We should be discussing why the other guests appear to find offense in me. When I catch the eye of a particularly distinguished noblewoman, her expression contorts in repulsion. "He deserves better than you," she all but spits, then whirls and vanishes into the throng.

I stare at the crowd, utterly baffled.

"What was that about?" Tuleen whispers in concern.

"I don't know. I—" A man in lavender robes snags my attention as he crosses the room—the royal physician. "Excuse me, Tuleen." I hurry forward to intercept him, slippers sliding across the marble in my haste to catch up. "Sir!"

He startles, glasses sliding down his nose as he turns. "Princess Sarai." The physician adjusts his robes self-consciously before casting his eyes briefly around the room. He is perhaps a decade younger than the king, ash gray hair combed to the side to hide his bald spot. "Is there something you need?"

A dancing couple jostles me from behind. "What is that tonic you were trying to give Father?"

"I'm not sure what you mean."

I level him a pointed look. "Sir."

He sighs. Bruises press the puffy skin beneath his eyes. I have heard he rarely sleeps more than a handful of hours, due to the involvement of Father's care. "It's nothing to be alarmed about. Just a remedy to help him put on weight."

When a particularly nosy attendee hovers nearby, I glare at him until he scurries elsewhere. This is probably not the best place to discuss Father's health. Quickly, I draw the physician into a shadowy nook for privacy. "So why won't he drink it?"

"He says it tastes vile."

I bite back a grin. That certainly sounds like King Halim. "Well, does it?"

"Of course it does!" The physician rubs his temples in exasperation. "There is little I can do about that. Some days, he will accept it. Most days, he won't. As long as he refuses to drink it, he will continue to lose weight."

"I see." Vile taste or not, King Halim would not want to appear feeble in front of his guests. No king would. It is the only argument in my arsenal. "What if *I* gave it to him?"

"At the very least, it's worth the attempt."

He discreetly passes me a small glass of green liquid. We part ways, and I visit the king at his seat. I bow as a sign of respect. "Father."

"Sarai." He glances over my shoulder with blatant disapproval. "Where is your betrothed?"

"Notus will be here." He promised. Yet I wonder how deep my foolishness runs, to trust the word of a god whose promises have become lies.

The king does not appear amused. "I was referring to Prince Balior."

I whittle my mouth into something resembling a smile. Of course he was.

"Firstly," I say quietly, mindful of the eyes and ears turned our way, "Prince Balior was never my betrothed, considering I had already promised myself to another. Secondly, I know you disapprove of my relationship with Notus, but please believe I am only doing what is best for Ammara."

"Best?" he hisses. "How can this be best? The South Wind is powerful, certainly, but he does not possess the information we need."

"As I said before, I am happy to discuss it with you—in private."

King Halim stares at me with all the indifference one would expect toward a particularly lazy hound, not his daughter. "It seems to me you have already made your decision. As far as I can tell, it would only be a waste of time."

It is not easy masking the hurt that rises, edged and bristling with points. "Is that how you view me? A waste of time?"

"You are putting words into my mouth."

"I'm only stating what you yourself have already established."

Father shakes his head in frustration. We have always bumped shields, he and I. "Don't you care for your life?" he whispers.

"Of course I do."

"Then why this farce with the South Wind?"

It softens me momentarily, to hear the pain in his voice. If the curse weighs on me, then it certainly weighs on him. I have often wondered if he blames himself for Ammara's precarious position, my impending death.

"I don't expect you to understand my choices," I say, "but I wish you would trust me enough to let me live a life that is meaningful, in whatever time I have left."

King Halim looks elsewhere. He is confused, torn in some way. Perhaps brokenhearted. But I cannot take responsibility for emotions that do not belong to me.

Tugging aside the fabric of my dress, I offer the glass of medicine. Father blinks in surprise.

"I know things have been hard lately," I say, "but the physician told me it's important for you to drink this. Will you do so, for me?"

His eyebrows slash low over his eyes. "Sarai—"

"Please."

And now I let those shields fall. I allow Father to see how I worry for him, how I lose sleep over nightmares in which I learn that he has passed without having said goodbye. King Halim is a hard man, but he is still my father, and he was willing to give up this kingdom for my life. That is something I will never be able to repay.

I'd like to believe my vulnerability placates him, since he gestures for me to come forward and downs the remedy without argument. When I whisper "Thank you," he drops his eyes.

"I'll come check on you shortly," I promise. Then I cross to the other side of the room, taking my place at Tuleen's side. The dull hum of conversation expands to a roar in my head. She glances at me in concern.

I sense the South Wind before I see him. A hot breeze invades the space, smelling of the desert at high noon. There, near the arched doors emptying into the garden—citrine robe, black trousers, ivory headscarf.

It feels like an inevitability, that his gaze should find mine from across the room. Notus strides toward me, and my heart flutters. I'm not ready for this. I need more time. There must be no indication that we are more than passing acquaintances.

Turning my back on him, I begin to engage Tuleen in inane conversation.

"Princess Sarai."

Notus' gruff voice lifts the hair on the back of my neck. He is close, the entire length of my spine warmed by his body. I continue conversing with Tuleen, ignoring him completely. Eventually, he moves off, though I find it difficult to focus on anything beyond his lingering scent.

"Who was that man?" Tuleen asks.

This answer requires a drink in hand. I pluck my abandoned wineglass from the windowsill and swallow deeply. The burn is as uncomfortable as it is necessary.

"The South Wind," I clip out. "He works for Father in safeguarding Ammara from the darkwalkers." I sigh, lean against the pillar at my back. Tonight's attendees mill about drowsily, like flies around a corpse.

She hesitates. "He appeared upset that you ignored him."

Well, he's going to have to deal with it.

After polishing off my wine, I signal to one of the servers for another drink. The full glass bolsters me with false confidence. Only then do I allow myself to search for Notus in the crowd. Too easily, I spot him. But he is not alone.

She is lovely. That is the first of my observations. A gown of liquid silver fans about her waist while a trio of ruby pins adorns her elaborately braided hair. They converse in what I imagine to be low tones, their heads bent, Notus angled toward her.

A hot wad of emotion fills my throat as his mouth curves in response to something she says. Not quite a smile, but close enough. It is so rare a sight I find it difficult to look elsewhere.

I have questions. Namely, who is this woman? How is she able to thaw his rigid features into something resembling affection? Why am I unable to do the same? I am his betrothed. Granted, it has yet to be officially announced, but that is beside the point. That he engages with another woman—unmarried, for her left hand lacks the opal rune— is a mark of humiliation and disrespect.

"Sarai?" The voice comes from behind. Oily and rich.

I do *not* need this right now. But I arrange my features as I turn, my expression blossoming like a flower bathed in sun. "Good evening, Prince Balior."

From the corner of my eye, I observe Tuleen glancing between us in curiosity. The prince carries a half-consumed glass of wine. "Can I steal you away for a moment?" His voice is low, beseeching. "There's something I wish to discuss."

Funny, how he is suddenly accommodating, now that his back is against the wall. "I don't want this to be more difficult than it has to be, Prince Balior. I've made my decision. Again, I sincerely apologize for how poorly I've treated you. It was unfair, and you did not deserve—"

"Is it about my research?" Carefully, he probes my gaze. "I know I haven't been forthcoming with you regarding my interest in the labyrinth," he says, "but I hope you know it was not my intention to withhold information from you. I've found myself in another king's realm, among people who are not my own, and I do not always know who to trust. Can you understand my concerns?"

"I can," I reply, and I'm startled to realize I am sincere. "But it's not that."

"Then what is it? I don't understand how someone can go from completely loathing a person, as you claimed to loathe the South Wind, to being in love with him, and engaged."

Tuleen sucks in a sharp breath.

Shit.

Prince Balior stares at me expectantly. "Well?"

I don't think anyone heard him but Tuleen, though I remain convinced that the guests regard me with cold judgment, gossiping with one another about something when my back is turned. The evening is not unfolding as planned, and I wish only for darkness and solitude.

"If you had been upfront about your interest in the labyrinth beforehand," I say to the prince, voice lowered, "maybe I would have seen things differently."

"But I *do* wish to share all that I know." He steps closer. Tuleen stiffens beside me. "Given enough time, I believe your trust in me will be rebuilt. I ask you for another chance to prove that my intentions are noble. I wish to bind my life to yours, and I hope you wish the same."

"Prince Balior—"

"Your father only wants what is best for you. He loves you dearly. The praise he sings of you behind closed doors? I only wish you could hear it."

A flutter of uncertainty alights behind my sternum. How can this be true if I have never witnessed it?

"Will you reconsider?" he presses, insistent now.

I don't know what to believe, but I say, "I will think about it." At the very least, it will get him to leave me in peace.

"Then we will speak again soon."

Before I'm able to respond, he moves off, drawing yet another unsuspecting individual into conversation.

Dread bleeds along my nerve endings. What is truth, what is lies? Was I unfair in prematurely judging Prince Balior's character? A loveless marriage is not exactly a death sentence. I believe I could grow to respect the prince, assuming I had time.

Unfortunately, Dalia appears, likely having been summoned by malevolent forces. She watches the prince depart with a salacious curl to her mouth. "You certainly know how to keep things interesting around here."

I do not have time for this. "What have you heard?"

"Something about a betrothal." Her eyes cut to the South Wind. "Only, not to the man your father arranged for you to marry."

My pulse rises, beating a staccato against my neck. There is a time and a place to reveal my engagement to Notus. This is not it.

I step forward. "Dalia—"

Tuleen reaches the woman first. Though she is of slighter build, the chill in her gaze is enough to cow even the strongest of war-hardened men. "What interest do you have with Princess Sarai? Because as far as I can see, your only purpose this evening is to spread gossip at court."

Dalia takes a step back from the future queen of Ammara, suddenly watchful. It seems her entourage has abandoned her.

"I believe it's time for you to leave," Tuleen clips out. She looks past Dalia, lifts a hand, and curls two fingers in a come hither gesture. Three guards approach. "Please escort Lady Yassin from the ballroom."

A hush descends. As one, the attendees crane their heads toward the commotion. All those eyes, all that judgment choking the air. Even King Halim observes from his perch.

Dalia appears to have swallowed a mouthful of sand. "Excuse me?"
Tuleen keeps her eyes trained on the buxom beauty. "You are a noblewoman. Gossip is below you. See to it that you keep the idle chatter to yourself." With that, Dalia is escorted from the premises.

Conversation explodes in the wake of the woman's departure. By the end of the night, everyone will know how Lady Dalia Yassin was dismissed by Ammara's future queen. But none will know that was due to my inability to defend myself. It is humiliating not to be able to stand on my own two feet.

"Princess Sarai?"

I grind my teeth, not in any mood to feign civility, and turn toward my brother's wife. How I wish she hadn't witnessed the ease with which Dalia caught me beneath her thumb. I should be stronger than that. I *am* stronger than that. "Yes, Tuleen?"

Gone is the tender queen-to-be, those green-flecked eyes like churned water. In her place stands a woman inflamed, jaw locked, mouth thin. "You do not like me very much, do you?"

All day, I must flatter and socialize, smile and preen. It is utterly exhausting, wearing my own skin. "It's not that I don't like you. It's that I don't trust you."

She regards me calmly. "Why not?"

"Because you are a woman of the court, bred to scheme, and as such, you and I will never understand each other."

"You sound certain of this."

"I am."

"Yet I just defended you from that horrible creature."

My reply disintegrates before it has the opportunity to form, and I shift uncomfortably in place. She is right. Then again, what is one favor? Who is to say she will not use this as leverage in the future?

"You are entitled to your opinion," she says, softly but not weakly, "but I do hope to prove you wrong, in time."

Before I can respond, Amir returns, pulling Tuleen against his side, a drink in one hand, the other curved around his wife's hip. Tuleen attempts to smile, but her unhappiness is plain. Guilt pricks at me.

Suddenly, Amir straightens. "What the hell is *he* doing here?"

My stomach plummets.

The king-to-be has locked on to Notus across the room. I stare as well. The woman draped in silver, plastered to his side still, always within reach. An onslaught of fury boils under my skin. Did he touch her, or did I only imagine it? No, I'm certain I saw his hand brush her lower back.

"Father has employed the South Wind's services," I explain. They are barbed, these words. I practically spit them out. "He arrived three weeks ago."

Amir looks as though he would enjoy nothing more than to set Notus on fire. "Since when does Father welcome traitors back into our realm?"

My sentiment exactly. Although without Notus, I would likely be dead, torn apart by the darkwalker in the library. He is here to protect Ammara. That, too, is important.

"You understand the pressure Father is under. The drought persists. Trade is in decline. Darkwalkers continue to multiply for reasons unknown. Notus' power is a boon to Ammara during this time."

"What does it matter that the South Wind has power if he flees at the first sign of trouble? There are others able to protect us. Others that are more trustworthy."

He is right and he is wrong. There are others, but none possess the South Wind's might.

"If Notus doesn't stop staring at you," Amir growls, "I will pluck out his eyes and feed them to the crows."

"Please don't," I say. "You've been drinking." As have I.

Tossing back the rest of his wine, he places the empty glass onto a table. A lethal gleam coats his eyes like a fine polish.

"Amir," I warn.

As my brother takes off across the room, I lunge for his arm. "Wait." He shakes me loose. I spin like a leaf in the wind.

"Amir!" I speed after him, nearly colliding with a group of governors in my haste to reach him. Notus' female companion, I'm pleased to note, has fled. Good riddance.

The South Wind greets my brother with a low bow. "Amir."

The king-to-be's expression hardens. "That's Prince Amir to you."

"My apologies, Prince Amir."

My brother bares his teeth. Tuleen tries to get his attention, but she may as well attempt to corral a wall of stone. Amir's will is unbending. We are alike in that way.

"You have a lot of nerve, returning to Ishmah," he spits. "Father may have his own ideas about what this realm needs, but the moment I take up the crown, I will banish you to the Wastes."

At this point, the majority of the guests have gathered to witness the affair, forming a half-circle around us. Notus does not fall prey to Amir's antagonism. Instead, his glittering black eyes slide to mine, and they hold a question. *What does he know?* I fear to answer.

Stepping between the two men, I push a hand against my brother's chest. "Amir, stop. As I said, Father requested Notus' return. You cannot fault him for answering the king's summons."

"I can, and I will."

Five fingers gently wrap my upper arm. Notus' hand is so broad he's able to encircle the limb easily. "Will you explain," he murmurs against my ear, eliciting a shiver from me, "or should I?"

"Take your hands off my sister," Amir snarls.

When Notus refuses to remove his hand, my brother lunges, but doesn't expect the South Wind to sidestep so quickly. A night sipping on wine has dulled his reflexes. He slams face-first into a nearby table. It tips, sending a group of spectators into a messy sprawl. Plates and cutlery topple onto the floor. Glass shatters.

King Halim watches the spectacle with mounting horror. Meanwhile, Prince Balior observes with arms crossed, mouth a pitying slash. The princess, the king-to-be, and the South Wind in a tangle? Such gossip will live on for years.

"We're leaving." My voice cuts low as I turn toward my sister-in-law. "Tuleen, please ensure Amir reaches his rooms safely." I gesture to a nearby guard for aid.

As Amir struggles to his feet, face curdled red beneath his beard, he draws his blade. And I am already in motion, stepping between the sword and Notus' heart.

14

THE SOUTH WIND'S ARM BANDS ACROSS MY CHEST, YANKING ME against his body as a wall of wind encases me so completely that when I reach out, it feels as if my palm presses against hard stone. A tremor runs through Notus' frame. His breathing possesses a ragged edge.

Only now do I realize what I have done: inserted myself between a weapon and its intended target. It shouldn't matter. Notus cannot die by a mortal-made weapon. Yet I moved without thought.

"Release my sister," Amir hisses. The tip of his sword scrapes the surface of the air-hardened wall.

"Your sister," Notus says gruffly, "or my wife-to-be?"

It is so silent I hear the click of my swallow. Then: whispers. They stir the air into a frenzy, until no area of the ballroom is left undisturbed by the rush and roar of this oncoming wave. *Did I hear that correctly? Princess Sarai and the South Wind? Engaged? What of Prince Balior? It cannot be true.*

Amir belts out a laugh. It is a loud, garish racket, made sloppy by the amount of wine he has consumed this evening. Tuleen shrinks in mortification.

"First," Amir sneers, gaze locked on the South Wind over my shoulder, "you deny a direct order from the heir to the throne. Now, you spout a claim that is so implausible it is borderline comical. Release my sister, before you embarrass yourself further."

"I will release her," Notus states with equal scorn, "when you lower your sword."

A few gasps ring throughout the ballroom.

The South Wind and I stand on one side of the barrier; Amir and Tuleen stand on the other, the attendees crowding at their backs. They are moths, drawn by the bright of candleflame. As such, no one notices the palace physician escorting King Halim from the ballroom. No one but me.

"Remember who it is you address," Amir snarls. "Release my sister, or I will have your head."

"You will not," I snap.

Amir's eyes flick to me in confusion. In this moment, he looks so much like Fahim that it hurts my heart. "Then we will duel, and whoever is left standing will be granted the honor of taking the other's life."

Notus unsheathes his scimitar. The curved weapon glints brilliantly, its edge nicked by many a battle. I have observed Notus whet and polish his blade time and again, with painstaking care. No one can best the South Wind in a duel. He is graced with powers far beyond those of any mortal. Should they lock blades, I am certain it will end with my brother drenched in a pool of his own blood.

"Put that away," I growl to Amir.

"He dishonors you in spewing these falsehoods." His sword does not waver. "I will not have it."

I glance around the room. So many eyes, so eager for blood. But one person in particular is absent: Prince Balior. "Notus does not lie," I admit quietly, hoping to diffuse the situation. "We are engaged."

Shock ripples through the crowd. Amir is like the sculptures lining the Temple District, those holiest of deities forever entombed in arid rock. "You think me a fool?" His lips have thinned to the point of being nonexistent. "I will not have it—"

"It is no deception," I snap as the tether to my patience begins to fray. My brother, the most stubborn of King Halim's children.

"Father gave you his blessing?"

"Not in those exact words, but he has always admired and respected Notus. It is a good match."

The information leaches through the gathering, first as ripples, then massive swells as guests begin to question the legitimacy of the announcement. *King Halim? His blessing?* Let them talk. None would dare question the king.

Eventually, my brother lowers his sword a fraction. "I don't understand." Much of his earlier scorn has depleted, too overwhelmed by confusion to endure. "You know the ways in which this god has wronged you."

I know. Roshar was not the only one who helped me gather the shattered pieces of myself after Notus vanished without a trace. Amir did as well. But I fear a greater threat to Ammara than a broken heart. The South Wind might be all that stands between this kingdom and utter ruination.

"Amir," I say pleadingly. "Put your sword away. Please."

I may as well have demanded he strip naked, so insulted does he appear. "Only if the South Wind sheathes his own weapon."

Notus' left arm is still banded around my waist. His right arm is held out, sword aloft. I touch the underside of his wrist in silent inquiry.

At once, the South Wind sheathes his sword. Amir follows, and only then does the wall of air dissipate. The room swells with a collective exhalation, numerous attendees fanning themselves, having found the display to be both exhilarating and alarming. It will, to be certain, be the most entertaining social event of the season.

Amir catches Notus' eye. "We're not finished, you and I."

The South Wind says nothing, only watches my brother storm from the room, Tuleen at his heels.

As the crowd begins to disperse, I jostle my way toward the refreshment table, snatching a cup of water and downing its contents in one swallow. Its bracing coolness washes the dryness from my throat. The display has shaken me more than I care to admit. What is a woman to do with her back against the wall?

I expect Notus to have followed me, but I spot him halfway across the ballroom, striding with purpose toward the corridor. The sight of his retreating form seizes my heart.

I'm moving before I'm aware of it, my cup abandoned, shoving aside guests left and right. I catch his arm before he reaches the hall. "Where are you going?" *To meet your mystery woman?* He was certainly moving with enough haste.

He glances down at me in impatience. "To the library. There's something I want to check."

At this time of night, the library is closed. Empty. An ideal location to meet an unmarried woman without danger of tainting her reputation.

My fingers fist the front of his sunset-colored robe. "We have things to discuss."

"Whatever it is, it will have to wait."

"It can't wait."

His eyes kindle in warning. "Sarai."

"Notus."

It is then his attention drops, locking on to my bracelet. His gaze darkens. The sight billows through me with breathless heat.

"It's a symbol," I explain, in anticipation of his question. "To represent our engagement." I'm pleased by my unaffected tone. Even I find it believable. "You did gift it to me, after all."

"I did," he replies slowly. "I didn't realize you still had it in your possession."

I'm suddenly aware of our proximity, the press of his hard thighs against mine, how the warm air feathers against my skin, ebbing and flowing in time with his breath. I have been here before. The most deliriously joyful time of my life. It does not bode well that already I struggle to keep my distance.

"As much as I'd like to discuss your choice of jewelry," he says, "there's something I need to do. It can't be delayed."

After a moment, I release him. Of course, he is going to meet this mystery woman. I am imagining his hands on her hips, her fingers in his hair, their mouths soft and open, mated fully. I crush a hand to my chest, above my thundering heart. "What is so important at a time like this?" My traitorous voice wavers. "I am your betrothed."

The South Wind studies me with too much knowing. For once, it does not feel so terrible to lower my guard. I trust him, though I fear it may be to my own detriment.

Tugging me into a dimly lit recess, Notus drops his voice, broad frame blocking the guests milling about from my view. "Did you notice that Prince Balior disappeared during the ball?"

I nod. "You think he went to the library?"

"Either the library or the labyrinth."

I'm so relieved that I barely flinch when he demands, "What did the prince say to you earlier?"

"Nothing of importance. Just that he hopes we'll be able to discuss this whole misunderstanding." I hesitate, unsure if I should go on, but then I say, "He believes we are an excellent match and that our realms are stronger together than apart. He wants to discuss how we might move forward."

The South Wind bristles. The sight pleases me. At least I'm not the only one affected by the sight of him seeking companionship in another. "And what did you say?"

"That I would think about it."

"And are you?" In the amber glow, flecks of color fracture the dark wells of his eyes. "Thinking about it, that is."

I frown and glance away. Does he ask only for the sake of Ammara, or something more? "I haven't decided."

Notus does not appear particularly satisfied by my answer. "The writing's on the wall, Sarai. Prince Balior has ulterior motives."

"I know."

"Do you? Because the Sarai I knew would never have considered making a deal with the enemy."

His words sting, which must mean they hold some truth. My life was different then. With Notus, I'd felt free. I'd revealed to him a woman hidden deep who yearned only for acceptance. When he was gone, I wondered if he'd even loved that person—the bright fire of the woman I'd been.

"The Sarai you knew is no more," I bite out. "Today is all we have. Do you understand?" The South Wind hasn't the slightest notion of how the curse burdens me. He does not know the dread of each arriving day. He is eternal.

Eventually, he sighs. "I understand." But it is clear he does not agree with me. "If you want to check the library, we shouldn't delay."

We make haste departing the ballroom. Four guards stand sentry at the library. They claim not to have seen Prince Balior, but I can't be sure that he hasn't bribed them. Inside the expansive atrium, all is quiet. An air of abandonment shades the area, with its vacated armchairs and extinguished fireplace. No scent of burning. No indication of any dark-walkers near.

After lighting a lamp at the front counter, I shuffle behind Notus through the back stacks, a palm pressed to his lower spine. The heat of his skin through his robes is the only warmth in this lightless place.

"This way," I whisper.

Down, down the gloomy hall where the air grows icy, my breath pluming as clouds before us. The special collections are still in disarray, books and documents stacked haphazardly along the walls. I direct him to the last doorway at the end of the hall, our single lamp wavering.

The room is empty. Everything has been straightened, the desk rightened. The shelves have been cleared, leaving bare walls behind. Not a book or scroll in sight.

"You didn't happen to clear this room," I ask Notus in unease, "did you?"

"No. I searched it but found nothing."

"No documents?"

"None."

That's what I suspected. If Notus didn't clear the room, who did? Prince Balior? The head archivist? I could demand a search of the prince's room, but what if I'm wrong?

"I suppose," Notus says, "I can do some research of my own, reach out to some old contacts to see if anyone has books or information regarding the labyrinth."

I nod in agreement. "I'll keep looking through the book I grabbed to see if anything else stands out to me." The more we know about the labyrinth, the greater the likelihood we stumble across material regarding my curse.

With no signs of disturbance, we return to the corridors empty-handed. My mood darkens the farther we travel through the palace. I have questions for Notus concerning tonight's ball, but this is not the place for private conversation. These halls echo.

A nearby door catches my eye. That will do. "In here." Dragging open the door, I shove him inside.

Darkness surrounds us, though a strip of light shines beneath the crack at the bottom of the shut door. Stacks of bedsheets, tablecloths, and towels stuff the shelves lining the cramped space.

"A linen closet?" Notus drawls. "Really?"

I lift my chin. "You have a better idea?"

His scoff wafts across my upturned face. The spice of his breath is so familiar it makes my teeth ache. We stand too close—the toes of his boots brush my slippers. Notus is a shadow before me, a ghost of my past, yet he is warm enough to rival the sun.

Once again, I understand the mistake I have made. This deity's presence clouds my thoughts and rips clarity from my grasp. There can be no worse place to have a conversation between former lovers than a closet, where his every breath becomes mine.

"What is this about, Sarai?"

That ugly, grinding sensation in my chest returns, shaving itself down to a vicious point. I think of Notus' promise, now broken. I think of that woman in the silver gown. I think of how lonely I am, how lonely I have always been, despite having been surrounded by people my entire life.

"Do you recall our conversation at the beginning of the week?" I say.

The South Wind regards me warily. "I'm not following."

He will make me spell it out for him. Very well. "About agreeing to the fake engagement. About being a little more *convincing*?"

His silence is telling. I sense rather than spot the pulse in his jaw. "I apologize for revealing our engagement. I understand why you would be angry about that. I should have discussed it with you beforehand."

"I'm not angry because you told the entire court about it," I hiss. The truth would have revealed itself eventually, with or without his aid. "I'm angry because you ignored me for the entire evening."

"I didn't ignore you," Notus counters, voice heating to match mine. "You were the one who ignored me."

A slow throb consumes me, a bright shimmer in my blood. Wounded Sarai is an entirely different beast. "Oh, really?"

"You were speaking with Tuleen," he growls. "When I attempted to approach you, you pretended I didn't exist."

My mouth clamps shut in surprise. He is right. I had forgotten how I'd ignored him in front of my sister-in-law. And yet— "Why didn't you approach me a second time?"

"Sarai." He shakes his head, the gesture of a man at his wit's end. "Do you hear yourself? If you sent me away, I would assume, as any sane person would, that you do not wish to be near me. Anyway, Amir was present. He hates me. You know this. I was trying to prevent a scene, which obviously didn't work. I was doing what I believed to be in your best interest."

Something claws at me with terrifying desperation. It wants to be seen, known, heard, soothed. Though I stand before Notus, it feels as if I stand before Father. I attempt to reach him, yet always, he brushes me aside. I do not feel understood. I feel burdensome.

"That's not what I wish," I croak.

"Then what do you wish?"

My twisted mind has the gall to misinterpret his inflection, the lowering of his voice to something decidedly more intimate. "I wish you would have come back to me." So that we might face this new world united instead of as separate parts. "Instead, I spent the entire evening watching you woo another woman despite the plan we'd made."

"What?" He's stunned. "Who?"

"Black hair, silver gown, huge chest. You don't remember?" How convenient. "You touched her back. I *watched* you touch her." My lips peel back as though I am a snarling dog. "Who is she?"

Again, this damned, dreadful silence. I fear his response, yet I'm no coward.

"I don't know who she was," he says.

"Lies."

Notus glances at the ceiling while muttering what I believe is a prayer. "You are quick to make assumptions, Sarai. Yes, it appeared that I touched this woman's back." He looks at me then. "Did you ask yourself why?"

What a foolish question. "Because you're attracted to her, obviously!"

"By the gods," he mutters. His hand slips to his beltloop and emerges clutching something long and tapered: a dagger.

I stare at the weapon. "I don't understand."

"I don't know who that woman was. I've never seen her before." He searches my gaze. Perhaps he wishes as desperately to understand me as I do him. "But I saw the shape of the blade beneath her dress. When I searched her, this is what she carried."

Prior to entering the palace, all guests save those who serve the royal family are required to remove all weapons. Additionally, each person is thoroughly searched. How did this woman manage to slip past?

"I was concerned she would use it against the king." After sliding the weapon into its sheath, he returns it to his beltloop.

"Where is the woman now?" I ask.

"Locked up for questioning."

I see.

Notus must recognize my skepticism, for he adds, "My duty is to the crown. You know this."

My chin lifts. Anger, that vibrant green shoot, leading always to fear rotting its roots. "And what of your duty to me? I am your betrothed."

He shifts his weight back onto his heels. I'm tempted to ease forward and close that bit of distance. "The engagement is a farce."

"Not to everyone else."

"Why do you care what others think of you?" he demands, tossing up a hand in exasperation. It accidentally hits one of the shelves, sending linens tumbling to the ground. "Why is their perception of you more important than your perception of yourself?"

I flinch back. "It's not."

"Isn't it?"

My lungs squeeze as I attempt to draw in air. I do not feel in control of my own emotions. On the contrary, I feel powerless against them. "Don't pretend that you know anything about what I feel," I say through clenched teeth. "We aren't talking about my emotions. We're discussing your failure to keep your promise to me."

"My failure?" He scoffs. "Again, you sent me away, Sarai. That's your own fault. Though now I question why you did it. Are you embarrassed to be seen in my company? Ashamed of me in some way?"

"Of course not." Nothing could be further from the truth.

"Then why is this an issue?" he demands.

"Because I needed you!" I cry. "I needed you and you weren't there!"

Notus goes still.

My gasps ricochet in the enclosed space. I don't know how we arrived here, with our knives locked and our past tinging the air in sour memories, but as our eyes catch and hold, the South Wind shoves me back. My spine hits the shelves. Something rattles loose as his hot, hungry tongue parts my mouth.

I moan, loud and long and full of want. Here, now, the transgressions of our past matter not. We are two bodies colliding in darkness, two pairs of fumbling hands, two mouths and two hearts fused. I despise him and ache for him, scorn him and fear him and hunger for him, hunger for this: the South Wind's anchoring presence, the security of his arms, the gentle pressure of his touch.

But there is no gentleness now. The darkness breeds hunger, cravings so acute I feel my very bones bend beneath its force. The South Wind has plastered himself fully against me, hands framing my face to stabilize my head as he steals every sharp-edged word from my mouth, every pointed insult, every scathing remark and daggered affront. He seeks to conquer me, but I will not go willingly. I eat at his mouth as he eats at mine, with thrusting tongues and vicious teeth, every pained groan drawn from his throat a spoil of war.

In this moment, Notus is mine, his body my realm. It has been long since I've explored its topography, but my hands remember, mapping the taut muscles and brute strength, the long line of his thighs leading to his abdomen, chest, shoulders, neck. Then down, sliding along his lower back, the taut globes of his backside gripped firmly in hand.

The wooden shelving at my back creaks as Notus rocks his hips forward. The length of his erection presses between my thighs, and I shudder, widening my stance so his cock nestles against the part of me that aches. The pleasure is mind-numbing, drenched in delirium. How could I have forgotten what it felt like to burn on a fuse before him?

A delicious sigh vibrates in my throat as I grind slowly against him. It's not fair that he should feel so irresistible when I have done everything in my power to maintain distance. Too easily, I have been dragged into the South Wind's undertow. I do not fight the pull.

With a pained groan, Notus rips his mouth free, stumbling back into the opposite wall. A stack of sheets falls onto his shoulders.

I can't catch my breath. My knees wobble, and I fear they will collapse beneath me, unable to bear my weight.

"I apologize," he whispers. "That was out of line. I—" Yet his voice dies. He hasn't the words.

The glitter of Notus' black eyes holds me in thrall. In the gloom, my gaze slips to the soft smudge of his parted mouth, the tongue that I have often dreamed of, despite my best attempts to push it from my mind.

Here is what I know. Desire is an animal. For years, it paced its cage. I did not feed it, not at first. Hungrier the beast grew. It crowded its pen. It knocked against the walls, the door, until it at last tore free.

Reaching out, I snag the front of his robe, haul him back, chest to chest and groin to groin. "Stop talking," I murmur, then crush my mouth to his.

He tugs my hair loose of its binding. The tresses fall free, and he slides the locks between his fingers, grazing my scalp with a delicious roughness that draws my nipples to peaks beneath my gown. I whimper. My spine curves, pushing me flush against his frame. The air dampens with the rising perspiration of two shadows entwined.

A low, throaty purr cascades out of me. I claw at his clothes, eager for his long, hardened shaft to enter my core. One of my legs curls around the back of his thigh in an attempt to drag him closer. He relents, hitching me into his arms. My legs wrap his waist as he braces me against the shelves. Something tumbles from overhead and shatters.

Arms wrapped around his neck, I tuck my face beneath his jaw and suck the heated skin there. The South Wind is pure, untapped power. It charges the surrounding air into static. His hips roll with leashed aggression, rutting against me as tension coils white-hot beneath my skin.

"*Sarai* . . ." Notus pushes harder against me, and I spread my legs wider. Delicious friction, unbearable heat. They twine into the tightest of knots.

And that has always been the problem, he and I. Our bodies fall into sync, into melody and countermelody. It is easy to forget what came before, his sudden departure. But that is what I fear most: that I will forget. That I will let him in. And then he'll leave. Maybe not now, but someday. Ammara is not his home. What reason has he to stay?

I break the kiss, my breathing ragged. "Put me down. Please."

He does so immediately.

I angle away from him, clutching the shelving with all the strength I possess. Collapsing into a puddle of emotion simply will not do.

"Are you all right?" Notus asks quietly.

"I'm fine."

"Clearly."

I cut him a glare. When Notus steps closer, my palm flies up, halting him. "This was a mistake," I say.

He stares at me. His lips are swollen, color reddening his cheeks. "The engagement?"

I grit my teeth. He is being willfully obtuse. "The kiss."

"I see." His unhurried response rolls forth with aggravating contemplation. "Because you desire me."

I practically choke on my own tongue. "Because you took advantage of me."

The South Wind snorts. "No one can take advantage of you, Sarai. But—fine. If you refuse to admit that you desire me as I desire you, that is your prerogative."

"Now who's the liar?"

He is still, this immortal. Darkness leaches from the air to cloud the space between us so that I struggle to see his face in full. "What, exactly, have I lied to you about?"

"If you truly desire me as you claim," I state, "you would have stayed all those years ago. But you didn't."

A blankness slides across his eyes, snuffing out the fire sparking within. I am sorry to see it go. Sorrier still that the past is present, this wound unhealed. When Notus retreats a step, my body goes cold.

"You're right," he says bitingly. "Then again, you always are." Nudging me aside, he pushes out into the hallway, blinding me with the sudden flood of light.

15

"YOU DID *WHAT?*"
Glaring at Roshar from where I sit curled in one of the oversized armchairs occupying his workroom, I shovel another pistachio cookie into my mouth. "Do I need to repeat myself?" I mumble, mouth full of crumbs.

The man is a coil of nervous energy. His long legs propel him to the window, the door, around the tables piled high with silk and muslin, wool and linen. The emerald fabric of his elegantly cut robe flaps around his shins.

"Oh no, my dear. I heard you perfectly the first time. I'm just beginning to question if I'm dreaming or if I am, in fact, dead."

Pacing and pacing. Yet more pacing.

"Roshar," I snap. "You're making me dizzy."

"Oh, *I'm* making you dizzy?" He halts in place, pivots to face me. His spectacles magnify what is a spectacular pair of hazel-green eyes, long-lashed and bright with undeniable irritation. "Let me get this straight. You kissed the South Wind . . . while being engaged to Prince Balior. Is that right?"

Calmly, I set down the plate of cookies. I am no stranger to Roshar's moods. They change more swiftly than the season's current fashions.

"Prince Balior and I hadn't solidified our engagement. We were only courting," I say. "I'm engaged to Notus."

Roshar shakes his head in denial. "I see what this is." He begins to roll up his sleeves with quick, perfunctory motions. "You're angry because I sewed that musical notation into your dress without your knowledge. Now you wish to surprise me in a similar fashion. I understand, my dear, I do. Roshar loves petty revenge as much as the next spurned bride, but I had hoped you would recognize those stitches as an act of love."

"Roshar." I wait until he meets my gaze. "It's the truth."

He doesn't *want* to believe me, but he must, and huffs in vexation. "Forgive me, Sarai. You can't spring this information on a person who has not even had his morning tea yet."

His fingers tear through his impeccably coifed hair. Then, as if realizing what he's done, he hurries toward the floor-length mirror and brushes the unkempt locks back into place.

My eyes meet Roshar's in the mirror's reflection. His expression is a kaleidoscope of emotion. Horror. Outrage. Intrigue. Outrage. Disbelief. Yet more outrage.

Voice hushed, he asks, "When did you and Notus get engaged?"

"Last week, before the ball."

He drops his arms, eyes comically wide. "Last week? And you didn't think to tell me?"

"It's not my fault you were called away on a commission, though I hear congratulations are in order."

"Don't try to change the subject."

And then I see what I have overlooked amidst Roshar's preening and dramatics, the flashy nature of his character. There is a wounded bend to his mouth. I have hurt my friend's feelings, though that was never my intention.

"I'm sorry," I say. "I was going to tell you, but it hasn't been easy." I flick the edge of the plate in frustration. It doesn't help much. "To tell you the truth, my father isn't supportive of the union."

His shoulders slump, and he frowns into the mirror. "I suppose that makes sense," he replies thoughtfully, "considering his plans for your arranged marriage have been tossed out the window."

I nod, relieved that he is able to see my perspective. "It was unexpected. Prince Balior is ... not pleased." An understatement. And there's his army to contend with as well. "I *am* sorry—"

"Please." He lifts a hand. "It's not your fault. It's none of my business, honestly. I'm just being a sorry sap, is all. It's bad enough I missed the social event of the season. And for what? To stitch a gown for a woman who is bat-shit insane? And I thought *I* had high expectations!" He abandons the mirror to slump into the chair opposite mine. The tray of cookies catches his eye. He grabs two and shoves both into his mouth. "Look at what she's turned me into. At this rate, I'll be up four trouser sizes by next month!"

I nestle deeper into the cushions. Gray steeps beyond the window— a rare fog blew in overnight. It hangs in filmy strips over the labyrinth. I'm certain something shifts behind the thickened mass, but when I stare at it for too long, my head throbs, and I feel compelled to look elsewhere.

After a time, Roshar settles. "Can I ask you something?"

"No, you can't borrow my lip rouge."

He huffs a laugh. "Different complexions, dear. Scarlet looks terrible on me." Then he sobers. "Why Notus? Your union with Prince Balior would have granted you more security than one with a god who has no ties to the realm. I thought you hated the South Wind." He searches my gaze. "Do you have feelings for him?"

The more apt question is, what feelings do I not experience when in the South Wind's presence? They are vast as Ammara is vast, full of unexplored depths. It terrifies me that I might be forced to dig deeper and face whatever pain still lingers.

"What I feel for Notus is ... complicated."

"You know you can always come to me, Sarai. I'm here to listen."

"I would have come to you," I say, "had I not spent the last few days hiding in my room avoiding Father."

Daily, King Halim sends me messages in a near-illegible scrawl, demanding I attend dinner, apologize to Prince Balior, rescind my engagement to Notus, present a public apology. What is worse, today would have likely been my wedding day, had Prince Balior and I both committed to the engagement.

But that is neither here nor there. I've slept poorly since the night of the ball. Twice, I have awoken standing at my bedroom window, peering down at the labyrinth below, though I have no recollection of slipping from bed. I have even begun to sleep with my lamp lit, for at times I am certain the shadows move. When I ask Notus if he's encountered any further darkwalker activity, however, he denies it.

"You know what?" Roshar waves a hand. "It doesn't matter. Yes, you should have told me, but I'm over it. Really. Now, on to more important matters." His smile stretches, cheek to cheek. "How was the kiss?"

Despite my best attempts at appearing unaffected, the blush rages red across my face. Last night, I fell asleep to phantom hands across my breasts, between my legs.

Calmly, I reach for my cookie, only to realize I have consumed it entirely. I draw the platter onto my lap. "It was fine."

"Oh, Sarai, *no*! Unacceptable." He snatches the plate of cookies from my grip. I squawk in protest.

Slipping a finger beneath my chin, Roshar draws my face toward him, eyebrows wiggling. "I see it all, my dear. Look at those lips. Pouty and swollen." To my horrified amusement, he sniffs my neck. "What is that woodsy scent you're wearing? Did he kiss you here?"

I shove him away. "You're ridiculous." When I reach for the plate, he holds it out of reach.

"Ah ah!" He holds up a finger. "Not until you tell me the truth."

Cookies, or my sanity? Today, I am weak. "All right, it was remarkable. Earth-shattering." As I knew it would be. That is, until I pushed him away. Days later, I regret it. He wounds me. I wound him. When will the cycle end?

Roshar takes pity on me, offering the dish of desserts. But my appetite has fled.

"I feared telling you," I admit, "because of your loose tongue. No offense."

He huffs. "Do you imply I would have spilled your secret? I would never!"

I level him with a long, pointed stare.

His fingertips tap the chair arm in a quickening tempo, rings winking with reflected light. "What evidence do you have of this?" he demands.

"Age fourteen, late summer. You told Jem I had a crush on him."

He crosses his arms. "A simple misunderstanding. I thought for sure he felt the same. I was just trying to help."

"Age sixteen, you informed Father I had abandoned the spring ball to practice for my upcoming recital." That had been a particularly nasty fight between me and Father.

"King Halim demanded to know your whereabouts. I could not lie to him—"

"Age seventeen, you told one of the noblewomen that I thought her nose looked like a warty squash."

He grows flustered. "Tell me you don't hold that against me. I mean, really, what was I supposed to do?"

"You also gifted her one of my gowns!"

"She offered me a Zarqan, Sarai. A Zarqan! Do you know how hard it is to get ahold of one?"

Only a mother's love for her child rivaled Roshar's obsession with the rare and beautiful handbags. "If you wanted a Zarqan, you could have just taken one from my wardrobe. I have plenty of bags I've never even touched." It's not uncommon for nobility to offer the royal family gifts of favor. Years later, they sit, gathering dust.

He emits a frail, choking sound, as though he has been brutally impaled. "A Zarqan is not *just* a bag. It is exemplary, of the highest standard in Ammaran fashion."

Of course it is.

Very soon, Sarai, we will meet.

My head snaps in his direction. "What did you say?"

Roshar lifts a curious eyebrow. "Only that a Zarqan is so much more than a bag?" There is a pause. "Are you feeling all right?" He presses the back of his hand to my forehead in concern. "You do feel warm. Have you visited the physician?"

"I'm fine." But I've heard that voice before. I hear it on the edge of sleep, when waking and dreaming become one. It is no voice I recognize, yet I fight its pull.

"Do you mind if I complete some reading while you work?" I ask him.

"Reading?" His expression folds into one of distaste. "Sometimes I wonder why we're friends." Then he springs to his feet and retreats to the other side of the room, soon disappearing behind a small mountain of cloth.

Reaching into the small bag resting at the base of the chair, I remove the book I saved from the night of the darkwalker attack. Seeing as it is the only resource I have at the moment, I've been wary of leaving it in my chambers. Already, I've read this volume thrice through, scanning for overlooked details, information that may benefit us. If Prince Balior intends to release the beast, then the only option is to kill it.

Cracking open the spine, I begin to read. Every so often, Roshar's mutterings pull me from my research. Occasionally, I hear the plink of a sewing needle hitting the floor.

After what feels like an hour, he uncurls from his hunched position, stretching his arms above his head with a yawn before wandering to the window. I'm rereading the beast's personal account when Roshar abruptly straightens, pressing a palm against the glass. "Sarai." He glances at me with enough severity to make me sit up straight. "I think you're going to want to see this."

Setting aside my book, I move to stand beside Roshar.

The labyrinth, with its curved walls and crisscrossing inner passageways, dominates the center of the courtyard. Notus advances toward it with a confidence some might mistake as arrogance. Upon reaching the entryway, he brushes a hand against a curtain of black tendrils seething beneath its massive door.

"By the gods," Roshar whispers.

The hair along my arms stands straight on end. Nose pressed against the glass, my exhalation rushes forth to steam the window.

The veil parts. The door opens. Notus steps through.

I gasp in alarm. When Notus said he would conduct his own research on the labyrinth, I didn't think he meant he would *enter* it alone. I thought we were working as a team.

Roshar turns to me, oddly mute. "What is the South Wind's interest in the labyrinth?"

There are things I can speak freely about to Roshar. This is not one of them. "I'm not sure," I say, pulling away, "but I'm going to find out."

Down and down and down the central staircase, before I burst through one of the doors leading out into a heat so thick my airway sears with each breath. The sun is blinding. I lift a hand to shield my eyes against it. Dust puffs beneath the heels of my slippers.

And then I am before the labyrinth. It is tall, it is wide, it is unknown. Notus has yet to emerge. Panic—I feel its roots, its slow-opening bud. What if he is trapped? The last time he faced the beast, he failed to kill it. His powers were not sufficient. How am I to know if he needs help?

Beneath the dense, pulsing shadows shielding the doorway are words chiseled into stone, a language the world has forgotten. The left pillar of the archway contains a large, round ruby. My eyes pass over it curiously. Strange. Never before has the jewel glittered in this manner, as though lit from within.

I glance around the courtyard. A few guards observe me warily, yet do not attempt to approach, likely due to fear of the labyrinth. I could go after Notus. But there is always the risk that I will lose myself in its twisting depths.

Hello, Sarai.

Won't you step into the dark?

This voice. It sings to me. It *knows* me. Reaching out, my fingers brush the coiling shadows. Frost prickles my fingertips. Rather than snatching back my hand, I allow it to sink deeper into the darkness, its chill coating my fingers, wrist, elbow. I step closer. The toes of my slippers brush the door.

A startling clang wrenches my attention skyward, and I stumble back, falling onto my bottom with an *oof.* The capital bell heaves. *One, two, three, four, five . . .*

Ishmah is under attack.

16

THE BELL CONTINUES TO PEAL, A BRIGHT, BRASSY CLANG PINGING against the slanted rooftops of the upper ring. The alarm is unceasing. It precedes the uprise of screams.

The ruby fixed into the labyrinth flares. I stumble back as shadows begin to seep out through the bottom of the door, coiling up the pillars that mark the entry. They move swiftly. If I'm not mistaken, the same shadow also drapes the darkwalkers' skeletal forms.

Sarai, a low voice hisses. *I await your arrival.* My mind blanks, engulfed in a sudden cold.

"Princess Sarai!"

I blink, and my awareness of the present returns. The courtyard has fallen into chaos. Attendants flee toward the palace, baskets of towels and crates of fruit abandoned to the sweltering sun. A door slams shut, locking from the inside. A harried woman bangs her fists upon its oaken shield with increasing desperation. But the rules are clear. In the event of a darkwalker strike, the palace doors, once shut, will not open. They will have to find shelter elsewhere.

One of the guards sprints toward me, scimitar drawn, and herds me across the baked stones. Meanwhile, additional sentinels pour in from the city beyond to station themselves around the labyrinth. My thoughts spin. Is it possible more darkwalkers have infiltrated the palace? If so, I must ensure my family is safe.

I'm halfway across the courtyard when I think of Haneen, the storyteller. I halt in place.

The guard glances around worriedly. "Your Highness, we must get you inside."

He is a young man, this guard, perhaps a few years younger than I am. The whites of his eyes, the sweat layering his skin—he is afraid. He is wise to be.

Another door closes with a startling bang—the east wing. Two more attendants managed to slip inside, but only just. Maybe I, too, can be like Aziza, the woman from the storyteller's tale, and draw courage from the place it has been buried.

"I need you to send a handful of men to the library," I tell the guard.

"Your Highness, we will, but first we need to make sure you're safe."

Generally, when darkwalkers are spotted in the desert, the bell rings briefly before quieting, to signal that the capital is secure. But the bell continues to peal, which can only mean something has malfunctioned with the city gates. The moment I enter the palace, the gateway will be barred until the threat has passed. I will shelter in my rooms: doors locked, windows latched, curtains drawn. No less than twenty men will guard my door—men better served protecting Ishmah's citizens.

"Your Highness," the guard presses urgently.

"Let the attendants inside."

"What?"

A dozen still remain trapped outside. They climb over one another, claw at the door latch, scream for help. The sight turns my stomach.

The young sentinel shifts his weight uncomfortably. "They are low-born, Your Highness." He watches two women yank the solid brass handles. One falls to her knees with a broken sob. He turns his face away. "Our duty is to protect the crown."

Low-born or not, they are my people. I have doomed them enough for one lifetime, I think. "The longer you wait, the more lives will be lost. Open the doors, and I will cooperate." It is exhilarating, I think, to use one's voice. To use it for *good*.

The guard mutters his dissent, yet he unlocks the nearest door without complaint. Pushing it wide, he allows the attendants to rush inside, then follows. He does not bother to check whether I trail him. He does not see how I have lied.

The moment the guard crosses the threshold, I dash toward the stables. There is a shout, the rapid footfalls of pursuit. After diving into the secret passage, I reach the Queen's Road in minutes.

Terror bleeds through the streets. The gates separating the upper and lower rings have broken open, sturdy hinges shattered from force of entry. Everyone, from the wealthiest aristocrats to the destitute families of the slums, floods the wide, paved roads of the affluent upper ring, their sights set on the gleaming palace atop the hill.

From my vantage point, I see the whole of Ishmah, its thousands of citizens teeming like a colony of ants. In the distance lies the capital gates, split wide. Darkwalkers prowl through, dripping shadow over jutting bones. The bell continues to clang.

Leaping over a stack of crates, I dive into the rush of cityfolk fleeing the streets. An elbow stabs into my spine, and I stumble with a cry of pain. Someone snags my dress and attempts to drag me toward the ground. I whirl, snarling, to slap aside the woman's hand. Her eyes widen in recognition before I plunge deeper into the current.

Eventually, I reach the lower ring. The crush of bodies is even more horrendous, bottlenecked at the souk entrance. Multiple stalls have folded inward. I pass a spice cart having toppled onto its side, yellow cumin and red-orange cinnamon draining out like the city's lifeblood. A dry wind courses through the crooked footpaths. It smells of a long-burning fire: sweet char and bitter smoke.

I've nearly reached Haneen's dwelling when screams erupt from the next street over. There is the unmistakable sound of tearing flesh.

Darting down an alleyway, I peek around the wall of a crumbling building. Darkwalkers, three of them. They block the road ahead, tearing through the throng of fleeing citizens, and there is blood, clouds of it, the dry earth sucking it down through its cracks, and limbs strewn about, and the whites of peoples' eyes rolling in fear. One woman shoves her child to the side, and the darkwalker snaps its massive jaws around her body instead. Someone attempts to hack it down with a rusted sword, but unless the blade has been coated in salt, it will fail to harm the creature.

In seconds, citizens fall prey to the beasts. The dead litter the street. Eight, eleven, fourteen—still more. A man falls. He curls onto his side, arms covering his head. The beast lowers its snout to his face and inhales.

It takes less than a heartbeat. When the darkwalker lifts its head, the man's body disintegrates on a puff of wind. My heart breaks clean down the center. I fear his soul may never know peace.

People attempt to retreat in the opposite direction, but the roads are crammed so completely there is little room to maneuver, much less breathe. It will not take long before they, too, are soulless.

"This way!" I bark. A few citizens dart into the souk, where the footpaths are threads, too narrow for darkwalkers to squeeze through. I spin, dart down a less crowded side street, fighting my every instinct to flee in the opposite direction. As I round a bend, a soft whimper draws my attention to two children huddling against the wall. They peer at me with tear-streaked faces coated in grime. Brothers, I assume, and crouch before them. "Where's your mother?" I ask.

The youngest sobs into his hands. The older brother holds his sibling close. "I don't know," he whispers. "We were separated."

A whirlwind of dust plows through the alley ahead, hurling a large shape against the nearest structure with a forceful *crack*.

Over the cacophony of the city, there is an unmistakable growl.

"Stay here," I tell the boys. Moving quietly, I slip around the corner to investigate.

Amidst a large pile of debris, a darkwalker rises to its spindly legs, whip-like tail thrashing. Tipping back its head, it releases a bone-shattering roar.

At the opposite end of the street, the South Wind appears, sword in hand. His robe whips around his legs. His black eyes, chipped into a face carved by the hands of some wretched divine, glitter with unbridled rage.

I crouch low near one of the faded doorways, fighting for breath. Suddenly, Notus is in a different position entirely, weapon ablur. Air spirals toward the darkwalker, hits it square in the chest. It launches backward and crashes onto the roof of a nearby building. The structure collapses beneath its weight.

The darkwalker is struggling to rise when a second beast appears, larger and more grotesque than the first, with a mouthful of broken teeth. It charges at the South Wind with its head bent low.

Only I am witness to the battle that ensues. God and beast. Shadow and sun. A bright force driving back the dark.

Ducking beneath the beast's legs, he shoves the sword into its underbelly. Fluid spits from the opening. The creature howls, swiping at the South Wind with one enormous paw, and Notus spins, but is unable to dodge the attack. I gasp as the beast's claws tear into his lower back. He twists away with a guttural cry, narrowly missing another swing. The darkwalker lunges. I scream.

A flash of silver, and the blade shears the darkwalker's head from its body. It folds in a pile of severed parts, blood pooling beneath stinking innards.

"Behind you!" I scream.

His head whips around. Dark eyes catch mine and hold. Even from this distance, the clench of his jaw is unmistakable.

As the first darkwalker returns from the collapsed building to take its fallen brethren's place, the South Wind blasts it across the street. Then, using his wind as ropes, he binds its limbs long enough to thrust his sword into the beast's heart. It twitches once, then falls still.

He turns to me then. The roiling emotion blackening his gaze gives me hesitation, but I point to the two boys huddling near a partially collapsed doorway. He follows me to where they cower, scooping them up easily with a curt, "Follow me."

We make our way to a less-traveled road. It is here the South Wind sets down the brothers, who race toward a woman in the distance. She drops to her knees, sobbing, and takes her sons into her arms.

Then I remember. "Your back," I gasp. "Let me see."

The South Wind brushes my hands aside. "It's fine." But the terseness of his reply exposes what is likely an immense amount of pain. Too much blood. It has soaked the back of his robe.

"Are you sure—"

"I'm *immortal*," he reminds me.

I glare at him. "As if I could have forgotten."

"I'm not even going to waste my breath listing all the ways this decision was foolish," he growls, his voice so low it is reduced to mere vibration. "You need to return to the palace."

"And I'm not going to waste my breath explaining myself. I'll return to the palace when I'm through here."

"This is not a discussion." His eyes flash with the might of a thousand beating suns. "Every moment in the city is a risk to your life."

He is afraid. The South Wind is never afraid. It softens what is hard within me.

Reaching out, I grasp his hand in reassurance. Its wide, roughened shape swallows mine. "The storyteller," I say, pitching my voice over the uproar. "I need to make sure she's safe."

"I don't care about the storyteller," he snarls. "I care about *you*."

Despite the madness overtaking the city, a wave of security enfolds me, and I absorb these words into my skin until I almost believe him. "I need to do this, Notus." Reaching up, I cup his cheek in one hand, thumb pressed against the bristle of his facial hair. "Will you help me?"

The intensity with which his gaze pierces mine is too much, yet I do not pull away. His is a strength I yearn for. "I won't be long," I promise him.

Notus utters a low oath under his breath, but he follows me without further argument. The chipped facade of Haneen's door comes into view. I rush inside to find it empty. "She's not here."

"Unsurprising." He paces the small area in evident vexation. "She likely fled deeper into the city. And we have wasted valuable time. Let's go."

"Wait." I pick up a long strip of fabric near her stool: Haneen's headscarf. I recognize the pattern.

Frowning, I peer down at the dirt floor, solidified by the press of a thousand feet over decades. Our footprints are marked fresh. But I see no footprints *leaving* the space.

And then I spot a curtain hanging from the back wall. It has been pushed aside to uncover a hidden passage.

The South Wind grips my arm. "I'll go first," he says.

Gloom shrouds the passage, which smells of minerals. Cracks run through the clay-hardened walls. Perhaps a quarter mile on, the tunnel empties into a small chamber, where the bard sits, a shawl warming her shoulders as she works her loom. She crisscrosses the threads and packs the weft with a large gazelle horn, utterly unconcerned by our presence. "Hello, Princess Sarai."

Notus plants himself in front of me. Sweet—but unnecessary. Once I've regained use of my tongue, I ask, "How do you know who I am?"

"Shall I count the ways?" With her threads secure, she begins the next row of color. "Your tread. Your scent. Your accent and choice of words. All these things reveal to me your status."

Her attention then shifts to the South Wind. Her wide, milky eyes rest somewhere to the side his face. "And there is a man who travels with you who smells of the desert. He has visited me before, but only once, and at a distance. Is he your guardian?"

The South Wind stands near enough that the heat of his body prickles my flesh, even beneath my sweat-dampened dress. I swallow. "Notus is my betrothed."

Haneen smiles. "See?" she replies. "There are plenty of things I still don't know."

"I was worried for your safety," I explain to her.

Her smile stretches wider. I have never seen a more serene expression at so violent a time. Indeed, she appears quite comfortable, nestled in her multicolored blankets and pillows. "What of your own safety, child?"

"I am well looked after."

"I can sense that." She angles her head toward Notus, who regards her with narrowed eyes. If I'm not mistaken, he is uncomfortable beneath the blind woman's scrutiny.

"Come with us," I urge. "You're not safe here."

"Because I'm blind?" At my lack of response, she chuckles. "I would argue that I see more clearly than those with eyes unclouded. Do not worry, my dear. I have survived nearly nine decades' worth of trouble." And she weaves another line of thread onto her loom with a complete lack of concern for the screams erupting beyond the passage walls. "The darkwalkers do not frighten me."

Daring, or foolish? I do not care to know. "Regardless, I don't wish to see you succumb to a brutal end."

Haneen lifts her gaze, copper hands resting atop the strung threads colored sapphire and ginger and blush. "There are worse fates," she says.

The South Wind steps forward. "You may come with us, if you wish, but if not, we must take our leave. There are others who may still be saved."

"You are correct, dear boy." At this, I fight a burgeoning smile, for I wouldn't consider a god who is millennia old a *boy*. "Go. Do not worry about me. I am as safe as can be."

Notus takes my hand. "We must go," he whispers to me.

Yes. But— "I'll be back," I inform the storyteller.

"I know," says Haneen.

Outside, the souk is even more crammed with people than it was minutes ago. Some roads must be blocked, forcing people to use the narrower footpaths. As a result, the majority of the stalls have been crushed underfoot.

"This way," Notus says.

"No." I stay his hand. He appears moments away from tossing me over his shoulder and taking to the skies, propriety be damned. "The city gates have malfunctioned. They must be shut."

"And they will be, once I've returned you to the palace."

I sigh. "Notus."

"*What*, Sarai?" He tosses up his hands, spears his fingers through the unruly locks of his windblown hair. A large family shoves their way past, followed by a small herd of goats. "I'm not taking you with me."

"I'm not asking you to." Despite the chaos unleashed, I remain composed. "You can leave me here."

"If you think I'm going to leave you while I head to the gates, you're out of your mind."

"That is exactly what I'm asking you." Someone jostles me in their haste to turn a corner. I tug Notus into a crumbling doorway, tucking myself against the length of his broad, muscled form.

He peers down at me. Gradually, as a red storm ebbs into calm, his expression smooths. "Asking," he clarifies. "Not ordering."

"Yes." Because one requires trust. The other, obedience. I know which I value more from the god who has risked life and limb to save me from, well, myself.

Notus presses his thumb into my chin. "Why?"

One word should not possess the complication it does. But it holds a story that spans the entirety of my relatively short existence. I have lived a safe life, a sheltered life, a life that, in many ways, was never mine to live. I can do good, I think, before my time comes to an end.

"These are my people," I explain. "They are my family. They are home. I would stop at nothing to protect my home, wouldn't you?"

Notus frowns. As I suspected, he is not happy about this. But for once, he does not argue. For that, I am grateful.

My eyes drop to his mouth. We alone stand still in the tide that surges through the souk. "Be safe," I whisper.

His eyes darken. "You, too."

The last I see of the South Wind, he is cleaving the crowd in two with a brute wind. He runs, leaps, catching himself on an updraft, which carries him far, far into the distance, and deposits him in front of two darkwalkers. A swift cut of his blade, and their heads are severed.

He then launches skyward, a cyclone of wind spiraling around his legs. It propels him toward the distant gates.

As for Ishmah's citizens, they need a miracle. And by miracle, I mean the palace.

"Everyone to the palace!" I scream, shouldering my way through the crowd. "To the palace!" Again and again, I cry these words, this plea, until the cityfolk join in accompaniment, my solo transforming to a trio, an octet, an orchestra, its crescendo driving those fleeing up the hill.

Reaching beneath my dress, I yank at the small pendant hanging around my neck until the thin gold chain snaps. I place it into the hand of a young woman whose hazel eyes are ringed in white. "Show this to the guards," I order, grip tightening. "Tell them Princess Sarai demands Ishmah's citizens be sheltered inside."

She nods and takes off.

My feet change direction before I'm fully aware of it. Toward Notus, toward the gates. The closer I get, the more deserted the streets become. More than once, I'm forced to leap over bodies strewn about the road. When I reach the gates, which have yet to be shut completely, numerous guards are attempting to shift what looks to be a jammed handle. I scan the area, panting, my dress sticking to every sweaty dip and swell. A wall of soldiers stretches across the entrance into the city, battling two darkwalkers attempting to pass. Notus is nowhere to be found.

"Your Highness?"

Two sentinels pause in their attempts at sealing the gate, mouths agape. This draws the attention of their superior, a captain with ink-blot freckles and a scowling mouth. "Does the king know you're down here, Your Highness?" he demands.

My eyes narrow. "Perhaps you should focus less on my whereabouts and more on closing the gate."

A nearby staircase leads up to the ramparts. I take the stairs two at a time until I reach the top. From my vantage point, I see the whole of Ishmah, its palace, that bright, diamond-hearted center from which all roads lead. But to the south, more darkwalkers—shadowed forms blurred against the rising dunes. Their swiftness is horrifying. They eliminate half the distance in a handful of strides.

"Any progress with the gate?" I shout down.

A man strains to rotate the rusted handle. "Still jammed." It emits a grating shriek.

My gaze leaps toward the approaching threat. Stride by stride, the distance between the darkwalkers and the capital lessens. Black tendrils stream from their mutated forms.

Suddenly, the captain knocks his subordinate aside, grasps the mechanism with both hands, and throws his entire weight against the handle. It shifts forward a hair before grinding to a halt.

I spin in place, searching for Notus. There—in the sky. He plunges toward the rooftops and vanishes momentarily. Two heartbeats later, he soars upward on a cloud of wind, sword held aloft, its blade coated black. From one palm hurtles a roaring gust, aimed at a trio of darkwalkers below. The South Wind is so fixated on defeating the beasts inside the walls that he remains blind to the threat beyond them. Only he can stop the flood, this roiling deluge of darkness and ruin.

Meanwhile, archers atop the ramparts shoot salt-tipped arrows into the darkwalkers advancing on the capital. One hits a soldier in the thigh. He collapses mid-run with a shout.

I whirl toward the archers. "Only shoot if you're certain you will hit your mark!" Below, the man crawls, face contorted in pain. I spin toward the nearest sentinel. "Send a horse, now!"

But a darkwalker reaches the man first. His scream is bloodcurdling. In the end, I'm forced to look away.

The man's death leaves me woozy. There will be another, and another—a mountain, a sea of dead. Soldiers continue to struggle with the jammed mechanism. In the time it takes their combined body-weight to shift the door closed another foot, three more beasts slip into the city.

"Get her out of here!" the captain barks.

Someone begins hauling me backward toward the stairs. I wrench free of the guard's grip. "Notus!"

The South Wind falters mid-throw and swings his head around. A brief examination of the area reveals naught but carnage. He can't see me.

Again, the guard reaches for me. "Princess Sarai—"

"Touch me again," I spit, "and I'll have your head."

The man halts, stricken. He doesn't attempt to stop me as I grab the rungs of the wooden ladder and begin to climb one of the towers. Below, those barred from reaching the Queen's Road cram themselves into homes or shelter between alleyways. Others bleed out in the sweltering heat, their feeble pleas gradually falling silent.

Halfway up the ladder, my foot punches through a rotting beam. I drop with a scream, clawing the wood as I swing wildly, my shoulder slamming against the stone wall.

From below, the captain's thunderous voice breaks through the uproar of battle. "Get up there and bring her down before she breaks her neck."

"But she said—"

"I don't care what she said," he snarls. "If she falls, it'll be both our heads."

My foot finds another rung. The ladder wobbles, but holds.

At the top, Ammara spreads before me, a gilded carpet pressed beneath a sky the blue of a jewel. Notus battles a group of darkwalkers, having contained them to a large dome of swirling air. They tear their hooked claws against the transparent barrier to no avail. It allows him to dart forward and thrust his sword through the heart of the smallest beast.

"Notus!" I pitch my voice higher, hands cupped around my mouth. "Notus!"

As another darkwalker plows into the half-closed gates, a chill slips into my bloodstream. *Sarai,* a voice whispers. *Why do you flee?*

My vision wavers. Blackness plumes before me. Is it a dream? A mirage? A cloaked figure materializes before my eyes, and I stumble back, the grit of the wall scraping the soles of my slippers.

"Who are you?" I choke. "What do you want?"

You know what I want, Sarai.

The cloaked figure flickers out of sight. Confusion sends me backward, but I fail to realize how close to the lip I stand. My foot slips off the edge, and I am falling.

17

I WAKE ON MY BACK, STARING INTO A SKY THE BLACK OF A CROW'S wing.

My chest heaves. My skin prickles from the bone-dry air wafting from an opening beyond sight. I blink once, twice. Neither stars nor clouds nor moon. It feels as if I lie underground, though I'm not sure how that is possible. Gingerly, I push into a seated position. I remember falling. The silvery arc of Notus' blade. Then: nothing.

"Hello?"

The sound gutters the moment it escapes my mouth. Whatever this place, the air hangs with an unfamiliar weight. It tastes of rust and damp.

After a time, my eyes adjust to the gloom. The space is small, hemmed in on all sides by pale stone. A tall mirror framed in silver leans against the opposite wall. There is a pull I cannot deny. It coaxes me to my feet, drags me nearer to the gleaming surface. When I reach out to touch the ornate frame, however, my fingers pass through. Not real, then. A dream.

It is real, Sarai.

I startle. My head snaps around, yet I am alone.

Except . . . *am* I alone, or am I simply blind to whoever else occupies this space?

"What is real?" I ask, continuing to scan my surroundings.

The mirror, says the voice that is everywhere and nowhere. *Look again.*

My attention returns to the looking glass. It casts no reflection. Instead, moving images emerge from beneath the silver surface. Over time, they alter in color and shape. I am looking at myself gazing out my bedroom window, my body masked in the black of mourning. My eyes are swollen, red-rimmed. These must be the early days following Fahim's death.

"What is this?" I demand. "Why are you showing me something that has already come to pass?"

The mirror shows what has been, what is, and what will be.

"And what will be?"

Look in the mirror and find out.

The image melts away, becomes something else. I stumble back in horror. The South Wind lies on his back, eyes closed, the grime and blood of battle sullying his robes. He does not appear to be breathing.

This doesn't make sense. Notus cannot die except by a god-touched weapon. If his downfall has been foretold, then what is fated to kill him? Why does that thought render me breathless with anguish?

I peer closer. No, he *is* breathing. But he is . . . asleep? And then I realize something else. The bed he lies in is mine.

The image fades, leaving me staring at my own reflection. I am pressing a hand against the mirror, relieved to find it solid, when something moves over my shoulder. I whirl around. A figure has materialized, broad-shouldered, cloaked in dark wool. A spacious hood has been pulled forward, veiling the face within.

"Who are you?" I dare ask.

You would not remember our initial meeting. You were an infant then, and sickly.

My eyes widen. "The Lord of the Mountain," I whisper.

So, you do remember. The Lord of the Mountain sidles nearer. Beneath the cowl of his hood, I glimpse an opening, like a mouth. There is a flash of white—teeth? *Do not worry, Sarai. I do not demand your life—yet.*

I intend to reply, yet another, more distant voice demands that I wake. It is familiar, this voice. It promises peace. I'm certain it shouts my name.

Again, I glance around. These alien walls. This sky that is not a sky. The musk of pressed soil. I must be dreaming. It's the only logical explanation.

"Why did you bring me here?" I ask the Lord of the Mountain. "To frighten me? You will have to do better than that." I must be mad, standing up to the divine. "Father banned black iris from Ammara long ago."

Do you think the king's policies will stop me from claiming what was promised to me? There is a pause. *Look into the mirror and see.*

The impulse is woven into my very core. As I peer into the mirror, my reflection dissolves. In its place stands the Red City. There are its curved archways and pillar-lined temples. There spring the grasses and sweet-smelling blooms of its abundant gardens. Yet I blink, and all becomes shadow, a smoke-like residue blotting out the shining rooftops and marble statues as darkwalkers flood the streets.

The Lord of the Mountain hovers over my shoulder, cold lips brushing my ear as he says, *It is coming.*

My eyes fly open, and I gasp. A white starburst floods my vision. The ground is hard beneath me, its heat scalding the length of my back, and the sounds of chaos descend, an assault on my ears following the quiet of that strange, unearthly place.

A large hand comes to rest atop my thundering heart. "Steady."

The low, even tone wraps me in warm threads, and I calm.

The brightness fades as my vision adjusts to the stretch of blue overhead. The South Wind leans over me, dark locks haloed by the sun at high noon. His eyes churn with such deep emotion that for a moment, the walls I have erected around my heart falter. He is always in control. Now? I have never seen peace so far from his reach.

Slowly, I sit up. "What happened?" I croak.

Notus looks away, jaw clenched. I lie in a patch of shade cast by one of the nearby dwellings. A handful of soldiers hover at a distance while additional guards direct residents down the street. When Notus refuses to respond, I look to them questioningly.

Only one of the soldiers is brave enough to come forward. "You fell, Your Highness." He glances at the top of the tower. It's a long drop, a few hundred feet by my estimate. None could survive such a fall.

I have no awareness of reaching for Notus, but I must have, for suddenly my fingers slide against his. Just as quickly, he stiffens, withdraws. Curling my hand into a fist, I shove it against my knotted stomach. If he does not wish to touch me, fine. I will not beg for scraps.

"The South Wind caught you before you hit the ground," the soldier adds. At Notus' cutting glare, the man falls quiet.

Understanding settles over me. What power must it have taken the South Wind to travel from one end of the capital to the other in the span of time it would take a body to tumble from that height? It is not a matter of flying faster than the wind. He would need to *become* it.

"Leave us," Notus barks.

The guards retreat, some helping to carry the wounded onto stretchers. I look to the gates, now shut and barred. Something massive slams them from the outside. They shudder, yet hold.

There was a time when darkwalkers only emerged under the cloak of night, sunlight poison to their existence. But something has changed. They grow stronger. One day, I fear the gates' protective runes will fail.

"Notus." I speak quietly.

The South Wind lurches to his feet. "You will need to see a healer," he clips out, unwilling to meet my eye. "It's possible you sustained injuries I'm not aware of." Then he scoops me into his arms, cradling me against his wide, solid chest. The crowd parts as he begins the return trek to the palace.

"Notus—"

"What in the gods' names would drive you to position yourself at the gates when the city is under attack? Do you have a death wish?" Each word emerges choked, a snarl. Despite this, he holds me gently.

"Do you think I would stand by while my people were slaughtered?" I snap. "Is that the type of person you believe me to be?"

"It was a careless decision." The Queen's Road curves, and one cannot ignore the extent of the damage wrought. Many have already begun combing through the rubble of collapsed homes, searching for family and belongings. "I thought you were smarter than that."

However sharp the hurt, I allow his judgment to drift over me. All I wanted was to help my people. What use am I to anyone shielded behind high walls?

"Think of me what you will," I tell him, "but I don't regret my actions. I would do it all over again. Ishmah is my home. I would do anything to protect my home."

He wavers, and a bit of that wild wrath diminishes, cooling to a far more levelheaded disposition. It does little to quell the turmoil sucking me down. "I apologize," he murmurs. "I shouldn't have said what I did."

It's too late for that. "Put me down." We've arrived at the palace gates.

"Not until we've reached the infirmary."

"Who goes?" someone calls from atop the wall.

"It's Notus. I've Princess Sarai. She needs to see a healer immediately."

The gates heave open with an ominous groan.

As we enter the main courtyard, attendants and hostlers halt their duties to watch us pass. If I were less drained, I might insist on walking myself. As it turns out, I'm perfectly comfortable in the South Wind's arms.

The rocking motion of his gait soothes me. The scent of his skin is intoxicating. Against my will, my eyes slip closed. Then, the bright clip of Notus' bootheels against the marble floors. After a few turns, a slightly astringent scent stuffs itself up my nostrils. My eyes snap open as he drops me onto one of the infirmary cots as if I'm no more fragile than a sack of rice.

"I need to check that the capital is secure," he says, glancing at the doorway where the royal healer has entered. Her eyes widen upon catching sight of me.

I shift to the edge of the mattress, plant my feet on solid ground. "There are things I want to discuss with you first."

"Can it wait?"

If it were at all possible to set someone on fire with a glare, I daresay the South Wind would be reduced to ash at this point. "No," I say through clenched teeth. "It can't." The situation has become dire indeed.

The royal healer departs as quickly as she arrived, likely sensing how the air thickens. Notus peers at the door longingly, then takes a seat in a nearby armchair.

And now we sit, god and mortal, ex-lovers bound by the false promise of our engagement. No matter how I attempt to loosen my posture, tension crawls beneath my skin. "Why did you enter the labyrinth without telling me?" I demand, the words hoarse.

The South Wind rears back in surprise. "I wasn't aware I needed to ask your permission to enter."

"You don't," I snap, and am mortified by how swiftly a blush paints my cheeks. Notus is correct. He doesn't *need* to ask my permission, but would it kill him to inform me of his intentions, especially ones so dangerous? "I thought we agreed to work together on this matter."

"We did." His dark eyes are watchful.

No, not watchful. Confused. Hurt, even, that I would repay him saving my life with aggressive accusations. "If I hadn't seen you enter the labyrinth," I explain, tone softening, "I would never have known you were in there. What if you hadn't emerged?"

The change to his expression is subtle. My pulse stutters, for I know what he will ask before he opens his mouth. "You were . . . worried about me?"

Too often I have lied. What is one more, in the end? But I know myself. I cannot lie about this. "Yes, I was worried," I sniff, patting the blanket into place across my lap. "So . . . please keep that in mind next time."

Gravely, austerely, he nods. "I'm sorry for worrying you."

"Apology accepted." Now onto the matters at hand. "Did you find anything?"

"No." He rubs a hand down his face. There is an unmistakable gray pallor to his skin. "The passages are too complex, and I feared I would lose my sense of direction. I haven't figured out a way to mark my path back to the entrance."

"How did you manage to escape the first time?"

He ducks his head in what I believe to be embarrassment. "Would you believe me if I said luck had everything to do with it?"

My mouth falls open. Then I snort, shake my head in disbelief. It lightens my spirits to see the smile stretch Notus' mouth. It is a rare sight indeed. "I suppose luck *would* have something to do with it," I say teasingly, and am pleased beyond measure to watch red paint the South Wind's cheeks.

Speaking of which— "I think the darkwalkers are coming from the labyrinth," I say.

The South Wind doesn't appear the least bit surprised. "Truth be told, I've considered the possibility," he says, easing into the chair's cushioned back. "But aside from the ones that entered the capital today, the only darkwalker I've encountered in Ishmah was the one from the library. What makes you think that?"

"I was standing at the labyrinth entrance when the warning bell rang. Shadow seethed beneath the door—the same shadow the beasts are made of. I'm wondering if they're escaping from the labyrinth underground, through a tunnel, maybe, that leads outside the city." The palace itself has numerous tunnels, many long forgotten.

Notus rubs at his temple, thighs spread, deep in thought. I've the inane urge to drape myself across his lap. I would have, once. "It's worth exploring, at the very least." His attention returns to my face. "Have you learned more about the labyrinth?"

There is the conversation I had with the Lord of the Mountain, of course. But seeing as it concerns my curse, I'm reluctant to divulge it. Perhaps I *should* tell Notus. But ... I don't know. It seems pointless. Maybe I have already accepted the inevitable. After all, one cannot escape fate. Foolishly, I believed myself capable of outsmarting the divine.

"No," I tell him. "Nothing."

He peers carefully at me, perhaps sensing I am not being entirely truthful. "I ask because one of my contacts from Mirash got in touch with me this morning. He has some information he thought we'd be interested in. The sooner we can speak with him, the better."

"The Festival of Rain begins next week," I remind him.

"I remember," he murmurs.

I wish it didn't please me that he remembers Ammara's customs, but I'm not as unfeeling as I try to appear. It does please me. It pleases me a great deal.

"The capital closes its gates in the days leading up to the festival." The cot squeaks as I shift my weight. "We won't be able to leave until the festival is complete." What is another five days, really?

"That shouldn't be an issue," Notus says.

I hesitate, irritated by my sudden indecision. I promptly squash it. "Seeing as we are betrothed, it would befit our situation if you were to accompany me during the festivities."

Now more than ever, my people are looking for certainty. They seek strength and direction. I will not let them down.

Notus lifts his head. His eyes are very dark. I feel as though I stare at my reflection, as though his pain is my pain, and this wound is shared. I fist the blanket across my lap, suddenly unmoored. "I would stand by your side," the South Wind whispers, "if I believed you wanted me there."

"I do want you there," I say. Then, hurriedly, "For the benefit of Ammara, of course."

The South Wind considers me for a long moment. Long enough that I grow uncomfortable. "If that's what you want."

I haven't the slightest idea of what I want. "Are you still angry with me?" I ask.

"I wasn't angry with you, Sarai."

"Weren't you?"

"Maybe it manifested as anger," he admits, "but at its root, always, is fear and sadness and shame. I have never known fear until the moment

I watched you tumble from the wall and believed I would not reach you in time."

I manage a quiet, "Oh." And slowly . . . slowly that long-standing wound inside my heart begins to close. He cares. Too much, I believe. Maybe it's time I stop fighting what *has been* and start embracing what *could be*.

"Is that all?" he says, pushing to his feet.

It is and it isn't. I am always hungry, always reaching, never soothed, never satiated. He's reached the door when I call, "Notus?"

He halts, turns to look at me. My heart squeezes itself into silence.

"I know you're angry with me," I whisper with heartfelt remorse. "I know I did not act in the safest manner. And I know it's your duty to protect me, but . . . thank you," I say, "for saving my life."

The softest wind grazes my cheekbone, akin to the brush of his callused fingertips. "I didn't save your life out of duty, Sarai. I saved it because . . ." He takes a breath. "Because I don't want to live in a world without you in it."

His words heal me even as they frighten me. I know this. I think I have always known this. But I haven't been prepared to accept the truth until now.

"Be safe," I whisper. Then he is gone.

The royal healer returns to examine me from toe to scalp, then forces me to drink some vile concoction she claims will help clear my head. If only she knew what confusions resided there: a dark shade— the Lord of the Mountain, who covets my life.

An hour later, I'm released with the instructions to rest and hydrate. I return to my chambers to wash, then open the journal on my desk. Twenty-three days. The longer I stare at the inked number, the tighter my chest cinches. Yet another reminder of how powerless I am.

Seeing as I do not care to stew in my tumult, I go in search of Father. I find him in his chambers, abed. Amir and Tuleen sit at his bedside, speaking in low tones.

King Halim's quarters are thrice the size of my own. They include an office, two sitting rooms, an impressive library, a bedroom, and a spacious bathing chamber. On the far wall, there lies the interconnecting door to the queen's chambers. Empty for the last twenty-four years.

Upon catching sight of me, Amir lurches upright. "Where have you been?" He rounds the bed, scouring me for injury. "We checked your rooms but found you gone. I feared you were in the city."

"I took shelter in the library," I say to Amir. "I came as soon as it was clear."

"Thank the gods for that."

Slowly, I approach the king's bedside. He is reduced, what remains when a body wastes. His drooping skin resembles moist parchment, and my concern morphs beyond the bounds I have drawn, a spiraling panic threatening. Still breathing—for now. I wonder who will leave this earth first: me or Father.

It hurts to witness, this slow deterioration. I have cried, I have screamed, I have begged and demanded miracles of the gods. It has made no difference. When the Lord of the Mountain demands a life, the when and where and how of it will not change.

"How are you, Father?"

He takes a sharp, wheezing breath. "I was discussing the laws of Ammara with Amir. There is much he still has to learn."

"Why talk of such things now?" I lean forward, hand curled into a loose fist, as if I might hammer it upon that which builds before my eyes, this reality in which my brother rules and our father lies dead in the ground.

"The writing is on the wall, Sarai. I can no longer delay for fear of leaving Amir ignorant and uninformed. We cannot leave our people vulnerable."

What of me? It is a soundless cry, voiced only in my mind. "Father—"

"Enough. We will speak no more of this. Am I understood?"

I look to Amir. He looks at me.

"Understood," we murmur in unison.

While Amir pulls the king into further conversation, I select the empty seat next to my sister-in-law and dip my chin in greeting. "Tuleen."

She smiles, though it lacks the ease I would expect from genuine pleasure at seeing me. It is likely deserved. I have shown no willing kindness toward Tuleen—my own mistake. There are some days I could absolutely use another friend in the palace.

"I wanted to offer you an apology," I say.

She is watchful, but she dips her chin, signaling me to go on.

"I was unfair to judge you. You have shown nothing but kindness toward me—"

"Why did you?" Curt, clear, but kind.

I drop my eyes. "I feared you might treat me like the other women at court." Nevertheless, I lift my head and regard her with respect. "But you are better than them, better than me. I'm sorry for how poorly I treated you. I want you to know how glad I am that you're part of our family."

Tuleen glances away, blinking rapidly. She swallows before turning back to face me. "Thank you," she whispers.

That she is so willing to forgive is more than I deserve. And she is not the only one who's forgiveness I need. But an awkward silence descends, broken only by Amir's voice twining with that of the king. I ask Tuleen, "Have you visited Roshar yet, for your festival gown?"

"Roshar Hammad?" Her eyes widen. "But he is the royal tailor."

"And you are Ammara's future queen. It's your right to request his services."

Tuleen hunches forward in the chair. The silken strands of her unbound hair slip forward over her shoulders. "I don't know . . ."

"He's a friend of mine. I'll send him a message," I say. "We'll meet with him in, say, two days' time. I need a dress for the festival as well."

"You're sure?" Tuleen asks. "I don't want to intrude on your friendship."

"There's no intrusion. You deserve a gown fit for a queen. My sister-in-law shall be the best dressed in all of Ammara." My smile makes an appearance. It is genuine.

"The darkwalkers have been quelled?" King Halim suddenly rasps, the words garbled by fluid.

Shifting my attention, I reach for Father's hand. His fingers twitch in my grip, yet he does not tear his hand away. My throat tightens. I can't remember a time when I did not crave his affections. "You can thank Notus for that."

"Glad to know he's adequate at his job," Amir drawls sarcastically, regarding me with crossed arms from the other side of the bed. "Can the same be said for his role as your betrothed?"

Oh, he's not happy I kept that information from him. "As a matter of fact," I reply with false sweetness, "it can." Swiping the washcloth from the bedside table, I wet the fabric in the small pail of water at my feet and begin dabbing sweat from the king's neck.

Amir glowers with childlike petulance. Typical. "You should have told me."

I snort. "So you could run him off at the first opportunity? I don't think so."

"Why would I need to run him off," he counters, "when he does that on his own?"

He's not wrong. But I feel the inexplicable urge to shield the South Wind from my brother's indignation. The history between me and Notus is ours alone. Amir has nothing to do with it.

"Speaking of the South Wind." I rewet the cloth, wring the fabric free of water. "He will be accompanying us during the Festival of Rain."

King Halim attempts to sit up, but his arms tremble from the strain, and he sinks back into the pillows with a sound of frustration. "How am I to explain his presence to Prince Balior? He's under the impression you will come to your senses."

This again. Gently, I wipe along the king's collarbone where sweat pools. With the curtains drawn, the air is stifling. "As I've already told you, Father, I've made my decision. My mind will not change."

"Sarai." He sighs. "You must reject the South Wind's hand for the sake of our people. Please. If you show genuine remorse for your actions, there might still be time to win him over."

"Oh, *I* should apologize?" I scoff, tossing the cloth back into the pail. "For what? I agreed to court Prince Balior, but we were not formally engaged when Notus asked for my hand. We have done nothing wrong."

"Except having made me look a fool, and our realm weak."

Because it always comes back to Father's image. No mention of my life, my impending death, though I suppose he would not mention that in Amir and Tuleen's presence. "You must know that was not my intention—"

"Then what was your intention?" he demands. "Because as far as I'm concerned, everything you've done has been completely selfish."

Selfish.

A tinny ringing fills my ears. I stare, and I stare, and I stare, but my bewilderment fails to lessen, only morphs, becomes something else, something white-hot beneath my sternum. *Not now,* I think. *Wait until you are alone, without an audience. It's not proper. It's disrespectful. It's what Father would want.* But what about what *I* want? And so all that I have buried these long, long years rushes up and out, rupturing at last.

"If *anyone* is selfish," I spit, stabbing a finger at him, "it's you, Father. You, who have done nothing but belittle me, insult me, tear me down. You, who care more about impressing a visiting sovereign than your own daughter. You, who have never once made me feel as though I am free to be myself, never once made me feel as though I am loved just how I am."

It is so, so quiet. Amir and Tuleen are frozen in shock. My vision is too blurred by tears to make out Father's expression. It is for the better. I do not wish to witness yet more disappointment.

"Does it bring you joy," I wheeze, throat swelling with emotion, "to crush your children's spirits? Have the gods promised you a favorable afterlife if you can successfully mold your children into the same stern, rigid persona you possess?"

A soft, rattling inhalation breaks the stillness. King Halim shakes his head. "Sarai, I—"

"Let me tell you something, Father. I have done everything in my power to become this ideal princess, this perfect reflection of you. All the while—" I choke, suck in air, try again. "All the while, I feel myself slipping farther out of reach. It's clear I'll never live up to your impossible expectations. So I wonder: Why bother saving my life in the first place? As far as I can see, it was nothing but a waste of time."

Tuleen gasps.

A hard breath shudders out of me, and another. Before long, the sobs will descend. I intend to be far from this room when that occurs. "It would have been better for you to let me die. At least then you wouldn't be living in a state of perpetual disappointment."

King Halim has never appeared smaller beneath the blankets, his mouth hanging open in dismay, eyes darkened by turmoil.

Quietly, I let myself out.

18

"You're sure this is all right?" Tuleen asks me, studying the plaque before us in uncertainty.

Roshar Hammad. Royal Tailor.

"Absolutely." A swift *rat-tat-tat* against his door. "And I want to apologize again for the scheduling hiccup," I say. We were supposed to meet Roshar three days ago, but Prince Balior insisted on a ride through the city, then another darkwalker was spotted lurking in the palace grounds, which forced Turleen and I to shelter in our respective rooms until the threat was quelled.

"It's no trouble, really," she replies. "I'm just happy Roshar was able to accommodate us."

Less than a heartbeat later, it swings open. Roshar's wire-rimmed spectacles magnify his long-lashed eyes. His robe is a bright shade of orange, his trousers a contrasting blue.

The man positively preens in Tuleen's presence. "Your Highness." He makes a deep bow toward my sister-in-law. "And Your Other Highness." A shallower bow to me, the oaf.

"Tuleen, I'd like to formally introduce you to Roshar Hammad." I gesture at him as he straightens, adjusting his hair to his liking. "Not only does he have excellent taste in clothes, but he has excellent taste in pastries as well."

Tuleen smiles shyly. "Please," she says. "Call me Tuleen."

First-name basis with Ammara's queen-to-be? Roshar looks about ready to faint. "Come. Let Roshar see what we have to work with."

Inside his workroom, my sister-in-law examines the numerous works-in-progress curiously. A high-collared robe studded with clear beads draws her eye. The breadth in the shoulders signify a male garment, and the embellishment suggests a significant event, likely a wedding or funeral. Meanwhile, Roshar snags his measuring tape and begins to circle Tuleen, lower lip caught between his teeth.

"You have a gorgeous figure, very petite." He stops, tilts his head this way and that. "I'm thinking empire waist, gossamer fabric at the bodice. No pleats. We don't want Ammara's future queen to look outdated."

As he speaks, he pulls a small notebook from his pocket and begins to jot down ideas with a piece of charcoal. Then he snaps the notebook closed. "Let me take your measurements, dear, then I'll gather some fabric samples. All right?"

Dazed, Tuleen nods, watching him waltz to the other side of the room.

"He has that effect on people," I say to her.

"Oh!" Tuleen startles, and both hands fly to her mouth. "I forgot to tell him my favorite color!"

I snag her arm before she can approach Roshar, shaking my head in disapproval. "I wouldn't," I whisper.

"No?" Her voice drops to match mine. "Why not?"

"There are only two things you need to know about Roshar. The first is that he hates the color gray. Absolutely despises it." Those who have commissioned him to design a gray dress or robe generally aren't heard from again, interestingly enough. "The second is that he does not like being told what to do."

My sister-in-law steps back in surprise. "But I'm not telling him what to do. I just thought if he knew my favorite color, it might make the process a bit easier for him . . ." Tuleen trails off as I slowly shake my head. "No?"

"No." Sweeping an arm around her back, I guide her away from Roshar, just in case she decides to act rashly. "You're making the right decision," I assure her. "Trust me. Roshar has never steered me wrong. He has a gift. Your gown will be stunning, whatever the color or style."

While Roshar busies himself cutting fabric, Tuleen and I take a seat in the armchairs near the window. Beyond the palace walls, the streets have already begun to transform for the festival. Thousands of flowers have been strung along the walkways, between the shop rooftops. My heart sinks as I scan the courtyard below. No sign of Notus.

"How long have you known Roshar?" Tuleen asks, settling in.

"About a decade, give or take. He was the only person aside from Fahim who was willing to put up with me." Ten years later, he remains my only friend.

She glances over her shoulder to watch him pluck at a stack of fabric, charcoal caught between his teeth. He rounds the table, muttering to himself, head ducked as he completes a brief sketch in his notebook. "He seems very passionate about his work."

"He's a passionate person in general, but especially when it comes to fashion. By the way, do you have a Zarqan?"

Tuleen faces me, clearly puzzled. "I do."

"Don't tell him. He's obsessed with them and may take it when you're not looking." I smirk to show that I'm mostly joking, and Tuleen laughs. "Don't say I didn't warn you."

Roshar calls Tuleen over to take her measurements. Alone, I stare out the window, my thoughts beginning to stew. I haven't spoken to Father since my emotional outburst. I've considered apologizing. But it hurts to scream into a void. Hurts more to know my voice might never be heard.

Minutes later, Tuleen resettles into her chair. "How are things with your engagement?" she asks quietly.

Oh, gods. My engagement—fake engagement—is not a topic of conversation I care to discuss. But I've treated Tuleen quite poorly since her return to Ishmah, and she's never been deserving of the poison I myself have swallowed.

"Honestly?" I slouch lower in the cushioned chair. "Not great."

Tuleen seems surprised by my candid response, though she does her best to mask it. "I'm sorry to hear that."

My mood darkens. The last couple of weeks have been absolutely excruciating. The torment of sleeping in the adjacent chambers to Notus, hearing every shift of his mattress through the wall . . . I haven't slept well since he moved in.

"It's normal, isn't it?" I lift a hand in a gesture of indifference. "Relationships take effort. We all have our rough patches, right?"

Ammara's queen-to-be does not seem to agree with the sentiment. "Forgive me if I'm overstepping," she says, "but . . . I sense there's a history between you and the South Wind." She searches my face. Kind eyes, yet keen. "Or am I wrong?"

I'm surprised Amir hasn't spoken to his wife about it. Then again, the South Wind isn't a topic of conversation my brother cares to discuss.

"We were lovers years ago. We . . . didn't part on good terms." Indeed, I wasn't aware we had parted at all until I found him gone. "I never expected him to return." My jaw clenches. I force it to relax.

Tuleen's face softens with a compassion I have not often encountered. It warms me even as I fight the urge to duck and hide. "You're angry with him."

At Notus, Father, my circumstances. The South Wind doesn't deserve my anger. I know this. I'm trying to be better, to let go. It would be so much easier if a part of me—a larger part than I'm willing to admit—didn't crave his affection.

"I don't want to go too much into it," I say, "but he broke my trust, and yes, we're engaged now, but I learned my lesson once before. How can I trust that he won't break my heart a second time?" And how pathetic I must look to Tuleen. I didn't intend to bare my soul, but it poured out all the same.

My sister-in-law leans back, legs crossed, head tilted ponderously. "From where I stand, it looks like Notus is trying hard to rebuild the trust between you both." When I peer at Tuleen in question, she elaborates, "When he looks at you, I see that he cares for you, deeply. But it seems to me you're keeping him at arm's length. He's your betrothed.

At some point, you will either learn to trust him, or you won't. And if you won't, it will in all likelihood destroy your marriage."

Little does she know we won't ever reach the wedding. "This goes much deeper than the surface, Tuleen. You claim he's trying to rebuild trust? I don't see it."

"Why should he look upon a shut door and believe himself welcome?"

"You don't understand," I choke, fighting the sting in my chest. "Of course I would not let him in. He *left*." And I had no one. My mother, dead. Fahim, dead. Amir, lost in the throes of grief. Father, too, distanced himself, as he had always done. "It's obvious he didn't want me."

"You asked him this?" She regards me calmly.

I did not, for I was afraid of what he might say. I suppose a small part of me always clung to the idea that he left for something I had no control over, something that had nothing to do with me.

"He gave me his answer a long time ago," I tell her.

She raises a sleekly groomed eyebrow. "Have you considered that he might be hurting too? Maybe he's equally afraid of rejection."

Maybe. But I have been blinded before. I dare not close my eyes for fear of it happening again.

For a time, she gazes out the window, and her attention eventually finds the labyrinth. She frowns at the structure, yet goes on, "I know how scary it is to place yourself in a vulnerable position, Sarai. Believe it or not, I experienced something very similar with Amir at the start of our developing relationship. It took him a long time to open up to me. I didn't think he ever would. I guess what I'm saying is . . . I don't want you to lose a world-ending love out of fear."

My lips quaver. I press them together until they vanish into nothing. "Notus was welcome," I growl, low and coarse. "He was always welcome. I wanted to be his home. I thought I was." I'd given him my heart. I'd given him *everything*.

"Maybe you still are," Tuleen murmurs.

I want to scream, or flee. I will run until my lungs crumple and my legs collapse, and let the desert do the rest. But—enough. I've had enough of these *what-ifs*. History has been written. I cannot expend any additional energy questioning something I know is untrue. Notus is not mine. He never was.

Stiffly, I push to my feet, brush the wrinkles from my dress. "Apologies, but there's something I must see to." Three strides, and I'm across the room, Roshar glancing between us in confusion. If anyone notices the tears streaking my face, I will simply blame them on the sun.

The annual Festival of Rain arrives with a slash of reddish light breaking through dense cloud cover to the east. It begins on Mount Syr at high noon, where an offering will be made to the Lord of the Mountain, a prayer to usher in the rains that Ammara sorely needs. It ends on the fifth day, with a grand ball hosted in honor of our most esteemed god.

After slipping on a light linen dress and settling a laurel crown on my brow, I dab color onto my cheeks, swipe kohl beneath my eyes. I purse my lips in the mirror. The puffiness above my cheeks can't be helped. Last night, I awoke twice. Once due to the Lord of the Mountain whispering in my ear, reminding me that my time nears. And again, to the sound of Notus' pacing. I wondered whether he had donned his sleep robe, or if he wore only trousers, or nothing at all. I'm not sure which thought haunts me more.

But I can't avoid the day. And so, girding myself for what is to come, I turn toward the interconnecting door, only to find Notus already framed in the doorway, form haloed in amber light.

I blink in surprise, my stomach lurching toward my chest. "You startled me." A second thought chases on its heels. "Were you watching me?"

He gives me a slow once-over as if in answer. My face warms. "You're already dressed."

I can't discern his tone. Is he suggesting he would rather I *wasn't* dressed? As soon as the thought manifests, I promptly toss it away.

He enters the room, yet another shadow among darkness. I retreat toward the window, dawn's pearly light visible through the dusty glass. From this angle, the rising sun drizzles orange light across the room, catching the green of Notus' robes, the curled strands of his disheveled hair.

"Why have you been avoiding me?" he asks.

Arms crossed, I regard him coolly. "Funny," I say. "I was under the impression *you* were avoiding *me*." I've seen neither hide nor hair of him since my visit to the infirmary. Not for lack of trying, however.

He regards me in puzzlement. "What reasons would I have to avoid you, aside from completing my rounds?"

I do not deign to answer, for I fear his reasons are many, though I do not want to know them. "You are aware our rooms share a connecting door? It's not difficult to knock if you desire my company."

"You didn't knock either."

"Did you hope I would?"

The question slips out. I swallow hard, well aware I cannot call it back.

Notus taps a finger against his thigh. His sword hangs alongside it. "And if I did?" His dark eyes meet mine. I wasn't expecting, well, *that*. I don't know how to respond to it. The immortal exasperates me to no end. I cannot bull my way to his surrender.

"If you want to spend time with me, all you have to do is knock," I say, pleased that I sound quite unaffected by this awkward conversation.

"It would be easier to approach you," he says, "if you did not act like I carried a pox."

Really? "I don't act like you carry a pox."

He levels me a pointed look.

All right, maybe I do act like that, just a touch. A smidge. A small bit. But that's only to avoid having to confront my body's urges when he is in close proximity—as he is now. "Fine. Should we hold hands then?" I suggest.

Notus shifts his weight, clearly tense. "Isn't that typically frowned upon in your culture? Displays of affection in public, I mean?"

My blush continues to crawl along my cheeks and neck. "An engaged couple may hold hands, even in Ammara. But you're right. It was a stupid idea. Forget I mentioned it." *Stupid, stupid, stupid.* "Let's get this over with, shall we?" If we play our parts well, hopefully we'll show the world—and Prince Balior—how truly in love we are. The prince will lay down his sword. He will swallow his surrender. And he will leave, taking his army with him.

Together, we descend the stairs to the front courtyard, where Father, Amir, and Tuleen have gathered, their horses readied for the journey to Mount Syr. Cheers erupt beyond the shut gates, Ishmah's citizens having assembled to line the streets. Behind them, the guards are positioned in rows of two, forty men deep.

My sister-in-law wears a simple olive dress that accentuates the green in her hazel eyes. She offers me a shy smile, and I return it, ashamed of the way I'd departed Roshar's workroom earlier in the week. I'll have to apologize when I get the chance.

I'm not certain whether Amir and Notus have made amends since my brother threatened to skewer the god with his sword, the fool. To my absolute horror, Prince Balior already sits astride his horse, observing me with a keen eye. When his attention falls to the South Wind, he frowns, but not before I spot the panic flickering across his expression.

The South Wind bows to the king. "Your Majesty."

"Father." I dip my chin stiffly, accepting Zainab's reins from the hostler. My mare stamps her hoof with a loud *clop*.

King Halim glances between me and Notus. My heart thuds sickeningly, for I am fully expecting a scathing remark or disapproving look, but to my surprise, there is a sad crimp to his mouth. If I were less of a cynic, I might believe it to be regret. "Sarai—"

"We don't want to be late for the start of the ceremony, right Papa?" I hold his watery gaze until he looks elsewhere. This is the last place I want to discuss the topic of our recent parting, especially with Prince Balior present. Today will be difficult enough. I must be blissful, engrossed, in high spirits, never mind the guilt surrounding this sham of an engagement, the regret I feel toward my father.

"Yes," Father croaks, suddenly doubtful. "You're right. It would be in poor taste to be tardy, and I do not want to offend the Lord of the Mountain." At last, he wanders toward the head of the procession, allowing me the space to breathe.

The South Wind dips his mouth to my ear. "What was that about?" he murmurs.

I shake my head, too inundated by emotion to speak. Zainab nudges my shoulder. I rub her neck, and the motion soothes me. With her, I can just be.

When I push toward the head of the procession, however, my hand is suddenly caught in a warm, solid grasp. My head snaps toward Notus, who gazes at me with deep, deep eyes. I hear what he does not say: *I am with you.* His hand, and mine, tightly clasped. It means more than I can say.

"I thought you didn't want to draw attention with public displays of affection?" I quip, though my mouth eases into a curve, no heat behind the words, just warmth.

The corner of his mouth hitches in reflection to mine. "Anything to hasten Prince Balior's departure, I figure."

He gives my hand a gentle squeeze before helping me mount Zainab. Seconds later, he swings himself into the saddle behind me, muscled thighs pressed against the outside of my own, wide chest brushing my back.

I stiffen as my eyes pop wide. "What are you doing!" I hiss. When I attempt to slide forward, the curve of the saddle forces me back. I remain in place, my position awkwardly held, wooden. "Where's your horse?"

"We'll ride together."

"That's not an answer!" When I spot Amir gazing at us with interest—and perhaps a bit of loathing toward the South Wind— I mellow my expression, wiping the shock and dismay from my features.

Notus and I are supposed to be in love. Happy. Comfortable in one another's company. A large part of me wishes that were so, that we did not have to perform for thousands. That I could be loved, just as Sarai.

"I intend to keep you close," he explains, and as I shift my head, his lips brush the shell of my ear. I bite my tongue so as to dam the whimper threatening to spill into the open. "After the last attack, I won't take chances."

Yes, yes, it all makes perfect sense, but it is a two-hour journey to Mount Syr. How am I to bear being pressed against the South Wind like a waxen seal?

The gates heave open like giants of old. Cheers peal out, Ishmah's brightest faces welcoming our procession with joyful greetings and flowers tossed into the streets. The Queen's Road slithers down the central hill, framed by thousands of citizens gathered for the festival. Flowers adorn every doorway, every cart and wagon. They are even twined around the necks of goats and dogs.

Notus and I rock side to side atop the mare. I do my best to ignore the brush of his chest against my back, but it has the irksome power of claiming my thoughts. One of his hands rests along my thigh, heavy with heat. The other clasps the reins.

Amir and Tuleen ride ahead with Father. As luck would have it, Prince Balior rides beside us on a chestnut gelding.

"Lovely weather today," the prince comments.

I offer him a close-lipped smile. "Indeed."

I hope this will put an end to the conversation, but Prince Balior then says, "Will you have time for a cup of tea this week?"

"Doubtful," the South Wind cuts in irritably. "Princess Sarai and I will be quite busy. I'm sure you can understand."

Prince Balior's mouth thins. "Of course." He glances between us, expression dubious. Notus and I sit stiffly in the saddle—like two thorn bushes rather than two people in love. I'm considering how best to respond when Notus' hand slides up my thigh to curve around my hip. I nearly choke on my tongue. The gesture is a claiming. It says, *Mine.*

With a curled upper lip, the prince faces forward, nudging his gelding into a trot. I expect Notus to remove his hand now that Prince Balior's attention is elsewhere, but he keeps it in place. I am painfully aware of his spread fingers, their heat through the fabric of my dress.

As we approach the gate separating the upper and lower rings, someone tosses a fresh bouquet onto the ground. Ebon petals, colored violet in the low light. Before I can fully process the sight, we trot past, easing around a bend in the cobblestoned road.

The first stirrings of unease ooze through me. Black iris. I recall that woman from the market over a month ago. It was my duty to report her. But . . . she wasn't hurting anyone, and so long as I keep my distance from the deadly blooms, I've no reason to worry.

We exchange the jeweled windows and stately homes of the upper ring for the cracked doors and dilapidated porches of the lower ring, refuse piled high in the narrower alleyways. The capital is still in the midst of reconstruction following the darkwalker attacks. Yesterday, Amir and I attended a meeting with the king's council to discuss what could be done to accommodate those who lost their homes. Funds will be redistributed to provide temporary shelter until the structures are rebuilt.

As though sensing my distress, the South Wind tightens his arm around my stomach in comfort. I waver, but eventually allow myself to sink against his chest with a grateful sigh. The thump of his heartbeat thuds along my spine. If I'm not mistaken, it picks up pace.

Hours later, we summit Mount Syr, where the earth is cracked and reddened, and the wind cuts the sand into glass atop the bluff. The heat is boiling. The sun is a brutal whiteness reflected across the hills and troughs of Ammara's dunes. Fanning out in a half-moon around the throne, the procession watches King Halim kneel before the dais, head bowed. Does he plead, as he did a quarter of a decade ago? Does he bargain, or demand? Whatever he offers our Lord of the Mountain, he doesn't speak it aloud.

Amir and Tuleen are next. Once they have spoken their prayer, they clear the area, and I kneel, easing forward until my forehead brushes the carved stone of the first step.

Lord of the Mountain?

A coarse wind cuts across my back, and I shiver, sensing his presence, though he does not appear.

Hello, Sarai. What have you come to offer me?

Out of the corner of my eye, I watch Prince Balior approach the South Wind. As they converse, the prince gestures with his hands in evident frustration. Notus, unsurprisingly, remains calm.

Returning my attention to the task at hand, I reply, *I'm not here to offer you anything. I'm here to beg for your mercy.*

The wind abruptly dies.

Members of the Royal Guard glance around in apprehension. Here, atop the bluff, the air is always stirring, building into distant storms. I wait, nape prickling, for the Lord of the Mountain to smite me down. Perhaps I could have worded my request with a bit more reverence.

Please, I press. *I don't want to die. I want to live, I—* My fingernails dig crescent moons into my soft palms. *You owe me nothing. I know this. But my father is a good man who only wanted to save me. Why must I be punished for something I had no control over? I was just an infant.* A terse breath hits the back of my clenched teeth. *I'm begging you. Please, won't you help me?*

But the Lord of the Mountain does not answer.

On our return to the palace, King Halim is stopped by a haggard woman clutching a swaddled infant to her breast. The child is sickly. Wan face and yellow eyes. Paces behind, I am frozen atop the horse I share with Notus, stricken.

"Please," says the mother, lifting her child toward the king. "I would ask for your blessing, Your Majesty. I have beseeched the Lord of the Mountain, but he continues to ignore my pleas. You are my last hope if my son is to live."

One of the soldiers begins shoving the interloper aside when Father lifts a hand. "Wait." Slumped forward in his saddle, he considers the woman before turning to one of his guards. "Help me down from my horse."

The South Wind dismounts as well, positioning himself nearer to the king for protection. I watch Father take the baby into his arms. I remember a time when he gifted blessings most generously. Monthly, he ventured into the city. Young and old, healthy and infirm, none were turned away. Following Fahim's death, he no longer paraded the streets, choosing instead to cloister himself behind the palace walls.

As Father bestows a kiss on the infant, a queue begins to form. The king's blessing, more valuable than coin. Slowly, he makes his way down the line, until his crown slips out of sight.

Meanwhile, attention shifts from King Halim and settles onto the South Wind. At first, I can't discern what the crowd is saying. The city sounds drown out but the nearest voices. Eventually, however, I catch their topic of conversation: my betrothal to Notus.

I hesitate before dismounting from Zainab, the Royal Guard driving back the gathering. "You are quite the person of interest," I murmur to the South Wind. From their saddles, Amir and Tuleen watch King Halim bless Ishmah's citizens.

"Give the princess a kiss!" someone cries.

The crowd stirs. Their mouths run away from them. *Kiss? Did I hear that right?* Holding hands as an engaged couple is harmless. Kissing is another beast entirely. Prince Balior still sits astride his horse, the clench of his jaw exposing his outrage.

"You say you're truly engaged to the South Wind?" another person calls. "Then prove it!"

Soon, a second voice piles onto the first, and a third, until the chant rolls over our party.

Kiss, kiss, kiss, kiss, kiss, kiss, kiss . . .

I clear my throat, shift my attention to Notus, whose eyes come to rest on my face. Strands of dark hair poke from beneath his headscarf. He looks . . . not terrified, exactly, but wary. My cheeks heat in the passing moments. We made an agreement, he and I. Notus vowed to help me until Prince Balior departed Ammara. Watching the woman promised to him kiss another man—it might be enough to drive the prince from Ishmah for good.

I'm not sure who moves first, but somehow, I find myself in the South Wind's arms, as though we have irrevocably agreed to do whatever is necessary to maintain this charade, damn the consequences. My vision momentarily blurs as his scent surrounds me. I sigh against his neck. Notus stiffens.

"It doesn't mean anything," I murmur, for his ears only.

Kiss, kiss, kiss, kiss, kiss!

"Right." He grips my hip with a broad palm. "It's for show."

I curl my hand into the front of his robe, drat its trembling. "Exactly." His eyes begin to heat. I do not think I'm imagining it. "What if . . ."

My lungs hollow out. "What?"

He shakes his head, and the bristle sketching his jaw scrapes my cheek. My stomach drops so swiftly I swear it splatters at my feet. "Never mind," he murmurs.

I can't help the feeling of disappointment that follows. I'd thought . . . but no, that's stupid. We promised to put on a show. And if it's a show the people want, it's a show they shall get.

Easing back, I peer at him through my eyelashes, our mouths a hairsbreadth apart.

"Do it," I murmur.

A chaste thing. A small, impersonal peck. That was the intent. But the moment Notus' lips touch mine, I open for him, drawing him as easily as a needle draws thread, into the velvet darkness of memory.

As soon as my tongue brushes his, something snaps in him. He growls low and gathers me close. His fingers spear through my hair. He tilts back my head, plundering my mouth of every sweet drop. His hunger is like mine: a bottomless pit. It pulls me down, and I go willingly, any semblance of modesty forgotten.

I didn't expect this, but . . . I want it. I want *him*, the way a river seeks the sea. The circumstances that have forced us together aren't ideal, but I can't deny I still feel things for this immortal. I *crave* him.

A collective "*Ooooh*" sounds, and we jerk apart like startled rabbits. The surrounding crowd is a streaming blur of color. My mouth feels tender, like a bruise. The South Wind's face is nearly as red as mine.

"Again!" someone shouts. "Kiss again!"

"I think that's enough for today," I state loudly, so it carries to the farthest reaches of the street. When Notus catches my eye, I hurriedly look elsewhere, fearing he can sense my erratic breathing.

This is going to be a long day indeed.

"Princess Sarai. A word?"

I turn to face Prince Balior. We arrived back at the palace less than an hour ago, my mouth still tender from Notus' kiss. The South Wind fled to his chambers as if pursued by death itself. I tell myself not to take it personally.

"I apologize, Prince Balior, but I need to change for dinner. Might we have this conversation over tonight's lamb?"

"All I ask is five minutes of your time." He steps closer, and a rush of clove-scented air barrages my senses. My eyes water from the strength of it. "Please."

There is an earnestness to his expression I have not seen previously. It looks ill-fitted against his features. The sooner we have this conversation, the sooner I can return to *not* thinking about the kiss.

I nod, gesturing him into a vacant sitting room. He sinks onto an armchair. I select its turquoise-colored neighbor. Through the tall, arched windows spanning one wall, Mount Syr thrusts upward to pierce the blue, blue sky.

"First," he says, "I wish to apologize for my behavior of late." He sits straight in his chair, gaze direct. "It has been difficult coping with the knowledge that even the best-laid plans can veer off course."

I nod in understanding, despite the disquiet worming through me. "I accept your apology."

He appears relieved, and relaxes into the cushions. "I also want to apologize for keeping you in the dark regarding my research, as I mentioned during the ball. I promised to help you find a solution regarding the darkwalkers plaguing Ammara." His foot taps once, twice, then stills. "I consider myself a man of my word, and I failed to keep that promise."

"It's all right," I reassure. "We have both been busy. I would not expect you to drop everything in order to cater to my needs."

"Regardless, I'm disappointed in myself." Leaning forward, he props his elbows on his thighs, fingers loosely linked between his legs. "I haven't put forth my best effort. Consequently, I sabotaged our relationship before it ever had the opportunity to flourish. And now the darkwalkers have attacked the city . . . I feel terrible. You could have been killed."

None of Prince Balior's men were reported among the casualties, as far as I know. Could that mean some level of involvement? Difficult to say. As for the rest, I do believe he is remorseful, but what's done is done. "Prince Balior—"

"Can I ask *why* you broke off our courtship?" He studies me in a ponderous manner, like I am something to be dissected. I've the inane urge to shield my chest with my arms. "When I thought deeply on the matter," he continues, "I couldn't believe that my research was the crux of it. After all, I've been open with you about my fascination with the labyrinth, haven't I?"

"You have."

Prince Balior nods, pleased that his hunch was correct. "Was it something I said? Have I offended you in any way, your culture or your people?"

This conversation feels far more fragile than I had expected it to. I do not wish to offend Prince Balior further. Neither do I wish to anger him. Ammara is unstable enough and cannot shield itself against additional strain. Has Prince Balior invited darkness into Ammara's heart?

"I know it may be difficult to accept," I say, "but the South Wind and I have a history, and while a union with Um Salim would provide certain advantages, the South Wind is still the most powerful being in the realm. Binding my life to his comes with undeniable advantages."

He shakes his head, mouth quirked in an emotion that is decidedly not humor. "See, that doesn't make sense to me. King Halim was quite aggressive in his pursuit of joining our realms. He was also enraged to learn of your deceit. It gave me the impression that there was another reason you rejected my proposal."

Since our conversation during the ball, I've questioned the next step. What is the good of trying to free myself if my people turn around and find themselves conquered by Um Salim? But maybe I've been navigating this all wrong. I've been acting on assumption only. Not truth. Not evidence. As a result, I've failed to give the prince an opportunity to defend himself.

"If we are to become husband and wife," I begin slowly, "then I would expect you to act with integrity. You must be someone whose word I could trust."

"You can't trust my word?"

Deep breath. In, and out. "I . . . came across certain information that made me question your motivation for agreeing to the marriage."

"Ah." His head drops forward, hand pressed against his mouth. "The army."

When he lifts his gaze, I've the distinct feeling of having been cornered, despite sitting in a spacious room, a hot breeze coasting through the open windows. I've a handful of seconds to determine how I might react.

I reply with a single word. "Why?"

He smiles, a little bit sharp, a little bit mean. "For the same reason your father stationed guards at my chambers and has a handful of his men shadowing me at every turn. I can't forget our history. Ammara and Um Salim have been politically strained for decades. Can you blame a man for requiring safety when visiting an enemy nation?"

As a matter of fact, I cannot. "Why did you fail to divulge this information to the king?"

"But I did."

"What?"

"With all the darkwalker attacks, I asked King Halim if my men might take refuge within the capital, and he agreed."

Never in my wildest dreams would I believe Father to welcome an army into Ishmah's walls. As his sickness worsens, I fear the deterioration of his mind.

"If it would ease your worry," the prince says, "I will remind him at tonight's meal that my men remain in the city. If he requests that the troops be removed from the capital, I will dismiss them without argument."

Admittedly, it would do much to ease the strain on my nerves. "Thank you."

"Is that enough reason for you to reconsider our engagement?"

My hands drop onto my lap. The lead bracelet gleams dully. "I don't know," I say honestly. And that is the best I can offer at the moment. "Whether or not this has been a misunderstanding, I'm still engaged to the South Wind."

"You've already shown how easily a promise can be broken." He levels me a pointed look.

And that, too, is a truth. Though I will need to think deeper on what I truly want, what is best for Ammara's future. "I will think on it."

"That's all I can ask of you."

Once standing, the prince dips his chin toward me, seemingly in better spirits than he was prior to this conversation. "Good day to you, Princess Sarai."

And so the festival unfolds. Each evening, following time spent in the city, offerings placed and markets attended, I return to my quarters, sunburned and dehydrated, yet filled with joy at spending time among my people. One night, Notus knocks on the interconnecting door between our rooms. I all but trip in my haste to open it.

"Hello," I say breathlessly, swiping strands of hair from my eyes.

The South Wind lifts an eyebrow in curiosity. "King Halim requests our attendance in his chambers."

My heart sinks. Right. Because of course that would be the only reason for Notus to knock. The last thing I need is Father challenging my engagement yet again. I'm not ready to speak to him just yet. "Can't we just . . . take a walk?"

I would like that, I think, to walk with the South Wind in the streets of Ishmah, and to blend past with present.

Soon we are strolling the King's Road, veering toward one of the public gardens. All is quiet but for the sounds of Ishmah bedding down. The stamp of horses' hooves. The din of merchants closing up shop. The snap of cloth, laundry hung out to dry on ropes woven from goat hair and strung between buildings.

"I heard you and Prince Balior spoke privately the other day," Notus murmurs, hands behind his back as we ease around a corner. Moonlight brightens the paving stones, gleams silver across the rooftops.

I fight the urge to look at him. "We did." My slippers scuff the hard ground.

He hesitates, and from the corner of my eye, I watch him fight the urge to look at me, too. "It's none of my business, but I can't help but wonder why you keep giving him the time of day, considering what we know of him."

I'm not sure whether to be pleased that Notus is affected by my conversation with the prince, or irked that he doesn't trust me. "Prince Balior doesn't surrender easily, and I'm wary of angering him now that he intends to stay. Better if he thinks he has a chance to change my mind about the engagement."

"Would you?" He pulls me to a halt in the middle of the street. The garden entrance lies only steps away, its wrought iron gates a shield over interlacing leaves. "Change your mind?"

"What?" I stare at him, completely flummoxed. "About Prince Balior?"

He glances away in what I believe to be embarrassment. "It's not that problematic of a question, is it?"

The longer I study the South Wind, the more certain I am of one truth: he cares. More than I realized, more than he is willing to admit. The thought warms me, ears to toes. "No," I say softly. "I suppose it's not."

"Do you feel anything for him?" His gaze returns to mine, imploring.

"Aside from mistrust? No." Then I do something utterly foolish, and glance down at his mouth.

It curves slightly, as though he senses where my attention has shifted. "I've actually been meaning to talk to you," he says.

"Oh?" I am calm, absolutely calm. "About what?"

"The kiss."

I tilt my head curiously. "Which one?"

The South Wind scans my face. His eyes drop, dragging across my bared neck to the neckline of my dress. Lower, to where the fabric bands across my breasts and waist. My mouth goes parchment dry. Only by sheer force of will do I manage not to faint. "Does it matter?" he asks.

I'm not a corpse. I've thought of both kisses an embarrassing amount. But I refuse to inform *him* of that. This immortal, who has more power over me than he knows. And now I question if the mistake was mine, to have invited him on a walk through the city at dusk, placing myself within arm's reach of his heat and scent.

"I'm telling myself to let it go," he murmurs. "To not look too deeply into something. But—" And then he lifts his head, eyes very dark. "I wanted it. And you wanted it, too."

The ground slowly slips from under me, the world skewed at an angle. "You're sure about that?" It's the first thing out of my mouth— and it's the wrong sentiment entirely.

Notus tilts back his head, scrubs his face, hard. I'm given barely a glimpse of his wounded expression before he strides ahead.

"And there you go walking away," I snap, stomach dropping toward my toes at the sight of his retreating back. "It's what you do best."

"That's unfair." He pivots, glaring with hot eyes. "No matter how many times I attempt to communicate with you, you either deflect or place undue blame onto me."

"Undue?" My eyes all but bulge from their sockets. "Are you ser—"

"Half the time, I don't understand what you want," he cuts in, tossing up a hand. "You want me close. You want me gone. You want me to kiss you. You want me to stop. You want my company, you despise my company."

Does he think he is alone in his confusion?

"Do you think this is easy for me?" I hiss. "I want to be near you, but then sometimes, I feel like I need to run. I can't explain it. It's like my body remembers what it was like when you were gone, and I need to leave before you make that choice for me."

He scoffs. "So this is my fault, is that what you're saying?"

"What? No!"

"So what do you want?" he demands.

"I don't know." The words are thrust through gritted teeth. "I'm trying to tell you—"

"You do know," he says. "But you're afraid."

Why do I fail to speak plainly? Stupid question. I know why. What might Notus think if he were to see how deep my fear of driving him —or anyone—away runs?

The South Wind stares down the deserted road, his expression cast in shadow. The public garden, so near yet so far. If only we had reached the iron gates. Might this miscommunication have been smoothed over? "I think I understand," he says.

How could he? If he knew my heart, he would never have left. So he must have seen something that he did not want, some flaw in me.

"You know what? This was a mistake." Arms crossed, I angle away from him. "We should return to the palace, discuss whatever it is Father wants to discuss." Though that only succeeds in plunging my mood into a darker place. "It might be better if we spoke with him separately."

He shakes his head. If I were not absolutely certain of Notus' restraint, I might worry that he would put a hole through the wall of a nearby shop. "And how will that look to everyone?" he demands, voice rising. "We're engaged."

"It doesn't matter!" I scream. "It was never real to begin with!"

I have misstepped. That is made absolutely clear as Notus' eyes shutter and he retreats a few paces. A small, pained sound falls from his mouth. It is too broken to be a laugh. "You know why I returned, Sarai? Not because your father sent for me. Because I believed our story remained unfinished. But you have made it clear since I walked through those throne room doors that I am not welcome in your life. So why do I continue to fight?" he grinds out, every shattered word forced from his throat. "Why do I continue clinging to hope?"

I fight for breath. It hurts to witness his pain. "Hope for what?"

"As if you don't already know."

I barge into my chambers with all the wrath of a storm. The door slams shut with enough force to rattle the picture frames along the walls. A single lamp casts amber onto the patterned rugs and heavy curtains.

I spot my violin case in the open wardrobe. It rests beside my music stand, which sags beneath the weight of études, sonatas, the occasional show piece, all coated in dust. Kneeling beside the case, I run my hand along its oblong shape. There had been a time when particularly tempestuous emotions would draw the violin toward my chin, hours spent in concentration until I calmed. The moment my fingers brush the metal clasps, however, something falters in me, and I shove it aside.

With a groan of frustration, I toss myself onto the mattress, limbs spread, staring at the ceiling. My skin is flushed, my nipples peaked. A dull pulse between my legs, and my eyes flutter shut as I cup my breasts in my palms, squeezing slightly. I'm not sure what is more humiliating: Notus hacking my defenses to shreds, or the fact that I still desire him despite his blasted refusal to explain why he left all those years ago.

Our hungry kiss before the public resurfaces. The engagement is a farce. It will collapse should anyone scrutinize it too closely. But we have history, Notus and I. It endures despite my attempts to kill it.

Sometimes, the best cure for sexual frustration is sexual vengeance.

I'm hitching up my dress when a floorboard squeaks from the other side of the wall.

Slowly, I push into a seated position against the pillows. The ground vibrates beneath the force of the South Wind's tread. His footsteps pause, perhaps near the window. I imagine he stares down at the labyrinth, as I have done, and questions its purpose and presence. Shortly after, clothing thumps onto the ground. Then, the creak of his bedframe: Notus, settling into bed.

The layout of our suites are reflections of one another, which means his bed shares a wall with mine. The realization sends my pulse racing. If needed, I could knock against the wall, and Notus might answer. I'm easing back into the pillows when a low rasp snags my attention. It comes again, a sound of drawn-out tension, a stifled groan.

The hair on my body spikes in awareness. My ears recognize what my eyes cannot. I straighten, blankets bunched in my hands.

The South Wind touches himself on the other side of the wall.

My sweaty palm slides down my torso, balls into a fist against my quivering stomach. When I was younger, I would lie awake in bed and imagine what might happen should the South Wind enter my room. I envisioned the hot glide of his tongue. I anticipated the heat of his breath, the flex of muscle, the thrust of hips.

As his bed begins to knock against the wall in a slow rhythm, I quickly shed my dress and undergarments, grabbing the small vial of oil from my bedside table drawer. Gods, I am too twisted for words. The South Wind is a man grown. He has a right to privacy. But I've my own release to tend to. A woman has needs. Surely none can blame me for scratching an itch?

Legs spread, I slip my oiled fingers down my drenched center. My flesh quivers in excitement as I guide my hand to the small nub shielded behind the thatch of dark hair. The slightest brush sends pleasure curling through me, and I whimper.

I stare up at the ceiling, imagining the South Wind's muscled torso arranged against the blankets. He would be naked, bronzed skin dusted in sparse black hair. His sex would hang heavy between his powerful thighs. His eyes, all pupils.

My core clenches in response, yet I do not allow the circular motion to falter. It propels me, higher and tighter and brighter. My toes curl. My heels dig into the mattress. Sweat dampens my skin, plastering the bedsheets to my flushed body. An ache spirals through my pelvis like a bowstring drawn taut.

Then there are his hands: wide of palm, thick fingers toughened by calluses. I imagine them slipping between my thighs, gliding through my wet folds. His fingers slowly penetrating my entrance, a feeling of fullness gathered there. As a trembling spreads outward from my core, I bite my lip, angle my hips nearer to my hand. More pressure. A firm pinch against the bud, and I cry out, the coiling in my pelvis exploding outward in a wave of warm, shimmering pleasure.

Sated, I sag into the mattress, among the wool blankets and cotton sheets. My eyelids begin to sink shut.

Someone hammers against the connecting door. I startle, a scream wrenched from my chest.

"Sarai?" Notus calls. "Sarai, open the door!"

I sit rigidly in place, face flushed, hand shoved between my thighs. My teeth grind in frustration. "What do you want?"

"Let me in."

"Oh, *now* you want to speak with me?" My voice cracks. "It's late, Notus."

"If you don't let me in, I'm breaking down this door."

My head falls back against the pillows, eyes squeezed shut. The heat of climax begins to disperse in the passing moments. "Just a moment,"

I croak. *Shit.* Snagging a clean cloth from my armoire, I wipe between my legs, beneath my damp underarms, before tossing the cloth onto my bedside table and hurriedly pulling my dress back on. Fumbling the lock, I heave the door open.

His broad figure demarcates the shadowy interior of his chambers. Loose trousers hang low on his hips, his muscled abdomen unfairly taut. The bare expanse of his chest fills my vision. I see nothing else. "What do you want?" I demand breathlessly.

"Are you all right?"

Only when I yank my attention from his pectoral muscles does my addled mind make sense of his question. "Excuse me?"

Notus stares at me as if I am a simpleton. "I heard a cry." At my confusion, he explains, "You sounded like you were in distress."

A subtle heat warms my cheeks. *Distress.* That's one word for it. I didn't realize my release had been so, well, exuberant.

"I'm fine, as you can see." I gesture toward my rumpled dress impatiently. "Now if you'll excuse me." I begin to shut the door.

His foot catches the jamb. Our eyes collide, mine cautious, his skeptical. One hard push, and Notus forces his way inside.

Arms crossed over my chest, I track his powerful form across the room. Beneath my dress, my nipples pebble to points. "Just because we share a connecting door does not mean you are free to come and go as you please. Shall I call the guards?"

Notus doesn't respond, instead vanishing into my study, apparently searching for something. Moments later, he reappears before venturing into my bathing chambers, then my sitting room. As his attention passes over my rumpled bed, however, he halts. I realize with horror that the cloth I'd used to wipe myself clean is balled atop the bedside table, the bottle of oil resting beside it.

Clearing my throat, I step forward, drawing his focus away from the damning evidence. "What do you want, Notus? I don't appreciate having my rest disturbed."

"No one is here?" he presses. "You are alone?"

I lift a hand, drop it. "Clearly."

Once more, his attention returns to the cloth. I've half a mind to toss it out the window, though that would certainly reinforce the truth of its purpose. But really, what have I to be ashamed of? Nothing. I was simply doing as the gods intended. Why should a woman not pleasure herself in the privacy of her rooms, as all men do?

Slowly, he angles toward me. I am not aware I'm holding my breath until the pinch behind my sternum forces me to exhale. "You were pleasuring yourself?"

My chest flares with heat. It is wrong for such filthy words to be wrapped in so rich a sound. "I was," I state. "As were you." When my eyes drop to the front of his trousers, I'm met with the unmistakable stiffness of his erection. "Do you deny it?"

And the South Wind says, "I do not."

Dark pleasure slides through me. Here are unexplored riches, and I wish to pry them open, plunder every delicious drop. "Did you think of me?" I ask, reaching for Notus, my hand cupping his erection through his trousers. I press my thumb against the wide head. It leaps in my grip, a hard, throbbing heat. "Did you think of my mouth on you? How it might feel for our bodies to relearn one another's? To think, we could have found release together, instead of attending to our needs separately."

Beneath my touch, his will weakens. I am glad of it. I will topple him stone by stone. And when all that remains is dust and ruin, I will begin the process all over again.

"Let me make something absolutely clear," he says. "There is only one person I desire in this life, and that is you." The low, gritty texture of his voice rakes across my skin like coarse grains of sand. "The thoughts I have of you . . ."

I swallow, hard. "Wh-what thoughts?"

His eyes are wholly black. "I wish to fill my hands with your curves. To clamp your ripened flesh in my palms and mark your skin with my mouth so that all who gaze upon you will know you're mine."

My mouth parts, the shock of his words staggering me.

"What do I desire?" he continues, easing nearer, one hand claiming the curve of my hip. "The sweetness of your throat poured into mine.

The clasp of your sex around my cock. The pliancy of your limbs, your breathlessness, the racing of your heart alongside mine. You ask what I desire?" His voice drops lower, if possible. "Everything that you can give me."

I can neither move nor speak nor breathe.

"Do you not see how I hunger for you, Sarai? Do you not recognize how I pace this cage, eager for whatever scrap of affection you toss my way?"

A pinch behind my ribs. I feel breathless with the understanding that it has caused him pain, this wanting and pacing and waiting and yearning. It completely overwhelms my defenses. "So why did you leave me? Because I'm not enough?"

He looks like I've slapped him. "No, Sarai." He is suddenly cold. "It's not you. It's me, it's . . ." Notus retreats a step—just one.

My heart sinks. "You're leaving." All I want is an explanation, honesty. Yet he is always running.

His gaze holds mine. I haven't the courage to break it. "We travel to Mirash at the end of the week," he reminds me. "Don't forget."

"Don't worry," I mutter to his retreating back. "I won't."

19

"I S THIS SUFFICIENT FOR YOUR SILENCE?"

The guard, his face shadowed, regards my outstretched hand in uncertainty.

Inwardly, I sigh. He drives a hard bargain, this one. Very well. A gentle clink as I drop another coin onto the pile rising from my palm. To the east, the sky begins to pale. I haven't much time.

"Your Highness—"

"What have I told you, Emin?" I understand his concern. Truly, I do. It is early, an unusual time to venture from the palace.

The capital sleeps. It didn't take long to slip from my rooms unnoticed and ready Zainab in the deserted stables. My mare stands calmly, tail lazily flicking at flies. Notus will not seek me out until seven—the time we agreed to depart. By then, I plan to be far from Ishmah's gates. I don't need an escort. What I need is freedom. Mirash is half a day's journey northwest, and I'm perfectly capable of traveling alone. Once I reach our destination, I'll wait for Notus at the entrance. Barring delays, we will return home by nightfall.

The young man's lips quiver. A tuft of facial hair sprouts from his chin. "That I'm not to address you by your official title."

"And?"

"And that you have the power to make my life very difficult if I do not obey."

I have taught him well. "Excellent." I add another coin onto the growing pile.

As Emin ogles the heap of gold, I glance over my shoulder, but the courtyard is deserted, nothing to interrupt the night sounds but the occasional whicker of a horse from the nearby stables. Tucked in the shadow of the palace walls, it is unlikely any guards completing their rounds will spot me.

"Emin?" He startles, and I gesture to the locked gate. "With haste, please."

His eyes flicker toward the gold, and I stifle a huff of laughter. Of course. Payment first. As I reach for his hand, however, a larger, stronger hand swallows my wrist, halting the motion.

Emin's eyes widen. My head whips around, and I am pinned. Two dark eyes glitter below a headscarf of flaming red. My heart leaps so forcefully I'm certain it has wedged itself inside my throat.

"If I recall," Notus says quietly, with that leashed patience I have come to know, "we agreed to journey to Mirash together." He regards me without blinking. "Have you changed your mind?"

We both know the answer to that question.

He shifts forward, his warmth bleeding through the frigid desert night. My skin tingles from his proximity, damn my traitorous body, but I remain in place, unwilling to give ground.

Emin glances between us in puzzlement. Right. Notus and I are supposed to be engaged. Foolishly in love.

Curling my hand into the ivory fabric smoothed across his chest, I peer at my betrothed through lowered lashes. The South Wind was not expecting this display of affection. Perhaps it's petty of me, but I feel pleased by the power I hold over this immortal. Angling my head, I tap my cheek expectantly.

Notus glances at the young guard, who promptly gazes elsewhere, granting us a bit of privacy as the South Wind leans forward to brush a kiss against my cheek.

The spice of his breath overwhelms me. I can't deny that a part of me wishes to shift my head and claim his mouth, as I'd wished to do after learning he had touched himself to thoughts of me in his bedroom.

214 • ALEXANDRIA WARWICK

"How did you know I would be here?" I demand.

"Because I know you," he murmurs.

At this point, I can't deny it. He understands my need for freedom. I understand his desire to share, and be known.

"How well?" I challenge, feeling suddenly bold.

He fights a smile. "You forgot your cloak." As he passes it over, he says, "Check the pockets."

I do so, pulling out two honey cakes wrapped in cloth, still warm.

Now it's my turn to fight a smile. What an unexpectedly thoughtful gesture. He must have gone into the city earlier, knocked on Nadia's door, and bought these for the journey.

Lifting my eyes, I ask Notus, "Did I ever tell you how I discovered Nadia's bakery?" I swear we've drawn closer together.

He smooths a hand down my arm. "Remind me."

Oh, gods. I press my hand to my forehead, soft laughter bubbling up at the memory. "Father forbid sweets after Fahim ate an entire plate of cookies in one sitting. It didn't stop my brother. He simply snuck into the city and acquired them himself. When he brought me back one of these honey cakes, I demanded that he show me the bakery." They were so mouthwatering, I *needed* them.

And so when I took Notus to the bakery for the first time, I was telling him without words what it meant to be able to experience joy without restrictions. After that, he would often bring me honey cakes, stashing them in my bedroom, the music room, the garden. It was our little game, our secret, a thread of our developing story. And I thought of him then as I do now.

Clearing my throat, I step back. The sky has begun to shed its gray pall.

"Open the gate," I order Emin before my attention shifts to the South Wind. "Are you coming or not? We mustn't delay."

I can't be certain how long Notus searches my face. Perhaps he, too, knows of this desire I continually subdue. Who will break, who will bend? Not me. Never.

After tugging the reins from my grasp, he places them into the guard's hands. "Return the horse to the stables," he says. "We'll be taking my sailer."

Half a mile west of Ishmah's outer wall, Notus' sailer rests beneath the scant shade of a parched date palm. The vessel is sleek, arrow-shaped: twin masts, white canvas sails. It appears out of place amongst the desert's rolling curves of tawny and rust red.

Sand hisses beneath our trudging footsteps as we ascend a particularly steep dune. Despite my struggles, the South Wind maintains pace at my side, shortening his strides to accommodate me. The gesture both infuriates and warms me in turn.

While Notus unties the sails, I climb aboard. A few crates have been secured to the floorboards with rope. The creak of the wood stirs a particularly vibrant memory. It rises like a leaf upon a forgotten oasis pool. Wind, the world blurred into color and light. A feeling as close to flying as I have ever experienced.

I sit cross-legged at the bow, wincing at the stickiness dampening my underarms. I pull my waterskin from my satchel and take a deep drag. Moisture washes the dust from my mouth, the bitterness of a bygone era.

It hurts more than I can say to sit here, in a place I'd once known. To know that time will never return.

I glance at the stern where Notus grips the rudder. Our eyes catch, and the world momentarily stills. *Do you remember those days?* I wish to ask him. *Do you remember our shared laughter, the vision of tomorrow we built? Do you remember?*

A cloud passes across the South Wind's expression. I sense his need to speak, but in the end, he faces forward, legs braced. A powerful gust explodes into the sails, and we speed into the dawn.

The vessel skips across the ground before blasting up the side of a dune. Higher and higher we ascend. My hands clamp the lip of the hull as the summit nears, wind roaring in my ears. And as sunlight emerges to greet a new day, we release our hold on the earth.

Laughter tickles my chest. I fight its rise, yet it bursts its cage. We soar, weightless, through the air. We cannot be stopped. I marvel at the wonder of it all.

Slipping down the back of a neighboring dune, I look over my shoulder at the South Wind. His teeth, rarely seen, gleam in the first pale rays of morning. Time slips its knot. I am eighteen years old, riding the South Wind's sailer beneath a star-flecked sky.

It was my first taste of freedom. The possibility of another life spun like madness through me. Imagine if there were no walls to retreat behind, all the earth my inheritance? What might I find? What might I learn about myself? But that life was never mine to claim. I could only view it from a distance.

Suddenly, my laughter fractures, and I clamp my teeth around a budding sob.

"Sarai."

Notus crouches at my side. The sailer skates at a brisk pace over the flattened earth.

My head hangs. Tears drip down my cheeks, plopping onto my cloth-covered thighs. Gently, he cups my face in concern, lifts it toward his own. "Why do you cry?"

My lips quaver as another memory escapes its confines. His gentleness in those quiet moments, tangled in bedsheets and each other's arms. It soothes me even as some bottomless wound tears open wider than before.

"Because the world is beautiful," I choke, "and I am a stranger to my own realm."

No, not to my realm. To myself.

Which makes me question if I have ever known myself. All my life, I was told what to wear and how to act and what to say and what to eat and when to sleep and how to study and who to be. I was, in all ways, faultless. But I wasn't me.

He appears saddened as he wipes my tears. But he lets me cry. He doesn't attempt to stifle the emotion. He makes space for it, just as he has always done. I am reminded of how easily I fell for the South Wind. He is still the same thoughtful god he's always been.

"I'm all right," I croak, sniffling. Despite the impulse to bury my face against his chest, I pull free of his embrace.

He considers me for a lengthy moment. Then, as if deciding I'm well enough, he rises to his feet and retakes his position at the rudder. And as Notus steers the sailer toward Mirash, I settle back against the crates, and I remember what it felt like to be alive and free.

If Ishmah is a red heart nestled amongst golden sands, then Mirash is polished ebony, all imperfections smoothed away. Long before Ishmah touted the honor of Ammara's capital, Mirash once held that title. When its oasis ran dry, however, its residents forsook the gleaming city. They chipped Ishmah from the adjacent cliffs and piled high the red stone. Rains wet the earth, and the Red City flourished, Mirash left in the dust.

After slowing the sailer to a halt beneath a cluster of date palms, Notus and I disembark. My hair is a scraggly mess. I grimace, attempting to pat the windblown strands into place.

As with all major cities in Ammara, Mirash is circled by a high wall, its gates carved with protective runes to shield against darkwalkers. From our vantage point, I'm able to survey the region in full. A sizable portion of the former capital has been carved from the massive cliff face stretching east to west: small dwellings with square-cut windows, whittled stairs worn smooth. I recognize the larger, more elaborate doorways as temples or shrines, the largest paying tribute to the Lord of the Mountain.

The southern edge of Mirash is all sprawl. Tents litter the cracked ground in white canvas, their numbers incalculable, displaced families huddling beneath the insubstantial coverings. The oasis is a spot of green wilting in the northeastern corner. Due to the prolonged drought, only a small, muddy pool remains.

Notus and I take our places at the back of the line of people awaiting entry into the city. I shift in place, lift a hand to shield my eyes. Seven years. Has it really been that long since I visited Mirash? I was touring at the time, here for a single night before my next performance led me farther west. I'd had little opportunity to explore.

"You are not to reveal your identity," Notus murmurs into my ear. "Let me handle this." He tugs the hood of my cloak down over my forehead.

When I turn my head, I find our mouths less than a hairsbreadth apart.

I lick my lips. The line moves forward, but the South Wind makes no effort to retreat. Neither do I. My attention drops to his mouth, its full lower lip, before flitting elsewhere. "Well?" I clear my throat. "Are we going?"

Notus steps away, eyes unreadable. Only when he has faced forward again do I release the breath I hold.

We reach the front of the line swiftly. After spinning a tale of visiting relatives in the city, the guards wave Notus and me through, completely unaware that Ammara's princess is in their midst. Truth be told, I prefer the anonymity. It is a freedom I do not often experience, to wander the earth unacknowledged.

The main thoroughfare, which runs parallel to the cliffs, is hectic at this hour. Due to the lack of space available on the perimeter, a few artisans have set up shop in the middle of the street, much to the frustration of Mirash's denizens. At one point, movement comes to a standstill as a farmer herds his cows across the road.

Continuing down the crowded lane, I can't help but notice the interest Notus piques. Mainly women, even those who are married, opal runes inked upon their left hands. I glare with all the ire I possess until the interlopers slink away.

Notus coughs into his fist, though it sounds more like a laugh.

"What?" I snap.

"Nothing." But his mouth ticks up at one corner.

"They should keep their eyes to themselves," I sniff. Notus and I are, after all, engaged. It's perfectly acceptable to stake a claim on the immortal I am to wed, charade or not.

"Careful," he murmurs, "or I might begin to think you're jealous."

"Then I'm playing my part well, because that is exactly what an engaged woman would feel when strangers ogle her betrothed."

As usual, Notus moves through crowds with an ease I fail to replicate. Always, he is searching, awareness of his surroundings touching upon smaller details I might overlook.

"You've been here before?" I ask him, nudging aside an elderly fellow lodged in the current of the market.

"Not in years." Notus leads me down a crooked alleyway squeezed between two stone structures with flat rooftops. I follow closely on his heels. "If you recall," he says over his shoulder, "I asked you to accompany me once."

He had. At the time, I didn't trust him, this unknowable god whose power was something I could not comprehend, though I could not stop my eyes from seeking the South Wind out at every opportunity. "I remember."

"You turned me down."

I press my arm against my nose as we maneuver around a pile of refuse, home to a thousand buzzing flies. It reeks of decomposed animal parts. "To tell you the truth," I say, "I thought you were only asking me out of service to Father."

"It was never out of service."

"I know that now." With the refuse behind us, I drop my arm, breathe in the cleaner air. Ahead, a spot of brightness signals the end of the alleyway. "I stopped by the stables that morning," I confess.

Halting, Notus turns to face me, his expression creased in confusion. A droplet of sweat wends down the side of his neck. I fight the maddening urge to lick it clean. "When?"

And so descends the urge to flee, fast and far, for as long as my legs might carry me. Yet paired with this impulse is the desire to be reassured and held close. If I were bolder, I might press the pad of my finger along the crease edging the South Wind's mouth. I image how the touch would burn. "Just after dawn."

"I looked for you," he says, searching my gaze in the gloom between the buildings. "I didn't see you."

"According to the gatekeeper, I missed you by a handful of minutes."

Notus appears deeply conflicted to learn this. Would it have made a difference if he had known? "I thought you didn't want to travel with me," he says. "If I had known you would show, I would never have left."

I had recently turned nineteen. I didn't understand why this worldly immortal would ask me to accompany him on a trip to a nearby city, though at the time, I wanted desperately to be worthy of his attention. With the competition fast approaching, I couldn't afford to take time off with practicing, but I hadn't cared.

"You would have," I say, unable to temper my bitterness.

"Why do you say that?" He sounds more curious than anything else.

"You had no loyalty toward me. You probably thought I was an annoyance more than anything else."

Notus looks positively perplexed. "That's not how I felt about you— at all."

Don't do it. But I have rarely taken my own advice. "Then what did you feel?"

He shifts his weight, taps the hilt of his blade. If vulnerability was difficult for me, it was far more difficult for the South Wind, a god who rarely spoke of his past, or his feelings.

"I valued what we had," he says. "It felt like we were building something that belonged only to us."

Felt. A word fixed firmly in the past.

But what of his recent confession to me? *There is only one person I desire in this life, and that is you.* One cannot return to their old life. I understand that. Too much has changed. *I* have changed.

Yet in this moment, I allow my armor to fall. Piece by piece, it surrenders itself. Notus can't know what it was like when he left, but I let him see. Daily, I stood at my window and looked upon the whole of Ishmah, hoping for a glimpse of the South Wind. I had never felt so obsessed, so alone, and so weak.

I shrug, my smile pained. "Pointless regrets." But as I attempt to brush past him, Notus catches my arm.

I *feel* the air change between us. Its subtle spike hardens my nipples. Immediately, I yank free of his hold, clamping my arms over my chest.

He glances at my chest. If I'm not mistaken, his eyes have darkened. "You regret not accompanying me?" he murmurs lowly.

The truth emerges whether I wish it to or not. "I regret many things, Notus, including not accompanying you that day."

But we're here now, in Mirash, together. Perhaps we can make the most of it.

An hour of wandering leads us to the ceramic district, with its glossy earthenware and clay-hardened pots. The stalls are tucked uncomfortably close, cluttered with cups glazed in rainbow hues of citrine, ruby, turquoise, aquamarine. As we continue beyond its borders, the city gradually deteriorates. Young families squat in murky corners, some having taken up residence in piles of rubble, those few structures that still possess standing walls. It hurts my heart. So many without homes or food or clean clothes. Were the rains to return, it would heal much of what is broken.

"What exactly do you know of this lead anyway?" I ask Notus as we round a corner. Every so often I'm certain I feel his hand on my lower back, a pale touch of reassurance. I'm likely only imagining it.

"Amad is a jeweler, well-known throughout the region. He is trustworthy."

"How can you be certain?"

We turn down a deserted street and stop in front of a nondescript building with a sagging roof. "One's reputation is built on their word. Leading me astray would risk more than my wrath. It would risk his entire livelihood." He jerks his chin in indication for me to follow.

Notus enters the shop first. The morning is bright, yet shutters cloak the windows, the air uncomfortably stagnant. Shelves along the walls cradle teardrop emeralds, moon-pale quartz. A single candle burns atop a nearby table, sputtering in a pool of hot wax.

The man at the counter regards us with the wariness of one who cannot afford to lower his guard. Two knives hang from his beltloops. A knotted scar blots the skin of one sun-darkened cheek.

"Meetings are by appointment only," he says, polishing a small oval of turquoise. "You will have to come back at another time."

Notus pulls back his hood, murmuring, "Amad."

The jeweler grunts in acknowledgment. When I remove my hood, however, he straightens in surprise. "Your Highness."

I incline my head in greeting.

Immediately, he bends at the waist. "I apologize. I wasn't aware you would be joining us." Hurriedly, he rounds the counter and locks the door.

"I trust that you've kept this arrangement to yourself?" Notus says as the jeweler, Amad, returns to the counter.

"Of course." This paired with a sincere smile, but if I'm not mistaken, tension lingers around his eyes. He is uncomfortable. It does not escape my notice.

Leaning over the counter, I ask, "Notus says you have information about the labyrinth. How did you come by it?" No matter this man's reputation, *I* don't personally know him. He must first prove himself trustworthy.

Amad casually eases back. He holds my gaze with confidence— a good sign. "I've a client who possesses a significant number of rare and obscure texts." He sets aside the turquoise, selects a yellow gemstone the size of my thumbnail. "We made a trade, he and I. When Notus reached out asking if I knew anything regarding the beast in the labyrinth, I happened to have this scroll in my possession."

My eyes narrow. I sense the South Wind's skepticism as well. "You just *happened* to have the scroll in your possession?" I say. "Sounds awfully convenient to me."

"Agreed," says Notus.

We stand shoulder to shoulder. Princess Sarai Al-Khatib, and one of the divine? The jeweler must realize what he's up against, for he drops his eyes.

"All right," he concedes. "It is true that I already had the scroll in my possession, but that's because someone else was looking for the same information you were."

Now we're getting somewhere. "Who?"

"Prince Balior of Um Salim."

My eyes close on a wave of apprehension. Notus swears softly. Here I thought we were steps ahead of the prince, when really, we were trailing at his heels. "Did you inform Prince Balior we were interested in the same information?" I ask the jeweler.

"No." He shakes his head adamantly. "I met with the prince before Notus wrote to me."

The South Wind and I exchange a heartfelt look. Then we're in the clear—so far.

Amad pulls a box of polished wood from beneath the counter. "The prince wasn't too happy with the information I offered him. You may find some interest in it, however."

The wood is quite old, bleached white and full of cracks, its face carved with dark whirls. When I brush a finger against the fine grain, my ears pulse from the low vibration running through the room. Neither Notus nor the jeweler appear to be affected.

The top opens with a soft creak. Inside lies a scroll tied with a strip of leather. Gently, I lift it from the box. A piece of parchment flakes off as I untie the binding and open the scroll.

My stomach hollows out. Lifting a trembling hand, I trace the musical notation arranged on the staff, quarter notes and eighth notes, accidentals and beats of rest gathered to create the whole of a melody I recognize immediately. It was one of Fahim's favorite pieces. Somehow, this connects to the labyrinth, though I haven't the slightest idea how. Notus is equally perplexed.

"The client you traded with to acquire this scroll," I say, lifting my eyes to the jeweler. "Do you have a name?" There must be something we're missing, some loophole. It is all eerily familiar, yet just beyond the threshold of comprehension.

"I'm sorry to say I don't. He was a trader passing through."

The heat and breadth of Notus at my side momentarily draws my attention from the notation. "May I?" he asks. I nod and pass it to him.

His brow creases as he scans the scroll. I allow myself a small smile. Many do not know that music is a language, and few are fluent in it.

He then peers closer at one of the corners. "Did you see this?"

"What?" I gaze over his shoulder to where he points. There is a simple sketch in black ink I hadn't noticed before. It showcases what I believe is a winged man. "Do you recognize it?"

"I can't be sure, I—" He shakes his head, skims a brown fingertip across the illustration. Amber light from the nearby candle ripples across the parchment. "I think I need to send a message to my brother."

"Boreas?"

"Eurus," he replies.

Interesting. This is one of only a handful of times he has mentioned his family. In the past, any attempt at learning more of his relatives was met with stony silence. It frustrated me to no end. "You think he has something to do with the labyrinth?"

"I'm not sure." The creases lining his mouth deepen. "Possibly."

I'd hoped we might discover a possible weakness the beast has, or a clue concerning whatever power it may possess once it's freed from the labyrinth. What are we to do with a scrap of musical notation?

Then I think deeper on the matter. There is something here. Something I'm not seeing. "Could this be related to my curse?"

Notus' head whips in my direction. "Curse?"

My eyes widen. I didn't intend to speak that aloud. "Ah—"

There comes a knock on the door.

The jeweler stiffens. The South Wind falls motionless, as do I.

A voice calls, "Princess Sarai?" The door rattles as whoever stands on the other side attempts to open it.

Notus draws his sword in one fluid motion. "You told me none knew of our arrival," he growls at Amad. The tension emanating from his body is a physical thing. It crawls beneath his skin, crests to pool in those dark-pupiled eyes. At last, rage cracks open that stony facade, and it is a glorious sight to behold.

Amad yelps as Notus prowls forward, and he scrambles to put distance between himself and the South Wind, using the counter as a shield. "It wasn't a lie!" he cries. "I swear it!"

Wind snaps at my legs and tears at my cloak. One of the precious stones on display tumbles from its perch and hits the floor with a sharp ping. Amad glances toward the jewel, expression stricken.

"Then why has someone shown up at your place of business asking for the princess?" A band of air whips out, snagging Notus' quarry around the neck and lifting him high. Amad clutches the noose, face purpling from lack of air. He chokes, wheezes out, "I promise you, I—"

"Sorry to bother you," the visitor at the door calls. "I've a message for Princess Sarai from Prince Amir. Someone claimed they spotted her entering this shop?"

My mouth parts in surprise. Amir? Quickly, I stride for the door. As I reach for the handle, however, Notus stays my hand.

"Let me," he says quietly.

Nodding, I step aside while he opens the door. A thump behind us indicates Amad has dropped onto the ground.

It's Emin. The poor lad is out of breath, drenched in sweat. "Your Highness." He bows, hands braced on his knees, and holds out the crinkled message. "Prince Amir's courier came to the stables shortly after you departed, looking for you. I did not wish to betray your trust by telling him of your whereabouts, but he said the letter was most urgent. So I agreed to deliver it myself."

For a handsome fee, no doubt. I shake my head in incredulity. "How did you find me?"

"You and Notus mentioned Mirash," he puffs. "I rode here as fast as I could, asked people in the streets if they'd seen a woman traveling with an armed man. That led me here."

And with little time to spare. "Thank you, Emin."

The moment the parchment brushes my fingertips, I break the wax seal and begin to read.

Sarai,

I'm not sure if this will reach you in time. It's Father. He is fast fading. Please come. I fear it is already too late.

—Amir

20

A HARD BREATH PUNCHES OUT OF ME. I DO NOT RECALL MOVING, but suddenly I'm stumbling across the threshold, into brightness and a hot, coarse wind. The din of my surroundings can't touch me, for I am distant, I am elsewhere, I am deep, deep in my mind. My heart trills fearfully. *Too late.*

My last image of Father swirls before me like a smoke plume. The broken pieces of his heart, which I shattered with my cruel words. How small he looked, how shrunken beneath the blankets of his bed. With my back against a wall, I lashed out. I wanted to wound him as he had wounded me. And now—

The dusty road crunches beneath my slippers, and I halt, swaying. Notus catches my arm with a murmured, "Steady."

Tearing free of the South Wind's grip, I rush blindly in the direction I believe leads to the city entrance. My legs propel me down the road, into the thick of the market. The crowds have multiplied since this morning. I weave around trundling carts and bypass beggars in rags. Notus and I traveled this way before, yet for whatever reason, nothing looks familiar.

"Sarai." The South Wind's shadow stretches over me as he catches up. "What's wrong? Talk to me."

When the swarm of marketgoers blocks the road ahead, I dart down a side street to circumvent the blockage, Amir's crumpled message wilting in my sweaty palm. As long as I continue moving, I will not be burdened by the fear of *what if*.

"Sarai." Notus grabs my arm.

"Don't touch me!" I snarl.

The South Wind retreats a step, palms lifted, confusion passing over his expression.

Only now do I recognize my posture: feet planted, braced as though to come to blows. We've stopped in the middle of the road, the crowd granting us a wide berth. Notus is not my enemy. We have moved past that, I think.

"I'm sorry, I—" My throat thickens, and I swallow down the shame that rises. "I'm sorry. I shouldn't have yelled at you." *Get it together.* But I have nothing to ground me, no anchor but my own spiraling thoughts.

"I want to help you," he murmurs, "but I can't if you don't let me in." Then he says, quietly and with feeling, "Let me in, Sarai."

A farmer dragging two goats behind him jostles my back. I stumble forward, nearer to Notus, the rock around which this current parts. Here is what I know. The South Wind is my betrothed in name only, but what we have mended and built anew is perhaps the truest thing in my life. He is here, I think. That in itself is enough.

Wordlessly, I pass over the message. My hand shakes.

He reads swiftly. A heartbeat later, Notus lowers the note.

"My father—"

He nods, though coolly, refusing to meet my gaze. "This way."

It turns out, I was traveling in the wrong direction. We backtrack as quickly as possible, but midday in Mirash, the road has overflowed its banks, the space between bodies so narrow one could not squeeze even a sheet of parchment between them. Eventually, movement grinds to a halt.

"What's happening?" I ask. "Why aren't we moving?" My attempts to put space between myself and those around me result in an elbow to my spine.

"I'm not sure," Notus says.

People crane their necks in curiosity, including a young boy draped in filthy rags. "What's happening, Mama?"

"Hush, child." She shushes him, yet gathers him close.

A scream splits the air.

All at once, the crowd fractures, heaving itself in the opposite direction, away from the entrance. I brace against the tide, Notus sheltering my back. One scream becomes three, becomes seven, becomes ten. Someone's boot crushes my toes. A man goes down and is trampled. Then I smell it: smoke on the wind.

"Darkwalkers," Notus says.

A cold wave of despair sloshes through me. Darkwalkers are widespread through Ammara, but I'd hoped we wouldn't have to face them, today of all days. It will take hours to return to Ishmah. Time is running out.

Notus turns to me. "Head for the entrance," he says. "Wait for me at the sailer. I need to send a message to Eurus, but I'll take care of this and be there as soon as I can."

I fight the urge to toss myself into his arms. He is a god, I remind myself. He can take care of himself. "Stay safe," I whisper.

He dips his chin. "You, too."

The South Wind flings himself skyward, propelled by a gust of air beneath his boots. When he vanishes behind the buildings, I race toward the entrance, dodging those fleeing to the best of my ability. Eventually, I pass beneath the archway, where Ammara expands in golden pleats. There is his sailer. Its twin sails flutter in a surprisingly strong breeze.

I pace before it, struggling to catch my breath. I think of Father. I think of Amir and Tuleen. I should be at his bedside, but I am far, as I have always been. Try as I might, I've never been able to close the distance between us.

The sun boils overhead and presses red onto my tightening skin. I'm not sure how much time has passed. An hour? Two? My eyes hunt the sky. No sign of the South Wind. Over time, the screams peter out. Still, I pace.

When a blurred figure passes beneath the archway, I squint into the distance. "Thank the gods," I gasp, and race toward the South Wind. "I was beginning to think something happened to you."

Notus limps past me without acknowledgment. I hurry to catch up, slipping and sliding through sand. "Are you all right?" I ask.

"Fine."

Fine is the word I myself have used when I am anything but. "You don't look fine. You're hurt." I trail him to the sailer. "This won't hinder your ability to get us back to Ishmah, will it?"

Notus slows, tossing a glare over his shoulder. He then turns and keeps walking.

I open my mouth, snap it shut. "That's not what I meant."

"I'm sure."

His dismissal stings. I *was* worried for the South Wind, but he is immortal, flush with power. My father is dying. One cannot liken a fish to a bird. They are from completely separate worlds.

"Here." I shove the waterskin into his hand. He takes a swig before passing it back. "Let's go." Leaping onto the vessel, I settle at the bow. The sails, however, hang limp.

I spin around. Notus leans against the hull, arms crossed, looking out at the distant dunes. "Did you hear me?"

He lifts his head, eyes slitted against the sun's harsh glare. There is no distinction between iris and pupil, only roiling black, a fury so hostile I retreat a step. "Give me a damn minute, Sarai."

I flinch, curl my arms across my stomach. "I'm sorry. You're right, just . . . we're running out of time, and—"

"I understand you're frightened," he growls, "but I'm trying to help you."

There is that, yes. Notus is doing everything in his power to help me, but even gods have their limits. "I understand," I tell him, "and I'm sorry. Take a moment if you need it. Let me know when you're ready to return."

But Notus asks, "Are you sure it's your father's health that calls you back to the capital, or is it something else I'm unaware of?"

"What?" I gape at him. "Didn't you read the note?"

He scowls. "I did, but there's more at stake than you're telling me. The sooner you lay everything out on the table, the sooner we can return to Ishmah."

Red douses my vision. If I was not certain Notus would disarm me, I would snatch his scimitar and fling it against the nearest palm. "My father is dying, Notus!"

"You want my cooperation? Then I need answers." Fire brightens his ebon eyes. "Let's start with the curse."

Something fractures inside me, this many-faced image of myself. A roar of noise overwhelms me. Is it the wind, which has begun to lash with increasing ferocity, or my own thundering heart? I can't leave Mirash without the South Wind's cooperation. Neither can I stop myself from crumbling. I can only delay my inevitable collapse.

"I was born a sickly child." I speak low and quickly. "According to the physician, I was not going to survive the night. Father went to Mount Syr to beg the Lord of the Mountain for my life. At first, Father believed him to be merciful. My life was saved, and I grew into a healthy baby.

"But that same year, drought decimated the realm, and the majority of the crops failed." I move to stand at the bow. The blue, cloudless sky, and beneath, the bronzed earth. "Father suspected something was amiss. He returned to Mount Syr to question the Lord of the Mountain, who revealed parts of the bargain he did not originally disclose." In my periphery, I watch Notus straighten, his attention fixed on my profile. "In exchange for my life, he claimed Ammara's nourishing rains for himself." Sweat trickles along my hairline. I dab it with the sleeve of my cloak. "That is my curse, my burden," I say. "The suffering I have placed upon my people."

For a time, the South Wind regards me, his face wiped clean of emotion. "That's all?"

While I don't want to deceive him, I see no other option. With so few days remaining, it seems pointless to inform him of my impending death. Perhaps it's time to accept the hand I've been dealt. I do not want him to mourn me. "Yes."

A particularly harsh gust snatches at my dress. Notus is trying his best to appear unaffected, but as time goes on, I see his cracks, just as I see mine.

"You understand how terrible this is," I press. "If the rains do not return, my people will perish. The last of our crops will fail completely. Our army will weaken. Ammara will be left defenseless." Any conqueror might waltz through Ishmah's gates and lay claim to the realm without ever lifting a weapon. There will be none to stand against them, or the darkwalkers.

He lifts a hand to his eyes, shielding himself from this truth that shines brightest of all. Then it drops, fingers balled into a fist. "How long have you known this?" When I do not respond, he growls, "How long?"

"Always." The word burns like a lit match in my throat. "I have always known. Father forbade me to speak of it."

He shakes his head, jaw clenched as he stares at the wood grain beneath his feet. "I didn't know." The words are spoken so softly, I initially believe I imagined them. "King Halim requested my return to help fight the darkwalkers, but I didn't realize a greater threat loomed." Then he frowns. "Why do you believe there to be a connection between the curse and the labyrinth?"

This, at least, is no falsehood. "The symbol on the labyrinth door is the symbol of the Lord of the Mountain."

His frown deepens, and the quiet stretches. "Have you warned your people of what's to come?"

Guilt descends with punishing ferocity. "No." Father and I fought over this. I wished to tell them. They deserved to know the drought was borne from dark forces. But King Halim wanted to keep the information private, between family. A curse threatening Ammara's livelihood? There could be not even an inkling of weakness or doubt toward his reign.

Yet I think of Haneen, the storyteller. I think of Roshar, my dearest friend, and Ibramin, teacher and father. I even think of Tuleen, whose friendship has only begun to blossom.

"I think you should tell them," Notus says.

That poisoned core in me, that festering resentment, lashes out. "Why do you even care?"

His head snaps up. "Have you considered that Ammara is not just your home, but mine, too?"

"That's not true."

"Who are you to say what is true?" The fury with which he speaks sends me backward a step. A strong gust whips at my hair and rattles the scraggly date palms shivering at our backs, long shadows cast across the arid ground. "It was my home, once," he growls. "And I was a fool to hope it might one day be again."

It spears me with the swiftness of an arrow to the chest. It is deep, this emotion, old as earth and weathered by much strife. "I don't understand," I force out. "You never showed that you cared for it before."

"Didn't I?" He stares at me until I drop my eyes. "I fought to protect your people. I adopted your customs. I paid respect to your gods."

He did. I suppose I never considered the ways one *made* a home. I'd always assumed it was something you were born into.

"When I was banished," he explains, "I had no home. And maybe I wanted to believe I was deserving of one—deserving of you."

My heartbeat stutters. "Me?" I whisper.

The South Wind gazes at me with an openness I have wished for in those hours before dawn. This powerful immortal, this undying god, is many things. Vulnerable, he is not. "Home is not a place, Sarai. Not for me."

"I'm not your home," I say, voice quavering. "I can't be."

I did not realize a brightness touched his eyes until it winks out, like a star extinguished. "Then we have nothing left to say to each other."

Notus climbs aboard to take his place at the rudder. I settle against the bow, stomach curdling with something resembling shame. I don't know whether to scream or cry, plead or fall mute.

In silence, we depart, launching across the dunes. I stare at my arrow bracelet, trace its delicate leaden curve as the winds strengthen, jostling the boat. Neither the heat nor the glare of midday can touch me. I imagine it is a cool, dark room I retreat into, drapes drawn, door barred. If I wrap myself in blankets thick enough, perhaps reality cannot touch me either.

Here is what Notus doesn't understand. I once lived a life where I loved and lost two people I held dear. So I told myself I would live a life where I had no future. I would live a life where I would love no one, because if I didn't love anyone, I wouldn't lose anyone.

So that's what I did. I closed my heart. I turned my back on *I wish* and *I want*. I belonged only to Ammara, not to the world, which owed me nothing. Maybe Notus does—did—see a home with me, as I saw a home with him.

As our vessel cuts through the great sandy valleys, the wind pitches into an eerie keen. My head snaps around. At Notus' back, a great red mass gathers, stretching seam to seam across the sky.

"Red storm!" I scream.

The South Wind grits his teeth, fighting to remain on course. The wind is so powerful it yanks the sails taut with a loud snap. The sailer rattles. The air is deafening. Notus attempts to guide us into a trough between two dunes but is forced to redirect as the whirling cloud overtakes us and the sun goes dark.

We veer wildly, unable to maintain our course. When I glance up, I notice the sails have been shredded, the thousand grains of sand having sliced the canvas to strips. "Notus!" I point to the sails.

He nods with grim-faced resolve. "Grab the rudder!"

The stern slides out, pitching me into the mast. My shoulder makes impact, and I bite back a pained cry, yet manage to hook one arm around the post long enough for Notus to yank me against his chest and position my hands on the rudder. "Got it," I say.

While he struggles to patch the holes in the sails, I use my weight to hold the rudder steady. It sounds as though the sky is shattering overhead. The most vicious of red storms can stretch for up to fifty miles. Our only hope is to claw free of it before we're dashed to pieces, or worse—buried alive.

As we lean hard into a turn, another gale wrenches me sideways. I slam against the crates. One of the ropes snaps. Two boxes go flying, a third exploding against the hull. Wooden fragments pelt my face, and my stomach heaves as I'm flipped over, dragged backward over the vessel's edge.

Something solid pins my shoulder against the sailer. My legs hang over the railing, toes skimming the surface of the sand. Through the hazed debris obscuring his face, Notus' eyes burn into mine with unmistakable fear. He hauls me back into the sailer and directs me to the mast.

"Grab hold," he growls.

Once I've anchored myself, he returns to the rudder. The air is so choked with particles I can't see even a foot in front of me.

A burst of speed propels us toward the dune's summit. As we fling ourselves off its crest, arrowing through debris, another battering gust snaps the vessel around. We spin. My hold on the mast breaks, and I'm falling. "Notus!"

The last thing I see is the South Wind's eyes. Then he, too, is swallowed up.

21

MY SHOULDER SLAMS INTO THE GROUND, PAIN RUPTURING AT the joint. The squall steals my cry. It drives daggers into my eyes, wrenches the fabric of my dress with sharp hands of greed. Down, down it hammers, shoving me deeper into the sand, the dense cloud of particles razing my skin. In seconds, I am buried.

My thoughts white out. Staggering upright, I fight to maintain balance against the vicious gales. A step forward, and my knees fold. Sand piles atop my body with frightening speed as the earth demands flesh.

I shake my head, grip fistfuls of sand in an attempt to stabilize myself. *Focus!* I need to reach higher ground. Caught in the valleys between the dunes, the sand will accumulate, and I will be unable to climb free. A heave, an arduous push, and I am once again standing. I slog headlong in some nameless direction, unable to see, or hear, or speak, until eventually, the ground begins to ascend.

Eyes slitted against the debris, I search for a broad shape among the red-gray slew. Notus should be somewhere nearby. I couldn't have fallen far. But there is nothing.

"Notus!" I scream. Yet the wind snatches that, too.

Again, I shout his name. The storm's roar bleeds so thoroughly across the landscape it would take a miracle if he could hear me.

"Sarai?"

The bellow is faint, but it is the anchor I have desperately been searching for. "Notus!"

"Where . . . you?"

I spin around desperately. "I'm here!" Still no sign of him. I stumble in the direction of his voice, sinking knee-deep into sand. "I can't see you."

Hunched against the brutal winds, I continue to trudge through the sand that sucks at my shins and licks stinging tongues at my face and neck.

Sarai.

I halt, a hand lifted to shield my eyes. The air churns and churns. Now the voice is coming from *behind* me—I think. A glance over my shoulder. The cloud parts momentarily. There, a dark form manifests on the fringe of my vision: the South Wind.

You're going the wrong way.

"Well it would help if you kept calling for me so I knew where you were!" I cry back.

This way, Sarai.

I lurch forward, arms swinging to maintain my balance. It feels as if I make no progress toward the blurred figure, which, curiously enough, seems to stand taller than the South Wind, but the air shifts so rapidly I can't trust my vision. "I'm here!" A mirage? An illusion?

Hurry. You don't have much time.

You'd think the South Wind would *help* me, instead of hovering just beyond reach. He, too, has power over winds. Yet he watches me struggle.

"Sarai!"

My head snaps around. "Notus?" This voice, different now. Rougher, its texture akin to a raw, unpolished stone. I waver in uncertainty, my legs trembling from overexertion. I need to rest, but to rest is to die.

Something slams into my back. I hit the ground face-first, legs crushed beneath a heavy object—a tree or block of wood. The sand heaps too quickly. My thighs, buried. My stomach, buried. It continues to pile higher: breasts, shoulders, neck. Though I scramble to dig myself free, I succeed only in submerging myself deeper.

"Notus!" I cough, spitting out a mouthful of sand. "Notus!"

No reply, just a roar, a quake of energy drilling deep into my ears. My eyes slip shut. Gods help me, I don't want to die. Not like this. I doubt anyone would ever find my body.

When I open my eyes, however, I gasp. In the distance, the South Wind trudges toward me, shoulder braced against the storm, using his powers to divert the worst of the wind. When his gaze locks onto mine, my heart feels as if it might burst, so overwhelming is the relief. He is the South Wind, and he has returned.

Arms extended, Notus shoves back the flying debris. Eventually, he carves out a small pocket of air to combat the storm's force. On the other side of the transparent barrier, the squall gnashes its fearsome teeth.

Notus punches his open palm toward me. A current lifts the heavy wooden slab from my body and flings it elsewhere, pain rolling down my legs as the weight vanishes. The second I'm free, he yanks me into his embrace.

"Are you hurt?" His mouth brushes my ear, the low, deep tones thrumming with power.

"No." I fist a hand into his robe. His body heat seeps through the fabric, into my skin. "I was looking for you, but the storm—"

"I know." His arms tighten, deliciously hard with muscle. "You're safe now."

Gradually, my trembling subsides, the chatter of my teeth tapering off. "Where's the sailer?"

His fingers splay across the small of my back. "Gone. In pieces."

My stomach plummets, dragging my heart along with it. That vessel was our only means of reaching Ishmah before nightfall. Before . . .

I hide my face against his shoulder, a dark pall blanketing my thoughts. This cannot be the end. There are things I must say to Father. So many months of illness when I did not sit with him, eat with him, speak with him, comfort him. What if he leaves this life before our relationship is fully mended?

"We can't delay." I am clinging to sanity by frayed threads. "If the sailer is destroyed, then we'll need to travel by foot."

"Sarai," he says. "You know that's impossible."

Improbable, maybe. Not impossible. If Notus can maintain the protective dome, we should be able to cross the dunes with relative ease. Water is the greater concern. We'll have to wait until nightfall and use the constellations as a guide. Even then, I fear too much time will have passed.

Heartbeat after heartbeat, we stand together, wrapped in one another's arms. It's the safest I have felt in years. "Look," I say, "sometimes dire circumstances force difficult decisions. A red storm might pass quickly, or it might squat in place for days. Father doesn't have days. We can travel through the storm using the dome as a protective measure."

"It can't be done," Notus says.

My back molars grind together. He's not even *attempting* to see this from my perspective. "I say that it can."

"My powers are not infinite," he explains. "Eventually, they will deplete, likely before we ever reach Ishmah. When that occurs, we will have no protection from the elements, or from any darkwalkers we encounter along the way. I would rather we seek shelter and conserve my power for when we really need it."

"And I would rather we take the risk." As for shelter, there is none, only the dunes, an eternal rise and fall of sun-bleached sands.

"Stop it," he snaps. "You're being ridiculous."

I stiffen. "So my needs are ridiculous?"

"That's not what I meant, and you know it." A huff of air—pain, or frustration—punches from his chest. "If you go out into that storm, you will die."

He is not wrong. "And if I were to tell you I will do as I please?"

"I forbid you."

My eyes flare, and I retreat from the shelter of his arms. "I am Princess Sarai Al-Khatib. *You* bow to *me*." If I so desired, I could request his head on a spike and no one would stand against me.

Notus swipes at his face with the sleeve of his robe. It is subtle, but our small, domed barrier begins to sink inward. "Think about what is at stake, Sarai. This is a *red storm*. It has flayed the flesh off men and beasts alike. Even my power struggles to repel it—"

"Father is dying!" I scream. "I must go to him!"

"I don't care about your father!" he cries. "I care about *you*." His fingers tear through the disheveled locks of his black hair. "Do you think I would let you walk into certain death? I could not live with myself knowing something happened to you that I could have prevented."

"Stop." But the word quavers. "You don't mean—"

"Don't put words into my mouth. Don't tell me what I feel."

I am pinned. Frozen by my own feelings of inadequacy, the lies I spin.

He is quiet when he asks, "Why is it so hard to believe that I care for you?"

To my horror, hot tears spill down my wind-abraded cheeks. Notus lifts a hand, thumb smoothing away a watery track.

"Because I'm afraid," I say hoarsely.

"Of what?"

I cannot say it. And yet, it feels inevitable, each interaction having led here, to this moment of heartbreak and peril and dread. "What if I let you in again," I whisper, "only to turn around and find you gone?"

Sadness tugs at the South Wind's mouth. There would have been a time when he hid the emotion from me, but I like to think we have both evolved. "I know that I left," he murmurs. "I know that it hurt you. And I'm sorry—deeply, profoundly sorry—for the pain I have caused you. That is something I regret to this day." He steps closer. The pull is there—to fall into him, to forget. It takes all my courage not to retreat. "But I would protect you to the best of my abilities, and that means delaying our journey to Ishmah until the storm passes."

He's right. It would be a senseless decision, yet— "You don't under-stand," I choke out, swiping at my eyes. "I said horrible things to Father. I have to apologize. I have to tell him—" That I love him. That I have never understood why *I* felt unloved in turn. "I have to see him before it's too late."

"I hear you, Sarai, and I understand. We will travel to Ishmah as soon as it is safe. But don't think of sneaking off on your own. If you leave this shelter," he says, expression stony, "I will find you. Do not make the mistake of thinking no one cares for your life."

My knees wobble. Slowly, I sink to the ground. I am made of cracks, and all that I have struggled so hard to dam begins to leak through the slivered openings. For now, I can only wait, and pray the storm will pass quickly.

Hold on, Father. Hold on.

Eve falls, and still the storm howls, squatting over our fragile shelter like a territorial beast. The absence of sun draws a chill from the earth, and I shiver. With the protective dome intact, Notus managed to salvage pieces of the sailer, planting them deep in the sand to form three unstable walls. Miraculously, he recovered my satchel, which still contains my waterskin and two bruised peaches. I'm not sure that it makes a difference. In all likelihood, I will succumb to this squall before ever reaching Father.

Seated beside me against the shattered hull, the South Wind scans the area. His shoulder braces mine, and I fight the impulse to ease against him and draw his strength into myself. This god, whose presence has caused so much turmoil in my life. Yet Notus would happily gift me comfort, if I asked.

Reaching into my satchel, I remove the waterskin and offer it to him. He hasn't drunk in hours.

His glare rakes over my body with borderline affront. "I am immortal," he growls. "Drink."

"Prickly," I mutter, yet I pour the tepid water down my throat. I've only a few mouthfuls left. I will need to ration them carefully.

Every so often, the hull rattles at our backs. I try to ignore it with varying levels of success. Over the hours, our domed barrier has dwindled. Though Notus' power is vast, it is also finite. I question how much longer it will hold.

"I'm still mad at you," I quip.

"I know."

"You should have let me go."

He shakes his head. "I already made that mistake once. I do not plan on repeating it."

In the farthest reaches of my heart, I want to believe him. "If you say it's a mistake, then why did you?"

Because I did not want you.

I stiffen, the words carving into me like sharpest teeth. My molars clench so hard it drives a painful twinge into my temple. "If that's how you truly feel," I snap, "then why are you here?"

Notus regards me in confusion. "What are you talking about?"

"You just said—"

"I didn't say anything." He searches my face with a combination of puzzlement and concern. "Are you feeling all right?"

Do not believe this god. He will lead you astray.

Deep into the sand my fingers sink, into the coolness awaiting beneath the surface. That voice, it has visited me during my dreaming and waking hours. The figure cloaked in shadow from my vision. The Lord of the Mountain. How did I not realize how similar his voice was to the South Wind's?

"Sarai."

I startle. "What?"

"Where did you go?" Notus asks.

In my younger years, I would occasionally hear from the Lord of the Mountain, though I did not know it at the time. In recent months, however, his voice makes itself known far more often, sometimes multiple times a week. I am afraid of what it means.

"Nowhere." Tugging free of his grip, I ease onto my side, my body contouring to the soft sand beneath. Round and round my thoughts spin. I have been so focused on the Festival of Rain, traveling to Mirash, uncovering potential leads about the labyrinth, that I completely forgot what day it is. Eight days hence, my nameday will arrive. The Lord of the Mountain does not want me to forget.

I doze for a time, albeit fitfully. The desert chill dives beneath my dress, stippling my flesh. Even Notus' body heat fails to banish it.

It seems as though no time has passed before I'm shaken awake. My eyes peel open, slitted against the unexpected glare: dawn, breaking over the horizon.

"The storm has passed," Notus says.

"And?" I bite back a groan as I sit up. The aches and pains of yesterday's fall have settled into my joints. "The sailer is still broken." As for my father, I do not know whether he survived the night.

The South Wind does not remove his touch as I expect him to. Rather, he cups my nape in one large hand, thumb pressed against the side of my clenched jaw. "Will you look at me?" he whispers.

He asks with a compassion I cannot deny. Shifting my position, I tilt my face toward his.

Dark tresses fall in unruly layers around his ears. In the youth of our relationship, I recalled how their silken threads slipped between my questing fingers. I recall, too, the quiet strength in his gaze, and I fear the power it holds over me. His eyes promise a lifetime of peace. I have yearned for such things.

"I'm sorry," he murmurs, "for my behavior yesterday. I tried my best to protect you in the only way I know how, but I fear my methods lacked the proper compassion. I was not open to your concerns."

His apology is an unexpected balm. "Father is dying, Notus." A thin, depleted plea. "I must go to him."

"We will reach your father," he says, squeezing my hand in the warmth of his wide palm. "I promise."

He has made plenty of those. We both have. I'm too fatigued, too beaten down, to challenge him.

After helping me to my feet, Notus examines the remnants of our shelter. I scan the landscape, awash in the brightness of early sun. The dunes have shifted location. They lie flat, like dogs in the sweltering heat. Ammara, smoothed of imperfections.

Notus pries a wooden beam free of the hull with a sharp crack. I watch him with crossed arms. "What are you doing?"

Shrugging off his robe, he begins to tie the arms of his garment around the end of the board. "Making do with what we have."

He proceeds to fashion a platform, mast, and sail from the remains of the sailer. A thin tunic hits mid-thigh beneath his robe, sweat-dampened fabric plastered to his skin. Despite my best intentions to avert my gaze, I fall prey to what I hunger for. The South Wind's body is beautifully crafted, and I admire beautiful things.

"Sit here." He gestures toward the makeshift platform, large enough for two people to squeeze onto. Once I'm settled, he slots into place behind me. "Tuck your knees against your chest. Now lean back." A strong arm bands around my waist. Cradled between his bunched thighs, I sink against him. "Try not to make any sudden movements."

Wind crams the makeshift sail, launching us forward. I hold tight to the arm around my waist as we soar across the dunes, toward Ishmah, toward home.

22

W E REACH ISHMAH BEFORE SUNDOWN. FLINGING MYSELF OFF
the makeshift sailer, I sprint for the capital gates, only to find
myself barred by the line of sentinels stretched shoulder to shoulder
beneath the great archway. I rip away my headscarf, baring my face.
"Get out of my way," I snarl.

Their eyes widen in recognition, and they instantly fold at the waist,
allowing me to pass. I dart toward the small stable yard obscured in the
shadow of the wall. "I need a horse!"

One appears in seconds. The mare is fractious, high-spirited, her
coat a rich mahogany in the fading light. I mount, reins clamped in
a trembling hand. One of the soldiers—a captain—steps forward in
concern. "Your Highness—"

"Clear the roads," I command.

He rushes off, barking orders. When I attempt to guide the mare
down the street, she tosses her head, skittering sideways with nervous
energy. "Drat it all," I hiss. "Move!"

Someone catches the reins. I've half a mind to strike them down
when the panic-induced fog clears, and Notus' unruffled gaze fills my
vision. Gray colors the drooping skin of his face. The long hours of
travel have sapped the majority of his power.

"Let me," he says.

I do not fight him on this. In truth, it is the greatest respite to pass the responsibility of navigating the city onto him. Once the South Wind has settled at my back, he digs in his heels, and we spring forward, hurtling down the street with a sharp clatter of hooves.

Up, up into the upper ring, down the broad Queen's Road. Notus directs us not to the central palace gates, but to a smaller entrance nearer to the king's quarters. The moment we are through, I slide from the saddle.

"Sarai."

I glance at Notus. He is magnificent atop the horse, the deep pools of his eyes welling with all the emotion he cannot speak. Perhaps he, too, regrets what was said in the desert.

Then he shakes his head. "Go." And that is the last I see of him, for I plunge into the cool palace interior, past green alcoves and burbling fountains. My legs twinge with fatigue, yet I take the stairs three at a time to the third level, swinging myself around a pillar. By the time I reach the king's chambers, I am near collapse. I stumble inside, gasping for air.

The shades: drawn. The lamps: sputtering, wicks charred black. King Halim's quarters are substantial, burdened by the opulence of hanging silks, the air having curdled with the reek of old sweat. Despite the lethargic warmth of the room, the king's bed is piled high with blankets, Father buried beneath. Amir sits at his bedside, head bowed, clasped hands pressed to his forehead. He is still, both shadow and man.

I step forward. "Amir."

No movement. My heart quavers. I press a fist against it, trying to ward off the rising hysteria. "Amir!"

He stirs and lifts his head. In the muted glow of a nearby lamp, the skin around his eyes is inflamed, revealing what has likely been hours of weeping. The sight steals what little air remains from my lungs.

My brother manages to stand, with effort. His robe is a wrinkled mess. I wonder when he last bathed. "Sarai."

At last, I close the distance, saying, "I came as soon as I could." I brush Amir's shoulder tentatively. He is fragile, my brother. Soon, his life will change, the crown passed onto his brow. "Where's Tuleen?"

"I sent her away," he mumbles, eyes lowered. "I do not wish for her to see me like this."

It saddens me, though I understand Amir's sentiment. That is how our family has always handled uncomfortable emotions. We strip them from our expressions. We scrub them from our skin.

I glance at Father. "Is he—?"

"No." Amir looks toward the window despite the curtains shuttering the view. "But he doesn't have much time."

I'm afraid of peering closer at the body wasting beneath the thick blankets. It is a blight upon my mind. But it cannot be ignored. And so I turn, and gaze down at Ammara's king.

His eyes are closed. The lids droop, and sweat clings to his brow. "Father." But the title is too stiff. It has never sat comfortably in my mouth. "Papa."

His eyes crack open. A white film clouds their pupils. "Sarai," he rattles. "I'd hoped you would come."

I bite my cheek. How many times have I wished to hear these words? I could never have imagined it would be on his deathbed.

The king's thin chest stutters, a sound of liquid in the lungs. "Where is Amir?" he wheezes out.

"I'm here, Father."

He nods, the motion stilted. "That is good. You are . . . together, as you should be."

Settling into the vacated chair, I grip Father's hand with both of mine, as if I might shelter its frailty, the dulled rings that had once gleamed. "I'm sorry I was not here sooner. Notus and I were delayed. A red storm destroyed his sailer, and—" And this was a gift I may have never received, to bid Father farewell. There are more important things to discuss than my delay. I have no idea where to begin.

Slowly, Amir lowers himself into the chair next to mine. I take a breath. "Papa—"

"Do you know what I wish, Sarai?"

I stare down at our father, who watches me unblinkingly. The full force of his attention unnerves me. "I don't, Papa."

"I wish that I knew for certain you'd be safe after I was gone. That Ammara and Amir would be safe as well."

My lips part, then close, no words to come. I see what this is about. "I admit, I've made a mess of things."

"If you were to marry Prince Balior—"

"I *won't*. Please, just—" I sigh, eyes closed. "You will have to trust that I'm doing the best that I can. If you knew—" But I'm not sure now is the time to reveal what lurks in the shadows. It would certainly not ease Father's passing.

"What?" King Halim presses. "If I knew what?"

I look to Amir. He stares intensely back.

"What are you keeping from us, Sarai?" my brother demands.

Fear makes fists of my hands, which I press into the edge of the mattress. This is not how I wanted to spend my last moments with my father.

"I know you had your heart set on a union between Prince Balior and me, Papa, but I don't trust him. I believe his motives in agreeing to the arranged marriage to be nefarious."

Amir gapes at me. "What are you going on about?" He never considered Prince Balior to be the enemy. None of us did.

King Halim says to Amir, "Leave us."

My brother doesn't move. "Whatever it is Sarai knows, don't you think I should be informed, considering I'm your heir?"

"Leave us," he repeats more forcefully.

The slow pulsation of Amir's jaw is the only indication of his indignation. To my surprise, he doesn't argue. With a final glance at us both, he departs, closing the door softly behind him.

"Papa." I speak quietly, as I might communicate with a child. "I believe Prince Balior intends to free the beast from the labyrinth."

"What!" The king struggles to prop himself against the headboard. "Sarai, this is ridiculous."

Gently, I press him back down onto the mattress. He glares at me all the while. "It's true."

He shakes his head, looking elsewhere. Eventually, as though unable to deny the absurdity of my claim, his attention returns to mine. "Prince Balior is an honest man. I don't want his reputation tainted due to idle gossip. Do you have proof of this?"

So I start at the beginning. At this point, I have nothing to lose. I inform him of the records I found, the information unearthed about the beast, its personal account of the events leading up to its imprisonment, Prince Balior's interest in the labyrinth. Despite all evidence laid before him, however, King Halim's doubt is palpable. "Sarai—"

"He has brought his army into Ishmah," I state, the last card I have to offer in this terrible game of leverage.

Every bit of color drains from King Halim's face. "What?"

I feel ill. Prince Balior lied to me, though I should not be surprised. He never asked for the king's permission to allow his army access to Ishmah, and it was not granted. Father's shock proves it. "I saw it," I say. "Thousands of his men have made camp in the western reaches of the city. Tell me: Why would he bring them inside the gates if not to use them? Once he frees the beast, I imagine he will use his army to quell any potential retaliation. He will take control. I think it's clear by now that I don't plan on marrying him. So why does he continue to lurk around the palace, unless it's to enter the labyrinth and release the beast?"

For a time, all is quiet. The lamplight wavers. "This is . . . not good." With a weary sigh, King Halim sags deeper into the pillows, naught but skin and bones. "If I were to stand against Prince Balior, he would unleash his army upon Ishmah without question." Then he frowns, expression ponderous. "I doubt he would strike so soon. Not until I am gone, at least." Another long pause follows. "It's possible he might move during Amir's coronation. I will warn the sentries. We have too few men. Much of the city will be unprotected during the ceremony."

A distorted sound squeezes from my throat, caught between laughter and a sob. "And what of me?" Always, I stand alone in the cold looking in. "My life will end in eight days, Papa. Eight! I *should* have died at birth. That was my fate. You cannot change it."

"Your fate was not to die on that day. Your fate was to live, Sarai, and live fully. That is what I hoped for you."

I shake my head, voice emerging low and hoarse. "Then I have failed you."

A stillness swathes the room. It reminds me of the goats butchered in the market square, a slow drip, drip of lifeblood leaking out.

"In what way?" he asks with a softness I have rarely witnessed.

Tears wind salted tracks down my cheeks. Even as I hold tight to strength, my grip weakens. "I have tried, Papa. All these years, I have tried to be the princess Ammara needs." Tactful, diplomatic, perceptive, judicious, an outstanding leader. I could risk not one imperfection. "But I fear I have fallen short in the eyes of my people, and of you."

"What—" His second attempt to sit up in bed is met with defeat, and he sinks down into the pillows. "What is this talk of failure? Of course you have not fallen short. The people love you, as they should. And with Amir taking the throne . . . he will require all your support."

Mutely, I nod, even as I feel myself folding inward. Just once, I wish I knew what it felt like to be heard by the man who'd raised me. "Can I ask you something?"

He nods, though warily, as if sensing a shift in emotion.

"What do you love about me?"

Father recoils into his sweat-dampened pillow. "What kind of question is that?"

"Just answer it. Please."

King Halim appears as if I have caused a great injustice for daring to request of him this one, small thing. He cannot know how desperate I am to hear his words.

"I love that you are diligent," he says gruffly. "I love that you are a leader. I love your complex mind, your dedication to the people of Ammara."

With every spoken trait, my heart sinks lower. Shaking my head, I pull away from him. "But that's not who I am."

He stares at me. "I don't understand."

"I became those things," I say, "because I felt pressured to be this flawless, faultless version of *you*."

Papa huffs. It stings, this disbelief. "You can't believe that, Sarai. The things I have done for you and your siblings over the years! All of it to ensure you would be looked after, cared for."

"That is my truth," I say. "It has been my truth. I haven't wanted to accept it for fear of failing you." How sad that Father never truly knew me, or saw me for what I was, rather than what I was not.

"I don't understand what you want," he grinds out.

A wild-eyed tightness squeezes my chest. Never have I spoken these words aloud. I have gathered them, secreted them into the smallest folds, so small they are pressed into nothing. I have carried them all the years of my life. And now, I let them unfurl.

"To be free," I whisper, voice wobbling as more tears fall.

Father tightens his hand around mine as I feel those ill-fitting pieces of myself slide into place.

"I wish to know the world," I say. "I wish to cultivate a life of courage and authenticity. I wish to shed the obligations of my upbringing."

King Halim looks terribly saddened. "Why did you never tell me?"

"Because I was afraid," I choke out, "that no matter what I did, I would never be enough for you. All I wanted was to play violin. But even that lost its allure." For Fahim took his life, and my love of music along with it.

Backbreaking sobs send me into the bed. I feel so lost, so completely alone. Father is dying. We have never seen eye to eye, but I do not wish for him to go.

"Sarai." A gentle touch on the back of my head. "Look at me."

I lift my head, wipe my dripping nose. To my astonishment, tears sheen Father's eyes.

"You are my daughter," he says softly. "My greatest and most unexpected gift. If you truly believe you are not enough, then I have failed you as a father. I have always been proud of you, Sarai. Always. I'm sorry I was never able to tell you."

I nod, unable to speak amidst the weeping.

"You ask what the realm needs?" he says. "Sarai. Just Sarai. That's who Ammara needs, who Amir needs, who Notus needs."

Notus. I wonder where he has gone. "He hurt me when he left. I feared he did not care for me." Feared he did not love me, as I loved him.

"I understand why you would feel anger toward Notus, but the fault is not solely his. Fahim played a large part in his departure."

Only the rattle of Father's lungs interrupts the quiet. A peculiar numbness begins to spread across my face. "What are you talking about? What does Fahim have to do with Notus leaving Ishmah?"

"You didn't know?" Father searches my eyes. "Fahim demanded that Notus leave. I was not aware they had spoken until Fahim told me what he had done later that evening."

"He—" I falter, suddenly unsure. "Fahim sent Notus away?" I always assumed Notus *chose* to leave. Father never refuted it.

I snatch my hand from his. "Why?" I croak. "Why would Fahim send him away? He knew what Notus meant to me. He knew that I loved him." Loved him still.

"I don't know Fahim's reasoning," he says, voice weakening, "but I do know he was remorseful after the fact. He dispatched scouts to search for the South Wind in the weeks that followed, hoping to call him back, but Notus was never found."

For what reason would Fahim make this decision? It was not his life. Neither was it his business. Perhaps he feared my happiness, feared who I was when I was loved and free. Was it because he was unable to experience the same, as heir? Because it was yet one more thing he must give up to be king?

Yet even as my ire grows, I deflate. What does it matter anyway? Fahim is gone, and what's done cannot be made undone. Though I question why Notus never mentioned this to me; not once did he fight the words I'd weaponized against him. He allowed them to land where they would inflict the greatest pain.

"Why didn't you tell me about this?" I whisper.

Father is momentarily lost for words. Rarely am I allowed to witness such deep emotion as the sadness and regret now painting his features. "When Fahim was discovered," he says, a quaver to his words, "my world changed. All of ours did. It didn't seem important to fixate on the past, knowing he would not return. And ... I suppose a part of me wished to shield him from your anger, even though he was no longer with us."

A lengthy moment passes before I have the strength to speak. "Does Amir know?"

"No. He took Fahim's death quite hard, as you know. I did not want to taint the image he had of his brother."

It's too much. To learn that the anger and resentment I've held on to has been misdirected? That it was Fahim's decision that carved this hole into my life? Yet Notus didn't fight my brother on this. He left, in the end—without me. How do I go about repairing that hurt? How do I heal?

"Papa." I wipe my streaming nose with the back of my sleeve. "What will happen when you're gone? Who will teach Amir how to rule? Who will guide Ammara through darkness?" And what will happen once my nameday arrives? How am I to protect our realm if I am no longer alive to stand between Prince Balior and the labyrinth?

"Sarai." He grips my hand with surprising strength. "Brightest and fiercest of my children. I am confident you will find a way."

"I don't know ..." A shudder runs through me, and a coarse, wounded sound falls from my mouth. "I don't want to face this alone."

"You are strong. Stronger than you believe. This I know." Together, he lifts our hands, brings them to my damp cheek. "Promise me you will not mourn me when I am gone. I have lived a full life, fuller than I believed was possible. You and Amir will find your footing, in time."

No matter my efforts, I fail to control my mangled weeping. There is so much we haven't said to each other. "Papa—"

"Promise me."

All at once, the fight goes out of me, and I press my face against his reedy chest. "All right," I whisper. "I promise."

23

I T IS A FLAT GRAY MORNING WHEN KING HALIM TAKES HIS FINAL breath.

We gather at his bedside—Amir and I. Tears wet my brother's cheeks, but I avoid making eye contact to offer him some semblance of privacy. Instead, I stare down at the lump beneath the blankets. I have been carved hollow of feeling. This man is not my father. King Halim was fiery, animated, beloved by all. This? It is a pile of old bones.

We sit in silence until the priest bestows the blessing that will grant the king safe passage into the afterlife. Shortly after, he takes his leave. I'm not sure what to say. I have lost a mother, a brother, and now a father. Soon, the curse will claim my life, Amir forced to rule alone atop the earth where our bodies are buried. Already, I ache for him.

Reaching out, I take my brother's hand. His fingers curl, gripping with bone-breaking strength.

"I miss him," Amir chokes out, before descending into another round of fitful weeping.

I understand, for I have missed Papa my entire life. He always extended his greatest efforts toward his sons.

But I rub Amir's back. I soothe him with murmured nonsense words. I tell him things will be all right, not now, but someday. I remind him that he is strong, enduring, and most of all, loved.

With King Halim's passing, the official period of mourning will commence at sunset this evening. Amir's coronation is set for the end of the week. He will need all his resilience, all his strength. He has time neither to process nor grieve. I would not wish that duty upon anyone.

A knock sounds. The door eases open, and Tuleen pokes her head into the room. "The council wish to speak with you, Amir, when you have a moment."

Ammara's future king clutches me tighter, face tucked against my neck. "I don't want her to see me like this," he murmurs.

So do all who guard their hearts as fiercely as King Halim's children. "You don't give Tuleen enough credit," I whisper in response, meeting the queen-to-be's eyes over Amir's shoulder. "She is understanding and kind. More importantly, she's your wife. Let her help shoulder this burden."

A shudder wracks his frame. Tuleen hovers near the doorway in uncertainty, heartbreak whetting her fine features to points.

"Amir." Gently, I untangle myself from his arms. He peers at me through red-rimmed eyes, his face a mess of snot and tears. "There is no shame in grief. We all experience these things at some point in life. Let Tuleen help you. Let your wife," I repeat, "help you." I wipe his cheeks dry. "Go on," I soothe. "It will be all right."

Hesitantly, Amir shuffles toward Tuleen, who takes him into her arms. She, too, holds him close, shushing him as one would a child.

As they speak in low tones, I wander toward one of the open windows. The air is cool despite the rising sun. It comforts me, knowing Papa's final view before darkness claimed him was the glorious spread of golden dunes.

The snick of the door draws my focus from the desert. Amir has departed. Tuleen, however, remains.

"May I?" she says, gesturing to the sitting area.

I dip my chin and select a chair facing away from Father's bed. Tuleen settles across from me. Ivory drapes her form, a thin, beaded headband strung across her smooth brow. She balls her hands in her lap, mossy eyes dark with sorrow.

"I'm so sorry, Sarai."

My eyes flutter shut on a fresh wave of pain. A tear slips out, which I wipe away. "Father's health has been in decline for months," I whisper. "I thought I was prepared. I thought I'd communicated everything I wished him to know. Now that he's gone, I realize I could have taken three, five, seven more years to speak with him, and know him, and lo—" I open my eyes, lift a hand to my mouth as my voice cracks. "Love him."

Wordlessly, Tuleen offers me a square of cloth, which I use to dab my eyes. "I hear you. My parents have both passed. Every day, I miss them."

Grief, I understand. I have stood on its banks as the murk of its waters dragged at my ankles and shins and calves. For a time, I was free of it. Notus' return brought frustration, confusion, yet also warmth and security and healing. But a tide always returns.

"Amir will take this hard," I inform her, though she's likely already aware. "He—" Gods, I hate this. "There was much he admired about our father, and they grew closer in the years following Fahim's death."

"I know." Tuleen's attention falls to the tea set arranged on a nearby table. "Tea?"

She does not await my answer. That's fine. I watch as she pours from the beautifully wrought silver teapot, then passes me the teacup. Bitter. The leaves have steeped for too long.

After pouring her own tea, she eases back, saying, "I worry about him." *Tap-tap-tap* goes her nail against the porcelain cup. In the end, she sets her drink onto the table untouched. "King Halim was a good man: honorable, well respected, admirable. You know this. It's why his children are such upstanding citizens of the realm."

My heart flutters from the praise, for it is something I did not expect. Still, I remain quiet, waiting for her to continue.

"But I want you to know how this has impacted Amir. He would not want me to tell you, but I'm of the opinion he needs more support than he realizes, especially during this transition . . ." Tuleen hesitates.

"Go on," I urge. "I'm listening."

"Amir often speaks of Fahim. Although I never met him, I can see how loved he was by our people. He was charming, upstanding, diligent. Favored, clearly. Amir never anticipated inheriting the throne. He never wanted it. Unfortunately, circumstances changed. He believes himself a disappointment, having failed to fill Fahim's shoes. It was the reason we extended our honeymoon for as long as we did. Your brother was terrified of returning and being proven a failure."

I consider my sister-in-law for a moment before looking elsewhere. "I see." I didn't realize Amir's insecurity was the catalyst for their extended honeymoon. Here I was, resentful of his freedom, while he, too, fled from our father's impossible expectations.

"We had conversations, the king and I," Tuleen goes on. "I mentioned my concerns about the pressure he placed on Amir."

My head whips around, eyebrows drawn all the way to my hairline. "You challenged Father?" I thought only I dared to challenge him.

"I did." She ducks her head, fingers continually moving, fiddling with a pleat in her dress or tugging on a stray thread. "Though I'm not sure it did much good. He didn't seem to understand that Amir was not Fahim. More sensitive, less dauntless. Unfortunately, with his advanced illness, King Halim didn't have the luxury of easing Amir into his station. It has been . . . a lot," she says, rubbing her brow in weariness. "Too much, I would argue. There wasn't enough time to learn all of the information required to lead the realm before he passed."

"There never is." Then I sigh. Poor Amir. He has a long road ahead of him. There are things that must be done. For the next seven days, Ammara's denizens will place offerings at the temples and shrines. The capital gates will close. The markets will shut down until the crown is inherited by another.

"I know we aren't close," Tuleen murmurs, "but I want you to know that I'm here, should you need me." And now she takes my hand in hers, offering it a gentle squeeze. I accept the comfort for what it is: a grace. "You are my family, but more so, you are my friend. If ever there is a time when you feel you don't know who to turn to, please come to me."

A wave of gratitude moves through me, and I bite the inside of my cheek hard enough to draw blood. My family does not speak of such things. We do not divulge hardship. We expose neither unhappiness nor suffering. What a relief that this woman has entered our lives, allowing us to tread new paths.

"I appreciate that," I whisper. She cannot know how much.

It is not so bad, I think, *having a sister.*

Time passes, and I find sanctuary in the gardens. Dawn and dusk, I find myself enveloped in green, doing all I can to avoid interaction. The white marble bench cold beneath me. The fountain burbling behind a shield of interlocking laurel leaves, and bougainvillea clambering up the face of the stone wall at my back, its buds painted in sunset shades of orange, rose, and lavender.

Today was particularly heavy. I could not stay in my quarters a moment longer. They are too vast, all that space for my spiraling thoughts. Here, the dense foliage piles and climbs. It enfolds me in the scents of loam and sweet nectar.

The crunch of pebbles underfoot draws my attention to the entrance. The South Wind, his violet robes blending into the shadows and his hand resting on the hilt of his sword, hovers beneath a cluster of trumpet-shaped flowers. Even in the near gloom, his dark eyes possess a remarkable brightness.

"You're up late," I say. The midnight hour fled ages ago.

"I was finishing my rounds." This low, careful manner of speaking holds a slow rhythm. "I thought I might find you here."

The comment brings a small, sad smile to my mouth. Because he knows me, I realize. Perhaps better than I know myself. "I couldn't sleep."

"That's understandable." There is a pause. I sense his indecision even as I sense it within myself. Notus is one such person I made an effort to avoid. "Roshar's looking for you," he says.

"I know."

Earlier, Roshar knocked on my door. I didn't answer. He left a note, along with an apricot tart, stating he would seek me out tomorrow. The tart sits on my desk, untouched.

The South Wind comes forward a step—just one. The stretch of darkness between us feels alive. Always, that push and pull, to fall or to flee. The truth is, I do not wish to be alone. His presence is not unwelcome.

"May I sit?" he asks.

My throat tightens, yet I nod, sliding toward the end of the bench to make room.

"I would have come sooner," Notus whispers, angling toward me. "But I wanted to respect your need for privacy." His expression twists in helplessness. "I'm so sorry, Sarai."

I nod numbly. These passing days have been spent organizing his funeral, preparing for Amir's coronation. One king exchanged for another. I've barely slept. "Fifty-seven years he ruled Ammara," I say. Papa was only a boy of twelve when he inherited the throne.

"He was an honorable king."

Indeed, King Halim was honorable, loyal, fair. Ammara's citizens will remember his generosity and goodwill. As for me, I will cling to those few memories, the rare times I had Father rather than a king.

When I do not respond, Notus asks, "How is Amir?"

"As well as can be, given the circumstances." The next words emerge before I have the opportunity to fully process them. "I know you don't exactly care for him, but it's important that we show the realm a united front, at least until Amir has settled into his new role." Not that I will be here to witness it. "He would appreciate your support."

"He told you this?"

"Well, no." I clench my hands in my lap. "But I spoke with Tuleen, and I just want you to be aware of how difficult a transition this will be for him. He's too proud a man to ask for help, and your acceptance would go far in alleviating some of his concerns."

The South Wind sighs. "Amir and I have never seen eye to eye, and we likely never will. That doesn't mean I don't believe he is good. That doesn't mean I won't support him." He is earnest as he says, "Amir will bring positive change to Ammara and build a legacy your father would be proud of. This I know."

So few words, yet they help alleviate my worry before it has the opportunity to hook too deeply. I nod, slightly abashed. "Sorry."

"No offense taken."

How does he so easily forgive? I have insulted his character not once, but again and again since his return. The gods must have thick skins.

"Sarai." At last, Notus' hand engulfs mine, thawing the chill of my icy skin. My heart twinges. His touch has always grounded me. "What do you need?"

Perhaps I have been waiting for this question. There was a time I would have responded with lies of every possible shape and shade. But in this moment, I trust that I will not be brushed aside. "I wish for company, even if we do not speak."

"Then I will sit here with you for as long as you need me to."

And that is exactly what he does. This, too, heals me. To expose some deep-seated wound, and to be welcomed for it, to feel seen. "Will you tell me of your family?"

I asked him about his family multiple times during our previous relationship. Notus never deigned to answer with any depth. It frustrated me, for I only wished to know more of this unknowable god. I wished to know all that he could give me and more.

"If you're looking for some tale of comfort and familial love," he warns, "you won't find it in the story I'm about to tell you."

I wasn't, as a matter of fact. I was looking for something real.

Gently, I squeeze his hand. His eyes leap to mine, swirling with vulnerability, the fear of being seen. I understand him. I see him. I know him, as I know myself.

"I was never close with my father," the South Wind begins. "Boreas was the eldest, the favored child. Zephyrus was cunning, too clever by half. He often meddled in others' affairs—not that he was ever punished for it. Eurus was . . . troublesome. He loathed our father and did everything in his power to make his life as difficult as possible. Of the four of us, Eurus received the most abuse."

At this, the South Wind falls quiet. If I'm not mistaken, he appears unsettled, perhaps guilty, though I cannot imagine why. "I, however, am not like my brothers. A god who chose to spend his time with books rather than in combat?" His mouth curves bitingly. "They called me weak. Soft."

Notus is the last person I would ever consider weak. There are soft parts of him, as there are soft parts of us all. I appreciate those pieces, for they are the most stable and secure. "You are a superb swords- man," I assure him. "A protector in every sense of the word. There is no one stronger, no one else I would wish to guard Ammara." Or my heart.

His head is bent, but his eyes crease in a way that suggests he is touched by the sentiment.

"I didn't take up the sword for glory," he says. "I took it up out of necessity. Without a weapon in my hand, I would be looked down upon, ostracized. As a result, I fell into the trap of changing myself to fit the persona others had created for me. This is why I struggled so greatly throughout my childhood. I never felt true belonging in the City of Gods.

"When I was banished to Ammara, I wandered for many a year. But one day, I heard of the sacrifice that would be made to the beast in the labyrinth. Seven men sent to die. And I thought, if I could kill the beast, perhaps I could prove to my father how great a leader I was. I'm not sure why I did it, exactly. Following the coup, my father was bound to the Chasm and would never again be free. But a part of me still sought his approval, even then."

"I never understood why you stayed," I say. "You're immortal, more powerful than the most powerful mortal man. Why kneel before a king that wasn't yours?"

He studies me for a time. "Maybe he wasn't my king initially, but I came to respect your father. He was fair, just, if exceptionally hard on his children." He sighs. "But to answer your question, I believed your father wanted a man like Eurus, or Boreas—a born fighter. I told him I wasn't interested in shedding blood. I wished to help the people of Ammara. Your father respected my stance. He did not seek to change me."

I had no idea Notus struggled so. Here I was writing my sad, sad story, having failed to share it with someone who might truly understand.

"And you brothers?" I ask. "What happened to them?"

"I admit, we lost touch a long time ago."

"How long?"

"Many centuries," he says.

I nod, feeling terribly sad for him. It means something to me, that he has opened himself in this way, and shared these shadowed pieces of himself. I wish to know Notus wholly, deeply. I wish to touch his heart as he has touched mine.

"Do you miss your brothers?" I ask him.

"To tell you the truth, it's hard to miss them without ever having truly known them. Of course I knew my brothers to a certain depth, but it never went beyond that. They never wished it to."

Sometimes I think of these things. I know of my brothers only what they show me. I wish Amir and I were closer. I wish Fahim had trusted me enough to share his struggles.

Lifting pained, tear-filled eyes, I whisper, "Why didn't you tell me Fahim sent you away?"

A sharp, driving inhalation cuts the air. At first, I don't believe Notus will respond, but then he says, "Your father told you?"

I nod.

Notus grips both my hands. "Because," he says, voice so quiet it's nearly lost to the fountain spray, "I knew you still grieved him. I didn't want to taint your image of him. He was a good man who was only doing what he thought was best for you."

But Fahim must have realized the mistake he'd made. Is that what drove him to kill himself? Did the guilt of my despair eat at him? Or was it another burden he carried: the pressure of our father, the impossible pursuit of perfection?

"He didn't know what was best for me," I say, "and neither did you."

He nods, expression pinched. "You're right. It wasn't fair to make that decision for you. I should have known better."

"What exactly did he say to you?" Even if Fahim had demanded that Notus leave, I would still expect a goodbye. They had gotten along well, Notus and Fahim, at least—I assume—until my brother discovered my relationship with the South Wind.

This immortal, this god, studies his hands, which rest in his lap. Strong brown fingers marred by white scars. He balls them into fists. "You were preparing for a competition at the time," he murmurs. "Fahim told me it was your last year of eligibility. You were to age out the following spring. If you did not win," he says, lifting his eyes to mine, "you would likely lose your only opportunity to see the world."

There was truth to his words. The King Idris Violin Competition, founded by Ammara's first sovereign, attracted hundreds of elite violinists from lands near and far. The winner was granted the opportunity to tour with orchestras beyond Ammara, beyond even Um Salim, to those realms in the north and west and east. One such realm, Marles, boasted the world-renowned St. Laurent Symphony. Performing with them was something I had dreamed of since I was a young girl.

Notus goes on with an urgency that implores I listen. "Fahim opened up to me. He told me how painful it was to have sacrificed music for duty to the crown. It *destroyed* him, Sarai, and I . . . I couldn't live with myself if I was the reason you lost your dream."

I shake my head in disbelief. I hear him, but . . . "You could have talked to me about it. We would have figured something out."

"Your brother had a point. It was unfair to string you along when it was unlikely I would stick around. Ammara wasn't my home, no matter that I wished it were. A clean break was best for everyone."

"Best for everyone," I counter, "or best for Fahim?"

Notus opens his mouth, pauses, then closes it. A sweet breeze rustles the nearby laurel trees. "I know it was unfair," he says, "but I'd hoped the letter I wrote would explain everything."

My focus suddenly sharpens. "What letter?"

"The letter I asked Fahim to give you."

Silence, broken only by the burbling fountain. "Notus," I say. "I never received a letter."

His expression twists into confusion, and I expel a pained breath. This message, another secret Fahim hoarded. I remember the anguish of Notus' departure, how it ate me alive, these questions that had no answers. I remember elusive sleep, my days squandered. I lost years of my life in months. An entire summer, gone.

"If I'd received the letter," I whisper, "maybe it would have helped me move on. But . . . it was unfair for you to leave without saying goodbye."

"Sarai, I *never* wished to go, never wished to leave you." His expression is made of layers: regret and misery, shame and remorse. He takes my hand. I haven't the strength to pull away. "You must understand. I was a stranger in a strange land. As a princess, you are expected to marry for influence and power. I could not offer you anything resembling security. Yes, I am a god, but I have no ties to your culture, your people, your realm. And . . . people talked. Some of the things they said were not kind. I thought it best to remove myself from the situation entirely."

"Since when do you care what others say about you?" My voice is hoarse, each word a shard of glass in my throat.

"I don't." He meets my gaze squarely, with challenge. "But I care what they say about *you*."

It is just like him to think of me in place of himself. It makes it difficult to be truly angry with him. "You don't know what it was like after you left." A low keen wells in my throat. Five years of anguish, heartache, regret. "I failed to compete that year. I couldn't even make it past my bedroom door. You were gone, and then Fahim died—"

"I'd heard. There was an accident—"

"It was no accident."

Notus has fallen quiet. "What are you talking about?"

Gods, he will make me say it. "Fahim wasn't killed in a hunting accident," I choke, though that is the story my family disclosed. Fahim Al-Khatib, diamond-bright, fell from his horse, and broke his neck. An honorable way to die. "He hanged himself."

The South Wind is so still it is difficult to separate him from the shadows at his back. His dark eyes are pearled, sheened by a shattering heartbreak. "Sarai," he breathes.

A coarse moan of despair deflates me, and I hunch lower onto the bench, hands shielding my face as Notus gathers me into his arms. I do not fight it. In truth, I am far from this place, this shadowed greenery.

"Two weeks after you left," I whisper, "Fahim didn't come down for breakfast." To this day, the smell of fuul—beans with lemon and salt—makes my stomach turn. "This was unusual. Most mornings, he was first to the table."

There we sat: Amir, Father, and I. Four chairs placed at a table large enough to seat sixteen. Every so often, one of the king's advisors entered the dining room to deliver a message. At the time, Father was in negotiations with Um Salim about a possible marriage contract— my marriage to Prince Balior.

I wish the memory stopped there. But one cannot stop a flood in motion. Softly, I continue.

"After breakfast, I went to Fahim's bedroom to check on him. He'd mentioned not feeling well the previous week." Fool that I was, I'd believed it to be an illness, not some poison rooted in his heart and mind, a darkness that was his alone. "I found him swinging from the ceiling rafters," I push out, "a noose around his neck."

Notus stares at me, horror having petrified his features. "Sarai."

And just like that, I break.

Father never discussed Fahim's death. Neither did Amir, neither did I. We moved forward, each carrying that unseen burden. There were times I thought my spine would break from it.

Five years following Fahim's suicide, I am still no closer to healing than I was. What, then, have I been doing all this time? Running. After so long, I am weary. I seek only to rest.

Notus tightens his arms around me as I sob into his chest. "I'm so sorry." He smooths the damp strands of hair from my tear-streaked face. "I know we can't turn back time, but I'm here now," he says. "I'm here."

The tears flow fast and hard. I cry for Fahim. I cry for Father. I cry for my mother, whom I never knew. But mostly, I cry for myself. For all the turmoil, all the hardship, all the instability, the impossibilities I have faced, the battles. I allow the South Wind to comfort me. No, I welcome it. His arms, so solid and secure. Gradually, my sobs quiet and my body calms.

I pull away, just far enough for air to slip between us. My eyes drop to Notus' mouth. His lips part, and the spice of his breath wafts against my face. We are unfinished, he and I.

"Notus." Lifting a hand, I press two fingers against the flesh of his lower lip. I trace it to one corner of his mouth, then the other. I don't want to ask permission. I want to take, to conquer and claim. And I want to give, to feed his hunger as he has fed mine. To give life—and receive it.

Leaning forward, I brush my nose against his, a velvet touch. His eyelashes flutter, and a low growl of need rises from his throat. The sound drags up my spine like a sharp nail. My nipples pucker; warmth travels through my belly—lower.

Our mouths open, become one. His blunt teeth. My eager tongue. Sliding his hands down my back, the South Wind fills his palms with my backside. I moan and press closer. Notus tastes like no one else in the world. He is like the sun, that pulse of brightness, which all creatures great and small gravitate toward. I have missed him more than I can say.

Deeper the kiss delves, plundering hidden depths. My mind blanks. I forget what has come before this moment. I know only the drive of my heartbeat, the shimmer in my blood. Soft strands of his hair slide between my questing fingers as the press of his body drags me into memory. We'd had this, once. We'd shared the intimacy of togetherness, belonging. We had trust then, and love.

"Wait." Notus suddenly pulls back, sending me off balance. I clamp his shoulder to avoid tumbling into a nearby bush. "I don't think this is a good idea," he says, breathing hard despite having not moved from his seated position.

It stings. Despite this, I plaster on a winning smile. "We're engaged, Notus. We can do whatever we like."

He is grim-faced. "You're mourning, Sarai. I won't take advantage of you."

What mourning does he speak of? Today, or all the days of my life? "You're not taking advantage of me." If anyone is taking advantage of the situation, it's me.

He shakes his head, adamant. "You need time to heal."

"Isn't that my decision to make? I need this." My fingers skim the worn softness of his robe. They curl into the cotton, and I anchor myself to him. "I need to feel *alive*."

"I understand, but—"

I graze the front of his trousers with the palm of my hand, trace the length of him, feel it stiffen beneath my touch.

The South Wind wavers. To pull away? To lean close? I understand these conflicting needs. He is not alone in experiencing them.

But he removes my hands from his body, expression pained. "This isn't the answer."

My face scalds. I'm so overcome with humiliation that I have to physically fight the urge to flee the garden. Notus is right. I hate that he's right. Maybe it would feel good in the moment, to give our bodies to one another. But I don't want sorrow to taint the intimacy we would share. In the end, the rejection is no less painful.

Mouth pinched, I shove to my feet, adjusting my dress. "Very well. I bid you good night, Notus."

He watches me with a sadness he does not attempt to hide. "I don't want you to leave," he murmurs. "You shouldn't be alone. Not tonight."

Ask me to stay. But I fear voicing this desire. I am afraid in so many ways, and the grief, freshly bruised, is another complication. Perhaps it's better for both parties if I take space.

I do not say goodbye as I depart the garden. But I do think of all that I regret.

Later, after crying myself to sleep, I wake to a knock on the door. My swollen eyes open the slightest crack. I blink, peering blearily into the gloom. What time is it? With the curtains drawn, it's difficult to say. The knock doesn't come again.

My joints creak as I slide from bed and shuffle across the room. I still wear my dress from earlier, having been too exhausted to change. "Hello?" I press my ear to the door.

No response.

I open it to find a small bunch of wildflowers on the ground, a note tied around their stems. As I pick the flowers off the ground, I open the message.

I'm sorry.

Notus' handwriting. My mouth wobbles, and I seal my lips together in an attempt to regain control of my emotions. Perhaps I was too rigid, too hostile. He's right. I *am* mourning. I wanted to feel close to him, but desperation overrode logic in the moment. I'm glad he stopped me before things went further.

I'm placing the bouquet in a vase of water when a sting darts through my finger. I glance down, vaguely noting the blood beading on the pad of my thumb where it sliced against the stem. Then I recognize the flowers I hold. Their velvet petals, so deep a violet they are nearly black.

Black iris.

I lunge for the door, but my vision blurs, smearing into shadow. The handle slips from my hand. As I slam onto the floor, my racing pulse beginning to falter, the Lord of the Mountain makes himself known.

Sleep, Sarai, he soothes. *Sleep, my beauty.*

PART 2

THE BLOOM

24

I AM SIX YEARS OLD. I STAND AT MY BEDROOM WINDOW, PEERING down into the courtyard below. Beyond the sleeping labyrinth, King Halim speaks with a wiry man carrying an oblong leather case on his back. I lose sight of them as they enter the palace.

"Sarai." My handmaiden, an elderly woman named Hoda, emerges from the washroom, having finished drawing my bath. "Come. We must make you into a proper lady."

I do not understand what *proper* means. Why can I not meet this man, this violinist, in my trousers? Why must I squeeze myself into a dress?

Hoda ushers me into the washroom, where I am scrubbed and swabbed and scoured until my skin gleams.

I am twelve years old. Violin clasped in hand, I tremble in the wings of the massive concert hall, the eyes of a thousand spectators glinting in the sinking western sun. A full orchestra commands the stage, their tuning nearly complete.

Sweat leaks beneath my arms. I have prepared for this moment. Six years of weekly lessons, hours upon hours spent honing my technique. My fingers are fluent in scales. My bow hand is adept at all manner of articulation. And here, now—my debut. The piece, aptly named *Chatter* for its rapid spiccato, is a bright hum in my pulse.

"Are you ready?"

I turn to face my teacher, Ibramin. At eight years old, he had already performed with the realm's most distinguished orchestras. Now, decades following his solo career, he is Ammara's most sought-after pedagogue.

"I feel sick," I whisper.

Soft creases enfold Ibramin's kind black eyes. "That is normal. If you were not nervous, that would mean you did not care."

The maestro enters upstage to exuberant applause. He bows, climbs onto the podium. When he catches my eye, he smiles in encouragement. My stomach lurches. "I don't know if I can do this," I murmur to Ibramin.

"What do you fear, exactly?"

"That I will err. That all my work will be for naught, and I will fall apart with thousands to bear witness."

"That everyone will learn you are imperfect?"

I clench the instrument's neck, dampness from my palm transferring onto the violin's fingerboard. That is correct. But what does he expect? Father dictates I practice for a minimum of four hours daily. I cannot remember when I last had a respite.

In an attempt to settle my nerves, I search the hall for the royal family. There is Fahim and Amir, both dressed for the occasion. King Halim's chair is empty. "I don't see Papa."

"I'm sure he'll be here," Ibramin reassures.

But the maestro looks to the wings. I take a slow, deep breath, and another. At his nod of encouragement, I step onto the stage to thunderous applause.

I am fifteen years old. Dressed in a long-sleeved, sapphire gown, I perform the second movement of Harimir's Violin Concerto in D minor. The strings cut into my callused fingertips, a slight vibrato wavering the notes as adagio eases into unhurried grave, a countermelody to the horns. I cannot release pressure on the bow for fear of losing the string's resonance. The sound must carry to the very back of the hall.

And when I reach the movement's emotional climax, when the orchestra joins in a sweeping crescendo that rings throughout the amphitheater, my own tears rise, for here is joy and grief, awe and suffering, marvel and anguish, peace and sorrow. The people will know Sarai Al-Khatib. They will know music.

I am eighteen years old. The throne room is as cold as it is vast: white marble, red stone. I shift uncomfortably in my chair. I should be practicing. I've a competition before the year's end. If I were not certain of Father's wrath, I would have slipped away hours ago.

Biting back a groan, Amir tilts his head back, eyes squeezed shut. "I don't know if I can survive two more hours of this," he mutters.

I snort. "You and me both."

Once a month, King Halim meets with Ammara's citizens to heed their grievances, an event that often stretches well into the early hours of evening. Fahim, Amir, and I are required to attend. Stupid, considering we're not allowed to participate.

"This is what you have to look forward to, Fahim." Amir waves a hand toward the woman currently complaining to the king, in great length and extraordinary detail, that her crops have failed yet again. "I, for one, am thankful I was the second-born." He slouches back with a gratified sigh.

Fahim's lack of response draws my attention. His form is carved from granite, his face frozen into blankness. Five hours we have sat here, yet he has not spoken once.

Reaching out, I rest my hand on his arm. Though Fahim is older than me by six years, we share much, including the tendency to armor ourselves. "Everything all right?"

Two heartbeats pass before his eyes slide to mine. Something painful flickers in those gold-flecked irises. My stomach clenches in unease, for the distress there has surfaced often these past months. Each occasion, a darker blemish, a deeper void. "Fahim?"

"I'm fine." He jerks his arm away.

I glance at Amir, who is too preoccupied with cleaning his nails to notice Fahim's waning spirit. Regardless of my brother's claim, I do worry. I worry a frightening amount.

I've accepted my fate of death by boredom when the doors to the throne room open. A rush of desert air infiltrates.

I straighten in interest. The man who enters bears an impressive physique, with broad shoulders and a wide chest stretching the ivory fabric of his robe. His strong torso reminds me of sturdy oak. A scarf veils the lower half of his face. Eyes the color of rich earth glimmer beneath black eyebrows.

Deliberately, King Halim rises to his feet. "So. You are the man who believes himself strong enough to slay the beast?"

I frown in response to this unexpected information. Rumors have sprouted in recent weeks of a newcomer promising to kill the beast imprisoned in the labyrinth. I believed it to be folly. Fahim, too, frowns in light of this announcement. Even Amir seems to be invested in the conversation.

The man bows low at the waist. "I am, Your Majesty."

Deep and resonant is his voice, with a pull that reminds me of Ishmah's lowest temple bells. Though he is but a single person, he possesses the presence of a thousand men.

"And how, pray tell, do you intend to do that?" King Halim demands.

My left hand taps a rhythm on the chair arm. A reasonable query. Either this visitor is a fool, or we are to underestimate him. Seven men have already been selected as sacrifice to satiate the beast's growing hunger. Seven men every decade. They are to enter the labyrinth in less than four months' time. This man believes himself capable of slaying the beast? It cannot be done.

"I would prefer to discuss that privately, if it's all the same to you, Your Majesty."

Father considers the visitor for a lengthy moment. Then, as if agreeing to the man's request, he swings out an arm. "My children. The eldest and my heir, Prince Fahim, finest horseman Ammara has ever seen."

Fahim dips his chin in acknowledgment. The man returns the gesture with respect.

"My second son, Prince Amir."

Amir rolls his eyes good-naturedly, for he has never received the praise Fahim does. Such is the bane and blessing of the second-born.

"Lastly, my daughter, Princess Sarai."

The man's gaze shifts to mine. My breath catches.

"Princess Sarai." The visitor's voice, a complex upwelling of sound, is music I dearly wish to know more of. "I was once granted the opportunity to attend one of your recitals. You performed the Variations on a Theme of Three Ammaran Dances, if I recall."

I blink in surprise, for that recital took place nearly three years ago. I am particularly fond of that piece.

When the visitor returns his attention to the king, I'm left oddly bereft.

Two days later, I learn the visitor's name: Notus.

He is smoke in the halls. Some days, I am only able to catch a glimpse of his shoulders as he turns a corner, or hear the click of his bootheels against the marble floor. It is enough to hunt him in the pre-dawn gray each morning, peering through my bedroom window to where he trains in the courtyard below. There, he is a study of movement. Sword drawn, chest bare, he stabs and retreats, ducks and whirls, hacks and parries. His body is beautiful. It is particularly alluring when glazed in sweat.

In the week that follows, I become so consumed by Notus that I begin to neglect my practicing. Rare it is that I skip a day, but three mornings pass before I realize I have not touched my instrument. The attendants talk. They claim King Halim has offered Notus accommodations in the palace until he is to venture into the labyrinth. Of course, I must see for myself if this is true.

One morning, when the sun blisters the dunes into waves of burnished umber, I don my finest dress before descending the stairs to the central courtyard. The morning bell tolls the seventh hour. A cool mist dampens the gray stones underfoot.

Notus is a darker silhouette against the shadow cast by the labyrinth. Beads of perspiration slide down the grooves of his abdomen. He sidesteps, his back to me, cutting in a brutal arc of molten silver. The bunch of muscle in his shoulders arrests my attention, wholly and completely. I stop a healthy distance away and clear my throat. "Good morning, Notus."

Midway through his exercise, he stills, arm outstretched. It is almost unnatural how rapidly he turns toward me and bows at the waist. "Princess Sarai." Low and rich, his voice shivers across my skin. It contains an accent I cannot trace.

"I understand the need for formality in the king's presence," I say, "but *Sarai* will suffice when we are alone."

In a liquid motion, Notus sheathes his scimitar. He does not even appear winded. "I was not aware that we were friendly enough for the informality."

It takes a great effort to keep my attention above his neck. This would be much easier were he not carved to perfection. "We are friendly enough." I do not give him the opportunity to negate this claim, charging forward with all the subtlety of a bull. "Am I correct in assuming you were not born in Ammara?" Though his coloring is similar to my people, the narrowed shape of his eyes suggests he was born elsewhere.

"You are."

He offers nothing else. But I have cracked tougher shells.

"So what brought you here?" I ask, and can't help the way my eyes rove over this man, every part of him. His fingers are strong and broad, the color of baked bread. To the east, opaline sunlight flutters across the Red City, brightening his left cheek.

"I suppose," he says, frowning, "I am no longer welcome in the place where I was born."

It is a start. But I am eager to know more. "Why?"

To this, he offers no response. Very well.

"If you will not gift me with an answer," I say, "then explain to me why, out of the thousands of people here, you believe yourself capable of slaying the beast."

His eyes—ebon stars shaded by thick lashes—glitter above the scarf shielding the lower portion of his face. Beyond his shoulders, the labyrinth looms, as it always does. A shallow tug in my gut compels me to approach. I ignore it.

"I am a god," he says.

"A god." Somehow, I know it to be true despite lack of evidence of his claim. "What are you a god of, exactly?"

The smallest pebbles clatter underfoot as he widens his stance. Our shoulders brush briefly, and my heart kicks hard against my rib cage. Then Notus stretches out his arm. The air stirs against his palm.

"Many know me as the South Wind," he says. "I am responsible for the summer winds."

I stare in wonder. He sends a gentle breeze to stir the strands of hair curled against my neck. My eyes leap to his. He does not shy away.

"If you're a god," I press, "then I can only assume that means you are immortal?"

"You would be correct."

For a time, all is silent, snuffed out by the thickening mist. "I wish to know your thoughts."

Notus looks to me with thinly veiled surprise. I imagine the curve of his mouth behind the scarf and wish for the barrier to be removed so that I might see his expression in full.

"I am thinking that it is quiet here," he says. "I am unused to this weight, this . . . open stretch of flattened land."

The wind gusts, its hollow timbre in my ears, a twining of pitches high and low. I pull my arms to my chest, wrapping them around my stomach for additional warmth. Every so often, one of the guards makes his rounds.

"What else?" I demand, angling my head just so. I wish to know all that he can give me.

He looks at me then. "But I have told you."

"Tell me again," I say.

"Sarai."

I startle, Ibramin coming into sharper focus. He sits in his wheeled chair near the window of the music room, violin resting on his knee. Mine is tucked between my left shoulder and chin, bow hovering over the string.

"Your scales," he says with evident irritation. "D harmonic minor, if you please."

I comply, ascending and descending the scale with ease. My daily sessions always begin with scales. After nearly an hour, we move on to études. We spend so long on technique that my lesson comes to an end before we're able to review my concerto.

As I tuck my violin back into its case, Ibramin rolls his chair toward me, face grave. "Sarai. The competition approaches. You must focus."

"I understand." Loosening the hair on my bow, I slip it into the case as well.

"I'm not sure that you do."

I straighten, considering my teacher with new eyes. A brisk, biting tone—that, I am not used to. "Is something on your mind, sir?"

He traces the large wheels of his chair, as he often does when deep in thought. "I'm concerned that the time you spend with the South Wind is disrupting your focus."

It takes an effort, but I successfully smooth the coarseness from my breathing. The old man hasn't a clue what he's talking about. "I appreciate your concern, but I have everything under control."

"Do you?" Ibramin regards me with a disapproval I would expect from my father. "Can you look me in the eye and say, with complete confidence, that you are putting all your effort and attention into the competition?"

As a matter of fact, I cannot. The South Wind is due to enter the labyrinth tomorrow. As we have grown closer these past months, I have begun to fear for his life. It is silly. He is, after all, immortal. He cannot die except by a god-touched weapon. He told me so. But who is to say what powers this beast possesses?

Last night, I did not return to my rooms until dawn. I wished for that night to last forever. It was cold. The sky was black, chilled by a thousand icy stars. Standing beside Notus in the courtyard, I opened to him in a way I had opened to no one else. I told him of my upbringing, of music, of my desire to see the world. I shed the bonds that made me small.

"I want great things for you, Sarai," Ibramin says. "Your gift has only solidified the king's commitment to your success in the endeavor. The King Idris Violin Competition will open so many doors for you."

He does not have to inform me of Father's intention. I know. I have always known.

But here is something I have told not a soul. Sometimes, I want more from life. It would be mine alone to paint with whatever hues I saw fit. Or maybe I would not use paint at all, but a sculptor's tools, a weaver's loom, a storyteller's quill and ink.

But that is neither here nor there. "I do my best, sir. I am diligent in my studies. You know nothing is more important to me."

"I am glad you recognize this. Whatever distracts you will surely pass, but music will remain. You alone are responsible for your future."

I shut my case with a loud thump, struggling for breath. For the first time in years, I feel a connection with someone as unknowable as myself. I cannot bear to think of him leaving.

"I appreciate the concern, sir," I say. "However, you forget that I am a princess of the realm. I will do as I see fit." I depart without delay, shutting the door with a quiet snap.

It is a long, sleepless night.

Only hours ago, the South Wind entered the labyrinth with only his scimitar and his winds. We parted with a heartfelt embrace. I cried. I never cry. Six men followed to meet their fate.

I'm not sure when or if he will emerge. Inside lies a complex tapestry of winding corridors, or so I have heard. It is possible he will not return at all.

The idea renders me breathless. Lying spread-eagled in bed, I stare up at the obscured ceiling, thinking back on these glorious months spent in the South Wind's company. It has been a reluctant unfolding—for both of us. But I do feel seen by this deity. It is something I hold close to my chest.

After a time, I slip out of bed and move toward the window. Due to the sacrifice, additional guards have been stationed in the torchlit courtyard below. They wait to see if the shadows seething beneath the labyrinth doorway are soothed. If the beast has been satiated for another decade.

Then—movement. Notus staggers forward, having emerged from the labyrinth's gloom. He hits the ground. His sword skitters across the stone. I gasp and fly from my room, racing down the hallway and stairs, out into the courtyard where the guards have gathered around him. I shove them aside, seeing only the weeping cuts marring the South Wind's purpling face, the tattered state of his robe, the unnatural angle of his right arm. Nothing else.

He lifts a hand to cup my cheek. Even wounded, his touch is gentle. When he speaks, he says but one word.

"Sarai."

"Can you get away?"

Partially shielded by a thicket of ivy, I turn toward Notus, who has appeared at the garden's entryway, its abundant flowers and sweet-smelling blossoms hemmed in by tall hedges. Generally, the grounds are unoccupied in the evenings, but today is King Halim's nameday. The palace has opened its doors. Wealthy aristocrats, government officials, longstanding families at court—all are present. The South Wind is Father's honored guest. He failed to slay the beast in the labyrinth, but he survived—the only person to have ever done so.

Notus angles his ear toward me, though continues to scan the guests milling about on the patio separating the garden from the ballroom, its doors open to the evening breeze. "Don't you tire of sneaking around?" he murmurs. "Your father will find out soon enough."

Shielding my developing relationship with Notus is the only way I can ensure it stays mine and no one else's. "I'll tell him, just . . . not now."

"When?"

"After the competition." Once I win first prize—and I intend to win—Father will be far more amenable to the idea of my relationship.

"Sarai."

I startle, whirling around. "Fahim." My back hits the hedge with a sharp crinkle of leaves. "I thought you were with Papa."

My eldest brother steps forward. Behind him, couples spill out onto the patio in their refined robes and elegant gowns. "I need to speak with you about something." He sounds pained, though there exist no outward wounds that I can see. "Please."

I glance at Notus, who is doing an excellent job of staring straight ahead and pretending we had not just exchanged words. "Sure. Can you just . . . give me a minute?"

Fahim glances between Notus and me, suddenly suspicious. He knows. How can he not? The desire I feel toward the South Wind is palpable.

"Is there something you wish to tell me?" he demands.

My stomach bottoms out. These hedges rise high. Too high to climb. "Please, don't tell Papa," I whisper. It is too frail, this bloom. Too young to withstand any external force.

Fahim sends Notus off with an abrupt wave of his hand. I bite back my protest. As heir, Fahim has authority over the South Wind, but I do not appreciate that he treats him so disrespectfully.

When we are alone, Fahim demands, "How long has this been going on?"

I stiffen. "That's none of your business."

"How long?"

He bristles with aggression. This has become more common of late. Fahim is as docile as they come, but the last six months have bred rising tempers, frustration, outbursts fueled by contempt.

"As I said," I reply coolly, "it is my business."

"Ibramin claims you've been spending a lot of time together."

Fact—and fuel to these flames. "It is not Ibramin's place to share the details of my private life."

"But it is his obligation to inform me of his concerns regarding your studies," Fahim counters. His next word comes low. "Well?"

Arms crossed, I glare at him. I am beholden to no one. But this is my brother, whom I love, and who loves me. "If you must know, Notus and I have developed a friendship over the last few months."

My brother considers this. The darkness in his eyes is entirely foreign to me. "Has he touched you?"

I deliberate on ignoring this question altogether, but I'm afraid Fahim will do something rash, like attack Notus. "No." And what a frustrating thing that has been. The South Wind is honorable. Always, he stands an appropriate distance. His eyes neither wander nor linger. Sometimes, I question if my attraction toward him is one-sided.

But when we speak late into the evenings, I watch this god transform. He is warm and sturdy, gentle and open. Slowly, so slowly, I pry pieces of his story free, when he allows me to do so. I wish to know everything he is.

Eventually, Fahim sighs, rubbing his forehead with the heel of his palm. "Don't let him become a distraction, Sarai. You need to focus on music."

Sometimes I wonder if Fahim resents me for living out his dream in his stead. "I appreciate your concern, but it's fine—"

"It's not fine!" he cries, then draws me deeper into the garden as heads swivel our way. "Your competition is weeks away," he whispers, voice dropping to an inflamed hiss. "This is your chance. I just . . . I don't want the South Wind getting in the way of your aspirations."

I reach for my brother's hand, hold it tight. I understand him, I do. "You know I would never let that happen."

"Sarai—"

"Please, Fahim. I know what I'm doing. You don't have to worry about me."

He falls quiet, which makes my heartrate stutter for reasons unknown. In this moment, he is small and bent and defeated. Without saying farewell, he wanders off, and becomes night.

Later, when the palace has bedded down, there comes a knock at my chambers. With the guards dismissed for the evening, no one is around to witness me pull the door wide, allowing Notus entry. A flick of my wrist, and the lock is engaged.

My chest strains as I turn to face the South Wind. Immortal. Swathed in sapphire and shadow. This pull, which I can no longer deny. As if in a trance, my hand lifts to press over his heart. Its stoic, even-keeled rhythm grounds me. Stable as the earth.

Easing nearer, Notus lowers his mouth. His lips part mine with a hunger that dizzies me, for I have lain awake aching for his touch. The breadth of his hands spans my waist, the small of my back. I am spiraling. Down and down and down I go. A gentle tug, and he pulls me onto the bed.

I wake deliciously sore, body boneless, mouth sweetly bruised. Rolling onto my side, I glimpse the rumpled blankets, the imprint of where Notus had slept. I reach over, touch the soft white silk. It is cold.

A small pit hardens in my belly. Not that I'd expected Notus to remain until morning, but I had hoped he might leave some small token of remembrance, proof that he thought of me as I thought of him.

By the time I reach the throne room, I am in a foul mood. Fahim and Amir have already arrived, the latter dozing in his seat, the former appearing unusually troubled.

"All right?" I whisper to Fahim as I settle into my chair.

He shrugs without looking at me. "Just another day."

I mean to ask him about our conversation last night, but Father arrives before I get the chance. We spend the morning in meetings, then break for lunch. I use the opportunity to seek out Notus. He is not at the labyrinth. Neither is he in his chambers. Disappointed, I return to my quarters alone.

I've barely shut the door when there is a knock. Notus pushes into the room, hands grasping the front of my dress, the hot press of his mouth marking my neck and jaw as he kicks the door shut behind him. In the next breath, he lifts my skirts, hefts my legs around his waist, and enters me in one hard thrust.

I cry out, teeth clamping his shoulder as he drives into me. It is not soft, his loving, but I am not easily broken. The slap of our skin cuts through the stillness, my gasps muffled against his shoulder as he pounds into me with a desperation akin to my own.

And when it is done, his seed trickling down my leg, Notus takes me into his arms, holds me closer than I ever thought possible. "Meet me at the south palace gate," he pants. "Just after midnight."

Leaning back, I search his eyes. They hold a fear I do not understand. "Notus—"

"Don't be late."

I've barely righted my dress before he is out the door.

I press the back of my hand to my mouth. My lips throb. Whatever doubt his strange behavior has unearthed, I will not allow it to soil what just occurred. I pass the time practicing until the bell tolls the midnight hour, then don a cloak. Shadows shield me from the guards completing their rounds. The gate lies ahead. I sprint the remaining distance.

It's deserted.

An icy wind cuts through me. The stars mark the first hour of morning. Peering into the silhouetted courtyard, I search for Notus. Did I mistake the time we were supposed to meet? *Just after midnight*, he'd said. *Don't be late.*

The hours pass. The moon emerges white and full to brand herself against the sky's thin black skin. Pacing before the gate, I comb the gloom, the obscured alcoves, the doorways of the palace. The bell tolls the fifth hour of morning. My nerves begin to fray, for I fear something terrible has befallen Notus. Later, the bell tolls again, dawn bleeding color onto blank canvas. Still, I wait. And I wait. But the South Wind does not come.

Two weeks have passed since the South Wind's abrupt departure. Father informed me that Notus left Ishmah before the sun, on a horse pilfered from the stables. When I demanded answers, the king had none to give. Notus had, after all, failed to slay the beast imprisoned in the labyrinth, though that should not have mattered. *There is nothing to keep him here*, Father said. He could not have known how that wounded me.

I fled to my chambers and locked the door. I raged. I wept. I screamed for the South Wind. Then I screamed for justice, for blood. In the days that followed, silence was my only companion.

Now I stand at my bedroom window, wondering what I did wrong.

"Don't fret, my dear," Roshar murmurs from behind me. When he attempts to pull me into his embrace, I step out of reach, unable to bear his touch.

His expression wavers, then folds into disappointment, though he tries his best to remain upbeat, plucking at the voluminous pleats of his scarlet robes. "Sweet?" he asks, offering me a plate of confections.

"I'm not hungry." No, I am vastly empty these days.

"Sarai—"

"I don't want to talk about it."

He sets down the plate. "Very well." Low and somber. "Shall I go?"

I don't know. I'm paralyzed, a leaf spinning in the wind, with no knowledge of where I might land, or how.

When I do not respond, Roshar says, "What of Fahim? Perhaps he might comfort you?"

My frown deepens. Fahim did not come down to breakfast this morning. In fact, he has avoided me most days. I've failed to notice, so burdened by my grief of Notus' unexplained disappearance ... but perhaps he knows something I do not.

I climb the stairs to Fahim's room, push open the door, his name dying on my lips. There he swings, noose around his neck, back and forth and back and forth.

"Please play for me, Sarai."

Slouched in my chair, violin resting untouched on my lap, I peer out the music room window, open to the temperate breeze. In the distance, rare clouds blacken the horizon. I find myself doing that a lot these days— searching for what lies beyond. Always, my gaze seeks the south palace gates, as if I might spot a dark figure on horseback galloping through.

I turn my attention toward Ibramin, who sits on the other side of the large, woven rug gracing the floor. It hurts to meet his wizened eyes. To see how far I have fallen. The King Idris Violin Competition was mine to claim. And I failed. Could not drag myself out of bed. Could not motivate or encourage or inspire. I never showed.

"Can I ask you something, sir?"

Ibramin studies me in concern. I wish he wouldn't. I do not deserve it. "Anything," he says.

For the last three months, I have been unable to place the violin at my shoulder and draw my bow across the strings. First, Notus' desertion. Then, my brother's life cut short. If I had paid more attention, could Fahim's death have been prevented? Could I have eased whatever burden he carried?

"You mentioned that you once stopped playing," I say hoarsely. "Why was that?"

Ibramin glances down at the violin in his lap. A most generous donation from Ammara's Council of Arts. The instrument itself is nearly two hundred years old. "My wife and I married young, before I gained recognition throughout the realm. We were happy, then." A long, weary sigh, drawing forth a memory having grown brittle with age. "As the years passed, however, and my popularity grew, I spent less time at home. My rigorous touring schedule would not allow it. By the time I was twenty-four, I was gone for most of the year. It was then that I saw my wife for what would be the last time."

Silence trickles out. I swallow once, twice, before I'm able to speak without my voice cracking. "She passed?"

He plucks the E string. Its pitch fades, enfolded in a breeze unfurled. "She left, having decided our marriage wasn't worth the effort. *I* wasn't worth the effort."

"Oh." My mouth pulls. "I'm sorry to hear that."

"Don't be. The fault was mine." At my confusion, he explains, "She approached me many times requesting that we spend more time together. I failed to listen." A cloud of sadness drifts across the old man's features. "After she was gone, I didn't touch my violin for over two years."

Again, I glance out the window. The distant storm has since dissipated. No clouds. Not one. "What made you pick it back up?"

He shrugs. "It wasn't a choice, in the end. Music called to me, and I answered." For an uncomfortably long time, Ibramin gazes at me. "One day, you will rediscover the urge to play. And your soul will know peace."

It is a lovely sentiment, truly. But I am tired. I wish only for the forgetful veil of sleep. And so I return my violin to its case, where it will rest for the remainder of my days.

25

AM I DEAD?

The ground blazes a line of cold down my back. I blink. Darkness. It neither lifts nor lightens, this perpetual stretch of black across my vision. My rough exhalation hits the air, so cold it steams silver before dissipating. Then: more darkness.

I'd pondered this moment for many a year. I'd questioned what I might find on the other side, how I might feel. What I might say to the god who granted me but twenty-five years of life. I did not expect to feel pain: a throb up my spine, coiling tight around my neck.

In the passing moments, however, the dim begins to lift. My limbs move easily enough. I sit upright, glancing around. Bare earth. Its gray dust coats my fingers, reminiscent of ash.

No lamp, no candle, no fire to drive back the encroaching shadows. There is, however, an ambient glow, though I'm not certain where it originates from. There are walls I see now: curved, cut from pale stone, carved with symbols. The light appears to be coming from around the corner. It beams toward me, snagging my bewildered curiosity until I push to my feet and drift forward.

It's a mirror. The same mirror I gazed into when I last spoke with the Lord of the Mountain.

A woman fills the looking glass. Her sharp, mistrustful gaze meets mine, slitted beneath swollen eyelids, cheeks tracked by the salt of dried tears. But there is more: the defeated dip of her chin, the crimp of displeasure shaping her mouth. That layer peels away, makes room for another. The determined jut of her jaw, the stretch of her spine, mistrust shedding into some cold, hard, shining heart of strength. This woman is not defeated. *I* am not defeated.

I pinch my cheeks, the motion reflected back in the mirror. The sting makes me wince, and I drop my hands. I don't look dead, nor do I feel dead. I always imagined death to be burdenless. I would not feel hunger as I do now. My finger would not smart with pain where it was pricked by the small spine of a deadly blossom. But who can really know death's face? As far as I'm concerned, the curse was correct. On my twenty-fifth nameday, I met my demise.

The mirror's surface wavers then. It resembles a shallow pool of water rather than reflective glass, for my reflection bleeds out, reshaping itself to reveal a vast chamber, marble floors, opulent chairs atop a raised dais: the throne room.

A large audience fills the hall. They are seated on long benches arranged in rows, a blue rug unfurling down the aisle. In the mezzanine above, archers have drawn their bows, deadly iron points catching the light. The head advisor stands at the bottom of the dais. Slightly behind him, there rests a luxurious velvet cushion, and on that cushion, the crown.

Understanding dawns. This is Amir's coronation.

"Presenting Prince Amir Al-Khatib of Ammara."

As the audience rises to their feet, the doors open, and there my brother stands, resplendent in emerald robes, the sleeves and collar adorned with a painstaking weave of silver thread. There is no hunch to his posture, no inkling of grief. It is the most convincing mask.

His every footfall is deliberate. Ishmah's nobles and dignitaries and merchants and bakers—people from every walk of life—bow as he passes. Tuleen stands at the front, dressed in violet, eyes shining with love and pride as she looks upon her husband. No sign of the South Wind. I frown. Does the mirror show me what is, or what will be? Does Amir grieve me now that I am gone?

My brother kneels. The crown is lifted.

"All hail King Amir Al-Khatib of Ammara."

And when the gold circlet nestles in the thick locks of his hair, Amir stands, turning to acknowledge Ammara's citizens against swelling jubilation.

The image fades, becomes something else.

Ishmah's curved domes and spiraling turrets splash rust-red across the gilded dunes. An ugly smudge draws my eye skyward. A black plume, smothering the horizon. Smoke? No, *shadow*. It engulfs the rooftops, masking what teems below: darkwalkers.

They are too many to count, a horde, a stampede. They descend on Ishmah's population with a ravenous bloodlust, drawing people's souls from the broken bodies strewn throughout the streets. I spot the red robes of Prince Balior's soldiers sweeping across the crooked footpaths and cracked roads, swords wielded, funneling Ishmah's citizens toward the lower ring. The strangest sight of all, however, is Ishmah's gates. They are closed, likely due to the coronation. Which means the dark-walkers entered the city via other means.

I brush the looking glass with trembling fingertips. They warm with a sudden heat, as if someone holds a candle beneath the mirror. My city overtaken, toppled to rubble. Its people slain, raped, enslaved. I close my eyes, open them on a surge of distress. Ishmah's denizens continue to flee beasts and soldiers alike. Meanwhile, the same thickening darkness oozes across the dusty earth, laps the base of buildings, and is drawn up the walls and over the roofs to smother those inside.

I lean forward, palm flat against the mirror. It's not real, I tell myself. If I will it, perhaps that will make it true. But the scent of searing skin hits my nostrils, and I snatch back my hand with a hiss of pain. As I stare down at my reddened palm in bewilderment, blisters begin to form near the base of my thumb.

My heart sinks. If I'm dead, how can I feel pain? Why does Ishmah fall to darkness? Unless . . . has Prince Balior successfully freed the beast from its prison? In doing so, did he release the darkwalkers with it?

The image again transforms. I now stare down one of the palace corridors, its fluted pillars blurred by the smoke-like shadow dribbling through the open windows. Someone appears at the end of the corridor, moving with haste. I would recognize the broad-chested physique anywhere.

Notus turns a corner and begins to run. It's as if I'm running alongside him, watching through the mirror as he takes the stairs three at a time to the third level. I've never seen the palace so vacant. Where are the sentinels? Fighting the darkwalkers terrorizing the streets?

Eight men safeguard Amir's chambers. Notus lifts a hand, tossing the men aside as easily as matchsticks. He blasts the doors open with so formidable a wind they're wrenched from their hinges and crash into the opposite wall.

Amir stands at the window overlooking the city, legs braced, sword in hand. Tuleen shrinks behind him as the South Wind—banished god, features frozen into a chilling blankness—crosses the threshold. A crude wind snaps through the room, yanking books from shelves and toppling a nearby chair. My mouth goes dry at the sight.

Upon sighting Notus, Amir frowns. He doesn't lower his weapon. "What do you want?"

"Where is she?" He advances toward Ammara's new king. I imagine the floorboards trembling beneath the might of his tread.

Amir lifts his sword straight out. "Keep your distance."

The South Wind moves faster than my mortal eyes can track. By the time I process what has happened, he has already disarmed my brother, his own blade resting at the base of Amir's neck. Tuleen's eyes are wide, wide, wide. Two tears trickle down her cheeks.

"*Where. Is. She?*" Notus snarls.

Amir bares his teeth, but doesn't struggle. "Who?"

"Sarai. She was in her rooms last night, and now she's gone. No trace of her."

With impressive calm, Amir reaches up to curl his fingers around Notus' wrist. As a child, Amir was quick to anger. He was the youngest son, the weakest, always with something to prove. But here is iron where sand once stood. He will not be cowed. Already, the crown has changed him.

"Even if I knew where she was," Amir bites out, "I wouldn't tell you. Since you came into our lives, you have brought nothing but death and turmoil."

"What are you talking about?"

"We were fine before you came to Ammara. Yet within months of your arrival, Fahim was dead. You returned, and now Father's gone, too, and darkness spreads through our realm." The king bares his teeth. "Tell me you had nothing to do with it."

The South Wind's expression is thunderous. "Fool, I'm trying to *save* Ammara."

"Then why were you not at my coronation yesterday?"

Notus is taken aback, that much is clear. He frowns, lowering his blade a fraction. "I was . . . called elsewhere."

A cutting smile curls Amir's mouth. "I'm sure."

The sword point returns as Notus spits, "My brother called for aid. I left Ishmah briefly to help him, but I'm here now, and I won't hesitate to slide my sword into your chest, king or not." He twists the tip of the scimitar. A spot of red blooms beneath its point and spreads to clot the fabric. "Fahim tried to keep Sarai from me. I won't let you do the same."

Amir's eyes boil with unrestrained fury. In this moment, he has never looked more like our father. "Kill me, and you will not leave this place alive."

"I don't care for my life," Notus says. "I never have."

The South Wind whirls, sword raised to meet the descending blades of the guards pouring into the room. Tuleen yelps, cowering in a corner near the curtains, face bloodless against the gloom beginning to choke the room.

Amir attempts to stab the South Wind amidst the tussle, but a gale rips through the chamber, scattering parchment like a thousand leaves. The wind's intensity forces Amir to his knees. Tuleen claws the edge of a bookshelf to avoid being flung into a wall.

My heart throbs, and I swallow thickly. So, this is what it has come to. Notus will destroy Amir, the palace, the realm, so long as he believes they stand between him and my whereabouts. I can only watch the disaster unfold.

The soldiers regroup and charge. I gasp as Notus sidesteps a brutal swing, only to narrowly avoid another strike to his back. He releases a small cyclone of air, which hurls men into walls and topples furniture. Two guards are knocked unconscious. A vase explodes in a shower of clay fragments.

I'm leaning fully against the mirror, palms flat, the tip of my nose pressed to the warm reflective glass as though I peer through a window. Heartbeats later, Notus has successfully disarmed the guards. Amir lifts his sword, at the ready.

"Amir, stop." Tuleen grabs her husband's arm desperately. "Notus isn't our enemy."

"You're wrong, Tuleen." He attempts to dislodge himself from her grip, yet the woman holds fast. She is stronger than I believed. "It's because of this immortal that my family is dead, splintered apart."

"If you can't see that Notus loves Sarai," Tuleen snaps at her husband, "then you are blinded by more than pride." She's shaking—with fury, I suspect. "Darkwalkers *and* Prince Balior's forces overwhelm Ishmah. You know we can't fight them alone. If you're going to make an enemy of the divine, then I question your intellect as well as your capacity to rule."

Amir gapes at his wife even as my mouth quirks in approval. Tuleen has spirit. I admire that.

In the end, Notus lowers his weapon. "Please," he says to my brother. "Tell me where Sarai is."

Amir looks to his wife in frustration, then sighs and sheathes his sword. "Gone," he says, and begins to pace.

"Gone?" The South Wind looks to Tuleen, back to Amir. "Gone where?"

My brother's robe snaps around his cloth-clad legs. He strides toward the window, peers into the shadow-choked city, the sun flickering like a grimy orb behind the opaque cloud. "My sister's life was fated to end on her twenty-fifth nameday." Slowly, he turns to face the South Wind, expression etched by grief. "She's dead."

Notus is petrified, hollowed out from shock. Four, five, six heart-beats pass. Slowly, oh so slowly, he lifts his hands, presses his fingers to his temples. "If this is a jest—"

"It's no jest," Amir says. Again, he peers out the window. "I wasn't aware that Sarai had been cursed. Our father only told me shortly after I arrived back in Ammara. And now it's too late."

Notus shakes his head, faster and faster. I see the heartbreak in his eyes, a devastation that is total, a storm breaking over him. I lift my hand to my mouth with a soft cry of pain. "She can't be dead," he says weakly. "The curse was about the drought. She told me . . ."

"The drought was only part of it."

The South Wind doesn't appear to be listening. He is deep, deep within his mind, where no harm can befall him. "We fought," he whispers, and the agony contorting his features is a mirror of my own. "She wanted closeness, but I kept her at arm's length. Your father's death hit her hard. I didn't want to push her away, but—" He falters, gazing around the room with childlike confusion. "I tried to make it right. Last night, I sent flowers to her room by way of apology. I'd hoped to talk about it today."

Amir straightens from his slumped posture, suddenly keen. "What kind of flowers?"

Notus blinks, perplexed by the question. "Black iris."

It is quiet but for the crack of a scream in the distance. I close my eyes. Grief made me careless. I should have recognized the flowers. I should have recognized a lot of things. But what I most regret is wounding Notus so deeply. Would things have turned out differently between us, had he known of my early demise?

My brother then sags against the wall with red-rimmed eyes. "The touch of black iris is what was fated to kill her," he explains, voice hoarse. "How did you acquire them? Father banned them from Ammara."

The South Wind presses the heels of his palms against his eyes. A broken sound falls from his mouth, and another. Heartbeats pass before he's able to speak. "I ran into Prince Balior in the halls. I wasn't in the right state of mind and may have mentioned the argument between Sarai and myself. He offered me the flowers, claimed they were Sarai's favorite. I wasn't aware of the ban. If I had known it was a danger to her, I would never have ..."

His voice breaks. Tears slide down my cheeks, and I wish I could step through this mirror and comfort him properly. It is what he would do for me.

To my surprise, Tuleen comes forward, head cocked curiously. "You claim Sarai is dead, but I'm not so certain."

I straighten to attention. Notus and Amir do as well. Amir says, "If Sarai touched black iris, then she's dead. That is what was foretold."

His wife regards him calmly. "Then where, pray tell, is her body?"

"What do you mean where's her body?" he snaps. "It's ..." But he trails off in realization. He hasn't the slightest clue. I struggle to wrap my mind around the implication as well. My body *should* be in my room. But Notus visited my room and found nothing.

Both men regard Ammara's queen in stupefaction. It is almost comical, their wide eyes and gaping mouths. "When Amir told me of Sarai's curse," Tuleen explains, "I took it upon myself to complete my own research. The Library of Ishmah is, after all, one of the preeminent research institutions in the realm—"

"You?" Notus stares at her. He is scarcely taken off guard, yet this small woman has managed to do exactly that. "You were the one who visited the back rooms?"

Tuleen stands pillar-tall. "I was."

The candle. All this time I thought Prince Balior had searched the small, deserted office. How wrong I had been.

"Did you take any books?" the South Wind demands, eyebrows snapped over his straight nose.

Tuleen smiles as she says, "As many as I could carry. And I cleared the room following the darkwalker attack. I would rather the information not fall into the wrong hands."

Amir looks between them. Sweat wends down the side of his face and dampens the collar of his robe. "What is he talking about?" He angles toward his wife. "Tuleen?"

A warm flutter of hope swells inside my chest as she motions toward the office, leading the two men to its impressive collection of wall-to-wall bookshelves. One by one, she removes fat tomes, bound documents, the occasional scroll, to place them on the desk. "King Halim claimed the Lord of the Mountain would return to take Sarai's life," she says. "But as you can see, Sarai's nameday has passed, and there is no body to be found. Which makes me believe the curse has altered course—or has been misinterpreted."

Misinterpreted. I hadn't considered that. Is this not the afterlife, this mirror a means to observe what develops in the living realm? But she makes an excellent argument. If I were truly dead, where is my body?

"What do you mean *misinterpreted*?" Notus demands.

"It's clear from my research that there is a connection between Sarai and the labyrinth," she responds, flipping through one of the documents. "But I stumbled upon a translation that makes me wonder if King Halim possibly misunderstood the bargain that was struck." She pins her finger against a page. "In this translation, it's stated not that the Lord of the Mountain would return to take Sarai's life. It's that he would return to take *her*. Which makes me believe that Sarai is not, in fact, dead."

"If she's not dead," Amir cuts in, "then where is she?"

Tuleen lifts her head, face grave. "She's trapped in the labyrinth."

26

THIS IS THE LABYRINTH?

I turn in place, scanning the area, hemmed in by solid walls. Darkness brushes my skin with its primordial chill. It smells of the earth in decay, the arid perfume of the desert air smothered by rot.

I press a hand to my breastbone. Fear twines so tightly with relief that I'm not entirely sure *what* to feel. I'm not dead, as I had believed: relief. There's still time to save Ishmah: relief. I'm trapped in the labyrinth: fear. And the heaviest, the most potent: I don't know if I will make it out alive.

I return to studying the mirror. Notus has begun to pace. "How can you be certain Sarai is trapped in the labyrinth?" he asks Tuleen.

Amir, however, continues to stare at his wife with a mixture of confusion and betrayal. "Why didn't you inform me of this sooner?" he insists. "Why would you keep this from me?"

Tuleen is a small woman, bird-boned, and—I had thought—brittle. But she appears to grow three feet in the span of a single breath. "Your father was ill. I did not want to place yet another worry onto your shoulders." She begins to cough, blinking rapidly through the thickening smoke. "We haven't time for your dramatics, darling. Darkwalkers are turning the city to rubble—the forges to the west have already collapsed. Ishmah is burning down as we speak. You know now. Let that be enough."

Agreed. There are more pressing matters.

Ammara's new queen turns to the South Wind with a keen eye. "What do you know of the labyrinth, Notus? You yourself have walked its passages, have you not?"

He crosses toward the window, pivots, and returns to the door, head dipped in thought. "I know that the labyrinth was built to contain the beast, which hails from the City of Gods. A sacrifice was made to the beast every ten years."

"Yes, a sacrifice." Tuleen glances between Notus and Amir pensively, the latter of whom looks utterly befuddled by the conversation. "Have you ever noticed the ruby that marks the labyrinth entrance?"

Amir frowns, but Notus says, "I have." He continues his anxious pacing, hands linked behind his back, tired boots appearing out of place against the opulent rugs embellishing the floor. "What of it?"

"According to my findings, the ruby is supposedly linked to the beast's hunger." She opens a small journal, where she has jotted down some of her notes. "The greater the hunger," she says, scanning her handwriting, "the brighter it gleams. But yesterday, when I passed by the entrance, I found the ruby dull and lightless. I believe something was placed inside the labyrinth to feed the beast."

My stomach drops. Or some*one*.

Gods. Was this to be my fate all along? Locked in this tomb with no hope of escape? For reasons unknown, I've always been drawn toward the labyrinth. If the curse was truly misinterpreted, I was destined for this prison regardless.

"You think Sarai was taken into the labyrinth as a sacrifice for the beast?" Amir says lowly. "Is that what I'm hearing?" He dabs the sweat from his forehead. When another fitful cough explodes from his wife, he passes his headscarf to her. Tuleen wraps it around her face for protection.

"Yes, darling," she wheezes, the back of her hand pressed to her mouth. "That is exactly what I'm saying."

Nervous laughter tickles the back of my throat. It's not funny. It is the farthest thing from funny. But if I don't laugh, I'm afraid I'll break, and that is simply unacceptable.

My brother swears, and shoves the heels of his palms into his eyes, and sags onto the edge of his massive bed, red silk robes already kissed by falling ash. "So what do we do?" His hands drop. His eyes are wet. "I can't leave Sarai to die in the labyrinth, but Prince Balior has unleashed his army upon Ishmah, and darkwalkers are ravaging the lower ring. People will be looking toward Tuleen and I to guide them to safety."

"I will go to her."

Tuleen and Amir's heads whip toward the South Wind, who stands frozen in the middle of the room, mouth taut with grim determination. My heart flutters in gratitude. I do not deserve this brave and loyal immortal.

The young queen plucks another book from the stack sitting precariously on the corner of the desk. "Before any decisions are made, I think you should read this." She offers Notus the slender volume, which he accepts. After flipping to the bookmarked page, he scans the material, then lifts his head in confusion.

Tuleen regards him expectantly.

Notus speaks as he reads the inscription. "According to this account, there is more than one entry to the labyrinth. Deep in the center of the maze lies a doorway leading to the realm of departed souls—"

"The Deadlands," Tuleen provides. "Have you heard of it?"

Notus huffs a short laugh of disbelief. He shakes his head, cheek caught between his teeth. "The Deadlands." He snaps the book shut. "My eldest brother's realm, though I have not seen Boreas in centuries."

Tuleen explains, as she gently pries the volume from the South Wind's grip, "I believe the labyrinth is connected to the Deadlands. Potentially other realms we are unaware of, too. In our culture, there is what we call *the unseen*, places where there is a thinning of the fabric between realms. The land on which the labyrinth was built is likely one such area."

"That would explain why darkwalkers have overrun Ammara," Notus says. "They are utilizing the doorway inside the labyrinth to enter Ishmah. They had to have come from somewhere. And since the labyrinth is within the city walls, they're able to circumvent the protective runes on the gates."

Beyond his shoulder, the sky continues to blacken. Smoke drifts in thicker globules across the rooftops. No shade of blue to be seen.

The South Wind strides toward the window again. It's as though I peer over his head, for I see the whole of the courtyard, its eerie desertion, pockets of dim light wavering behind shadow and smoke. Notus stares at the labyrinth with disquieting intensity, as if he might crumble the structure with but a thought. "I'm going after her."

Tuleen nods, having likely expected this. Amir, still seated on the bed, runs both hands through his ash-caked hair.

"Once you enter the labyrinth," my sister-in-law says, "there is a chance you may become trapped there with her."

"No god, man, or beast will keep me from Sarai. I will bring her back. I promise you this." Notus' attention flicks between the king and queen. "Will you both be safe?"

A perpetual wind smooths even the roughest of edges. Whatever came before, the vitriol spewed and suspicion fed, in this moment, Amir casts it aside.

"Tuleen and I will retreat," my brother replies. "We've a safe place to shelter while I call upon our allies for aid. If Ishmah falls, we will flee to Mirash and regroup." He hesitates, looks at Tuleen, who nods in encouragement. "Thank you, Notus, for your sacrifice. When you find Sarai, tell her that I love her."

Not long after Notus' departure, the mirror darkens. The ambient light, however, remains, pulsing from the wrought silver frame.

I touch the opaque surface of the looking glass. How could this mirror have known that I wished to view my loved ones above all else? Can the labyrinth sense my heart's desire?

These past weeks have held murk and depths, but at last I have clarity. All these months, during which Prince Balior placed his pawns. Now he is in the unique position to overtake Ishmah, his army positioned to finish what the darkwalkers began. I wonder if, in having touched the black iris, I somehow unlocked the labyrinth and its roiling darkness, which now leaks through Ishmah's streets. The only question is: Have I released the beast as well, or does it still pace its cage?

Whether or not Notus successfully finds me in this treacherous maze, I can't risk standing still. An opportunity to escape may present itself, if I am brave enough to face the dark unknown. Choosing a direction at random, I begin to walk.

The air knits close as I follow the dim corridors, hitting dead end after dead end. The shush of my slippers no longer dies a muffled death, but brightens sharply, bouncing off nearby walls. Eventually, the pathway empties into a chamber with a round table placed in its center. There, I'm startled to find a violin nestled in an open case, cushioned by gray velvet. Tears sting my eyes, for here, too, is another locked door. I remember this varnish, red like the sunset sands. The violin is not mine. It is Fahim's.

My pinky catches the A string and lightly plucks. Flat. It must be tuned. If I recall correctly, the peg that wound the A string was perpetually loose, slipping with a frequency that would often frustrate my eldest brother. My breath hitches at the memory. I was not the first prodigy in my family, but I was the first to become known.

I brush the ebony pegs, trace a line down the fingerboard, across the arched bridge, over the slope of the tailpiece. I think of how painful it must have been for Fahim to watch my rise from afar, this destiny that should have been his to claim.

Something scuffs the ground behind me. I whirl, unconsciously planting myself in front of the violin. I carry no weapon. I've no knowledge of combat. Whatever I face in this labyrinth, I face alone.

Large and formless, the creature shifts in those lightless pockets, too dark for my mortal eyes to penetrate. A slow exhalation stutters across my tongue. I'm not dead. Not yet, anyway. "Who are you?" I demand. "What do you want from me?"

"I'm surprised you do not know," responds a voice. How cold. And how familiar.

A figure leans forward, revealing a sharp nose, followed by the thin curve of an unsmiling mouth and two amber eyes.

I recoil in shock. "Prince Balior?"

The long, emerald robe parts around his legs as he steps toward me, shedding the shadows at his back. "Were you expecting someone else?"

"How—?" But that is the wrong question. Rather, the question is *why*. Except I know the answer. At least, I *think* I do.

"You didn't come here to marry me," I tell him. "You came for the labyrinth."

He angles his head in deliberation. I have always considered Prince Balior handsome, yet in the obscured interior of the labyrinth, the planes of his face appear almost skeletal, cheeks sunken and jawbone sharp enough to cut. "On the contrary, I was willing to secure Ammara through marriage. This land has its faults, but acquiring your realm would help expand my vision for a new world."

"I was merely a tool."

"Well, yes and no." He spreads his arms wide. The corner of his mouth tics upward. "You are lovely, willful, loyal to a fault. Why should I not desire a partner by my side when I am finally granted what I was promised all those years ago?"

The air is cold, but the prince's words bring an unsettling finality, shaved down to the thinnest of points. "What are you talking about?" What, exactly, was promised, and by whom?

Pressing the tips of his fingers together, he begins to circle the room, his gait so smooth he seems to be gliding on ice. I shift to avoid exposing my back. "My research on the labyrinth goes back more than a decade. From a young age, I was fascinated by its presence. A prison for a hellish beast. Seven men to sate its hunger. It's quite the tale.

"One year, I came across an obscure manuscript, which I found at a border town south of Um Salim. To this day, I don't understand how a jeweler came to be in possession of the document, but he was more than willing to part with it—for a price. It was in this manuscript that I learned the labyrinth's true nature: it is a doorway to another realm."

His sharp eyes slide to mine, and I retreat, the heel of my slipper sending a small pebble clattering toward the wall. It hits the stone with a sharp ping. "I see from your expression that you are already aware," he says, his smile terribly hungry. "Good. That will make it easier."

If I thought I had any chance of escaping Prince Balior, I would already have fled. I have wounded his pride. I have insulted him, embarrassed him, deceived him as he has deceived me. He has every right to want to bring me harm. But it would be too easy to kill me outright. I imagine he wants my suffering most of all.

"You may not remember," he continues, "but I visited Ishmah about ten years ago. King Halim invited my father and I to attend his nameday celebration as a token of faith and healing between our peoples."

I do have a vague recollection. There was talk at court about a visiting prince, though I didn't think much of it at the time. I was more concerned with my upcoming recital.

"You wore an ivory dress and your hair plaited in a crown atop your head. You were to perform for the guests that evening. While everyone gathered, I used the opportunity to slip away to the labyrinth. The guards were half-asleep. So lazy and irresponsible. I stepped inside with them none the wiser.

"It was there I met the beast. I'd timed my entrance perfectly. A few days before, a sacrifice had been made. It was sated, and with a full belly, it was able to regress to its humanoid state long enough to talk with me. It told me of its needs. I told the beast of mine. We reached an understanding, the beast and I."

I will not give him the satisfaction of asking what this understanding is. I know he is eager to tell me. So I wait.

"By combining forces, we would be able to achieve so much more. The beast wished to break free of its bonds. I sought power and influence, security for Um Salim's future, a stake in the region. The beast agreed to bestow that power upon me if I vowed to help it escape. So I put my plan in motion. I would need to be invited back to Ammara.

I was, by that time, already a renowned scholar. All I had to do was create a problem only a scholar could solve. So with the beast's help, I unlocked the doorway into the Deadlands and released the dark-walkers into Ammara."

Dread descends over me. Prince Balior continues to circle me as a vulture would a rotting carcass. It is becoming increasingly obvious that I have been a fool in more ways than one.

"Over time, the darkwalkers multiplied. Drought continued to plague your realm. Eventually, it became too much. King Halim hoped that I might unearth a solution to Ammara's troubles in my ancient tomes and proposed that our two realms become one. It was the opportunity I'd been waiting for. I would return to the labyrinth, and the beast, to fulfill the promise I'd made all those years before."

I shake my head, for I see the end of this long, treacherous road: ash and ruin. Father had hoped Prince Balior would banish the dark-walkers, alter fate. Instead, he invited a traitor into his kingdom. "Think about what you're doing, Prince Balior. If the beast is imprisoned, it's likely for a good reason." Though the beast was locked away due to no fault of its own, I do not doubt that it is dangerous. "There's still time to change things."

"It cannot be stopped," he says, spreading his hands wide. "My plan is already in motion."

As if on cue, the ground trembles. Grit rains from the ceiling. I hurriedly snap the violin case closed to protect the instrument.

"We could have been happy, Sarai. With my promise to the beast fulfilled, I could have kept your people safe from ruin. But you spurned me, and for what? A man whose promises are worth no more than bits of worthless copper?"

"Notus' promise is worth more than your word," I snap. "Your word is poison."

"Which you have gladly swallowed. Do not deny it."

I deny nothing. "Do you know what comes from placing your trust in immortals? They take advantage. As soon as the beast no longer requires your help, it will dispose of you."

"I'm not so sure about that." He veers closer, forcing me nearer to the wall. I change direction to avoid being cornered. "You see, once the beast has escaped," he says, "it will slowly return to its humanoid form and regain the powers it once had as a demigod. But it will be vulnerable during the transition. I've promised to protect the beast until it can enact its revenge on the one who trapped it here."

"And when you've conquered Ishmah, what next?" I glare at the prince, wishing I had the power to set him on fire with a look. "Um Salim's army may be vast, but it is still finite. How do you expect to maintain control over Ammara while you're helping the beast? Do you honestly believe my people will bare their bellies to your blade?"

At this, Prince Balior emits a low chuckle. I can't believe I ever thought him handsome. He is rotten to the core. "If they value their lives, they will kneel."

I bite the inside of my cheek so hard blood slinks across my tongue. When I bare my teeth, I imagine them lined in scarlet. "You won't leave Ishmah alive," I snarl. "I may not survive the labyrinth, but Notus *will* find you. He won't stop until you are dead."

The prince shrugs as if he can't be bothered by the threat, however thin. "Take comfort that, long after your body perishes here, your mind will live on in the labyrinth, forever haunted by your past. Eternity is a long time, after all."

I lunge forward with a scream, swiping at Prince Balior's eyes. He sidesteps and tosses up a hand. A sphere of darkness leaps from his palm, hitting my chest and launching me backward. I crumple against the ground.

Slow, deliberate footsteps approach. A fresh wave of aches settles in my joints as I push upright, wary of this strange power he wields. I've never seen anything like it. How am I to fight against something I do not understand? "You can't take Ammara from me," I cry hoarsely. "I won't allow it."

Prince Balior peers down at me pityingly. "Sarai," he says. "I already have."

He gestures to a mirror leaning against the wall I'm positive wasn't there previously. The surface fractures into a thousand ripples. When it settles, I watch, horrified, as Amir and Tuleen attempt to bar their bedroom door. Something slams against it. Through the crack that forms in the wood, a black wisp slinks into the room, extending toward Tuleen's ankle. She screams and whacks it with the book she clutches.

Amir shoves her behind him, sword drawn. The door bows with a groan. A sharp crack precedes splintering wood. Tuleen retreats, quickly scanning the room for salt, the only means of protection against the darkwalkers, aside from runes. She finds none.

I watch as my sister-in-law races for the open window to peer below. She will jump. It is three stories high, but she will jump. Behind her, Amir braces his shoulder against the door, stabbing his sword at the beasts salivating on the other side.

Where are the guards? Dead? Souls sucked dry? As I watch Tuleen climb onto the windowsill, the mirror goes dark.

All at once, the breath leaves me. *No.*

I whirl around, diving toward Prince Balior with a ferocious cry, but he vanishes before I can reach him. I'm not certain how he manages to disappear. I only know that shadows enfold him, and he's gone.

My breath shortens, my mind spirals. Tuleen and Amir: my only remaining family. Someone has to know Ammara's monarchs are in peril. If not . . . if not, I must trust Amir's proficiency with a sword. And pray that someone, somehow, comes to their aid until I can reach them.

But there is no way out. The shadows that Prince Balior escaped into have somehow sealed the tunnels of the labyrinth shut. As I search the room, my attention falls to Fahim's violin. I have spent my entire life allowing others to dictate how I must live, what I must eat, what I should wear, how I should speak, where I may wander, and when, and with whom. But I remember Ibramin's parting words to me all those weeks ago.

Music is grief, yet it is also healing and wonder and joy. Remember that. Remember the ways it has shaped you. Remember how it nurtures and heals.

My hands move before I'm aware of it, snapping open the case to brush the silver-wound strings, pulling the bow free of its recess and tightening the horsehair. Then, the violin itself. Its heft is familiar as my name is familiar, a knowing stitched alongside my heart.

Tucking the instrument beneath my chin, I drag the bow across the open strings, slowly tuning using the pegs. The strings are old, but they ring as if they have been recently broken in, resonating with a velvet depth. And then? I play.

Here is what I know: grief never truly lifts. It may alter its shape, it may shed its skin, but no matter the attempts to live your life around the hole of what was, inevitably, the pain penetrates the shield you have erected around yourself. I did not realize that in erecting that barrier, I barred my heart from joy and curiosity, awe and tenderness. I became stern, bitter, full of sharp stones. There was no remedy to smooth their edges. I did not wish for one. I did not ask.

But here, now, the shield crumbles. Music encases me in its soft presence, and flows without impediment. It soothes my weary, grief-stricken heart.

If I could speak to Fahim now, I would say this: I'm sorry. I love you. I understand you. I miss you.

As the melody crests, my fingers shifting higher, tears slip down my cheeks. And that, too, is healing.

I've nearly reached the end of the piece when something moves in my periphery. I turn, staring into the shadows. Nothing. Perhaps I only imagined it.

Yet when I continue the piece, the flash and flutter of light comes again. A door, arched and wooden, has materialized across the room. As soon as I halt my playing, however, it vanishes.

A sign? Is music the answer to escaping the labyrinth? If so, I'd like to think it is Fahim guiding me to freedom.

So I slip into a jaunty tune. The melody springs beyond my control, spiraling into one of the showpieces Fahim used to perform when we were young. By the time I reach its conclusion, my fingertips throb, tender to the touch. But the door remains clear, gleaming like a dawn-kissed mist. For too long, fear has kept me small. Whatever awaits me on the other side, I'm prepared to meet it.

Pushing open the door, I cross the threshold before my courage flees. And I take the violin with me.

27

SOMETHING STALKS ME.

I can't say for certain how many hours have passed while I have wound through the crisscrossing passageways and broken corners of the labyrinth. Every so often, I hit a dead end and am forced to backtrack. Time moves strangely in the dark unknown. But it was not long after I began to explore that I first heard it, a steady *clop clop*, like a metronome.

I clutch the violin case to my chest. Seeing as it has significant heft, it could be used as a weapon, if needed, though I fear harming the instrument nestled safely inside. Stupid, that I care more for this violin than I do my own life. The quicker I escape this place, the sooner I can help those I love.

Eventually, I reach a crossroads. Right, or left. The passage walls, carved with a language of the ancients, rise like highest cliffs, shielding what lies beyond the white stone. The sound fades, but always, it returns: *clop, clop, clop*.

My ears strain. It sounds closer than before. I turn right, my sweaty palm grasping the leather handle of the violin case. I veer around a corner, then another. Whatever stalks me—the beast?—it sounds enormous.

Ducking behind a wall, I spot an area in the stone that has been carved away, providing a crevice wide enough to offer a hiding place.

I manage to squeeze myself into the cramped space, eyes fixed on the tunnel ahead. A quick scan of my surroundings reveals small stones lying against the base of the wall. I snatch one up, breath held.

From out of the distant shadows, there emerges the beast.

Its body is a slab of pure muscle, tapered to four long, bony legs with curved, ebon hooves. Bristly hair roughens its snout and the insides of its wide pink nostrils. Its shoulders are akin to boulders rupturing through its sloped back, and short dark hair patches its body. It looks to be a bull, though from the odd shape of its head, I can tell it once had the appearance of a man. It sniffs the ground along the opposite wall. Too close.

This creature once possessed enough lucidity to transcribe its thoughts, the shame of its existence. This beast, whom over a dozen men have been sacrificed to—did it once have a name? Family? Looking at it now, I understand it is too far gone to listen to reasoning. Here, I am prey.

With a short prayer, I heave the rock as far as I can into the distance. Its sharp clatter draws the bull's attention, and it charges after the disturbance.

I'm up, pushing my flagging legs into a sprint. I reach a fork, turn right. Another passage, another split, another choice that may lead me to salvation or ruin. At the next bend, I ram into something solid, steeped in shadow.

With a scream, I slash my nails across the hulking shape, only to have my wrist clamped as I'm hauled close, arms banded tight across my upper back to stifle my struggles.

Sarai, a voice coos.

A shudder encases my heart and lungs and ribs. "Let me go." I twist in the creature's grip. My breath comes short.

Why do you struggle, Sarai? Why do you struggle, my daughter?

I freeze. The cold begins to climb my skin. Daughter? A forceful shunt, and I shove free of the figure: a woman.

I know her, though we have never met. I recognize her face, its regal oval shape and wide, pink lips. The high brow and rippling black hair, the dimple in her chin. Her portrait hangs in the throne room alongside Father's: Queen Khalise of Ammara, who died at only thirty-three years of age.

But this is not my mother. Rather, it is some twisted version of her. Her skin is naught but shreds of cloth, excess fabric sagging off her bones. She wears a shapeless white dress. Her long, ebony hair hangs in wet hanks down her skeletal back.

I've been waiting for you, Sarai. She reaches for me. *Where have you been all this time? Why hide from fate?*

I recoil from that bony, outstretched hand as her mouth parts. A low, gurgling wail peels out. Black fluid gushes from her rotting gums, and I scream, stumbling back, only to find her sticky fingers have latched onto the violin case.

A sudden *clop* snaps my head around toward the tunnel I'd emerged from. Even from this distance, I hear the beast lurking somewhere beyond sight. It must have caught my scent.

The clacking of its hooves tumbles into a loud rattle. I attempt to jerk the case away. The phantom folds forward, skin oozing across her bones, soft as candlewax. *Not my mother,* I remind myself, and punch the phantom creature in the face. She splatters across the ground.

Snatching the case, I dart down another side corridor, putting as much distance between myself and the bull as I can. I'm not sure how much longer I can run for. The case slows me down considerably.

Though perhaps I am doing this all wrong. The violin helped me once. Perhaps they are connected: this labyrinth, Fahim's violin, me. I do not know the how or why of it, nor do I particularly care. Halting in the middle of the passage, I flip the locks on the case, pull out the instrument, set the bow to the string. The creature's ragged breaths seethe on the opposite side of the wall.

What do I need? Protection. A means of defense. The violin created the door that led me here. What else might it call into existence? I will build a wall of sound, of music. I will play until it breaks through the darkened ceiling overhead.

And then I remember the piece of musical notation the jeweler from Mirash showed us. I recall its melody and begin to play. It wells, bell-like, down the throat of the corridor. As I shape it with intention, a barrier assembles, stone materializing in a misty shimmer, stacked higher and higher still.

On the upper section of the barrier, the stone transforms, becoming transparent. Glass, thick enough to become walls. Construction is nearly complete when the bull appears, barreling around a corner. The melody ends, yet I return to the beginning of the piece, moving through the measures, praying my fingers do not falter. Steps from the wall, it skitters to a halt, its yellow eyes like fogged sunlight. Steam curls from its wide, slitted nostrils.

It paces alongside the barrier. A low grunt of frustration emanates from its chest. I fear that the moment I cease playing, the barrier will vanish. Once the wall is fortified, I shift my attention toward creating a long, brutal spear. It hovers above the ground to my right. A crude head, a sturdy haft. It will do.

"Sarai!"

My fingers falter. The wall flickers; the beast shoves its broad head against the barrier. I hurriedly continue to play, and the wall solidifies, bleeding into the shadows overhead. "Notus?"

"Keep calling out to me," he cries. "I'll find you."

My heart lifts in tentative hope. His voice. I have missed it, though it feels as if only a handful of hours have passed since we last spoke. With effort, I hone my concentration on the task at hand: felling this dark beast.

Slowly, the spear lifts higher off the ground. Using a series of rapid sixteenth notes, I pull back the weapon and release.

The spear cuts clean and true. I will the weapon to pass through the barrier, and it does, sinking deep into the animal's bulky shoulder. A guttural scream wrenches from the beast's mouth. It stumbles, blood pooling beneath its hooves, then rams the partition, its snarling face plastered against the surface.

So long as I continue to perform, I am safe. The trouble is, it's impossible to focus on two tasks as the same time. With my attention on the spear, I'm unable to reinforce the wall, and when the bull strikes the barrier with its blunt horns, it smashes through in a shower of glass.

I bolt, abandoning the violin case in my haste to flee. It's impossible to play and run at the same time, but I manage to tuck the instrument beneath my right arm, left hand gripping the neck. I pluck the strings with my right hand, the sound frenzied, as the stitch in my side hooks deep. I stagger, heaving for breath.

Then all at once, the sound of hooves in pursuit stops.

I slow, head tilted back, throat open to suck in air, saliva clumped at the edges of my mouth. I have no idea whether I'm closer to escape than I was moments ago. Dare I venture forth into the labyrinth, these corridors which haunt me? In the end, I haven't a choice.

I return the way I came, violin tucked beneath my chin just in case. Rounding a corner, I spot the beast, its massive form steeped in shadow as it battles the South Wind.

Scimitar in hand, Notus lunges, weapon a blur. The hacking blow arcs downward, bright silver in the gloom, yet rather than wounding the beast, the sword seems not to touch it at all.

Shock stiffens Notus' expression. The bull lunges. The South Wind leaps up and over the bull, propelled by a gust of wind. If I'm not mistaken, his sword failed to penetrate the beast's hide. It slipped through as if the creature were made of smoke. Except . . . it's *not* made of smoke. It collided with the wall I'd erected, and my spear wounded it. So how is this possible?

And then I understand. Music. It was harmed only by what I conjured with the violin. As such, Notus' blade cannot touch it.

The bull rears. From its hooves, a cloud of darkness blasts toward Notus, who rises to meet it, legs braced, sword raised. Shadow collides with the arid desert air. A concussive boom shatters the labyrinth walls, god and beast hurled in opposite directions. Notus flips midair to land on his feet. The bull rams into the far wall. Grit showers its crumpled form.

The South Wind swipes a forearm across his face, ebon hair disheveled, coated in a fine layer of dust. Again, he sends a powerful wind toward the bull. It ricochets off its haunches, completely harmless. He swears, powerless in the face of this foe. It is the closest thing to mortality the South Wind has likely ever experienced.

"It won't work," I shout.

Notus startles, whipping toward me. His eyes widen.

"Corner it against the wall," I order. "If you can keep it there long enough, I might be able to send it elsewhere."

He nods, lips pressed into a grim line. Using his power, he corrals the creature into a corner while I begin to play. Three, four, five drop chords rattle the air, and a void blooms at the beast's back—an abyss. Notus hurls a spiraling wind toward the beast, which flings it into the cavity. The void stitches itself shut the moment I remove my bow from the string. Where I have sent it or how long it will remain there, I haven't the slightest clue.

"Sarai." Notus hastens toward me, sweat drenching the front of his robe. His eyes are wild. "Are you all right? Are you hurt?"

A low, wretched sound tears free of my throat. This immortal, who has stolen my heart, and whom I believed I had lost. "You came," I sob, and collapse into the South Wind's arms.

He dips his head close. The fragrance of his breath warms my mouth, and I inhale eagerly, desperate for his scent. He is here. We are here, together, and as he murmurs words of comfort and reassurance, I break. I cannot remain standing. I cannot brace myself against an all-powerful wind.

"I thought you were dead," he whispers.

"If it makes you feel any better," I manage, the words garbled, "I thought I was, too."

There is no sound but for my broken cries. I sense his desire to eliminate this fragile barrier between us. Perhaps I would do so myself, if I were not so consumed by adrenaline, this marriage of life and death hovering over me.

"I didn't know about the black iris," he says. "You must know I would never intentionally cause you harm."

"I know." His concern touches upon my skin like a physical ache.

He knows, and he sees, and I cannot bear it, this feeling of being exposed down to the bones. "I should have known my destiny would lead me to the labyrinth." I shake my head. "Say it," I weep in earnest. "Say how foolish I am to have trusted Prince Balior. Tell me—" A bright keening snags behind my teeth, a sound of continuous tension. "Tell me I have not learned."

My body tightens, girded for that inevitable blow.

But the South Wind only tightens his arms around me and says, "I'm here, Sarai. You're not alone." And it lifts from me an unbearable load, because I have felt so lonely all these years, and I do not feel strong, or wise, or clever, or whole. How could I, when my entire life I was told I must be someone else? What an incredibly damaging thing for a child to think, that they, at their core, are flawed, or lacking.

But this man, this god, this generous, forgiving immortal, who has inserted himself into my business as if he had a right to do so . . . "I can't stand against it," I whisper.

He is quiet. "Stand against what?"

"You."

His mouth brushes my ear. A shiver rolls down my spine. "Then don't," Notus says. When I fail to respond, he pulls back, though not enough to completely disentangle our arms. Dirt smudges his face, sinks into the creases bracketing his mouth. "For so long, I didn't believe myself to belong—anywhere, really. So when I came to Ammara, I drifted. I accepted the idea that I would have no home. That perhaps I did not deserve one."

"Oh, Notus." My heart breaks for him.

"But home can be built," he whispers, and I'm startled by the quaver in his voice, an undercurrent of that fear he's carried with him. "It can be found and nurtured in another." As his dark eyes hold mine, he says, "And I found a home with you."

I blink rapidly, but the tears sting regardless. His words are beautiful. In them, I see the whole of his heart.

A heart that is mine. A heart I will cherish and defend. A heart I will shelter, if he will allow me the honor.

"I'm sorry for pushing you away." I fight that old shame, which tells me in no uncertain terms that I am unworthy of Notus, this one good thing. But I am, after all, human. I am imperfect. I am unfinished and always will be. "I was not in a good place, as you know, and I suppose I felt insecure about myself."

He cups my face in his broad hands, thumbs smoothing away the tears that trickle like rivulets. "Insecure in what way?"

Despite my attempts to stifle the emotion, it rushes up and out. The words emerge as a croak. "I feared that you would leave, that you did not want me."

Notus' eyes soften, and warm. "Sarai." My name is a sound of relief and completeness and deep knowing. It makes my knees quake. "I have never wanted a single thing in my life, but I saw you, and I fell, and not even the gods could stop me."

The stony emotion obstructing my airway eases, and I swallow, hard.

"I have always loved you," he says, resting his forehead against mine. "I don't think you truly understand how deep my feelings for you run. I am enthralled by you. Wholly, stupidly, madly in love with you. *You*, just as you are in this moment. Just as you have always been." The corners of his mouth drag downward into a frown, and he searches my gaze. "But I have spent many nights lying awake wondering if those feelings were reciprocated."

That fault is mine. I have given no reason for Notus to trust my word. After all, my actions have not always showcased my true feelings—rather, the opposite.

"Shall I tell you," I begin, "what excruciating torture it has been since you arrived? To watch you practice in the pre-dawn mist and pretend I do not notice the sweat slicking your skin? To search for you in the corridors, to listen for the rhythm of your footsteps around every corner, across every room? Some days, I thought I was going mad from the obsession."

A short laugh chases my words, and I'm caught in the South Wind's eyes, sheened as mine are by emotion too great to contain. "Shall I tell you," I go on, "the ways that your kindness slowly chipped away my

armor? How your patience was sometimes the only thing that kept me
grounded? Or that you have inspired me beyond measure to grow and
face down those fears I harbor? The care you have for my people. Your
belief in me, gods ..." Without Notus, would I have even considered
leaving Ishmah? Would I have recognized how poorly Father treated
me, if I did not receive the South Wind's love and acceptance and
gentleness?

"You have absolutely stolen my heart, Notus. There's no way around
it. I loved you then, and I love you now, and I'll love you tomorrow, for
as long as you'll have me. You are all that I want. And . . . I hope I'm not
too late in telling you th—"

His mouth crushes roughly against mine. Our teeth collide. The
sting fizzles through my blood, and as he parts my lips with his tongue,
licking deeply, my thoughts scatter to the wind.

For here is hunger. The biting drive to consume, its descent into
madness. His taste, his scent, the power of his form, all combine to
create the headiest impression, sensation at the forefront. Our tongues
dance and our lips feast. He drags from me embarrassing sounds of
need; I wrench those deliciously low groans from his throat, the ones
that send vibrations through my sternum as I press closer, breasts
crushed against his chest. We have nothing but our past, our exposed
hearts. There is no need to shield, no reason to conceal. My appetite rips
wide. It demands *more*. I feed it eagerly.

Meanwhile, my hands map the South Wind, no part of his body
left untouched. The wings of his shoulder blades beneath the cotton
of his robe, which ease toward the curved spine, its lifted vertebrae,
leading to the taut curves of his buttocks, which I shamelessly clamp
with both hands. Pleasantly round, firmly muscled. I fight the inane
urge to catch his flesh between my teeth.

"I always did love your ass," I whisper into his mouth. That inane
urge? Not so inane, considering I've done it before.

Notus' warm chuckle teases out. "I remember." The tips of his
fingers skate across my hip, the slope of my lower back, pausing at the
rise of my rear. He goes no farther. It only serves to heighten my desire,

whet it to an acute point. "I believe I've told you plenty of times how I admire yours."

He has, hasn't he? "Do you stare at my ass often?" The warmth in my belly spills upward, my peaked breasts aching as their tips graze the front of his robe.

The South Wind smiles with his eyes. "Down hallways, as you climb stairs." Our noses brush. He exhales into my mouth. "Does that anger you?"

"No," I murmur. "But it might, if you don't touch me soon."

As he drags his lips along my jaw, the tingling sensation shivers through me, temporarily drawing my focus elsewhere. I wait, breath held in anticipation as Notus' touch wanders south. His heated palm strokes one ass cheek. Then, a sudden slap, a bright sting against my skin. I jerk against him, breathless laughter tumbling free. It's cut short as he claims my mouth, tongue plunging deep.

As our lower bodies shift into alignment, his erection presses between my thighs. I pull away, panting hard. His black eyes flicker behind a haze of desire.

"What do we have here?" I murmur.

I allow my palm to graze his turgid flesh. It surges hotly, and he bites back an oath. The sound is everything to me. The South Wind, so carefully contained, yet one thread is pulled, and he unravels at the seams.

It is an entirely instinctive gesture to roll my hips, dragging myself against the jutting length inside his trousers. One of his hands drives into my hair, fisting the long dark strands between his blunt fingers, my scalp smarting with a delicious pain. The desire is so thick the air is laden with it, and my pulse drives higher as the kiss spirals into rich, velvet carnality, our mouths so deeply mated I find our edges blurred, reduced to shadow and smoke and night.

Because the South Wind and I were never meant to remain separate parts. Sun and moon, earth and sky, forever caught in an endless cycle, a perpetual push and pull. Fate laid the stones of this road long before. Oh, how I fought every winding curve. But it was all for naught.

Time spins on its axis, yet I hold the South Wind close. Here is what I know: tomorrow is never guaranteed. There is no perfect moment. Lives are messy, unpleasant, chaotic. I don't know what awaits beyond the labyrinth. I'm not even sure we'll make it out alive. But I won't squander the time I've been given. It heals something in me, to give myself to this immortal in all ways: mind, body, soul. We will not be parted, not again.

After a time, I pull back, gently breaking our kiss. Notus searches my eyes for one, two, three heartbeats.

"You must understand," I say lowly, tracing his eyebrow with my thumb. "I'm selfish when it comes to you." It has always been so. His time, his touch, his voice, his presence, his desert scent. "I don't want one lifetime with you, Notus. I want a thousand lifetimes. As many as you can give me."

But my heart sinks. For while Notus is permitted that privilege, I am only granted one.

As though sensing my thoughts, he frames my cheeks between his palms.

"What will happen when this is over?" I ask. "If we survive, I mean."

He tucks unruly strands of hair behind my ears. Patient, always patient. "Do you ever think about marriage?"

I lean back, suddenly wary. "You mean to Prince Balior? I thought we already established I want nothing to do with him." Especially now, with Ammara in peril, and he the rotten seed beneath its soil.

"Not to Prince Balior," he clarifies with an odd shyness. "I mean . . . to me."

My eyes widen, and I clamp my mouth shut on a hard swallow. "Oh."

Slowly, Notus' eyebrows climb up to his hairline. "You don't sound enthused."

"No, it's not that." Marriage . . . to the South Wind. I wanted this at eighteen, and I want this now, at twenty-five, regardless of practicalities. "I'm just wondering, realistically, how that would work. You're immortal, and I'm . . . not." It was easier to ignore that glaring obstacle in my younger years, especially when I knew I wouldn't live beyond twenty-five, but I have endured the death of too many loved ones. I have toed that threshold myself. I can't put that grief onto him. It is such a hard weight to bear.

Notus brushes a kiss of reassurance across my cheek. "I'm not afraid of you aging, Sarai. It would be a privilege to live my life alongside yours, for however long that lasts."

"But I'll leave you," I tell him. "Maybe not now, but someday."

"Everyone leaves me, eventually." This, paired with a small smile. "But with you? It would be worth it." Before I can protest, he kisses my other cheek, my forehead, the tip of my nose. Beneath his touch, I calm. "After, when all this is over," he says, catching my chin, "I wish to court you properly. I wish to make you mine in all ways. I want the world to know we belong to one another."

Gods, I want that, too. More than I can properly express with words. "And how do you intend to do that?" I question. When he tilts his head in silent inquiry, I elaborate, "We're already engaged, remember?"

"But it's not real."

"It is real, Notus." I smooth my palm down his cheek. "Believe me. It's real." And I could not be more proud to bind my life to his in all ways. "I would love that. The courting. A proper engagement. And yes," I say. "Marriage."

The South Wind's smile is the brightest light. Here is safety, here is support, here is generosity, here is forgiveness, humility, evolution. Yet Notus bestows a trail of heated kisses across my cheekbone, along my jaw, chin, the curve of my neck where sweat has begun to bead. All the while, he is murmuring promises against my skin.

I love you. I adore you. I cherish you. I wish never to be parted from you.

They are more than words. They are a declaration, the promise of tomorrow. I know the South Wind speaks truth. I *am* loved. I *am* cherished. And I am worth more than my station. What a relief to know Notus accepts me as Sarai, just Sarai. I sag into his chest, safe in the knowledge that my walls need not rise again. They are free to crumble.

As his tongue twines sweetly with mine, my fingers dive beneath his robe, pressing into hot skin. It is a pleasure to watch his eyes cloud, hear the stutter of his breath. I may not be an immortal, but my touch holds power enough to weaken this god.

Tearing open his robes, I bare his erection to the cool air. Its dark coloring and the thatch of black hair at the base of his shaft draws me closer. Even as I watch, it twitches, as though already anticipating my touch.

My knees hit stone, and Notus inhales sharply, cupping the back of my head and guiding me forward. His powerful thighs frame my head, the cut of his abdomen blocking the labyrinth from view. A dip of my chin, and I swipe my tongue along the flared crown, catching the liquid beading from the slit. Notus hisses through his clenched teeth.

Glancing up through my eyelashes, I ask, "Good?"

"No words," he chokes out, eyes black with desire. "I have—" He shudders. Red cuts into his cheeks. "No words, except that I have dreamed of this, of you on your knees, pleasuring me."

My face warms in satisfaction. As it turns out, there is nothing I love more.

Gripping the base of his erection, I suck him down to the root. Notus mutters a low oath, his hands tightening in my hair, holding me in place momentarily. The dense black hair clumped around his shaft tickles my nose. I relax my throat, accept his full length.

The years have whittled down, yet I remember his taste: earth and salt. A little tickle beneath his cockhead, and the muscle leaps against my tongue. I work him over slowly. First with my mouth, then my hand, then a combination of the two. A rough, tortured groan cracks out, and his hips begin to move.

I tighten my grip. A long, delicious suck to the base before I withdraw, his shaft glistening with saliva. Again—and again. Notus locks his knees, expression contorted, head tipped back. "Sarai." My name, chased by a tortuous moan. He swells in my grip, his scent ripening as I draw him that much nearer to completion. Just as his body begins to coil, I release him with a loud *pop*, my smile stretching ear to ear.

The South Wind stares down at me, dazed. He then falls to his knees, takes me into his arms. Piece by piece, he discards my clothing, a gentle tug of my dress up and over my head, followed by the slow unraveling of my breastband, the removal of my undergarments. I feel as though I am a glass figurine, its cloth protection slowly unwrapped, to be placed atop a shelf or high mantle. It is the way Notus looks at me, my bared form. Like I am most precious to him.

Of course, I would be remiss if I didn't return the favor. I do so with leisure, baring his incredibly honed body. Notus is not particularly tall, but he is sturdy, square, powerful. Small, white scars dot his brown skin. I touch a crescent here, an asymmetrical ring there, and wonder what weapons bestowed these small hurts.

My touch drifts lower, skimming the rise of his hip bone. I frown, peering closer when the texture of his skin roughens. "I don't recall this one," I say, and trace the scar's raised edge, its dull shine. It's about the width of a sword blade, if I'm not mistaken. "How did you receive this?"

"My brother."

Concern draws my eyes to his face. Somehow, I know it was not an accident. "Oh." Back and forth, my fingertip trails. "Which one?"

"Eurus."

"Do I even want to know why?"

The South Wind leans forward, nips the side of my neck. My eyelids sink low as the heat of his breath dampens my skin. "I'll tell you," he murmurs into my ear. "Just not now."

My smile rises more readily. I suppose he has a point. Lower my fingers travel, the lightest graze down his firm upper thigh, inward to his jutting shaft. Notus shudders beneath my touch. "Are you trying to kill me, woman?"

"You're immortal," I remind him coyly.

"It makes no difference when your touch is fatal," he murmurs, "your tongue the sweetest poison." Then his gaze drops to the subject in question. Thumb pressed into my chin, he draws me forward, a soft kiss pressed onto my bruised mouth.

One eases into two, this kiss longer, wetter, deeper. When we separate, I struggle to catch my breath, piece my thoughts into something resembling order. My skin is so flushed the biting air feels practically balmy. "I've wanted this for so long," I whisper shakily. Gods, have I wanted. "Now that it's here ..."

"I know." Notus cups the side of my face. "Can I tell you what I wish for?"

I nod.

"What I wish," he says, thumb smoothing across my heated cheek, "is to pleasure you as I have longed to do since our parting."

And just like that, my heartbeat quickens. "What do you have in mind?"

In answer, he hooks his hands beneath my arms and, gently, eases me onto my back.

The ground: abrasive. The ceiling: a black hole overhead. But the labyrinth fades as Notus positions himself at my side, my head propped against his arm, my hip crowding his abdomen. Close, but not close enough. The tips of his fingers skim my bare breasts. My skin quivers, warm waves of sensation branching down my arms and legs. He pinches one nipple, rubbing it firmly with the pad of his thumb until it throbs painfully, rosy with blood.

He moves to the other breast, gives it a gentle squeeze. I watch his hand, mesmerized. A soft sound of need slips past my throat before he takes the nipple into his mouth, sucking gently, his gaze never leaving mine.

I bite my tongue, tilt back my head, but the moan pours out. It is ... too damn good. His tongue flirts with the tip in teasing strokes. Around and around and around, a tight coil of heat. Another gentle bite, and an answering pulse throbs between my legs. I'm seconds away from catching fire. I'm certain of it.

Down, down his fingers trail, the scrape of his calluses drawing bumps in their wake. My hips lift, seeking penetration. Instead, he slides his fingers through my drenched flesh and plucks at the small, sensitive bud before circling it with a fingertip. The friction causes my core to clench, this emptiness that seeks to be filled.

"Eyes on me," he says.

A delirious laugh tumbles free. "As if I would look anywhere else."

His eyes flare with satisfaction, pupils flickering like candlelight. It sends another wave of heat scorching my face, neck, and chest, yet as he plays with me, I dare not look away. For his expression is one of rapture. An exaltation reserved only for the gods.

My attempts to shift my hips nearer to his hand are thwarted, his low, rumbling laughter a joy to hear as he skirts the area, moving elsewhere for a time. I scowl and curse his name. He only laughs harder, which in turn ignites my own laughter—that is, until he touches me in a way that draws an exquisite shudder up my spine, rendering me breathless.

My legs fall open further. The brush of cooler air against my exposed center coils the sweet agony in my pelvis ever tighter. He brushes my entrance once, twice. A harsh breath stutters out of me. My heels dig into the ground.

"More?" he asks.

"Yes. Lower. There. Oh." My toes curl as the burn intensifies and the pleasure burrows deep. "Please don't stop."

His pace quickens, circling, always circling, dipping low to slide one, then two fingers into me. Notus withdraws, my wetness providing an easy glide across my swollen flesh. It is agony. Ecstasy. The South Wind forces me to the edge over which I now hover, pleasure-pain served to me on a knife point.

"You are, without a doubt, the most beautiful woman I have ever laid eyes on," he whispers. "To watch you come apart . . ."

My back arches off the ground. *Yes, this, more.* I am so, *so* close.

Clamping his arm, I tug him upright. "I need you inside me. Now."

The South Wind rises to his knees. The span of his shoulders cuts a darker shadow against the labyrinth wall. His body is beautiful. That hard, taut stomach, the bunched thighs that spread as he abruptly rolls us over, so that he lies on his back and I'm seated atop him, legs splayed over his muscled abdomen.

As our eyes lock, I fall into the memory of our first lovemaking. Then, it was new and undiscovered, the future cloaked behind the twisted sheets of our joining. What was then is also now, for I question what awaits us, should we escape the labyrinth. Ammara having fallen to ash and ruin? Or the dawning of a new day?

But then Notus says, "Sarai." So simple a thing, but never was a word threaded with so much love and trust and commitment. My apprehension settles, redirects to the strength of his body between my parted thighs, the curling hair coated thickly across his pectorals. Positioning him at my entrance, I sink onto him, slowly.

And it is an inexplicable joy to be stretched by this god, to feel alive and desired and seen. My position allows me greater control over the speed and depth of our union, and I use that to my advantage, drawing myself up, sinking down with slow deliberation, thoroughly enjoying the sounds of pleasure I draw from the South Wind. I watch his expression as the clasp of my body tightens around his shaft. The flicker of his eyes, which cloud with hunger. How the tendons in his neck draw taut.

And slowly, slowly the simmering begins to spark, driving us toward completion. Notus' fingers bite into my waist, wander up to my breasts, where they squeeze possessively. Together we rise and together we fall. The slap of my rear against his thighs ekes out its rhythm, and the roughened "Yes," Notus growls motivates me to quicken the pace.

Because the South Wind and I were never destined to smolder as coals do. We were destined for fire, for the white light of deliverance. I grow dizzy, intoxicated by the hot brand of his hands, the musk of his arousal, the sweat layering his skin, the heady perfume of our coupling.

His cockhead hits deep. I gasp, angling forward to prolong the contact. He dips his head, drawing my nipple into his mouth. And as he sucks, he snaps his hips upward, creating twin pulsations between my breast and drenched core.

A sound of unintelligible delirium chokes out of me. "Notus."

"You feel so good, Sarai." He stares at his shaft as it withdraws from my body, the glisten of wetness. "Impossibly good." He sheathes himself inside me with one powerful thrust.

He hits a spot that makes my eyes roll into the back of my head. Squeezing my inner thighs, I shift my hips, angling them so the bud between my legs brushes against his hip bone, twining the tension higher and sweeter and brighter.

One of his large hands sinks onto my rear. He holds me to him, allowing no space for separation. This was another thing I had forgotten: the duality of the South Wind, gentle and dominant, passionate and knowing. He molds my flesh with ownership, his eyes akin to darkened stars.

Another hard thrust, and he groans into my mouth. We move as madness, a drive toward the finale. And as we move, I understand how rare a thing it is, to find a love not once, but twice in one's lifetime. I have lost Notus before. I do not know if I could survive that again. And yet, that is the strength of our bond, forged and broken and reforged throughout the years. We are no green buds. We have weathered much. Our roots run deep.

When we at last come together, two bodies aligned, there is the most beautiful music.

28

I LIE IN THE CURVE OF NOTUS' BODY, HEAT BLANKETING MY SPINE, the hard thud of his heart reverberating against my back. Its sluggish tempo indicates deep slumber, yet in the passing moments, it accelerates, grave to andante to allegro.

"You're awake," I say.

He brushes a soft kiss onto my shoulder. "I am."

I can't help it: I smile. He is awake, as am I, our bodies intertwined, braced against the crumbling wall of the labyrinth. His hand catches mine, our braceleted wrists winking, lead and gold. He's tossed his robe over our bodies for warmth. The air feels alive against my skin.

Notus releases what I believe to be a huff of laughter. My smile widens. "What?"

"You snore."

My jaw drops, then clicks shut. "I highly doubt that. If anything, it's *you* who snores."

"Are you sure about that?"

Rolling over to face him, I send him a withering glare. "Quite sure."

Sleep creases the South Wind's brow and cheeks and mouth. His heavily lidded eyes are warm, always warm. When I tilt my face upward, he slips his mouth against mine. Wandering hands and drowsy kisses. It would be a luxury to continue exploring each other's bodies, but time continues to unfold, and darkness threatens all I hold dear. I cannot give in. I will endure. I must.

After disentangling myself, I sit up, facing him with crossed legs. "We don't have much time until Ishmah falls."

The South Wind's expression grows somber. "Failure isn't an option."

The truth is this: the Lord of the Mountain may not have claimed my life, but there is a very real chance I will die in the labyrinth. I may not be able to control the how or where of it, but Amir will remain. Ammara will remain. My people and customs and history, all will remain. As will Notus. He is the only one who stands a chance of saving the realm. "I want you to promise me something."

"No."

I blink. "No?"

"Whatever promise you're looking for, look elsewhere. I won't grant it." He holds himself in high tension, his right hand balled into a fist.

"Well," I clip out, tossing him his robe. "Good to know where your loyalties truly lie."

He shrugs it on. "Maybe you're quick to accept defeat, but I'm not. If we focus our efforts on escaping the labyrinth, we can return to Ishmah—"

"And then what? Last I recall, Ishmah was overrun by darkwalkers." And Prince Balior's army. "How are we supposed to escape this place? And the beast . . . I'm not sure what it did, exactly, but it gifted Prince Balior some sort of dark power. It's dangerous, Notus."

He shakes his head. When he speaks, his voice lacks the assured quality I've come to expect from him. "There is the library—"

"Which we have already exhausted."

He falls silent.

Something softens in me. I have witnessed my loved ones pass, but I, at least, will be granted the gift of meeting them again in the after-life, once my time reaches its end. What must it be like to always bear witness to the end of another's life, never to pass on yourself?

"I'm grateful for the time I was given. Twenty-five years," I say. "Many do not have that privilege."

"And you do not care to extend your life?" he demands, growing more fractious by the moment. "There is a way out. There has to be."

"You can't alter fate, Notus. The curse will take me, whether you want it to or not."

"I will not allow it!" he roars.

The South Wind has shoved to his feet. A harsh gust tosses grit down the long, murky tunnel. His chest contracts like a bellows. Then he begins to pace. I watch his long-legged stride calmly. Wall to wall, he wears a groove into the floor.

"Notus." When he next passes, I catch his hand. "Please sit. You're making me dizzy."

He's all but vibrating in place. "I can't accept it, Sarai. I won't." Yet the more he paces, the more I'm certain something shifts in the shadows at his back. I stiffen, squinting into the distance. He doesn't appear to notice.

"Notus," I whisper. He drops his head into his hands with a groan. "Notus!"

He turns toward me in frustration. "What!"

"Someone's there."

He whirls, sword drawn in half a heartbeat, a powerful gust erupting to spiral down the shrouded passage.

A strange expression crosses the South Wind's face. He lowers his sword. "Eurus?"

My eyes widen as a tall, broad figure strides forward, shedding the shadows like a second skin to reveal a long dark cloak fluttering around his legs. His hood has been pulled forward to conceal his face. The East Wind. Notus' younger brother.

Notus sheaths his sword. "You got my message."

The cloaked figure glides forward, and the motion is so eerily reminiscent of a serpent that a cold sweat prickles my spine. When he is within arm's reach, he halts. This is no mere mortal. He towers over us, the air around him vibrating with an energy that is his alone. Even this close, I fail to make out any identifying features. The darkness inside his hood is consuming, showcasing neither eyes nor nose nor mouth. It is a crater, an abyss.

"What can I do for you, Notus?"

The low rasp of the East Wind's voice shivers across my skin. I have heard it before.

The Lord of the Mountain.

I examine this cloaked god, my mouth dry as dust. Yes, it's him. I'm certain. I recall Notus studying the sheet music in Mirash, an expression of confusion stealing over him upon spotting the sketch of a winged man in the lower corner of the parchment. He sent a message asking Eurus to meet. And here he is.

"We're looking for information regarding a curse," the South Wind replies, moving to stand by my side. Hurriedly, I climb to my feet and brush the dirt from my dress. "Information I believe you possess."

"A curse." Eurus angles his head. It is a distinctly predatory gesture. "Elaborate, please."

"Notus," I whisper, gripping the South Wind's arm. "This is him."

"Who?"

Swallowing proves difficult, my throat narrowing with apprehension at what will occur should I confirm his identity. "The Lord of the Mountain."

For a time, all it quiet but for the staggered rhythm of my heart. Eventually, Notus whispers, "What?"

And so I tell him of the voice I've heard with increasing frequency these past few months. I tell him of what occurred when I fell from the outer wall. I had awoken, unbeknownst to me, in the labyrinth. I could never have imagined the Lord of the Mountain was in fact the East Wind, whom Notus once described to me as withdrawn, borderline violent. Some dark current ripples beneath the surface of this deity, some tumultuous past that has shaped him.

A rush of desert air pervades the space, battling back the damp that smells of the sea. "You cursed Sarai?" Notus growls. "You?"

The East Wind straightens, adding to his imposing height, as the opening of his hood angles toward me. My body prickles beneath a scrutiny I'm unable to witness, can only feel in an uncomfortable crawling sensation across my scalp. "You seem surprised, brother," he replies with a disturbing lack of emotion. "Isn't that why you sent for me?"

"I thought you might have information about the labyrinth. I didn't realize you were the one who put her here!" Notus roars. "How? How are you the Lord of the Mountain? How is any of this possible?" His fingers tear through the thick locks of his dark hair.

Hands behind his back, the East Wind begins to circle us, the hem of his cloak hissing along the gray stone underfoot. When he passes, the subtle scent of brine burns my nostrils. I ease closer to Notus, gaze wary. The suffering this god has put me through, put my family through, my realm. Absolutely disgusting.

"You lied to my father," I snarl at Eurus. "He thought you were benevolent, that you would save my life in return for building the labyrinth to imprison the beast. But you took advantage of a desperate man. You stole our rains. Cursed me to die on my twenty-fifth nameday. Likely sent darkwalkers to Ammara as well." My chin juts forward. "Do you deny it?"

"I cursed you to die?" He sounds curious.

"Yes," I grit out. "Cursed to die by the prick of a thorn from black iris, except I was brought to the labyrinth instead. Why is that?" Tuleen's suggestion of a possible mistranslation is strong, but I want evidence. Truth, from the deity who placed me here.

At last, the East Wind comes to a standstill. "I'm not sure what the king told you, but you weren't cursed to die, Sarai Al-Khatib. You were cursed to become a sacrifice for the beast. Black iris was the vessel that drew you inside its walls, and now here you are. If you're able to defeat the darkness of your heart, the labyrinth will let you walk free. Should you fail, however, you will remain trapped here for all eternity."

"You *bastard*." The South Wind plants his feet, palm out, an explosive flurry flinging Eurus backward through the tunnel. Before his brother hits the ground, however, a pair of massive wings unfurl from his back, layered in minute ebon scales. I gasp. He alights on the balls of his feet, and the wings vanish.

"Calm, brother." The East Wind lifts a hand, though does not sound apologetic in the least. "What is victory without it being earned?"

I rest a hand on Notus' forearm. Taut muscle, rigid bone. Blow to blow, I am uncertain which brother would triumph. Eurus is certainly larger, bulkier, but he lacks any emotion at all, his demeanor eerily flat. Notus' fury would drive him to victory.

"As for the rest of your concerns," the East Wind says, "yes, I took your rains. Seeing as I control the rainstorms and their winds, it is well within my right, and I required that power for a time. But I had nothing to do with the darwalkers. Your father built the labyrinth on an area of land where the fabric between realms was thin. The location was unfortunate for you, but I had no say in it."

Not only is Eurus pitiless beyond measure, he refuses to take accountability for his role in Ammara's suffering. "And how long do you intend to keep our rains?" I press. "Our realm is dying. We can't survive the drought indefinitely."

He shrugs: easy come, easy go. "Until I no longer have need of them. It may be months. It may be years. That was the cost of your life, the price your father was willing to pay."

On the contrary, King Halim was deceived. But I haven't the time to argue semantics. "What of the darkness Prince Balior has unleashed?" I demand. "The beast hasn't escaped yet, but it will, if the prince has anything to do with it. It has given a mortal man incredible power, and I fear the destruction it will bring. You're the one who imprisoned the beast in the first place. The responsibility is in part yours."

Though I can't see the Lord of the Mountain's eyes, I sense how they sharpen on me. "How do you know that?"

As if I owe him an answer. The East Wind may be Notus' brother, but I don't trust a hair on his head. "Where I acquired that information is none of your concern."

"Eurus." Notus is beseeching. "I have never asked you for anything. But I ask this of you now. Help us find a way out of the labyrinth. Help us stop the beast from escaping. Help us defeat Prince Balior—before it's too late."

There is a stillness to the East Wind that suggests he cannot fathom such a thing. I question what sort of face rests within the darkness of his hood.

"Even if I wanted to, I cannot help you," he replies. "The bargain was struck long ago. Your fate is in your own hands now."

I've half a mind to rip back this god's hood and stab him in the eyes. Amir and I have our battles, but I would never think to hold power over him. No wonder Notus rarely mentions Eurus. His brother is a complete ass.

"You don't understand," I say, my voice cracking. "As soon as the beast is free, it will have its revenge. Its darkness will spread. It will consume this realm, and all others after it." Because a beast unfairly imprisoned for decades? It won't stop at one god, one realm, one king.

"That is no concern of mine." Though he does not sound as assured as he did.

I shake my head, teeth clamped around the flesh of my cheek. "Your brother is a piece of work," I mutter to Notus.

His huff is nearly inaudible. I take it as agreement. "You really won't help us?" he asks Eurus.

"As I said before, you must conquer the darkness of your heart if you wish to escape the labyrinth alive."

"And how are we to do that?" Notus snaps.

The East Wind's hood shifts in my direction. "Your destiny is not mine," he says to me. "I cannot alter a path that is already laid."

Does Eurus speak of a literal darkness that must be conquered? A physical manifestation? Something symbolic? And what sort of god would curse a helpless child anyway? One whose morals are lower than dirt.

Suddenly, a rumble fills the space. The earth quavers, and grit spits from the ceiling. The ground lurches. I catch myself against the wall. A heartbeat later, the Lord of the Mountain has vanished.

My pulse sprints forward as the gloom deepens. The ground wrenches open with a bone-shattering roar, a great crevasse opening underfoot. I stumble out of range. To my left, another massive crack gouges the labyrinth, and dust plumes the air.

"Sarai!" Notus, who stands on the other side of the fissure, appears smudged behind the thickening shade. He waves his arms—I think. "You'll need to jump. Quickly!" And now the crevasse has widened. I tighten my grip on the violin and prepare to leap over the opening. With another ear-splitting groan, the edge of the stone floor crumbles, the space now too large to cross. Seconds later, a wall thuds between us, separating me from the South Wind.

"Notus!" I slam my palm against the rough stone, ears straining. Pebbles strike the ground with a clatter. The echoes stretch on. If he's calling for me, I can't hear him. I will have to find another way to reach him.

I dive down the tunnel at my back, the violin and bow cradled against my chest as I try to protect them from the falling rocks. I am a woman, mortal and prey. I am a princess, adrift and grieving. I am a musician without an instrument, a horse without its herd. I feel myself growing smaller, hemmed in on all sides by things I cannot change. My body bids me to yield. There is peace in surrender.

I clench my jaw. *No.* Surrender is not an option. I will find Notus, no matter the efforts. I will conquer the darkness before it conquers me.

"Notus?" Again, I scream his name and receive no answer. Not even the wind.

But there is a sound, a very strange sound. Tightening my grip on the neck of the violin, I release a breath, turn, and freeze. Darkwalkers, three of them. Their hollowed eyes glow in the swirling gloom.

My heart thunders so forcefully I fear it will skewer itself on a rib. A snarl cuts the air, and they charge.

My bow hits the strings to release a forceful wail as I imagine a wall enclosing me. Down my bow falls, over and over, a multitude of drop chords that ring discordantly. A wall flickers into existence. The first darkwalker crashes into it. I flinch, yet do not stop playing.

The second beast, larger, its fangs as long as my fingers, slams into its scrappier companion. Cracks splinter through the transparent partition. The third beast joins its brethren, and despite the weakening structure, I continue to grind out chords. *Solidity*, I think. *Walls, stone, defense, unyielding.*

Yet the cracks multiply and stream outward. I glance around, seeking an escape. When the wall gives, I'll need to make a run for it. Once more, the trio prepare to charge the barrier.

All at once, a swirling cyclone rips through the passage, punching through the barrier. It snatches up the beasts, flings them against the walls. They scatter, each vanishing down a separate corridor. Footfalls slap the ground behind me.

Two hands, warm and sure, curve around my front. "It's me," Notus soothes.

I am pinned, trembling, paralyzed by the ice locking my muscles, yet the South Wind's warmth thaws my frozen limbs and I turn, sagging against him, the instrument held off to the side to avoid crushing it between us. His heart hammers against my sweaty cheek. "Are you hurt?" he asks.

"No." I glance over his shoulder. Nothing. I see nothing.

But from out of the silence, there emerges the slow clop of hooves.

It drags forth, its rhythm so eerily precise it could be mistaken for a metronome. My heart hasn't slowed its pace since I woke to find myself trapped inside these walls, yet now it stumbles. I'm tired. I don't know how much longer I can evade that which has been sent to kill me.

Hand in hand, Notus and I flee quickly and quietly down the nearest tunnel. At the next fork, we turn right and promptly reach a dead end.

Pivoting, we sprint back the way we came. Left, then another left, a mindless, breathless scramble for the next bend. Eventually, the insistent gallop joins our rapid footfalls. Notus swings me behind him as, ahead, a massive, amorphous shape materializes through the gloom.

The beast steps forward, blocking our path. Shadows peel from its flesh, and I shudder. As its black head swings toward me, Notus unsheathes his sword. His blade whines as it cuts through the dark, warning the beast to keep its distance.

Then something stirs at the bull's back. Four, five, six darkwalkers materialize, snouts parted to reveal fangs oozing saliva. Notus swears, his features whitened by dread. "Go, Sarai. I'll hold them off."

"But—"

"Go!"

Fear is the blade. It cuts quick and clean, straight to the heart of me. I run.

29

My slippers slap the ground. Darkness bleeds before me. I am hurtling around sharpened corners and sliding around sudden bends. A distant shout rises, chased by a wretched snarl. My teeth clench. Though I long to return to Notus' side, I would be a fool to overlook my mortality. He has his winds, his strength, his speed. My only skill lies in the violin and bow clenched in my clammy hand.

Catching the edge of the wall, I swing myself into another passage and stumble ahead. Gradually, the South Wind's voice fades, eaten by darkness. My labored breathing grows coarse, throat rubbed raw. At times, I'm certain the beast is gaining ground.

I can't keep this pace forever. Already, my body screams for rest. I require temporary shelter. Some nook or shielded alcove that will grant me time enough to weave my notes into a form of defense.

As I round another hairpin turn, however, I halt, straining for air. I'm almost certain I spotted a figure in the tunnel I just passed. Turning, I hurry after it, slippers scuffing the gray stone. Carefully, I ease around the corner.

In the center of the passage, a man stands with his back to me. I gasp, my heartbeat growing increasingly erratic. It is hope and disbelief twined so tightly they cannot be differentiated. The man turns. His eyes are like mine, like Father's, like Amir's.

"Fahim," I whisper.

My brother smiles. "Hello, Sarai."

I step forward, dazed, so dazed I do not even register the impossibility of his presence. The gloom of the labyrinth vanishes, and I stand in Fahim's bedroom, his bedsheets twisted, documents cluttering his desk. "How—" But I haven't the words. Truthfully, I don't care how it's possible that Fahim stands before me. He's here. It is everything I want.

"It's been some time, no?" he asks tentatively, slipping his hands into his pockets. The points of his countenance—cheek, nose, jawbone—are softened by the low light.

A corner of my mouth hitches, more sadness than anything. "It has," I say. "You look good." He wears a yellow headscarf and matching trousers, a breezy robe the color of dates hitting him mid-thigh. It is his eyes, however, that claim my attention. They harbor no shadows, yet there is a deadness to them: windows without light. "Life has been so hard with you gone."

"I know," he says. "I'm sorry."

"Let's not fret about the past, hmm? We're together again." Another step forward. "We can make up for lost time."

Sarai!

I frown. Another voice, deep and warm and stabilizing, seems to echo from a great distance. But that hardly matters now, with my brother before me.

Shifting both the violin and bow to my left hand, I close the final stretch between Fahim and I. He does not appear particularly enthused to see me. It stings. At the very least, I would have expected an embrace, relief at finding one another again.

"There's so much you have missed, so much I wish to tell you," I murmur. And we have time now. It is a gift I refuse to squander. "I've been such a fool about so many things, and I don't know who to trust anymore. Ammara is in peril. The darkwalkers grow stronger, and—" I hesitate, then say, "Ibramin has departed the palace. I thought you should know. He's gone to teach a young boy with promise. I can't help but feel like he has abandoned me."

When Fahim doesn't respond, I reach forward to cup my eldest brother's cheek. His skin is like ice.

"You're chilled," I say to him in concern. My arm drops. "Are you ill?"

"Sarai." His gaze meets mine squarely. "Put down my violin."

I glance at the instrument. For whatever reason, my fingers tighten around the neck. "I found it," I say in slight confusion. But where, exactly? I know better than to enter Fahim's chambers without permission. I do not remember approaching his door. Nor do I remember knocking.

I shake my head. "I'm sorry. I know how you feel about me touching your things." Of course he would ask me to put down the violin. I'm not sure why that proves to be difficult at the moment. "Will you play for me?"

Our surroundings blur for the briefest moment. When I next blink, however, nothing appears out of the ordinary. I must have imagined it.

But Fahim . . . he has become a different person entirely, his face grooved, harsh and unfamiliar.

"It wasn't fair," he growls. "Why should I give up my gift when you had the freedom to pursue yours?" His sleeves stir as he lifts his hands to his chest. "And then to learn you were throwing it away, and for what? A man you hardly knew?"

I recoil from the unexpected venom in his words—and the truth he wields as a weapon. "I wasn't throwing anything away," I dispute. "You didn't even talk to me about what I felt toward Notus, or music. You made a decision without my input."

But Fahim isn't listening. "Please understand, Sarai. There are things I must do, responsibilities I must uphold." Once more, he glances at the instrument. "But I won't be able to do so until you let go of the violin." His mouth loses its curve then. "Let me take it off your hands."

I peer closer at my brother, disquieted. Why do his eyes hold such emptiness? Why must I release the violin?

Sarai, it's a trap!

My surroundings waver, a sheet of darkness momentarily blotting out the sight of my brother and his chamber, yet it snaps back into place. Only this time, Fahim has disappeared, and I peer down one of the bright, open corridors of the palace.

The setting sun is a jewel. It sets fire to the orange, yellow, and red mosaic tiling the far wall. At its end, I spot Fahim dressed in an ornate yellow robe, walking with a slump to his posture. His skin is wan, sickly. There, too, is the disheveled state of his hair.

"Fahim." My throat closes around his name, snuffing it out.

I watch my brother shuffle toward his bedroom at the end of the hall. Look at his hands, how tightly they clamp, and the rounded stoop of his spine. Evening will soon fall. Where are the guards?

As he reaches the door, I scream, "Fahim!"

My brother halts, hand on the doorknob, and glances over his shoulder, just once. He frowns, as if having heard my voice. But it is his eyes I notice most. They are empty, as if the light has already gone.

I lunge, yet am stopped short by an unseen barrier. My voice warbles as I call again, "Fahim . . ." A yellow robe trimmed in black thread. The same clothing he'd been wearing the day I found him swinging from the rafters.

The image fades. I am back in the labyrinth.

The despair is so much greater in Fahim's absence. I've lost my brother all over again. Is this the labyrinth's plan? Force me to relive the darkest days of my life until I am driven mad?

A shudder of unease shivers through me, yet I hurry down the passage, ears pricked for any unusual sound. Another turn, and another. At this rate, I would not be surprised if I were going in circles. But there, up ahead—a shift in the gloom. I press forward, violin tucked beneath my chin, bow poised to coax music from its strings. The crumbling walls fall away, and I step into another impossibility: a tapestry of curling vines, hanging branches, sweet-smelling blooms. The palace's eastern garden.

I glance around warily. In the distance stand two figures, male and female. It is night. Moonlight dribbles through the glass ceiling overhead, splashing the interlocking leaves, painting their waxy coatings in a high shine.

As I ease closer, I recognize the gown the girl wears. Fiery red trimmed in gold. Her hair is secured in a braid. I am both past and present in this moment. Twenty-five years of age, and twelve-year-old Sarai, following the evening of her solo debut. Which means the boy she speaks to is Amir.

It's not real. But it was, once. This memory, which I have locked away, now thrust into the open.

Following my debut, I'd returned to the palace with my brothers and Ibramin, elated by my performance, yet brokenhearted over Father's absence. I'd cried, of course. I had desperately wanted Father to witness this monumental accomplishment. Yet when faced with my tears, he only snapped "Stop crying," before reaching into his desk, pulling free a square of cloth, and tossing it to me. "Wipe your face."

I did so with a trembling hand. Whatever emotions surged toward the surface, I forced them down. Crushed them to dust.

Afterward, I'd sought solace in the garden, for it was deserted, calm. It was where Amir had found me hours later. He was angry. Apparently, my performance had upset Fahim, who did not wish to see me.

From my position shielded by the leaves, I watch this conversation play out. Yet suddenly, as young Sarai whispers, "I don't believe you," I am experiencing things through the eyes of my younger self.

My brother shrugs. It is of no concern to him. "Believe what you will, but I'm not sure Fahim will ever forgive you for taking music from him. It was what he loved most in the world."

Something wavers in my heart, for I have wondered if Fahim resented me, now that I alone carry music.

"Why are you like this?" I growl, fists clenched at my sides. If I were not afraid of injuring my fingers, I daresay I would wallop Amir in the face. "It's not my fault Papa made Fahim quit violin. If I didn't know any better, I'd think you were jealous."

"Jealous?" He barks a laugh.

"Yes. Jealous that I am known to the world, that Fahim is known to the world, while you are left in the dark." Fahim and Amir, both princes, but only one will carry the crown.

Sarai, can you hear me? Say something!

I ignore the distant plea, unable to look away as Amir's expression shutters. A long moment passes before he responds. When he does, his voice is so riddled with bitterness it eats at his words. "You're right. Fahim is heir, not I." He looks me up and down with noticeable distaste. "Then again, I haven't stolen music from him. I haven't paraded my accomplishments in front of him, this life that was promised. I'm not the one who forces him to face that pain daily."

Turning on his heel, he whacks aside the vines and plunges down the path, vanishing from sight.

I lift a hand, palm pressed to my chest, atop the fresh bruise that blooms in wake of his declaration. *It's not true. Fahim is happy for me. He's told me so on multiple occasions.*

As young Sarai collapses onto a garden bench, I charge through the garden, intending to speak my piece to Amir. Yet the stones beneath my slippers crack, and the sweet blossoms blacken, their scents curdling to rot. Two steps farther, and the garden begins to bleed out, the dense gloom melting into tall windows framed in drapery, an impressive desk that commands the center of Father's study. A younger version of myself hovers on the threshold of the doorway. Through the crack of the partially open door, I watch Father pen a message, nerves tumbling through my stomach. I know the rules. I am not to disturb Father in his study, but this is important. Lifting my hand, I knock.

His head snaps up, and he frowns. "Sarai. What have I told you about interrupting my work?"

I can see that child so clearly. Her wobbling chin. The uncertainty of entering Father's office despite the need to burrow into his embrace. *It's not fair,* she thinks.

But she takes a breath—for courage—and shuffles forward. "I'm sorry," I whisper. "I know I'm breaking the rules, but I wanted to ask you something."

"Where is Ibramin?" He looks beyond me, face grooved in displeasure. "Shouldn't you be practicing?"

"I already finished my lesson for the day. Papa—"

He rings a small bell on his desk. Two guards enter the study. "Sir?"

"Please take Sarai back to her rooms." He returns to his correspondence, not bothering to watch as I'm led away into the hall.

The image changes.

"Papa?" I sit up in bed, blankets clutched to my skinny chest. The darkness of my bedroom looms before me. "Papa!"

Quickened footsteps. I turn toward the door in relief, tears wetting my cheeks, but it is Fahim who steps inside, not Father. My heart sinks.

"Another nightmare?" my brother asks as he crosses toward my bedside. He's young, but not for much longer, toeing the threshold between boy and man.

"Where's Papa?"

"He's busy, Sarai." Fahim wipes my face with the sleeve of his robe. "Lie down. I'll stay with you until you fall asleep."

For the third time, the image alters. I'm running toward the dining room, pale columns flickering past. The moment I burst through the doors, King Halim turns toward me from his seat at the table, expression twisted in frustration. "You're late."

Amir and Fahim hunch further over their plates, attempting to make themselves as small as possible.

I dab the sweat from my brow, struggling to stifle my heavy breathing. "I'm sorry, my lesson ran long—"

"Sit down," the king snaps.

I look to my brothers for support, but they know what happens when one speaks against the king: nothing good.

My mouth clamps shut. I take my seat, as instructed, and I do not speak for the rest of the meal.

Sarai, please. You have to push through!

Why does that sound like Notus? Why would I conjure his voice now, of all times? Except I realize that the dining room looks different, as though I view it through a filter, fogged behind lost time. The smell of damp is real. It doesn't belong to the image spread before me.

Notus. The labyrinth.

I blink, and the dining room vanishes.

The bull stands at the opposite end of the shadowy passage, its bulky shoulders and towering height filling the space. Yellow eyes boil like feverish pustules. In them, I see its sorrow and its wrath, this immortal unfairly imprisoned through no fault of its own. An old pain rises in me, a kaleidoscope of memories emerging from the earth in which I'd buried them, and Father at the core of it all.

"Not now, Sarai."

"A princess must never show weakness."

"Go."

"Stop that."

"What did I tell you?"

"I don't have time for this."

Steam is expelled from the creature's wide, slitted nostrils. For a moment, I'm almost certain I glimpse something human in its face.

A sharp crack of air blasts the bull backward. It rears, hooves wheeling, and charges the South Wind, who has appeared at the other end of the corridor, dripping sweat and looking incredibly relieved to find me unharmed. In seconds, he smothers the beast with a column of wind that whips and shreds and flays, immobilizing it briefly. My hair tangles in the rush of moving air, and I have to brace myself against the wall.

You must conquer the darkness of your own heart if you wish to escape the labyrinth alive.

Of course. I'm not sure how I didn't see it sooner. This is no beast, I realize. It is a manifestation of our shadow selves, what we become when we allow others to dictate our character, our fate. So long as I continue to run, it will give chase. I will hit yet more walls. I will find my way barred. I will travel this maze end to end, my mind torn apart in attempting to rid myself of all the brokenness, the woe and resentment and bitterness, the agony and the strife.

I glance at the violin in my hand as the South Wind continues to pummel the bull with his power to no avail. Music is my protection, but ultimately, even if we kill the beast, it won't help us escape the labyrinth.

I think . . . I think I discovered Fahim's violin to remind myself that I'm still here, still fighting. I had dreams, once. I believed they'd died with my brother, but really, they'd died with me.

Because I did not fight for myself. Because I accepted my circumstances. Because I allowed others to write my beginning and middle and end.

"Sarai, help me!"

Notus won't be able to maintain that power indefinitely. He is waiting for my performance, the creation of melody and countermelody that will build some contraption strong enough to trap the bull a second time. But as his eyes meet mine through the dim, I gently tuck the violin beneath my chin and play not Fahim's melody, but the pain and grief locked away inside my heart. The music that is Sarai, just Sarai.

The South Wind cuts at the creature to no avail, his features twisted in horror. "What are you doing?" He swears and blasts the beast against the wall. It slams into the stone with a bellow.

"It's all right, Notus." I have held on tightly all this time. I clutched what *was* and what *could have been*. But we have only now. For the first time in years, I understand what it means to let go.

"What about the other melody? We need to confine the beast!" The words tear free of his heaving chest.

Briefly, I pause my performance. "Notus." His petrified eyes hold mine, swimming with confusion. "It's all right," I say again, softly.

Taking advantage of the distraction, the beast kicks out with a hind leg, catching the South Wind in his lower back. He falls forward with a bark of pain. The bull lunges, narrowly evading the sphere of wind Notus hurls at it. The strike of hooves on stone descends. I smile and let it come.

Here, in the black depths of the labyrinth, as I play out the darkness inside myself, I feel as if I have clarity for the first time. Do I continue to deny the truth of my heart? Do I reject myself, as I have done since childhood? Or do I welcome, shelter, embrace?

The beast is steps away. I understand, now, the harm I have inflicted upon myself in continuing to perpetuate the narrative Father wrote for

346 • ALEXANDRIA WARWICK

me. A story that dictated no room for error, exploration, or authenticity. But I have the power to rewrite my story. I will scrub the manuscript of perfection and precision. I grant myself permission to be messy, open, raw, vulnerable.

Lowering myself onto my knees, Notus screaming in horror, I close my eyes and let the darkness swallow me.

30

M Y EYES SNAP OPEN. GONE IS THE GLOOM OF THE LABYRINTH, its rigid walls and passages veiled by shadow. I stand before a plain of rolling hills, grass so abundantly green I'm convinced it must have been painted on. The damp air lacks the dust of Ammara. The ground, too, is unfamiliar: springy and moist, void of cracks and baked stone.

Although—*is* it unfamiliar? A murmuring hush draws my attention toward the east, where the sky has begun to darken, and a wide river interrupts the landscape. Its unhurried current carves a meandering path. Trees cast long shadows over the burbling water, and beneath the trees, crouched on the riverbank, is a small child.

I stare at that child, a young girl with dark hair, swallowed by the blue fabric of her dress. A sudden ache wedges my heart alongside my ribs. It can't be, but ... why not? That dress, I once wore it myself. Those mistrustful eyes and the fingertips marked by calluses, I know them too well. The smudge below her jawbone where the violin normally rests ...

The child is me.

Quietly, I approach. Young Sarai lifts her tear-stained face, and I falter, suddenly uncertain of my place.

The girl straightens, expression immediately pinching into something far more hostile. Her brown skin is a bit paler than usual. I assume it is due to the many hours spent practicing indoors. "Who are you?" she demands.

I bite back a huff of unexpected laughter. Of course the question would possess all the enmity of a blade held to one's throat. "I am a friend."

Her gaze narrows. "How can we be friends when we have never met before?"

A valid question. "We met long ago." Peering down at her, I allow my features to relax, if only to make her feel more at ease in my company. "You would not remember." I glance around. Whatever this place, it holds a peace I find incredibly soothing. "May I sit?"

Young Sarai continues to regard me in wariness. She is perhaps ten years old, and even then, has already begun to establish high walls. "No. Go away." And she faces forward, skinny arms crossed over her chest.

Well then.

I begin to walk in the opposite direction, not the least bit surprised by her response. I mean, she *is* me. And I can be absolutely ruthless when the situation calls for it.

But as I wander along the river, I think of this child, whom I once knew. She sits alone. Something troubles her. I always wished Father would sit with me, in silence or conversation. Most days, all I wanted was company.

The river broadens. I pick wildflowers from a shallow mound. On my return trip, I splash cool water onto my face, then go in search of my younger self. Her expression darkens in annoyance at my presence. As soon as she opens her mouth—likely to demand that I keep my distance—I offer the flowers.

The distrust in the girl's eyes hurts my heart. I know without asking that she questions this gift, its motive, whether it is safe to receive. For a second time, I ask, "May I sit?"

Eventually, she accepts the flowers with a shrug. "You may do as you wish," she grumbles. "I hold no ownership over the river." But her eyes brighten as she lifts the scraggly bouquet to her nose.

With a grateful nod, I settle onto the grass. The river is calm. Its waters are clear. Smooth pebbles line the bottom of the riverbed. A silver fish darts upstream.

After some time, young Sarai glances sidelong at me. "Maybe you're right," she says. "Maybe we have met before. You look familiar. Are you one of the ladies at court?"

I temper my smile. I do not wish to scare her off. "Technically, yes." Not that I ever relished the obligation.

She rears back in suspicion. "What do you mean *technically*?"

"Just as you are a lady at court," I reply calmly, "I am as well."

"Were you at Father's nameday celebration last month?"

"I was."

"Prove it."

If I am right in thinking that the girl is about ten, then Father would have been in his mid-fifties. The dress she wears . . . I spot a stain near the waist. Dark red—cherry juice. I wrack my brain, go further into my memories. I was supposed to wear that dress during a performance to celebrate Father's nameday—a disaster. Amir and I fought. I stained my dress at breakfast. Fahim ignored everyone, except for the girl he chased around the ballroom. Nobody had paid much attention to my performance. Except the king.

"You and your teacher, Ibramin, performed a piece for King Halim on the violin," I say. "He cried, your father."

The girl harrumphs. "I suppose you were there, but I really don't remember you."

That's all right. I do not need her to remember me. It is enough that I remember her.

"You are far from home," I point out, as a songbird flits onto a nearby branch. "May I ask what you're doing here?"

"You may ask." She drops the bouquet onto her lap. "Doesn't mean I'm obligated to answer you."

Was I really like this as a child? My tongue dearly loves a duel, but it doesn't seem productive to put my younger self in her place, especially when I know how fragile she really is. "Fair enough."

Leaning back on my palms, I watch the grass ripple beneath a temperate breeze. It cools the perspiration beading along my nape. I look to the sky, for it is vast and unknowable, yet always my attention returns to the river, its gentle hush. Water carries its own rhythm. Though I attempt to predict the cadence, it will forever remain out of my grasp.

In the corner of my eye, young Sarai hunches further over her knees. She opens her mouth, closes it, opens it again. "I don't know."

I angle toward her. We sit near enough that I could easily rest a hand on her shoulder, were I to reach out. Although, knowing my temperament as a child, I can't say I would trust that she wouldn't retaliate. "What don't you know?" I ask, my voice gentle, motherly.

"You asked what I'm doing here. My answer is I don't know." Her shoulders creep toward her ears, and she wipes at the stain on her dress to no avail. "I come here when I want to be alone. It's quiet."

Of course this would feel like a memory, because it *is* a memory. As a child, I would retreat inward. I traded fluted pillars and rigid marble for the expansive wilds of this space when the world became too much. I stared into the imaginary river and wondered where it might lead me: away from Father's expectations? A place of freedom?

"You're right," I say. "It is quiet." The birdsong, the river, the grassy hills. It holds its own magic.

"Was." My younger self glowers at me. "It *was* quiet."

I shake my head in amusement. "You're quite talkative."

She looks downright offended. "*I'm* talkative?" She tosses a hand in an impressive display of dramatics. Roshar would be proud. "You're the one who's talking to me!"

"Do you want me to stop?"

"Did I ask you to stop?"

"No." I smile at her, but to my dismay, her expression crumples, and she shields it behind her hands. A soft cry reaches me.

"Sarai," I whisper.

Her head snaps up, tear-filled gaze wide with bewilderment. "How do you know my name?"

I reach for her. How can I not? Taking that small hand in mine, I fold the chill of her fingers into the warmth of my palm, the only shelter I can provide. "Remember what I told you? We met long ago." Gently, I squeeze her hand. "What's wrong? Why do you cry?"

The little girl shakes her head. She can't express it. It is too dangerous to show vulnerability. But— "Because I'm sad," she whispers.

"About what?"

"Father. It was his birthday, remember? Amir and I were arguing, and somehow I didn't see the attendant carrying the plates of food, and I knocked into him, and the plates shattered and the food spilled, and Amir was laughing at me, and I was crying, and Father was so, *so* angry, saying I embarrassed him, dishonored him." Her chin wrinkles; tears slide down her cheeks. "When I tried to explain, he sent me to my room and . . ." A garbled wheeze catches behind her teeth. "It's not fair. Why am I always the one to blame?"

I remember now. It hurt at the time. I questioned my sanity and my character. I wondered why Father couldn't love me first.

"I just want a friend," she whispers, pained. "A real friend I'm free to be myself with."

"I'm your friend, Sarai." My hands cradle her sweet, sad face. "You can be free with me. You can let go."

As I draw the child into my arms, her voice cracks, and the sobs pour forth.

You are enough, I tell the girl, who feels slight and unworthy, desperate for a guide. *You are deserving, loved, safe, understood. You are important. You are most precious to me.*

Yet who is at fault, truly, that so young a spirit would believe herself to be expendable? Father did the best that he could. He carried his own traumas, his own failures, into parenthood. I can't imagine the difficulty in raising three children alone while grieving the loss of his wife. But what of myself? What responsibility do I hold for my unrelenting grip on resentment? Will I continue to move through life in pieces, or will I begin to work toward wholeness?

Here is what I know. Father is gone. I might never heal the hole he left behind. But I'm still here, still fighting. No matter where the road leads, I can mend the relationship with myself. I can be my own home.

And so my arms tighten around the child. *Things are hard now*, I tell her, *but you will get through this. You cannot be broken. I am here. I will never leave you. I will stay for as long as I am needed.*

At this, the girl weeps harder, fingernails gouging my lower back. I absorb that pain into myself as I rock her, again and again, whispering into her ear how brave she is, how strong.

But mostly, I tell her this: *I love you.* I give voice to what she desperately craves, this promise rarely heard from family. And I think, too, of Fahim. Did he yearn for these words? Might he still be alive had Father offered him an embrace rather than a crown? I might never know. But I press these words into the child's skin as rosin is pressed into the hair of a bow, until she has absorbed this truth into herself so that she never questions it again.

When her weeping has subsided, I pull away, brush the long strands of hair from her tear-dampened face. "Come with me," I urge, dark eyes full of mettle.

Young Sarai hiccups, frowns. She is uncertain. She dares not trust. But she places her small hand in mine, and together, we rise.

"Sarai?"

I startle, the South Wind's hoarse voice yanking me from the depths into which I sink. A rosy-gray light washes the walls of the labyrinth as Notus hovers over me, eyes wild, sweat and grime coating his skin, broad chest heaving for breath. Heat invades the space. The walls of the labyrinth have crumbled in places, opening a path to a doorway in the distance. Sunlight streams through the cracks that have appeared in the ancient stone.

"The beast," I gasp. "Where is it?"

The South Wind swallows and drops his head in a gesture of defeat. My heart sinks, down and down and down. Did I fail and this is yet another illusion, these cracks and sunlight and doorway out? "Gone," he whispers.

Gone? "As in dead, or . . .?"

"Escaped would be my guess," he says. "It ran straight through you, like you were a mirage. It disappeared down the passage."

Gingerly, I sit up, curling forward with a groan to relieve the pain seizing my lower back. "It worked," I say. Pressing my palm to my heart, I marvel at the lightness there, that absence of weight. The beast couldn't touch me. The darkness had no hold. Not when I finally embraced all that I was, every jagged-edged piece of myself, every cracked and weathered shard.

The South Wind regards me with worrisome solemnity. "You purposefully called the beast to you. Why? Sarai, I—" His fingers spear into his hair, as though they might rip those dark locks from their roots. "I thought I'd lost you. I believed you were gone. Dead. Do you know—" There is a sound I never wish to hear, a god giving in to an all-encompassing fear, a sound of finest cracks.

"I'm sorry." Taking his hand, I hold it to my chest, sheltering it as I would an injured sparrow. "There wasn't time to explain."

"Clearly." He's shaking.

I ease nearer, rubbing his upper back. It was not my intention to worry the South Wind so. There'd been no time to decide. I could only act and hope for the best. "Notus, look at me." I draw his chin up. Reluctantly, his eyes meet mine. "For the first time in years, I trusted myself. Do you know what that felt like?" I shake my head, mouth quirked in a wry softness. "It felt like coming home."

Notus, however, doesn't share the sentiment. His frown deepens. "Would it have killed you to inform me of your intentions beforehand?"

When he tries to yank his hand away, I hold tighter, saying, "It was as your brother said. I had to conquer the darkness in my heart and—" Then I gasp. "The violin!" I hurriedly glance around, but the instrument is nowhere to be seen. "Did it vanish?"

"Sarai," he growls.

Unless Fahim's violin was a part of my journey? If so, that explains why it's gone. It was a tool to help me, but now that I'm finally helping myself, I no longer need it. "The beast grew stronger the more we fought against it. That was the trap, don't you see? As long as we allowed fear to drive us, we were never going to escape. The beast is a symbol, a physical manifestation of the darkness we all carry. The only way to conquer it was to accept the whole of myself."

"And if you had been wrong?"

Notus appears so pained that I pull him to me, wrapping my arms around his wide shoulders. The weight of his body is comforting. "That was a risk I was willing to take."

"You are mortal, Sarai." His voice grinds with a budding frustration. "It could have ended badly. The beast . . . it took some of my power, do you understand? Drained it. I'm no longer at full capacity. To watch as it charged you—"

"You're angry with me, I know," I whisper against his neck, where the desert scent is strongest. "But I am well. The curse is broken. We are free." Pulling away, I gesture to the door at the end of the passage, light seeping through the bottom crack. Prince Balior claimed I would not escape the labyrinth alive. But he knew little of me and of my will. "We have a chance to save Ammara, Notus. We can save our home."

Unwittingly, his eyes soften. "*Our* home?"

A gentle warmth bathes my face, a pinkness below the skin. Of course he would notice the detail of a single word. "Yes." Because what was once mine is now his, this place I am ready to share, and build upon.

"What happened?" he asks. "Where did you go?"

I can't help but smile at the memory. "I saw myself," I say. "As a child." That precious girl, so lost and so small.

"I don't understand."

"I—" How to explain? "When I was younger, I would sometimes go to this imagined place inside my mind. I would sit by the river and keep myself company. It was where I found tranquility, where I could just *be*. But this time, I wasn't alone. A young girl was there, sitting by the river—me. And she was desperate for connection."

A tear tracks down my cheek, which Notus wipes away with his thumb. I didn't realize the ways I had neglected myself. I'd unconsciously made myself small in order to gain Father's approval. I'd hammered my corners and smoothed my uneven patches. But I wasn't me.

"How could I have been so blind to my own needs?" I whisper hoarsely. "Sitting with that part of me, holding her—it was incredibly healing."

Notus reaches for my hands. He wraps them inside his own, and draws them to his chest, flattening them to his heart, whose rhythm beats alongside my own. "I'm glad you were able to get closure," he says. "You are worthy of kindness and compassion and love. You deserve peace in your life."

For so long, I'd believed the opposite. My upbringing was the most ruthless knife. It carved me from impenetrable stone. But this shape was never mine to decide. Now look at me. A woman who doesn't know herself, and likely never has.

"I know Father meant well," I whisper, and the grief, still fresh from his passing, hollows my lungs. "But sometimes I wanted to scream for how little he knew me."

"I know," Notus says, likely thinking of his own childhood. "It hurts when those we love fail to see us. But we're all trying the best we can. Your father loved you as much as he could for a man carrying the weight of a realm. Don't let the resentment harden you." Reaching out, he cradles my cheek in one large palm. "I would not see your light dimmed."

"No." I shake my head. "I have hardened myself for too long, I think."

The South Wind studies me for a long while. This is perhaps the first bit of contentment I have experienced in . . . I'm not sure how long. Years, to be certain.

"I'm proud of you, Sarai. I know you'll find peace, one way or another." Then he brushes his mouth across my cheek.

I lost myself in the labyrinth, yet I found myself, too, in pieces, which I collected and placed lovingly into something given order and shape. Something resembling my true self. Now I must decide what comes next. Peril still threatens Ammara, somewhere beyond the door at the end of the light-filled passage. Prince Balior, and the beast, a threat I fear is too powerful to conquer. But I am not alone.

Reaching toward the South Wind, I ask him, "Will you walk with me?"

Something gentles in his expression. "Sarai," he says. "That is something you never need ask."

31

THE SKY IS A CHARRED RUIN, ITS SAPPHIRE EXPANSE BLOTTED out by smoke and shade that climbs, and writhes, and sparks red. The churning squall boils upward. It is teeming, *alive*. Through its screen, Ishmah's glittering rooftops waver behind a haze of slithering heat.

The labyrinth doesn't deposit us in the palace courtyard. Rather, we emerge from a cave on the outskirts of the capital, Ishmah spread below us like crumbling coals. I estimate we are some miles from the city. Despite the distance, the screams are unmistakable. The smoke seems to have originated in the western part of the city, an industrial area where most of the workshops and forges are located. Meanwhile, amassing shadow sits as a denser layer below the fumes, squatting like a territorial dog over the palace. The sight chills me.

Somewhere inside the city is my family: Amir and Tuleen and Roshar and even Haneen, whose stories dragged me from those darkest days of grief. Ibramin, blessedly, will have reached Mirash by now. Those that remain, the South Wind—they encompass the whole of what I love.

Slowly, I turn toward the god who has captured my heart. How depleted he appears now, on this threshold between peace and war, darkness and light. "How confident are you that you can defeat Prince Balior and the beast?"

He lifts a hand to his face, expression pinched, and drags at the corner of one eye. "The beast drained much of my power, as you know. And neither my sword nor the wind works against it."

Indeed, I've never seen Notus appear so weary. A nervous flutter captures my heartbeat in an irregular pitter patter. "That doesn't exactly answer the question."

He regards me for a long, drawn-out moment. In the end, he speaks only one word. "Sarai."

It's difficult to swallow. Miles we stand from Ishmah, yet the reek of smoke stings my nostrils, thin gray wisps skating over the sweltering earth. "Your sword couldn't harm the beast inside the labyrinth, but what about outside of it? Whatever hold that place had on the creature is no more."

He tears clawed fingers through his hair with a sigh. "I don't know."

I'm aware of what we face. I'm aware that tomorrow may not arrive for many, myself included. But … I'd hoped Notus would be strong enough to vanquish our foes. With limited residual power, he will need to take care of how much to use, and when.

I nod despite the fright cramming my chest. We will need all our strength to rid Ammara of this great evil. Our options are dwindling, few, but all is not lost. Not yet, anyway. "Now that the beast has been released, do you think it will do Prince Balior's bidding?"

Notus shakes his head. "It will take time for it to relearn the shape of what it once was. Until then, it has likely fled to a safe place until its transformation is complete. The good news is that it will be unable to use its power until it has transformed back into its humanoid form. However, we still have the darkwalkers to contend with."

"And Prince Balior's army," I add. "How much power would you need to take them all out?"

The South Wind's grimace pulls the skin of his cheeks taut. "More than I have at the moment, I'm afraid."

Despair drags at me. I stand firm. I will not allow myself to flounder.

"The beast likely hasn't gone far if it intends to use Prince Balior for protection," Notus says. "I'll go search for it. Meanwhile, we need to evacuate the city. It would be safest to head for Mirash. We'll need sailers, as many as can be spared. And horses. Do you think the palace could spare some of their mounts?"

Too easily, the uncertainty engulfs me. But I press a palm to my heart. I calm the child within myself. I assure her I am strong, that I will look after her in all ways. *Safe*, I think. *You are safe.*

"Amir would know," I tell him. "I need to find him. If—" No. I will not consider *what-ifs*.

"Then we'll find him," Notus says, "and Tuleen." His eyes blaze into mine with unswerving promise. "We'll make sure that they're safe."

Yes. Ammara's king and queen must survive. The future of the realm depends on it. "What of the darkwalkers?" I ask, voice low.

Notus stares at a point over my shoulder. A hot wind grazes the backs of my knees. Beneath the spreading darkness, shadow begins to blot Ishmah's lower ring. From this distance, those fleeing are as small as ants, bursting through the city gates, crossing the dunes on foot or by horse. The perfect meal for any darkwalkers roaming the desert.

"We can't kill them all," Notus says. "There are simply too many."

From the frequency of the screams, many will not escape with their lives. I watch a handful of citizens succumb to the creatures' soul-sucking kiss. Their bodies collapse in the sand. Seconds later, the ashes of their desiccated forms scatter in the wind. Never have I felt so helpless as I do now, watching my people fall. I am mortal, and I am weak. It is a bitter truth. "Can you call the Lord—your brother—back?"

Notus shakes his head with obvious frustration. "Eurus has no loyalty toward me, nor I toward him. I'm amazed he answered my call to begin with."

"What of your other brothers?"

"There's no time. It would take days, weeks, for a message to reach them. I doubt they would heed my call for help anyway. We were never close." A frown folds his brow, the baked skin around his eyes deeply furrowed, like cracks running through hardened clay. "We'll head to the palace—"

"It would be more efficient if we split up," I cut in.

"You're joking."

"You keep the darkwalkers at bay," I say. "Search for the beast if you can. I'll head to the palace to search for Amir and Tuleen." And Roshar, though the man has likely already fled the capital, his precious Zarqan in tow.

The South Wind stares at me as though I have suggested we strip naked in the middle of a red storm. "We're not splitting up. Wherever we go, we go together."

"We *must*," I urge. "You can't quell Prince Balior's army or the dark-walkers if you're busy protecting me."

"I also can't fight them while worrying about whether you're dead in an alley somewhere," he growls through his teeth.

I breathe out hard through my nostrils. I'm not getting through to him. The South Wind, as stubborn as they come. "I hear what you're saying, Notus, but there's no time."

He shifts onto his heels, then forward, agitation forcing movement into his body. Sand begins to swirl around his legs. "We'll head to the palace. Once we find Amir and Tuleen, we'll return to the g—"

"You're not listening to me," I snap, and my voice fractures, crumbling to bits. "I can't face the darkwalkers. You know I'm useless in a fight." The violin may have granted me an advantage in the laby-rinth, but it's gone now. It provided music, not miracles. "It won't be for long—"

"I can't lose you again!" he snarls. Then he looses a breath, and his shoulders slump, the fight going out of him. "Not again," he murmurs.

Death has dogged my heels my entire life. I am well acquainted with its mind-numbing fear. It is unfair, but *life* is unfair. This is what must be done. If we are to save Ammara, then we must part, only for a short while.

Reaching out, I gather his wide, strong body into my arms and pull him close. He's trembling.

"You won't," I whisper against his cheek. "I won't allow it."

It is easy as breathing, to part his lips with my own, gift him love and reassurance in this wordless form. Our bodies slot together like tiles in a mosaic. The strength of his arms encircles me: a hardened exterior armoring a soft heart.

When we separate, I lift a hand to his cheek, my eyes wet. We have come far, he and I. It is something I did not believe was possible. But I am no wounded girl. He is no exiled god. We belong to one another. We have built our own home.

"Clear a path toward the palace," I command. "I'll find you when I'm done."

Notus frames my face in his warm, roughened hands. "I love you," he says. "Do you trust me?"

"Yes," I whisper. "I trust you." Then, quieter: "I love you, too."

His eyes soften, and he gathers me into his arms. "Then it's time for you to spread your wings."

A vicious snap launches me skyward, and I scream, my dress billowing around my legs as I soar upward. Then, a plummeting descent, the air snatched from my lungs. Wind softens my fall. It cradles me in the middle of the sky before nudging me into an upright position as Notus shouts from below, "Run, Sarai! I'll catch up."

Of course he would use the last of his depleted power to aid my cause. That frustrating, wonderful, insufferable, doting god.

I run. The wind buoys me. It nudges me ever onward, my eyes stinging from the smoke as I near the capital, Ishmah in flames far, far below. The buildings are small blocks of red stone, like child's toys. The people are bright dots of colored fabric. Gradually, the wind begins to lower me toward the city streets. My heart hurts at what I witness. Chaos, everywhere.

I've never seen so many darkwalkers. There must be hundreds. They flock like flies to carrion. They tear into flesh and suck free the life and breath of the living. Meanwhile, hordes of townsfolk stream down the Queen's Road. They haul carts, goats, children, whatever they can carry. Some are not fortunate. They are slow, infirm, aged. Easy pickings. I turn my eyes away, only to catch sight of silver flashes through the shadow below. Prince Balior's army, corralling Ishmah's citizens like goats led to slaughter.

As my feet at last alight on solid ground, I hurry in the direction of the palace, swept along with the current of those fleeing. It feels like shoving through a wall of skin, so tightly packed are the streets. Sweat oozes from my pores, and breathing grows difficult in the thickening smoke, each inhalation a choked rasp, a stifled wheeze.

It is all grasping hands and bullish desperation, and I struggle to remain upright, my pleas to make room falling on deaf ears. Someone's cart rams the back of my knees. Another's elbow clips my hip bone.

As the road curves past one of the public gardens, the boiling air intensifies, drenching all in an orange light. Beyond the iron fence, the garden's many flowering plants succumb to flame, which leaps from tree to bush to flower bed. I hack a cough, my throat burning. Then: more screams. My head snaps around. Nothing behind. But—there. Two darkwalkers lope ahead, tearing into the crowd. The shrieks are bloodcurdling, the way forward blocked. I change direction, darting down a side street.

Unfortunately, many have the same idea. I attempt to squeeze past a large family when a scraggly woman turns to me, red-rimmed eyes streaming tears. "Where's my son?" she cries. "I need to find my son!"

She takes in my dress, my bare, sweat-drenched face. Her eyes widen in recognition.

"Princess Sarai." My title, whispered like some forgotten fortune. "Please. Help me." A claw-like hand latches onto my arm. She forces me against the wall of a nearby building.

"Get off me," I growl, yet I cannot shake her loose.

"It's Princess Sarai!" the woman shouts through her tears. "She's come to save us!"

The surrounding mob lurches toward us. It thuds into walls and clambers over piles of refuse.

Princess!

My sister is missing, Your Highness—

. . . do anything to help . . .

Black begins to blot the edges of my vision, for always, the smoke thickens, the fire spreads. I shove the woman back, gasping. She presses forward again, cornering me, an animal in a cage. "You need to let me through," I manage.

No one moves.

My eyes flick side to side, scanning the alleyway. Left: blocked. Right: blocked. But a nearby stack of crates provides a means of reaching the metal roof. If I cannot go forward, if I cannot go backward, then I will have to go up.

A forceful shove sends the woman back. Leaping onto the lowest crate, I scramble toward the top and heave myself onto the pitched roof, the boiling metal searing the skin of my palms. Its sting sends me to my feet, one foot placed lower on the incline. Turning, I peer down at the gathered crowd, their faces tipped toward me in hope. "I'm sorry," I call down. I can't help them all. I need to find my family, too. My heart clenches with guilt as I spin around and leap across the rooftops toward home.

It is a treacherous journey, stumbling across the fiery metal crowning the Red City. I take care with where I place my feet, avoiding holes or areas weakened by rust. Thankfully, the homes are pressed close, so it doesn't take long to travel to the upper ring. Eventually, I reach a gap too wide to cross and am forced to drop down onto the street.

The nearer I approach the palace, the thicker the shadow-smoke becomes. My skin, smothered beneath the drenched cotton of my dress, feels as if it is melting off my bones. As the breathable air continues to deplete, my visions wavers.

Another turn. The road skews beneath my feet, and I slump against a building, gasping. Ahead, bodies spoil the streets. My gaze maps the roads and alleyways. There, the narrowest of escapes, a thread of a path. I squeeze between two overturned carts and find myself on the eastern edge of the palace.

I sprint uphill, dodging escaped goats, harried mothers, soot-streaked watchmen attempting to direct traffic. Something explodes to my right. The cries are so numerous they bleed into a hum. Then— the palace, swarmed by citizens hammering at its rising outer walls in hysteria. Two women clip my shoulder in their desperate run toward the gates. They are firmly shut.

The guards have likely abandoned their posts, fleeing Ishmah with all the rest. None may enter. Which means I must find another way inside.

I shove through the crowd toward a row of nondescript buildings shaded by the towering wall. But my footsteps falter at the sight before me. *Oh, no. No, no, no . . .* This is where the tunnel leading to the stables is located, but a building has collapsed, blocking my path.

"Your Highness!"

I whirl, catch sight of a woman I recognize—one of the palace maids. Ash streaks her gaunt cheeks. "This way." She gestures me toward an alleyway across the street.

We slip into a concealed tunnel whose location I wasn't aware of. When it splits off, the woman points me to the left. "The throne room is that way. Good luck, Your Highness." She disappears down the other fork.

Perhaps a quarter-mile later, the tunnel deposits me into a storeroom below the kitchens. Dark, enclosed, rough stone walls. The dry air smells of sweet grain.

Before long, I'm climbing the stairs to the third level. I'm speeding across marble floors and careening around pillar-lined corridors, past gardens with still pools. No guards. No staff. Only smoke fills the palace halls.

Halfway down the passage, I skid to a halt, breathless with realization. The door to my right, its plaque askew: *Royal Tailor.* I shove inside. "Roshar!"

Colorful bolts of fabric litter the workroom floor and tables. But the space is otherwise empty.

The tightness in my chest eases, just a touch. *Good.* Wherever Roshar has found himself, better there than here.

Amir's chambers aren't far. I reach them in a handful of minutes, the doorway gaping like a mouth from when I watched Notus blast through the doors in the labyrinth mirror. Bedroom: empty. Study:

empty. All empty. I pace, and pace, and pace. Where could he have gone? The last I saw of Amir and Tuleen, darkwalkers were attempting to infiltrate their quarters. Except—not these quarters.

The king's chambers, which Amir would have moved to following his coronation, are located at the end of the hall. No guards flank his doors. The handle gives under my hand. It glides open on oiled hinges.

A window lies open on the far side of the room, curtains snapping in the smoke-heavy wind. The massive bed is neatly made. Everything is coated in a fine layer of ash. "Amir?" Slowly, I shuffle toward the library. "Tuleen?"

I nudge the door open. Unoccupied. Both sitting rooms are as well. Mounting alarm sends me through the connecting door leading to the queen's chambers. Those, too, are empty. Retracing my steps, I veer toward his study, and there is Tuleen, cowering behind the desk near the window, a gag cutting across her mouth. At my entrance, her eyes widen.

The door slams shut at my back.

32

"SARAI. THANK YOU FOR JOINING US ON SUCH SHORT NOTICE."
Prince Balior waltzes across the study toward where Tuleen and Amir have been shoved into a corner, bound, gagged, faces bruised and swollen. This high in the palace, we are among the clouds, the roiling smoke, a sky blistered black. Dense, particle-dusted air pours through the open window, but Prince Balior appears unconcerned as gray streaks across the room. I cough against the searing sensation in my throat. At his back: ash and flame.

Despite the dread weakening my knees, I force myself to straighten. No hesitation. No fear. "Have you lost all sense? What good is this kingdom if you burn it to the ground?" I point toward Ammara's king and queen. "Is this how you intend to treat people under your new regime? Disgraceful."

His upper lip curls. "Your attempts to shame me will not work. Be grateful these two are still alive. The woman in particular was quite vicious." He gestures to a gouge near his eye that weeps blood.

A deep sense of pride wells in my chest. Tuleen is a fighter. "Let them go. They've done you no harm."

"Do you think me a fool?" He runs fingers through his hair. "No, I think I'll keep them here for the time being."

I lunge toward my family, but a shadowy tendril slithers along the ground, wraps around my ankle, and hauls me backward. My spine hits the wall. I drop with a heavy *oof.* The shadow recoils, returning to the prince's outstretched palm, where it fades.

"Princess Sarai." One step forward, and a gloom pools beneath his boots, as though he steps in puddles of ink. "Unfortunately, your manners seem to have deteriorated in the time we've been apart. Let me explain. You are hereby my guest for what will now unfold. You move if and when I tell you to."

It's not real. But the screams are too piercing to mistake, and the whites of my brother's eyes, Tuleen's eyes, roll with desperation and fear.

Warily, I push to my feet. Prince Balior is no god, but he wields the power of one—a gift from the beast he set free.

"What do you want?" I demand.

He tsks. "I admit," he says, "I did not believe you would escape the labyrinth alive. But that is neither here nor there. I welcome a larger audience. I am nothing if not accommodating."

I examine the prince carefully. He appears larger than when we last met. His black eyes seem to absorb light rather than reflect it. His teeth catch his lower lip: dazzling white. His cheeks swell like ripened apples, their rounded tops brushed a healthy pink.

"You've done what you came here to do," I say roughly. "It is done. Leave Ammara to its people. Let us rebuild. It was never yours to take."

Prince Balior regards me as one would a particularly senseless child. "I don't care for Ammara. I never did. What use would I have for a realm in slow decline? Your basins run dry. Your crops wither. I have no reason to stay. On the contrary, Sarai, I'm *waiting.*"

For who? But I already know.

The smallest of smiles curves his mouth. "Notus is a sensible person. He would not wish the family of his love to be needlessly killed." That smile widens. "Leverage, my dear."

I understand then what I have done. My presence, a boon to Prince Balior's plan. Three hostages as opposed to two. I feel ill, woozy from the choking smoke. My vision blurs, and I crouch low to the ground, seeking the untainted air.

"You won't touch a hair on his head," I hiss. "I won't let you."

Casually, he slides his hands into the pockets of his trousers. "Who is there to stop me?"

I glance around in desperation. Amir struggles to stand, but the prince kicks him hard in the abdomen, and he falls, a guttural scream muffled against the fabric stuffing his mouth. Tuleen sits quietly, expression blank. I haven't the slightest idea where Notus is or what state he's in. I have no means of defending myself, or my family. But I have faced adversity before. Who am I? A survivor through and through.

I whirl, snatching a candlestick from a nearby table, and fling it as hard as I can at Prince Balior's face. Shadow explodes from his palm, knocking both me and the candlestick aside simultaneously.

Slowly, he advances on me, his features frozen with inhuman rage. I scramble backward until my spine hits the wall.

His ebon power grasps hold of my body and slams me once, twice, thrice against the stone. Pain ruptures at the back of my skull, and I see stars. A muted scream cuts through the ringing in my ears. Tuleen, or Amir?

I slump in the shadow's grip. The agony is so great my stomach lurches. My head feels as though it has burst. A trickle of wetness dampens my hair—blood.

When I manage to open my eyes, I am met by Prince Balior's handsome features less than a hand's width away. "Please believe me when I say I do not wish to harm you," he whispers, cool breath skimming across my mouth, "but should you continue your refusal to cooperate, I will have no choice."

He releases me. My limbs fold, and I slump against the wall, whimpering at the pain pressing into the backs of my eyes, digging down into my neck. With effort, I manage to shift my attention toward Amir and Tuleen's huddled forms. My brother's gag is tied so tightly it cuts white lines at the corners of his mouth.

"Or perhaps I should punish your family instead?" the prince continues, veering toward Ammara's monarchs. "Will that make you reconsider?" He lashes toward my brother. Blackness swarms Amir's face. He lurches wildly from side to side, arms and legs bound, unable to claw free.

"Stop, please!" I fall forward, crawling toward Prince Balior. My arms tremble beneath my weight, my surroundings fading in and out. "I'll cooperate, I will, just . . . please, don't hurt them."

The prince considers my plea, perhaps weighing its desperation. He shapes a fist with his hand, and the shadow vanishes. Amir collapses on the ground, gasping for air, his eyes wild. My chest tightens. If I had not been so consumed by my resentment toward Notus, would I have identified the prince's insidious intentions? If I cannot kill him, what am I to do?

"I'm glad to hear of your change of heart, Princess Sarai." He peers down at me pityingly. "All I need is an audience with the South Wind. I can't risk him killing the beast I've unleashed and ruining my plans. You understand, I'm sure."

"And what are these plans?" Aside from spreading darkness across the mortal realms.

"Unfortunately, I can't tell you."

Arrogant fool. "You've been deceived," I say, voice unwavering. "You are a tool to this beast, nothing more. You've granted it what it desires—freedom—and now it has no use for you."

I watch the words hit with satisfaction. There is a subtle twisting of his features. "The beast requires my protection until it is of sound mind, its transformation complete. Without my protection, it is vulnerable."

"And when it has regained full use of its faculties?" I press, watching those shallowest cracks run deep. "Who is to say it will not call back the power it has gifted you?"

He raises a hand, a dark look in his eyes, but the door blasts open, hurled clear across the room to slam into the bookshelves with an explosive crunch of wood. Heavy tomes collapse onto the desk, toppling the piece of furniture. Tuleen gasps through her gag as Prince Balior yanks me against his chest, a shadowy tendril banded across my waist.

The South Wind ducks into the smoke-heavy room. An immense wind shrieks and howls, tightening into a swirling vortex of smoke, ash, and debris. A moment later, the wind dies. In silence, Notus takes everything in at a glance. Ammara's monarchs, bound and gagged. Me, restrained against Prince Balior's chest. Notus' robe hangs off his frame, naught but scraps. Blood and ash powder his skin, his hair. They are empty, his eyes. Completely devoid of emotion.

"I will make this simple," Notus growls in a voice so riddled with rage I hardly recognize it. "Release Sarai and her family, and I will make your death a swift one."

But the prince only grins. "Welcome, Notus. So glad you could make it." He gestures toward the study, now a mess of broken wood and parchment, soot coating every available surface. "Though I'd hoped our meeting would take place under more, shall we say, agreeable circumstances."

Notus steps closer. "Release Sarai, now."

The prince tilts his head in contemplation. He glances between Notus, Amir, Tuleen, and myself. Then he sighs gustily. "Well, you do drive a hard bargain." The prince is all smiles. "Very well." He gestures toward the South Wind's waist. "In exchange for your betrothed's freedom, I will take your sword. And your life."

Notus' hand drifts toward the hilt. The weapon hangs protectively in its leather sheath. "You're mad if you think I would hand this over to you," he growls. "Last time. Step away from Sarai, if you value your life."

Prince Balior laughs and laughs and laughs. "You want me to step away? The solution is simple: your sword."

"I've already given you my answer," Notus grits out.

"I don't think you understand just how truly dire the situation is," Prince Balior replies. The shadow encasing my body migrates up my chest, higher, to wrap lovingly around my neck. Deliberately, the substance tightens. I grasp hold of its slithering shape, yank at it to no avail as the noose draws taut. Dark spots overwhelm the sickly light. I wheeze, my strength waning.

There is a roar, a crash of sound. The noose vanishes, and I drop, a throb of pain shooting through my skull as I hit the floor. Scimitar raised, the South Wind hacks at Prince Balior, who tosses up a shield.

The blade skitters off its wisped surface. Notus regroups, hurtling a thin shard of air at the prince, who dives toward the floor.

He hits the ground and rolls. A heartbeat later, he's on his feet, drawing forth a protective dome. Wind makes impact with a sharp crack. Shadow bursts from Prince Balior, a many-armed creature of darkness, lashing its multiple tentacles toward Notus. It grips his wrists, legs, waist, chest. He snarls, attempting to free himself. Wind daggers its way through two of the arms. They dissolve and immediately reform.

The men vanish behind the increasingly thickening smoke. I use the opportunity to crawl toward Amir and Tuleen, their ash-coated faces white with fear above their gags. I've nearly reached Tuleen's side when a ball of shadow shatters the bookshelves. Her eyes widen, and she frantically shakes her head. Something wraps my waist from behind and yanks me backward. I slam into Prince Balior's chest.

"Enough of this," he snaps, and a long steel dagger materializes inside the darkness pooling in his outstretched palm.

I stare at the dagger. My brother leans against the wall, his arms positioned at awkward angles, one of his shoulders having been wrenched from its socket in his attempts to unknot his bonds. Tuleen, meanwhile, glares at Prince Balior with utter loathing. Whatever fear sent her cowering against the ground, it has hardened, become something obdurate, uncompromising.

"Where did you get that blade?" Notus asks. He stares at the hilt in mystification: cut gemstones, tarnished steel.

"I conjured it from the realm of the gods." He slips the edge beneath my jaw, pressing it to the pulse point in my neck. I flinch from the metal's icy kiss. "Now you see how serious I am. With a god-touched weapon, I can kill you myself if I have to, but I am giving you the opportunity to end your existence on your own terms. Refuse me, and your precious love dies."

I clench my teeth, fighting tears. The agony carving open the back of my skull has become unbearable. I feel close to passing out. "Why are you doing this?" I hiss to the prince. "Why not leave Ammara as you came? Return to Um Salim and let us rebuild what was lost."

"I do intend to rebuild, Sarai." He grazes the wound on the back of my head. I recoil with a soft cry. "But the land will be different now that the beast has been freed. With the power granted to me, I can rule Um Salim and extend our borders, share our prosperity with smaller developing nations. I can ensure our realm will never bow to a greater force."

"You fool." The South Wind's voice is pure thunder. "Do you have any idea what you've done? The beast will rain fire over your realm, and all others beyond it."

Prince Balior gazes at him blandly. "I'm not concerned with your opinion of me, Notus. I'm aware of what the beast is capable of. I'm aware of the revenge it seeks. And I can't risk you driving your god-touched sword into its heart once it returns to its humanoid state."

Because Prince Balior's power is dependent on the beast's life, I realize. Though not a god itself, the beast is descended from a divine bull. Vulnerable to god-touched weapons.

As the prince drags the dagger point along my collarbone, he says, "We can do this the easy way, or the hard way. Your life, or Sarai's. Choose."

The South Wind is frozen. A muffled cry bursts from Amir's mouth. He crawls forward on his knees, but a whip of shadow unfurls, snapping his head sideways. The sight surges through me. My struggles grow more violent. The prince spits out an oath. The tips of his fingers dip deep into the place where my neck and shoulder meet, forcing me still. I'm panting, wild-eyed with despair.

"I won't ask again," Prince Balior says.

The South Wind considers his adversary. It matters not that he is a superior swordsman. The prince has the upper hand. "I will agree to the bargain," Notus replies. "On one condition. I do not wish to die by my own scimitar, for it has been a friend to me these long centuries. I will trade my sword for your dagger, and with it I will take my life in exchange for hers."

I stare at him, mouth agape.

Prince Balior is equally taken aback, judging by the silence that follows. But he is a man of greed. He wants what he wants. "I accept."

"Notus, *no*." My voice breaks.

He glances at me, eyes incredibly sad. My lungs twist onto themselves, rendering me breathless. Smoke lies as a dense veil between us. Why does it feel like he is already gone?

"Try anything," Prince Balior warns, "and I will snap her neck."

"Wait!" I renew my struggles. Prince Balior drives his fingers deeper into my shoulder, forcing me still, the shadow a subtle tightening around my waist. "This isn't the answer. Notus, *please*, just ... think about what you're doing." Higher and higher my panic mounts. There must be another way. A loophole. But I am powerless in this moment, little more than an animal pacing its cage. "It can't be undone."

He bows his head in surrender. "If the choice is between your life and mine," he says, "then it is no choice at all. I would gladly give my life for yours, Sarai."

As the South Wind offers his sword hilt first, the prince's dagger floats through the air and into his outstretched palm. Notus stares at it, the dull shine of its blade, the sharpened point. He looks to me. I understand, then, the decision he has made. I clench my teeth, trembling, tears already sliding down my face. "Don't go," I whisper.

"Forgive me," Notus says, and plunges the dagger into his heart.

There is a scream.

It is a shrill, splintered sound, drawn from the blackest depths of grief. On it goes, and on. I don't realize I'm the one responsible until the strain in my throat forces it closed, cutting off the shriek.

Blood pours forth, sopping the South Wind's robes. A hard exhalation punches out of him, wet and torn. His spine folds forward, like the toppling of a great stone tower. I lunge, catching him before he hits the ground.

Prince Balior peers down at the fallen god dispassionately. He then looks to Amir. "Tell Notus' brother the beast is coming for him." He oozes into shadow and is gone.

My heart feels like it will tear free of my chest as I lower Notus onto the floor, the rug already soaked with blood. He will leave me. He does not wish to go, but I must watch him vanish regardless.

374 • ALEXANDRIA WARWICK

A low curse briefly draws my attention from Notus. Tuleen shakes her arms free of the rope, having managed to pick the knot. After freeing Amir, she stumbles over to me, wrenching the gag from her mouth. "How can I help?"

Through his labored breathing, the South Wind stares at me. There is a glaze to his dark eyes, which have begun to lose focus.

"Find a healer . . . if you can," I whisper. She flees the room, Amir in pursuit, likely to ensure his wife does not come to harm. And then we are alone, Notus and I. His form blurs behind a stinging haze of distortion as tears well, and fall. The air is sharp, edged. It hurts to breathe, and takes a monumental effort to lift my hands, rest them against the roughness of the South Wind's ashen cheeks.

"Why?" I choke out. "Why would you do this?"

"Shh." One large hand curls around mine, quelling the trembling that has spread outward from my core. "Do not despair."

His eyelids flutter shut. The sight sends me forward with a sharp cry. "Notus!"

His eyes crack open, and I release a shaky exhalation. "I thought . . ." I can't say it. I can't make it real. "What should I do? How can we heal this?" I glance around. The smoke is quite thick now, making speaking, even breathing, difficult. I cough into my shoulder, swipe at my leaking eyes.

"You can't," he says quietly. "Death by a god-touched blade cannot be reversed."

My heart, that diamond-encrusted organ, plummets to my feet and shatters into a thousand fragments. "No," I whisper. "No, no, no, no . . . you're immortal. You can pull through. It's just a stupid blade."

"It is god-touched."

"But you—you're the South Wind. You can do *anything*," I whisper as the anguish hooks deeper. "I've seen it. You're unstoppable, resilient—" My voice cracks, and I duck my head, my eyes so choked with tears the South Wind's features have become a hot smear.

"It's not fair," I cry. "I just got you back, I—" *I can't lose you.* Now that I will live, how am I supposed to accept this cost? My chest strains, and

I press a fist against it, my face twisting as another broken sob bursts from my mouth. "Why do the people I love always leave me?"

"I'm not leaving you, Sarai."

"Yes, you are."

"No, I'm not, at least not willingly. Look at me." He draws my chin upward, searching my gaze. "I'll be right here. Always." He touches two fingers against my heart. "Please listen to what I'm about to tell you."

My fingers slide against his like the tightest weave, knotted into forever. "I'm not—"

"*Please*. I don't have much time."

My teeth clamp in an attempt to dam the scream that hammers against my locked jaw. Helplessly, I nod.

"I have . . . regrets," Notus begins, the words sluggish and muddled. "Had I known my home was with you, I would have stood against Fahim. I would never have left you behind. You are my heart in every sense of the word. The woman I imagined I'd spend my days with."

"It's all right," I soothe, wiping away a tear that squeezes from the corner of his eye. "I forgive you. I understand why you left."

"I was weak. I thought your brother knew best, thought *I* knew best. In leaving, I denied myself the person that was most precious to me. And now I'm leaving again," he whispers as the strength fades from his voice. "My one worry is who will look after you, if you leave Ishmah. Who will shelter you, reassure you? Who will love you?"

I wipe at the tears that drip endlessly. The truth is, I worry about that, too. I worry about being alone. How far will I drift this time before I'm able to pull myself from that black nothingness, if I have the strength at all?

But I won't burden Notus with these thoughts. So I tell him all will be well. I reassure him that I can look after myself. I have Amir, Tuleen, Roshar. I have our memories. "I know who I am," I say. "I'm not afraid."

Some of the apprehension eases from his face at hearing this. I did the right thing, I think.

"Never forget that you are strong." His fingers slacken, sliding from the hilt of the dagger protruding from his chest. The emerald pommel dulls beneath a coating of ash. "You are Sarai Al-Khatib," Notus chokes out, the words garbled, blood trickling from his mouth. "Do not let the world tell you otherwise."

"I won't," I sob, head bowed. "I promise. Just . . . stay, for a little while longer." All the stories I wish to tell him, the laughter we might share.

Blood slinks over our grasped hands, slips down into the cracks between. "Tell me of your childhood," I urge. "Tell me of your favorite sound in the world. Tell me . . . tell me what it was like to visit Ammara for the first time." These things, which I believed we'd have the leisure to discuss. This future that will never be.

His expression pinches as he draws forth the recollection. "Ammara was beautiful. I had never come across a land so vast, so effortlessly raw. There was power here, power beyond my wildest imagination, though it came from no god that I could see."

His chest judders, and he shifts his head toward me.

"And then I saw you," he whispers, "and I realized the beauty I'd beheld in the desert was a pale comparison to the brightness of your smile, the intelligence in your gaze. You speared the very heart of me, Sarai. You still do."

I cry harder, face pressed into his shoulder. "Notus." My fingers curve around his wrist, the unyielding bone my only anchor against the ebbing tide. As I have learned, life will go on. The sun will rise, the moon will cycle, yet I fear a world that lacks the South Wind's steadfast nature. "What can I do?"

"You can live your life, Sarai. Be happy." He brushes the side of my face. "It's all I've ever wanted for you."

"I don't want to live it without you."

"It will only be for a short while," he whispers, eyelids sinking low. "We will meet again. If not in this life, then the next."

"Notus." I grip his hand tightly enough to bruise "You must stay awake."

"Sarai," he slurs. "I will dream of you."

The South Wind is gone.

33

DESPITE THE BRIGHT ORB THAT IS THE SUN, I SEE ONLY SMOKE.
Ishmah—charred, crumbling Ishmah—is a smoldering ruin
in the weeks following Prince Balior's attack. The fumes are horrendous. My eyes suffer in a constant state of irritation, though I don't
know whether it's from the smoke or the hours I have wept. Ishmah
has weathered much, as have I, as have all who claim the Red City as
their home.

Flesh heaps the streets, human and darkwalker alike. From the
window of my study, I watch people drag bodies from collapsed buildings: mothers, cousins, uncles, friends. Loved ones fall to their knees in
anguish. They scream and tear at their hair. They plead to the gods, to
anyone who might listen. When this occurs, I press a hand to my heart
and wish them peace in the afterlife.

Twice, I have ventured into the city, seeking comfort in Haneen's
tales of friendship, adventure, and triumph. Since the beast's escape
from the labyrinth, Amir is all but buried under reconstruction efforts.
If he's not in meetings with the council or helping rebuild the lower
ring—where the worst of the devastation occurred—then he's organizing functions to distract the court from what they've lost, the knowledge
of a great evil unleashed.

I don't attend these functions. Neither does Tuleen, who is with
child. While Amir does his best to piece our broken city back together,

I remain behind closed doors, my mind tearing itself apart in an effort to think my way out of a situation that can be neither altered nor wished away.

I have written letters. I have placed offerings at every crumbling temple, every scant, forgotten shrine. I have read every book, tome, scroll, and letter housed in Ishmah's vast library. I have beseeched the gods. *Save him*, I plead. *Save this god, whom I love.*

The South Wind, who lies still in my bed.

Perched on the edge of the mattress, I lean over him, brushing the hair from his forehead. His broad chest swells and contracts with gentle exhalations. His skin, when touched, is warm.

He did not die, as I had assumed after he pierced his chest with Prince Balior's dagger. When I realized he was still alive, I wept tears of gratitude. But the days passed, and he didn't wake. Somehow, he is caught in an endless sleep.

In so many ways, I have failed him. So much wasted time. A wealth of bitterness and misdirected anger. If I had not been so utterly entrenched in the black cavity of my trauma, perhaps fate would have unfolded differently. As it is, there are no answers, no cure.

A knock sounds at the door. "Sarai?"

My eyes sink shut on a sudden wave of exhaustion. "Come in."

Queen Tuleen Al-Khatib of Ammara enters my chambers, dressed in the black of mourning. The door closes with a soft click.

Rather than approach the bed, she moves toward the windows, their panes of glass shuttered behind the drawn curtains. Grasping the heavy fabric, she looks to me for permission. "May I?"

I shrug, and she pulls back the heavy drapes. Streams of frail sunlight pierce the gloom.

She then refills my glass of water from the pitcher resting on the bedside table. "Drink," she says, offering me the glass. I accept it without complaint, draining every drop until it's gone.

After settling onto the chair located on the opposite side of the bed, Tuleen regards me in concern. "Any changes?" she asks tentatively.

"No." No matter my efforts, the South Wind will not wake.

She studies his smooth, unlined face. The skin around her eyes is puffy, signaling lack of sleep. "What are you going to do?"

"I've done all that I can." I must now ask myself what comes next. Do I allow Notus to sleep? Is it fair to keep him in this half-state when there is no hope for resurrection? How will that impact my life? Will I be able to move on, or will I obsess over Notus' affliction as I'd obsessed over my own?

Tuleen eases back into the chair. "I didn't think you were one to give up so easily," she murmurs.

I stiffen. "I'm not giving up, I'm just—"

Ammara's queen quirks a brow.

Giving up.

Helplessly, my lips pull into a smile. Crafty woman. She's right. It's not a question of accepting his condition. Rather, it is a question of how far I will go to bring Notus back. And I realize there is one thing I haven't done, one thing that may wake the South Wind from his cursed sleep.

I shove to my feet, skin buzzing with an emotion I dare not name. "I'll be back."

She dips her chin, mouth curved in satisfaction. "I'll keep watch over Notus for you."

As I suspected she would. As for me . . .

I need a horse.

Hours later, I summit Mount Syr. An arid wind plucks at my hair, and I promptly dismount, Zainab wandering to graze whatever scant weeds shove through the cracks in the earth. The sky overhead is a great, swallowing mouth, poised to engulf the world whole. In the distance, Ishmah shimmers behind waves of heat, a blurred spot of red.

No time to waste. As I imagine Father did long ago, I kneel before the great throne overlooking Ammara, this holiest of sanctuaries. I'm so overcome by desperation I feel woozy. What if this does not work? Then again, what if it does?

"Lord of the Mountain, I beseech you. Please, will you grant me your time?"

The air flickers, and when I next blink, the Lord of the Mountain —Eurus—becomes visible, gracing the massive throne. He is prodigious, immense. Two spots of brightness burn inside the shadowy cowl of his hood.

Hello, Sarai. The low rasp of his voice scrapes along my nerve endings. *I did not expect to see you again so soon.*

Neither did I. Leaning forward, I allow my forehead to brush the eroded stone of the bottom step. Today, I am strong, and for all the days after. "Lord of the Mountain. Twenty-five years ago, my father prostrated himself at your feet, begging you to save my life. Now I have come to ask for a similar favor."

The god is quiet. He watches me with predatory stillness.

"Notus has succumbed to eternal sleep," I say. "I need to know how to reverse it."

A hot wind skates over the barren earth. It smells not of the desert, but of sweet rain. When I glance skyward, however, I find not a cloud to mar the blue stretch.

How did this come to pass? the god asks.

Briefly, I explain the circumstances leading to the South Wind's current state.

Describe this dagger.

"It was old, tarnished. There was an emerald set into its pommel."

He straightens—the only indication of interest. *Emerald, you say?* I nod, curious. *If that is true, it seems this Prince Balior managed to acquire a god-touched blade himself. The emerald pommel is indicative of any blade owned by the god Sleep. He coats them in a powerful elixir, which Notus has succumbed to. Unfortunately,* the Lord of the Mountain goes on, *it means Notus is beyond my help.* He does not sound at all upset by this, though I suppose I should not be surprised, considering the brothers' most recent interaction. *Not even I have the strength to overpower Sleep's influence.*

"Then who does?" Because if there's one thing I've learned about the divine, it's that there always exists one of greater authority.

It doesn't matter. You are mortal and are not permitted to speak with them.

"Says who?"

The Council of Gods.

If I'm not mistaken, Notus once mentioned this council. They were responsible for the Four Winds'—the Anemoi's—banishment. Notus and Boreas, Eurus and Zephyrus, all exiled to opposite corners of the world. The odds are not in my favor, but I refuse to give up. "Please." Once more, I lean forward until my forehead skims the stone. "I know you have no loyalty to your brother, but do you not have loyalty to yourself and what is right?"

The silence speaks. It tells me this god considers my words, albeit reluctantly. *I can't help you,* he eventually says, the voice inside my mind riddled with cold, *but there may be someone who can. Boreas—our eldest brother.*

I sit upright. The sun is most bright. "How can I find him?"

You already know how.

"I assure you, I don't."

He drags a finger down the arm of the stone chair. *There's nothing more I can give you. The rest is up to you.*

He claims I already know how to find Boreas, a god I have never met. All I know of him is that he rules over the Deadlands, the realm of the darkwalkers.

And then it hits me. There is a doorway to the Deadlands somewhere within the labyrinth. I must have traversed every inch of that infernal place, and not once did I see such a door, no way out . . . except the mirror.

What was it the Lord of the Mountain once told me? *The mirror shows what has been, what is, and what will be.* What if the mirror was the door all along? After all, it transported me to my memories. It displayed the fire and smoke of Ishmah under siege. Who is to say it cannot transport me to the Deadlands?

Though I cannot see inside the Lord of the Mountain's hood, I'm certain his eyes seek mine. A feeling of pins prickles across my skin. Maybe Notus' brother isn't as heartless as I had first assumed.

"Thank you," I say, and bow low as another rain-drenched gust buffets my back.

Good luck to you.

Leaping onto my horse's back, I guide her down the trail edging the mountainside. Hours later, we arrive at the palace, and I dismount, sprinting toward the courtyard where the labyrinth squats. The area is deserted. Unsurprising. Many of the guards were killed during the attack. Others, gravely wounded and currently recovering in the infirmary. Thus, the labyrinth's arched entryway lies open for any who dare enter.

Palm pressed against the symbol cut into the door, I push it open with a creak of aged wood. Fear is beyond me. I am keen, eager for what awaits, what I might change. Cool, whispering darkness grasps at me. It enfolds me in its frigid embrace, and drags me into high stone walls cloaked by a heavy gloom.

There the silver mirror hangs, as though awaiting me.

Staring into the reflective glass, I see a woman who has pushed herself to the very brink of what it means to be a daughter, a princess, a citizen of her people. She is twenty-five years of age, yet lines carve years into her face.

But it is her shoulders that I study. Where is the downward slope? Where is the hunch to her spine from carting heavy burdens? Gone. And as I straighten, I understand something else. Here stands a woman who has lived. Her life has been both ease and suffering, trial and triumph. She knows what she wants. She is no longer afraid to demand it.

I reach out, fingertips brushing the cool surface of the looking glass. Ripples drag outward, revealing a doorway leading into depths unknown. My mouth curves.

I step through.

I stand in a wide stone corridor marked by countless doors. They are constructed of glass and wood, plaster and mud and iron tipped in frost. Some possess round windows of colored glass. Others, minute tiles fashioned into breathtaking mosaics. And still there are more, painted lilac and scarlet, even one carpeted in clambering vines.

The icy air stings my nostrils. It holds no familiarity. Even its scent is foreign, bright and crisp, a snap against my skin. Slowly, I spin in place. Has the mirror brought me to the Deadlands, as I had hoped?

With a frown, I begin to walk, slippers hissing against the gray flag-stones. At the end of the hall, I turn right. More doors, dozens of them. I open the nearest one, its battered wooden face covered in peeling white paint. I stare in shock. Snow-covered mountains, the glimmer of a frozen waterfall. I close that door, open the next one. A cramped lane leading to a market square. I shut it and hurry onward, without the slightest clue as to what I'm looking for.

"Who are you?"

The demand lashes forth, and I whirl, catching sight of a woman at the end of the corridor. In her arms, she shelters an infant swaddled in blankets. At her knees, a little boy clutches the hem of her moss-colored dress. She does not appear to be Ammaran, though her complexion is as dark as my own.

The woman steps forward, dark eyes flashing in warning. "Speak quickly, if you value your life. Who are you? How did you get in here?"

My stance is a reflection of hers: braced legs, squared shoulders. "My name is Princess Sarai Al-Khatib," I say, in a declaration fit for this vast stone hall. "To whom do I have the honor of speaking?"

Through narrowed eyes, she demands, "How did you enter my home, Princess Sarai Al-Khatib?"

An excellent question, though she failed to give her name in response. Not that I blame her. "I realize this might sound odd, but I entered through a doorway in my own realm."

The woman's mouth curls in suspicion, the large scar on her right cheek pulling taut. Her boots, I notice, are scuffed with age. She is no coddled woman. "And what realm might this be?"

"Mama." The boy reaches his small hand upward. The woman grasps it in wordless comfort.

"Ammara," I say. "Specifically, I hail from Ishmah, the Red City."

"I see." She frowns as her son attempts to climb up her legs, and the child she holds in her arms begins to fuss. "It is true these doors lead to other realms. However, that doesn't explain how you came to find yourself here. I wasn't aware others could enter of their own volition."

If I had even a shred of something resembling an explanation, I would offer it freely. As it stands, I have only the truth. "I don't know how the labyrinth works, exactly, but I'm looking for someone in particular. I think that's why it brought me to this specific location. Maybe it sensed that you could help me."

"And how could we help you, Sarai Al-Khatib?"

"I'm looking for Boreas."

Her eyes sharpen, and she wraps an arm around her son, shielding him. She glances over my shoulder, shaking her head slightly, but when I turn to look, nothing is there, only a flicker of light.

Quietly, she demands, "What business do you have with Boreas?"

Seeing as this woman appears moments away from either stabbing me or calling for reinforcements, I decide to lay everything out on the table. "I'm in love with his brother, the South Wind. He's one of the—"

"Anemoi," she says. "I know."

We stare at one another with combined wariness and reluctant interest. A strange thing, a very strange thing, that I might look upon this woman, a stranger to me, and feel as if I am glimpsing a reflection of sorts. "What do you know of Notus?" I ask.

The woman hesitates. Her caution is plain, but curiosity is a much greater force. Holding the swaddled infant close, she murmurs something to her son until he lets go and drops to his feet, pouting. "My name is Wren," she says. "Come with me."

I'm led down an ornate staircase with a gleaming banister. Every hallway, marked by doors. There must be hundreds, thousands in this stone palace. Rounding a corner, we enter a library with sleek, curved walls bearing an impressive collection of books. Her son races across the library on stubby legs, screaming, "Papa!"

A man unfurls from a cushioned armchair near the window. The boy leaps. The man catches his son midair, swinging him into his arms with deep, rolling laughter. His alabaster features are carved from marble, his eyes the pale shade of frost. As soon as he catches sight of me, however, his expression shutters.

"Hello, my love." Wren tilts her head up for a kiss, which he bestows with a gentleness that contradicts the aggression he suddenly exudes. When she tries to pull away, he tugs her close, positioning himself as a shield in front of her and their children.

"Who is this?" His voice slithers out, low and pocked by cold.

"This is Sarai Al-Khatib." Seemingly unconcerned by his attempt to protect her, Wren offers him the blanket-swaddled infant, who emits a small cry of distress. "She's our guest."

"Yes, but who *is* she?" He gently bounces the child until it quiets, scanning me from head to toe with slitted eyes. "That name tells me nothing."

"I just told you," Wren says. "She's our guest."

"She was not invited."

Wren sighs and turns to me, mouth quirked wryly. "My husband, Boreas, the North Wind." She gestures to the glowering man, who appears as though he would rather stab fiery pokers into his eyes than converse with the likes of me. "I promise, he's not as scary as he looks."

So, this is Boreas. He could not be any more different to Notus than a bird to a fish, both in appearance and demeanor. If Notus is a grounding safety, then his brother is shaped by the blackness of winter.

"I've come to plead for your help," I tell them. "Notus is in trouble."

The North Wind straightens, appearing even more stiff in the frame, if possible. "What news have you of my brother?"

I shake my head. "It's not good."

"Please, sit." Wren gestures me toward a nearby armchair, then calls, "Orla!"

A pleasantly plump woman dressed in a plain dress bustles into the library. "Yes, my lady?"

"Can you put the children to bed, please?" Boreas passes over the wrinkled bundle. Their son pouts, yet dutifully grips the woman's dress, well aware of what *bed* means. "Thank you."

As the woman exits the room, I blink in stupefaction. Do my eyes deceive me? That is most certainly candlelight I spot through the woman's body—her *transparent* body. "What is this? She—I can see through her body."

"Orla is a specter," Wren responds, taking a seat in the chair beside her husband, "as are all who pass into the afterlife. As overlord of the Deadlands, Boreas is responsible for Judging the dead. They are quite harmless, I assure you."

I look to Boreas. "And you have always judged the dead?"

"Since my banishment, yes. Though we don't know what will happen once Wren and I pass, whether our children will take over, or if the Council of Gods will appoint another successor."

"You are not immortal?" I ask the North Wind in surprise.

He looks to his wife before answering, "I haven't been immortal in over two years now."

The information sinks into me, oddity and realization both. I wasn't aware that shedding one's immortality was possible. I believed it to be inherent, of the blood.

The North Wind settles in, one long leg outstretched, a lock of black hair sliding over his brow. "What has happened to my brother?" he asks quietly. "I assume he still lives?"

How does one define life, really? What is the point of living when one cannot wake? "He's trapped in an eternal sleep. A darkness has been released into my realm."

Wren and Boreas exchange a look of silent communication, the softness and love evident between them. Wren quirks an eyebrow. Boreas frowns. She playfully rolls her eyes before turning back to me. "I sympathize with your plight," she says to me, smoothing a hand down her thigh, "but I'm not sure how you expect us to help. We have never traveled to Ammara. We know nothing of this darkness you speak of, nor of whatever curse Notus has found himself under."

"It's none of our business," the North Wind adds.

"Really?" I say. "Because from what I've gathered, the beast that escaped the labyrinth knows of you . . . and has a bone to pick with your brother, Eurus."

"Eurus?" This from Boreas, his suspicion suddenly whetted. "What, exactly, is this darkness you speak of? What beast?"

"In my realm, there's a labyrinth that was constructed a quarter of a century ago, built to imprison a beast that hails from the City of Gods. The beast blames Eurus for its imprisonment and has allied itself with a prince named Balior, who has now gained a dark new power. Prince Balior intends to help the beast enact its revenge, and spread darkness through the realms. Darkwalkers have multiplied in Ammara over the decades. We believe there is a doorway connecting the Deadlands to the labyrinth, which has allowed the darkwalkers to escape."

Stillness swathes the vast chamber of books. Wren stares at me in horror. Boreas is more difficult to read—I suppose that runs in the family. After a moment, Wren turns to her husband and whispers, "I thought the darkwalkers had been cleansed."

"They were."

She gives him a pointed look. "All of them?"

"As far as I know, yes." Boreas' confusion gives way, makes room for a distressing realization. "The Chasm." At his wife's puzzlement, he elaborates, "All of the darkwalkers were cleansed—except those imprisoned in the Chasm. I assume that's where they're escaping from." He runs a large hand through his hair. "I remember this beast. I remember how deeply Eurus' loathing for it ran. I'm not sure how he managed to cast it out from the City of Gods, considering we'd been banished for centuries at that point. But I suppose he found a loophole."

"Regardless of how your brother managed to imprison the beast," I say, redirecting the conversation back to the issue at hand, "there are very few people powerful enough to fight this darkness. Notus is one such person. If there is any hope of defeating it—"

"You love him," Wren says, eyes soft.

A harsh breath unspools from my chest. Gods, do I ever. "Yes." After a moment, I go on. "I understand that we've only just met, and that you have no loyalty to me, but I'm begging you to help restore Notus to a conscious state. Is there anything you can do? Anything at all?"

Wren taps a finger along the arm of her chair, head canted, expression ponderous. The rhythm pauses. "The Council of Gods."

Boreas scowls with more animosity than I have ever witnessed in a single person. It's quite impressive. "They're not an option. You know this."

She shrugs, completely unperturbed by her husband's reaction. "It's worth the attempt."

"It is a waste of time."

"Ever the pessimist."

I slide to the edge of my chair. Eurus mentioned them as well. "How can I speak with this Council of Gods?"

"You misunderstand," Boreas replies with a glare in my direction. "Speaking with them is not an option. It's prohibited."

Which is exactly what the Lord of the Mountain told me. But if the labyrinth sent me to the Deadlands, there must be a way around that. "Why are you so reluctant to help your own brother?"

"It's not that I don't want to help him," Boreas snaps, his cheeks flushing in irritation. "I *can't* help him. We were banished from our homeland, all of us. Our pleas will fall on deaf ears. There is nothing I can do."

Though I am much smaller than Boreas, I lift my chin, peer down my nose at him. Former deity or not, the North Wind will know of my displeasure. "So what you're saying is you're useless?"

Wren snorts, a hand slapped over her mouth. "I like you," she says to me, much to her husband's exasperation.

Pushing to my feet, I begin to pace. I must. If I am in motion, the shadows cannot touch me. "I need to speak with this Council of Gods."

"I forbid it," the North Wind growls.

Wren kicks his shin with a warning glare. Boreas mutters an oath and falls quiet.

Then the woman turns to me. I see myself in her. She may have this home, this love and security, but it was not always so. Beneath the softened edges, I see those points that were once sharpest of all.

"My husband will deny it," Wren says, "but every god has its weakness. What can you offer the council that they do not already possess?"

There had been a time when I would have said this: nothing, or little, or few. The divine desire power above all else, and I have none to give. But my hands are not as empty as I would believe them to be.

"There is something I have to offer," I say, ignoring the twinge in my sternum. If that's what must be done, then so be it.

"Then we have no time to waste," Wren says.

I'm led from the library, trailing the North Wind and his strong-willed wife down numerous corridors. Eventually, we halt at a door wrought in gold, one of dozens lining the hall. Boreas studies the ornate handle with remarkable distaste.

"Whatever occurs beyond this door," he informs me, "whether punishment or reward, I'm not responsible. Is that understood?"

I nod, my blood buzzing with a dangerous hope.

The door opens. Warm sunlight spills through.

"Good luck," Wren whispers.

34

THE TEMPLE IS A BREATHLESS EXPANSE, HEWN FROM WHITE STONE. Fluted columns reinforce a peaked rooftop. The stairs leading to the entrance are wide, reminiscent of curved bands of moonlight. Beyond the temple, laurel trees cluster in the valleys between great mountains, a shining city nestled in the distant foothills, glimmering like a golden coin.

Now matter how proud I am of Ammaran architecture, Ishmah's temples pale in comparison to this. I can all but feel the land pulsing beneath my feet. This stone is ancient, and this land, and this forest. I never thought I'd have the privilege of visiting Notus' homeland. I've never seen so much green in my life.

But I can't delay the inevitable. Rallying my courage, I press forward, climbing the temple stairs until I reach the top.

At the back of the temple, atop a broad dais cut from the same white stone, there is a long dining table surrounded by what I assume to be the Council of Gods. Laughter pings against the pillars. Animated conversation chases the sound into the surrounding trees. If the divine are anything like Father, they will find my late arrival impolite at best, offensive at worst.

My slippers whisper against the hand-tufted wool rug leading toward the dais, though no one notices my approach. They have much to distract them. The table itself is heaped so abundantly with food it noticeably sags in the center. There are at least five types of meat, including an entire roasted boar, its belly split open. Freshly sliced fruit piles in fine ceramic bowls. The breads are equally varied, accompanied by an assortment of spreads: butter and hummus and marmalade and soft cheese. An enormous cake topped with berries perches on one end of the table. A sizable chunk has already been carved away.

And paired with food is wine. The divine drink from their goblets with abandon. As soon as a bottle is depleted, another materializes to take its place. Some have discarded propriety entirely and eat with their hands, leaving scraps scattered across the gilded surfaces of their plates, utensils be damned. I spot a burly god whose face is spattered in blood snagging the thigh bone of a roasted turkey and slurping the marrow from inside.

Now that I'm closer, I count twelve deities total, their chairs designed specifically for each individual. A goddess dressed in a long white robe sits on a winged chair, an owl perched on its back. A god with blue-gray skin lounges on a throne studded in shimmering jeweled scales, a three-pronged weapon resting casually against his chair arm. Each god is uniquely striking, lovely beyond words.

My focus shifts to the opposite end of the table, then backtracks. I was mistaken. Not all are lovely. There is one individual, skin marked by soot, whose features are so unsightly that I question whether he truly belongs.

Steps away from the dais, I stop. A glass shatters; a shriek of laughter grates upon my ears. I stand for so long, I wonder if the council can, in fact, see me, but eventually, a god draped in red silk pauses mid-chew, having detected my arrival. "A *mortal*?"

The clinking of cutlery abruptly cuts off as twelve pairs of eyes take me in, painted every shade of horror and disbelief.

It is a pox, that word. *Mortal.* It sweeps with brushfire swiftness across the table between one breath and the next. My knees wobble. I cannot afford to falter now. I may be mortal, but I, too, was born into greatness. Sarai Al-Khatib. Princess of Ammara.

"How did you come to our place of council, mortal?"

The question comes from a hulking, broad-shouldered god seated at the head of the table. Candlelight gleams along the curves of his smooth, muscled torso, dark ink tattooed upon his golden skin. His gaze is watchful. A tall basket of flickering lightning bolts rests at his enormous sandaled feet.

My eyes meet those of the lightning god. Their leader, if I am correct. Both god and king.

"How I came here is irrelevant," I say, for I will not betray Wren and Boreas. "But I come with goodwill and a request." Not a plea. The last thing I need is for the divine to take advantage of me.

"A request!" One of the gods barks out a laugh. He hunches over his meal, mouth stained red. No less than seven goblets are cluttered around his plate. "What delightful impudence you bring to our table." Easing his chair onto its back legs, he laces his fingers behind his head. The goddess sitting across from him, a dark-skinned woman with softly lined features, rolls her eyes.

The lightning god regards me curiously. "Obviously, someone told you how to find us. Did they mention that our business is with the divine only?"

"They did." His gaze, I hold squarely. "I chose to ignore it."

A few eyebrows creep upward. Still, I do not fold, no matter how I tremble. Only fire can contend with fire. I'm likely the best entertainment they've had in centuries.

"I may not be of divine origin," I say, "but my business concerns someone who is. If you would—"

"Silence, mortal." This from the blood-spattered behemoth. "Or your next words may be your last."

My teeth clench. My scalp crawls beneath the touch of so many eyes, yet I lift my head, meet their disdainful expressions. I've held my tongue for too long. The years I have wasted, standing idle. They are proud, these deities, blinded by their own eminence. I will not make myself smaller, or less than, or other. I can ask nothing more of myself than to remain true of heart.

"I ask that you allow me to speak," I say, a crisp declaration. "Or do you fear the power of a mortal's voice?"

The lightning god straightens in his chair with a dark glower. No one speaks, though if I'm not mistaken, the lightning bolts sizzle and pop with increasing vigor inside their basket.

He lifts a hand. "Take her away."

Four burly immortals clasp me by the arms, having suddenly materialized around me. My pulse leaps, and their grips tighten. I struggle to no avail.

"By the gods, let the girl speak."

My head swings in the direction of the voice. A towering, buxom goddess wrapped in an elegant dress cuts an impressive silhouette where she lounges at the end of the table, one hand propped on her hip, the other pressed to the tabletop.

"You would think, after millennia of this shit, you would have better things to do than claw for petty wins against mortals." She speaks in a soft, rolling purr, her yellow cat eyes slitted against the sun. "Pathetic."

Whoever this goddess is, I decide she is someone I would absolutely love to know.

The lightning god does not share the sentiment. He sighs and lifts his eyes to the vaulted ceiling, long blond hair falling in waves across his chest. "Do you have something to say, Demi?"

"As a matter of fact, I do."

There is a round of groans from the table. A few pour themselves another drink. The goddess with the owl perched on the back of her chair plucks a cherry from a bowl and feeds it to the raptor, gray wings folded across its back.

Lifting her arms in a dramatic display of passion, the goddess Demi exclaims, "I know we love to think ourselves courageous, worldly, resolute. But this woman has obviously traveled far to speak with us. Not only that, but she has *crossed realms*, a feat few mortals have accomplished."

"Yes," snaps a pointy-chinned goddess with luscious black locks, "because it is *forbidden*."

Demi's head whips toward the other woman. "When was the last time you did anything so heroic, love? And no, gazing into the mirror without face paint doesn't count."

A round of snickers sweeps the table. The black-haired goddess sneers, arms crossed in defiance.

"At the very least," Demi goes on, "we should hear her plight."

"Smells like a mortal sympathizer," someone mutters.

She ignores the comment. "Why punish bravery when we can reward it? The girl doesn't ask for much. She just wants the opportunity to speak."

With a loud sigh, the lightning god bows his head, the bridge of his nose pinched between two tattooed fingers. No one is more surprised than me when he lifts a broad hand and says, "Speak then." His attention cuts to the goddess. "Sit down, Demi."

Her yellow eyes capture mine, and she winks at me before taking her seat.

With her performance complete, everyone turns to face me. I release a slow, inaudible exhalation. Now or never, do or die.

"I've come to save the life of the South Wind," I proclaim. "He was pierced by Sleep's own dagger, and will not wake."

A hollow wind slithers between the pillars. *"South Wind?"* someone whispers. The wine-addled god pours his eighth—ninth?—glass of wine with a muttered, "And the day keeps getting better."

The lightning god leans forward in his seat, perhaps considering whether to hurl one of those jagged bolts through my chest. The council members look between us nervously, a few avoiding eye contact.

"Unfortunately," the lightning god thunders disdainfully, "we no longer recognize the South Wind in the City of Gods. You have wasted your time."

I anticipated this. I am aware of Notus' banishment. He told me his story, just once. I have not forgotten. Following their banishment, the Four Winds were struck from the books. Their titles were stripped. To the Council of Gods, they no longer exist.

I'm not normally one to yield, but this is no ordinary meeting. I am a mortal woman who has come to beseech these highest deities for their assistance. Argument will not get me far. My pleas will not sway them. There exists only one thing I can offer: myself.

"Where is the god Apollo?" I call. My voice echoes against the stone and flees beyond the temple, into the sunlit greenery.

A handful of the council members descend into fits of laughter. A dark-skinned goddess with a braid crowning the top of her skull manages, "Who does this mortal think she is, making demands?" Her hazel eyes lock onto mine in revulsion. So strong an emotion for someone she has never met and knows nothing about.

"You misunderstand," I say once the commotion has calmed down. "I ask because I wish to offer him a gift."

The council members lean inward over the table while speaking in hushed tones, darting occasional glances in my direction. As mortals, we beseech, we pray, we plea. Demand, we do not. Eventually, someone pushes back their chair and comes forward.

This god possesses a fair complexion and is dressed in a flowing white robe that hits mid-thigh. A circlet graces his brow, glinting against the threads of his yellow hair. Apollo: god of sun, music, and light.

Notus has spoken of how this golden god once crossed paths with his brother, the West Wind, who lives in the forest-cloaked realm of Carterhaugh. According to Notus, Apollo lost a loved one many centuries ago and never quite recovered. It is this break I seek to heal, this rupture I hope to repair. Grief, after all, is seasonal. It may abate for a time, yet when the rains arrive to douse the parched land, it inevitably springs up until the weather again turns.

Apollo circles me, hands behind his back. The goddess, Demi, steals a berry from her neighbor's plate without their notice. "What do you wish to gift me, mortal?" he asks.

What a musical voice he has. Light in its purest form. "If it's not too much trouble, I require a violin. To demonstrate."

A brief whisper of conversation peaks and dies. A mortal playing the violin—for the god of music himself? The divine shake their heads, having already decided that I will embarrass myself, in addition to wasting their time.

The lightning god angles toward me with an expression of unexpected intrigue. "A violin? Why?"

Because I have dearly missed it. Because it was where I first learned to tell stories. Because I am not Sarai Al-Khatib without it.

But I only say, "Because it is my voice when I cannot speak myself."

Apollo regards me for a long moment. Unlike the rest of the council, he doesn't immediately dismiss my request. Does he recognize our shared grief? Does he see the holes alongside my heart?

In his hand appears a violin case, which he sets on the ground at my feet. I crouch, open the case, remove the violin and bow. After sliding the shoulder rest onto the body of the instrument, I tighten the bow hair and push to my feet.

I look to Apollo as the council watches on. A few whisper to their neighbors with light sniggers. I ignore them. "If it's acceptable to you, I'd like to perform the Unfinished Concerto."

"The Unfinished Concerto." Apollo rubs at his jaw thoughtfully. Sunlight gilds the tips of his bright hair. "It's been some time since I've heard it, but—" He nods, just once. "Very well. If you think yourself capable of the task."

My mouth quirks. It *would* be fate that brought me here to present this piece to Apollo. Having remained incomplete due to the composer's untimely death, it's not widely known. And yet, it was the concerto I sought to perform at the King Idris Violin Competition, were I to have attended. The last piece I ever played prior to Fahim's death.

I begin on the lowest string as my eyes flutter shut. No matter the years that have passed, my fingers remember. It is a slow build toward the emotional climax. It is the rising sun, the setting sun. It is the erosion of stone. The slow topple into love, security, trust. These moments of creation and wonder and completion, all shaped from musical notation. Sound bleeds out, not even vibrato capable of smoothing it, but I let it come.

This farewell to Fahim, and to Father. One last *I love you* and *goodbye.* And when it is done, the last note fading, I turn toward my audience.

Tears stream unchecked down the twelve deities' faces, as they stream down mine. Even the lightning god, with his hardened exterior, wipes the corner of his eyes, the tip of his nose red. For that is the power of music. To reach into our hearts and touch those pieces of ourselves we are too afraid to acknowledge.

Carefully, I return the instrument to its case, saying, "This is what I offer you, should you wake Notus from his eternal sleep: my gift of music."

Apollo regards me with the eyes of a man who could not conceive of such an idea. "Your mastery over the violin is unlike anything I've ever encountered." He appears torn between confusion and awe. These emotions toward a mortal, of all people, likely leave him feeling uncomfortable. "You would sacrifice your gift for the South Wind?"

"I would," I say.

"Why?"

"I would choose a life without music if it meant a life of love," I say. "Wouldn't you?"

Apollo looks to the violin, clearly hesitant. It is another moment before he finds the proper words. "After Hyacinth's death, I feared music was forever gone from my life. But to hear the things you can do with that instrument . . ." He shakes his head in wonder. "The way you played portrayed exactly how I felt. How I still feel, at times." Another tear wends down his cheek, a clear droplet against his golden skin. "You may be mortal," he says, voice wavering, "but you also understand the pain of a broken heart, a broken spirit."

"I do," I whisper. More than he can possibly know.

Apollo dips his chin, tugging at his lower lip in thought. He glances at his fellow council members, who watch on in doubt and disbelief. "Your performance was everything I could hope for, but I am only one voice of the council. I alone cannot decide."

"It's not enough," states the lightning god, stepping off the dais. He towers over me by at least two feet. I have to crane my neck to look at him. "The South Wind's life for a mortal's musical gift? You are forgetting that Notus was banished because neither he nor his brothers could be trusted not to work against us, after the old gods were overthrown. Why should we grant him this favor for so little?"

"Because you're a decent person?" I suggest with an expressive shrug.

To this, the lightning god throws back his head and releases a great, booming laugh. The council cackles in response. "Who knew mortals had a sense of humor!"

Right. These are the divine I'm dealing with. They are not swayed by promises of power or love or security. They already have everything they need. So how to convince them to agree?

"What more do you want?" I ask.

Apollo exchanges a wordless glance with the lightning god, who says, with a knowing smile, "To gain his life, Notus must give up something in turn: his power and immortality. He will live out his days as a mortal man."

The thought of what would be taken from him ... I feel sick, knowing he will be stripped of these things. It would be a true sacrifice.

Would Notus agree? Is it right for me to make this decision for him? If our positions were reversed, what would I want him to do? What would he want for himself?

You are my heart in every sense of the word. The woman I imagined I'd spend my days with ... in leaving, I denied myself the person that was most precious to me.

A surety settles over me. Notus would do everything in his power to share a life with me, as I am doing now. I can picture our life so clearly. The places we will go, the things we will see, the love we will nurture. I would not have to age while he remained in his prime. We would have the privilege of growing old together.

"All right," I say. "I accept."

Apollo turns toward a god wearing a bronze helmet, two wings shaped over his ears. "Send a message to Sleep," he orders. "Tell him to reverse the effects on the South Wind, by order of the Council of Gods." He then turns toward me. "Once done, mortal, the action cannot be undone."

Notus will live. It is enough. "Thank you," I whisper.

"On the contrary, it is you I should thank," Apollo says, "for giving music back to me."

35

THE SOUTH WIND LIES ON HIS BACK, SHORT BLACK HAIR GROOMED, fingers linked across his bare stomach. A thin, pale scar cuts across his left pectoral where the god-touched dagger pierced his chest. Even in slumber, he strikes a magnificent form. Lamp light cascades over the shallow indentations of his muscled abdomen in waves of rich amber. Between his softly parted lips, his breath unspools.

It has been hours since I returned from Notus' homeland. The Council of Gods assured me it would not take long for him to wake, though I question if it was all one elaborate deception, to steal my gift of music, offering nothing but an empty promise in return. Seated at his bedside, I tend to him as the lamps burn low, piling additional blankets onto the bed to combat the chill. Beyond the open window, the constellations shift horizons. The moon pulls away from the earth.

There is a tentative knock at the door. "Sarai?"

"You can come in."

Roshar enters, bearing a tray of tea, small sandwiches, and apricot tarts. Tonight, he is dressed in frilly white bedclothes, his dark hair set in small curlers. After placing the tray on a nearby table, he takes a seat in the chair beside mine and asks, "How is he?" Quiet, demure. Very *un*-Roshar.

I brush a lock of hair from Notus' brow. At all hours, I scour his face for some sign of life, but—nothing. "As well as can be, I suppose."

"I see." He speaks in a tone that suggests he absolutely doesn't believe a word I say. "And how are *you*?"

I stare at the pillows supporting Notus' head. They look uncomfortably flat. I fluff them from the sides. There. That's better. Or . . . have I made them too lumpy? Oh, what is even the point of this? I drop my hands in frustration. "I'm frightened, Roshar."

His fingers catch mine, and tighten. "Of course you are, dear." Reaching out, he tucks a strand of hair behind my ear. "Love is a scary thing. But you've found something worth fighting for. That's a privilege many do not get to experience in their lifetime."

And what if it goes no further? What if this is the end of the road? What if the South Wind does not wake? How am I to move forward with my life? I can't spend yet more years grieving. I've experienced enough grief for a hundred lifetimes.

"But you're healthy, I mean? Unhurt?" When I regard Roshar questioningly, he explains, "People are saying you were trapped in the labyrinth. Is it true?"

Ah. The truth would have exposed itself eventually, but I hoped I'd have a *little* more time to prepare before that occurred. "It's true."

"By the gods." He lifts a hand to his chest. "And you escaped? Alive? How did you manage that? Actually—" He shakes his head, bats the question aside. "I don't need to know. What matters is that you're safe."

Am I safe? Or will Prince Balior one day return to conquer Ammara?

"Although . . ." His twinkling eyes slide to mine. "I'm curious about what happened to Prince Balior. No one in the palace has seen him. Some claim he died, though I think the man is too crafty for that." He pats at his hair in satisfaction.

"Gossip, Roshar. Really?"

"Well, no, not exactly." At my pointed look, he bats his eyelashes at me. "All right, yes. But can you blame me? Ishmah nearly gets devoured by some unexplainable darkness. It's the most exciting thing that's happened in decades!"

The last thing I need is people worrying about things they do not understand. Even *I* don't know the full implications of the beast having escaped the labyrinth. "All I know is that Prince Balior has left Ishmah and is likely on his way back to Um Salim." To plot out his long-term plans. Now, we must wait to see where the cards fall.

Roshar wrinkles his nose in disappointment. He'd hoped for a novel, a masterpiece to divulge with those at court. I'd granted him a brief message, too short to be of any worth for gossip. "Hmph! Honestly, good riddance. He wasn't that good-looking anyway." My friend crosses his arms, mouth pursed in further consideration. "Well, mostly. I mean, his butt was quite nice, but his nose, eh."

I snort. Now that he mentions it, Prince Balior's nose was a bit large for my taste. Not to mention the gross entitlement. "I appreciate you, Roshar. More than you know." This, paired with an affectionate smile. "Thank you for always looking out for me."

"Of course, Sarai." He appears touched by the sentiment. "That's what friends do."

My attention wanders to the open window. How velvet is the sky, how icy are the stars. "Yes, well, I don't have many friends, as you know."

"What about the queen?"

I pick at a stray thread edging the blanket. The idea holds a warmth that was not present months ago. "I . . . suppose Tuleen is my friend," I murmur tentatively. And what a joy it is to know this.

Roshar glances at the South Wind again before turning to me. "I wish I could stay, but it's been a long night. I'm meeting a new client tomorrow, and I absolutely want to look my best."

My mouth quirks. "Understood." I would not dare get in the way of Roshar's beauty sleep.

Quietly, he departs, and I eat one of the sandwiches while passing the time. I pace, window to door to bed. A second sandwich finds its way into my mouth. As the lamp burns low, my nerves wear thin, because the night has waned, and Notus continues to sleep. But I can wait. I will wait for as long as is necessary—

With a low, rumbling sigh, the South Wind wakens.

Immediately, his eyes seek mine. Their earthy shade holds a startling clarity. I bite my lower lip, fighting tears. But the ache twists and sharpens, rendering me breathless. My hands unclench. My armor falls.

Frowning, Notus lifts a hand to my cheek. His thumb cuts the water in its tracks. "I do not like to see you cry," he whispers.

Oh, his voice. How I have yearned for it. "If it makes you feel better," I wheeze, the words mangled, "they are happy tears." Relieved tears. The most gratified tears. My teeth sink harder into my quivering lip. This man, this beautiful man. "I've missed you."

Notus closes his eyes at my words, as though they are his own music. "I've missed you, too." Then he draws me onto the bed.

The blankets sigh at my legs as his strong arms band across my back, his face tucked against my neck, the dark, heady scent of him embracing me. There is no singular emotion claiming space inside my chest. It is all layers, each adding newfound depth to what is already present. It is deeper than hurt, deeper than the sharpest agony. It lives and breathes beneath my skin.

"I feared you were lost to me," I whisper, tears coursing down my cheeks.

His arms tighten, and I burrow down into him, where sanctuary lies. "Not lost," he murmurs, with enough conviction to reassure me. "Never lost. Temporarily misplaced, perhaps."

I emit a watery chuckle into his chest. Temporarily misplaced, indeed.

"You must know," he whispers. "Surely you must know."

I slide a hand up his back, comforting us both. "Know what?"

Gently, Notus pulls away to look at me, his gaze earnest. Over his shoulder, the lamp light sputters, its wick eaten down. Whatever shadows emerge, they are harmless. The sun will return soon enough. "In any realm, no matter the obstacles, no matter the hardships I must endure, I will find you."

My lips quiver. This face, this strong, beautiful face. The face of the one I love. "Don't leave me again."

"I would not choose to do so. You must know that I would not."

I do know. Perhaps I have always known. Perhaps I would have accepted it sooner, had I not allowed fear to guide my life.

For a time, we sit in companionable silence, his heartbeat the lowest drum against my ear. It is too precious a sound. Twice, I have lost this man. I do not think I could survive a third parting.

"Sarai," he whispers. Something in his voice pokes my awareness: a childlike confusion. "Why can I no longer feel my power?"

His pulse drives forward when I do not immediately respond. He questions, he doubts, he suspects. But I anticipated this. In the hours of waiting, I arranged the relevant information into something palpable, easily swallowed. This conversation is, after all, fragile. An unexpected change. It must be handled with care.

Easing back, I cup one of his broad hands in mine. "What do you remember?" I ask.

Notus searches my gaze. Perhaps it is then he understands. Or perhaps the tightness of my grip reveals this difficult truth.

"I remember you bound by shadow," he says slowly, "your throat bared to Prince Balior's blade. I remember the helplessness, the terror that I would be forced to watch you die. And—" His hand lifts, presses over his heart, shielding the thin white line where the prince's dagger sank deep. "I remember thinking it would have been worth it, to take the blow in your stead. That I could not live with myself, knowing your life was cut short." He takes a ragged breath, swallows, yet I see how his distress rises like floodwaters, this prospect that was so close to being made real.

And just like that, my love for him deepens. Just as he reinforces my weakened parts, so too will I be the steel of his blade, the stony ground when all yields to sand. "I'm here, Notus," I remind him. "I'm right here. You're safe."

The South Wind expels a great, heaving exhalation. "I couldn't be certain at the time, but the dagger looked like it belonged to Sleep, the god who is responsible for half of mortals' lives. I'd hoped that was the case. His blades, though god-touched, are not like our other weapons. They're coated with a powerful elixir that sends whoever the blade nicks into endless sleep."

405 THE SOUTH WIND • 405

"Prince Balior didn't know," I realize. "He didn't know the dagger he held belonged to Sleep." Otherwise he never would have agreed to the bargain.

"In the end, it was to our advantage," Notus says. "I hoped the elixir would be enough to thwart death, at least for the time being."

It is a decision I would have made, had our positions been reversed. I would have given my life a thousand times. Nothing would have stopped me.

After a moment, he sits upright against the pillows. I pass him a glass of mint tea. He drains it in two gulps. "Let me guess," he says, rather dolefully. "Prince Balior found a way to drain my power."

I wince. "No, that's not it."

"Is he dead?"

If he were, I daresay it would make our lives infinitely easier. "He escaped. I'm not sure where he's gone." Would he return to Um Salim? Or would the beast dictate their journey? "Do you have any idea as to their destination?"

A long, heavy sigh sends him wilting into the mattress, eyes fluttering shut. "Marles. Eurus' realm."

I frown at him. "Because—" Ah. Because the beast seeks to punish the god who played a hand in its imprisonment. With King Halim having passed on, the East Wind—the Lord of the Mountain—is all that remains. "The beast will take its revenge on Eurus," I say slowly. "And Prince Balior will aid him."

Notus stares out the window. Hours from now, riotous color will infuse the sky, every grain of sand a golden coin set glinting beneath the sun. "I will need to reach out to Boreas," he says begrudgingly. "Perhaps he'll know how best to combat this threat." Then his attention slides back to mine. "But none of this explains why I'm awake, and why I no longer feel my power."

And thus the story unfolds. I tell him of my crossing into the labyrinth. I inform him of the mirror, which allowed me to travel between realms. I describe to him the Deadlands: a fortress with countless doors.

The South Wind isn't the least bit happy to hear that I visited his brother's realm. "Tell me Boreas did not attempt to kill you. I know my brother. He stabs first, asks questions later."

"Actually," I say, "he seems pretty tame compared to his wife."

"His wife." Notus rubs at his jaw, eyes thinned, skeptical of my claim. "I wasn't aware he had married."

"He seems happy." At least, that was my impression during the brief moments when he did not appear overcome with suspicion. "I quite liked his wife—Wren. They have two young children. And ... he is mortal."

His eyes snap to mine, wide with shock. "Mortal." The hand on his chest twitches before dropping onto the blanket. "And am I? Mortal? Is that why my body feels so ... burdensome?"

I hesitate, yet in this hesitation lies the truth. What's done is done. "Yes."

He takes in this information. I can't quite read his expression. There is sadness, as expected, but nothing compared to the devastation I witnessed through the labyrinth mirror when Notus believed he had killed me with black iris. "How?" he asks.

"I bargained with the Council of Gods to restore you to a conscious state, but they required something in exchange: your power and immortality." At this, my expression folds, throat squeezing my apology into silence. I force it out, an old croak. "I'm sorry you weren't given the opportunity to decide your fate. I took it upon myself to decide for you. It wasn't my place, but ... I would have done whatever it took to save you from that half-life," I say, pressing closer, face hidden against his neck.

His chest pulses, and my heart plummets. He is unhappy. I'd chosen wrong. It was never my place to decide. I knew this, but I didn't care, and—

"I'm sorry, Notus," I murmur. "It's not fair, I know, but please believe me when I tell you I made a choice—"

A choked sound vibrates against my ear, and I frown. "You're ... laughing?" I rear back, mouth agape as the South Wind struggles to suppress his mirth. A brief shake of my head. "I don't understand."

"There's nothing you need to apologize for," he says. "I would have made the same decision."

I wait with anticipation. "You're not upset?"

He peers down at his upturned palms. Layered in calluses and deeply grooved. "There is loss, of course. But it's not as strong as I anticipated it would be. I never revered my own power the way Eurus does, never used it as a shield, as Boreas did, or reveled in it like Zephyrus. What's done is done."

I take those wide palms into mine. *Yes*, I think. *It is.*

His mouth gathers in sudden thought. "Did the council require something of you as well? I can't imagine they would honor your request without a proper exchange."

My heart throbs, like a bruise. For a moment, I swear I feel the phantom weight of the violin against my shoulder and neck. "They did."

New lines crease his face: grave crow's feet and pleats of unexpected melancholy. Notus knows. Of course he knows. "Music?"

I nod, unable to speak.

"Sarai—" He sighs then. "I wish you had not done that."

"It was my decision to make."

"But was it to your benefit?" he counters.

What a stupid question. "Of course it was to my benefit. How can you say that?"

"I'm only thinking about your best interests."

He picks an odd way of showing it. "As if I would live life without you."

"Stubborn woman," he growls, fisting the blanket. "That's not how this works. Everything I've done has been to keep you safe, loved, whole. I have lived my life. I have lived it a thousand times. You are given but a temporary existence, precious, without guarantee. Why would you give up music? It is everything to you."

"As are you," I say.

For whatever reason, Notus ducks his head, his expression torn. I grant him space, yet continue to maintain connection through touch.

"I can't be everything to you, Sarai." Eventually, he tugs his hands from mine, smooths the wrinkles from the blanket, adjusts it in place across his legs. "You know that, right? You have to live your life for yourself first."

"I think you underestimate just how significant a part you are in my life," I tell him wryly. When he does not share in my humor, my smile wilts. He's right, after all. In making one person the whole of your world, you consequently lose sight of yourself.

"You are not everything to me," I say, quieter now. "But you are comfort when I sorely need it, kindness after years of slights, security when the world feels too dangerous to face." But there is more, so much more. "All my life, I have known only the inconsistency of Father's affections. You are balance, dependability, refuge, support. You *see* me." All those rough edges, all the jagged, unhealed wounds. "And that is something I wish never to take for granted.

"Because I see you, Notus. You, a banished god without a home. A man who understands the pain of having to earn a family member's approval. A loyal companion whose heart is true." I straighten as, brick by brick, my spirit is rebuilt, the crisp night breeze wafting in through the window. "You're right. You aren't everything to me. But you are everything I want. The choice I made . . . I do not regret it."

Because a sacrifice must hurt. The absence of what you give up must be enduring, for only then will the weight of what you've lost equal true appreciation for what you've gained.

"Just . . . tell me this. Have you looked at your violin since then?" His eyes rove my face, seeking answers I do not wish to give.

But I release a sigh. "Once." It had become a child I no longer recognized, its curves bulky in my grip, my fingers unwieldly. When I drew the bow across the string, an awful shriek of protest had sounded. I flinched, returned the violin to its case, and cried myself to sleep.

Notus must witness the dark cloud of that moment drifting across my expression. "Sarai—"

"Enough." I will not bend. Not for this. "It is done. I have no regrets. I would do it again. I would do it a thousand times if it meant building a life with you." I grip his hand as tightly as I can, and reveal to him the iron strength within me. "Look at me, please."

A muscle bunches in his jaw. But he raises his head, brown skin warmed in tawny light, so many lines of tension marking his countenance. All will be well. Perhaps not today, nor tomorrow, but eventually, in time.

"The gods have always underestimated mortals," I say to him. "Half the time they are so blinded by their own arrogance they fail to see what lies beneath their very noses. The other half, they're eating their own young for fear of losing whatever power or leverage they hold."

Notus tucks his tongue into his cheek. "That's actually an accurate representation," he concedes.

Of course it is. As it turns out, royalty and the divine share similar tendencies toward self-sabotage. "They believe music to be a singular object that, once taken, cannot be replicated. It's simply not true."

"But it is what you *love*," he grits out. "And now it's gone."

It is only a partial truth, really. "I have mastered the violin once," I whisper. "I will do so again, when I am ready. But you—" Reaching out, I frame his face between my palms. "You cannot be replicated, dear heart. You are my home. It has always been so. And I love you."

"Sarai." He leans forward, pressing his forehead to mine. Our mouths find one another's. The kiss is languid, dreamlike in its sweetness. When Notus draws back, color stains his cheeks. "My heart is yours," he says. "You know that it is."

Indeed, I do. "Will you come with me, and see the world as I wish to see it?"

"My home is with you, wherever you wander."

It is settled then. We will travel west, then north, then east. We will climb mountains and cross the expansive plains. We will witness the might of the sea. And then? Well. Fate is such a funny thing. I cannot know for certain what our future holds, but tomorrow, the sun will rise. Who knows what the winds may bring.

EPILOGUE

In which the South Wind
Attempts to Read a Map

"WE'RE LOST."

The declaration dripped reproach. Notus, who scanned Marqa's central square, with its singular well and plethora of penned goats, turned to regard Sarai calmly. "On the contrary, we are exactly where we are supposed to be."

Her mouth curled in an expression he knew well. After an hour spent wandering, dust and sweat layering her skin, she did not appear amused. "And where is that, exactly?"

"Marqa," he clipped out.

Sarai clacked her teeth together. It was a sound he had heard with increasing frequency these last few months as they explored Ammara north to south, east to west. The hairs on the back of his neck lifted in warning. He, the South Wind, a once-powerful immortal, quailing under the threat of his wife's temper. Imagine that.

"I'm aware this is *Marqa*," she growled, dark eyes flashing. "What I wish to know is where the souk is. That is where we're headed, isn't it? Or are we to wander in circles for the rest of the morning?"

Marqa, a town to the far north of Ammara, was their last stop along the Spice Road. Due to its remote location, few travelers visited. It was a quaint village surrounded by oases, its streets lined with date palms offering scant shade from the sun that boiled down. Some of these oases were known to possess healing properties, but that was not why Notus desired to visit.

"Yes, we're looking for the souk." He wiped the sweat from his brow, glaring and trying to ignore the passersby eavesdropping on their conversation. "Don't give me that look."

She batted her eyes, the image of utmost innocence. "What look?"

"The one that says you know best."

A comment that would, of course, draw defiance into Sarai's spine, shoulders squaring beneath her sapphire dress. Wisped strands of hair spiraled around her face, crimped in the insufferable heat.

"As it turns out," she said pointedly, "I *do* know best."

There was no point in arguing with the truth. However—

"You said you wanted adventure," he reminded Sarai. And look where it had taken them: the Spice Road, beginning to end, the cities that studded its brilliant route, from the arid valleys of the south to the plateaus in the east, the high cliffs of the west. Each region, a striking facet of the place he called home.

"Yes, but I would prefer not to melt in the process, if it's all the same to you."

A smile softened the creases around his eyes. Notus reached for her left hand, placed it upon his chest, over his beating heart. The opal rune that signified their marriage marked her skin. The lead bracelet, twin to his gold, adorned her wrist. "Is that any way to speak to your husband? The man you love most in the world?"

Sarai scoffed. "You think quite highly of yourself." Yet color pinkened her face.

"Do you deny it?" He tugged her closer, lips pressed to her sun-warmed cheek. Then her brow, nose, mouth, where he lingered for a time. Sarai relaxed against him—surrender, however brief.

"No," she murmured. "I deny nothing."

Her ear found his heartbeat. In the evenings, Sarai often rested her head on his chest, as though to confirm he was still breathing. The thought that he might never have awoken were it not for the sacrifice his wife had made tightened his throat with an unbearable pain.

Nevertheless, Notus had never seen her shoulders so unburdened as they were on this journey. He thought perhaps this was the happiest Sarai had felt in a long time. As he well knew, freedom was a gift.

Prior to departing Ishmah, they had wed in the palatial gardens, under a pergola of black iris, with King Amir, Queen Tuleen, and the newborn Prince Raj as their witnesses. They had exchanged vows, and kissed, and sealed their commitment to one another until the end of days. Notus had never felt so full, both in heart and in soul. He was hers and she was his. He wanted nothing else.

"I'm beginning to question your ability to lead us to whoever this merchant is before sundown, Notus." The frustration in his wife's voice was plain. "Who are we meeting again?"

"A family friend." Technically, a friend of the royal family, though Sarai did not need to know that. It would absolutely spoil the surprise, a plan that had been in the works for months.

"You keep saying that," she murmured, pulling back to scrutinize him. "How much longer must we wander?"

"Not much." He hoped.

Sarai pursed her mouth, an eyebrow raised. Clearly unconvinced.

"Look," Notus protested. "It isn't easy navigating these roads. Half of them aren't on the map." He would know. He checked every three minutes.

"Let me be the first to remind you that, were it not for me, we would have likely found ourselves stranded, with no civilization for hundreds of miles." Her smile sharpened. "Give me the map."

She snatched for the oiled parchment, which he held out of reach. "You said I could handle it."

"That was before I realized you didn't know how to read one."

Now, that wasn't entirely true. What need had he for maps and directions when the wind identified east or north, south or west? Unfortunately, since losing his power and immortality, he felt strangely detached from his environment. The wind was little more than sensation, a brush of air against his skin. It spoke to him no longer.

It was a small price to pay for the life he shared with Sarai. His wife was joy, she was comfort, she was security, she was companionship, affection, belonging, *home*. He would do it all over again, give it all up, in order to live out his days with her.

"My map-reading abilities are perfectly fine," Notus said, with only a small amount of indignance.

Sarai tossed up a hand in exasperation. "Why won't you just admit that we're lost?"

"Because we're not."

Head bent, she pinched the bridge of her nose between two fingers. "Well, when you figure out where we are, come find me." And she stomped off.

Notus watched her vanish down a side street. That was fine. At the very least, it allowed him to read the map in peace. Which was exactly what he did.

The luthier should be somewhere nearby—maybe. His shop was located at the end of a road just east of the main square. Unfortunately, multiple roads cut through the town, whereas the map only designated one. His only hope was to wander until he stumbled upon it by happenstance.

Notus selected a street at random and began to walk. Upon reaching a dead end, he retraced his steps, chose another chaotic road, which eventually led to a small, open-aired stall marked by a wooden sign. It boasted no wares but for a single bow resting lengthwise atop the table.

The luthier hunched forward in his chair, slowly carving into a piece of wood. From the curved ridges, it appeared to be the scroll of a violin. The man himself possessed frazzled, storm-cloud colored hair. The channels of a thousand smiles creased his bronze skin.

What were the odds of multiple luthiers in a town so small? "Are you Hassan Odeh?" Notus asked.

The man set down his carving. "I am."

Notus passed over a message bearing the king's seal. He had carried it all these months, hidden in the front of his robes. The luthier would be expecting him—the message was to simply confirm his identity.

Wordlessly, the gray-haired man drew out a leather case from behind the stall and placed it on the table. "The violin hails from the realm of Marles," he said. "I acquired it from a traveling salesman last year. It possesses a fine sound, bright and full, perfect for the solo performer." He hesitated, then said, "Any luthier would be honored to have their instrument played by Sarai Al-Khatib."

"Notus?"

He turned. Sarai was now wending toward him through the crowd. She appeared uncertain, gaze leaping between Notus and the luthier in silent inquiry. Upon catching sight of the case, she froze. "What is this?"

It had taken months of correspondence. Notus had first approached Amir prior to their departure from Ishmah six months before. He wished to gift Sarai music, as she had gifted him her heart. An instrument she could carry on their travels. A means to heal this wound she now bore.

Sarai had known nothing. A feat, to get anything past her. But Notus had been so, so careful, all to witness this moment, of the luthier opening the case to reveal the contents inside. Nestled in soft velvet there sat a full-size violin.

His wife lifted a hand to her throat, and tears streamed down her face. Notus' lungs ached, for he remembered, in the way of painful things, their departure from Ishmah. As they'd packed their bags, Sarai had removed her case from the back of the wardrobe, knelt with it on her bedroom floor. There, she'd touched her violin, and wept. As steadfast as she was in her decision to save his life, it hurt her, to live without music.

"I know it's not the same as your violin back home," he said, suddenly fearful of having overstepped. "But this is the best money can buy."

Mutely, she brushed the strings. Pulled the lowest one, a hard pluck.

Fifteen months had passed since Sarai had lost her gift of music. He recognized the hole in her heart, even if she herself denied it. Maybe she no longer possessed the aptitude of a prodigy, but there was today, this fresh, radiant morning. She could begin anew.

"You don't have to accept it," he said, "but Amir and I covered the cost. It's yours, if you want it."

Again, she plucked the strings, lowest to highest. Her hand trembled. "It's in tune." Sarai glanced at the luthier. "Do you have a shoulder rest? Rosin?"

As the man gathered the requested materials, Sarai threw herself into her husband's arms. "I love you," she choked out, teary-eyed. "That you went through all this trouble . . . you didn't have to do this for me."

On the contrary, he absolutely did. "I will do everything in my power to bring you happiness," he murmured into her hair. "This I promise you, for all the days of our lives."

Sarai trembled with a soft cry of pain. "Thank you," she whispered, "for sharing this life with me. I just . . . love you."

He pressed a kiss against her ear. It was no hardship. Indeed, loving Sarai was the easiest thing he'd ever done. "I love you, too."

By the time they pulled apart, a small crowd had gathered. Even now, he caught a few excited whispers, their eagerness to hear her perform sparking the dry air like static. Sarai Al-Khatib, Princess of Ammara. The realm had known her. The *world* had known her. Of course people would remember.

After sliding the shoulder rest onto the body of the violin, Sarai tucked the instrument beneath her chin, curved her fingers around the frog of the freshly rosined bow. Yet she hesitated. "It feels . . . strange." She searched his gaze, her indecision plain. "What if I sound terrible?"

How could anything born of the heart be terrible? "You won't." Notus smiled at his wife in reassurance, his heart near bursting. "Play," he urged.

Sarai Al-Khatib placed the bow upon the strings, and played.

ACKNOWLEDGEMENTS

THIS BOOK WAS DEEPLY PERSONAL TO ME. TO GIVE SOME INSIGHT, I have played the violin for over twenty-seven years now. I began when I was six years old, pursued violin performance in university, and continue to perform professionally as an orchestral musician to this day. It is something I love with my whole heart. I am a writer, yes, but I am firstly a musician, for that is where I first learned to tell stories.

Music guided me in crafting Sarai and Notus' tale. But it was refined by the guidance of my amazing editors, it was made known by the dedicated and insanely talented marketing and publicity departments, and it was championed by not only my publisher, but my wonderful readers, whom I never take for granted.

First, a huge, *huge* thank-you to my editors near and far. Thank you so much to Anthea, as always, for your extraordinary enthusiasm and support, and for being such a light and a joy to work with. Thank you to Jéla, whose insight brought this story to greater heights, and for all your efforts in honing this blade into something sharp and memorable. Thank you to Charlotte for such smart and clever insight that I sometimes feel like you've somehow looked inside my head while writing the story! Thank you to Lizzie for your brilliant storytelling instinct, and dusting off all the unnecessary bits so the heart of the story shines all the clearer.

To the entire Australian, UK, and US marketing teams, publicity teams, sales teams, and production teams. Thank you so much for all the hard work you put in to bring this series to readers around the world. I value every idea, every post, every email, every effort you take to place these stories, which mean so much to me, into readers' hands. You have my gratitude.

To my husband, Jon. I love you more than I can say. Thank you for never failing to stand by me. Every day spent with you is a gift.

To my family for their continued support, especially my mom, for being the emotional pillar I need when deadlines are looming. I love and appreciate you.

Lastly, I cannot write a book about music without acknowledging the man who helped it bloom. So, my deepest, most profound gratitude goes to Mr. Simmons. You are no longer with us, but I carry your spirit with me. May the heavens be always filled with Bach and Rachmaninoff, Tchaikovsky and Beethoven and Mendelssohn. From the bottom of my heart, thank you for gifting me music. I very much look forward to the day we meet again.

ABOUT THE AUTHOR

Alexandria Warwick is the author of the Four Winds series and the North series. A classically trained violinist, she spends much of her time performing in orchestras. She lives in Florida.